DOWNING DORA NINE

Written by MATTHEW PATRICK

Illustrated by JOHN PATRICK

PARADROME PRESS
CINCINNATI, OHIO

PUBLISHED BY PARADROME PRESS
CINCINNATI, OHIO
WWW.PARADROMEPRESS.COM

FIRST PRINT EDITION

ISBN 978-0-9913260-2-0

Book Design by Terry Patrick
Published in the United States of America
Printed in China

ACKNOWLEDGEMENTS

I would like to thank the following individuals for their help and support in turning this dream into a reality: Terry Patrick, Fay Patrick, Susan Leonard, and Michele Giuliani.

For our father,

Morris E. Patrick

CONTENTS

ILLUSTRATIONS

DOWNING DORA NINE

ESSENTIAL CHRONOLOGY

Boston, Massachusetts

February 6, 1788

Samuel Adams	*Nay*
Capt. Samuel Grant	*Nay*
Dr. Thomas Rice	*Nay*
Isaac Snow	*Nay*
John Sprague	*Nay*
David Sylvester	*Nay*
William Symmes Jr.	*Nay*
Charles Turner	*Nay*
James Williams	*Nay*
John Winthrop	*Nay*

Delegates to the Massachusetts Ratifying Convention vote to reject the proposed United States Constitution. An attempt at compromise, led by John Hancock and Samuel Adams, has failed; ten men who might have voted for the new constitution did not, thus tipping the scales against ratification.

June 21, 1788

New Hampshire, a vociferous proponent of states' rights, follows Massachusetts and votes to reject the proposed United States Constitution.

June 25, 1788

Persuaded by the arguments of Patrick Henry, and by the example set by Massachusetts, Virginia votes to reject the proposed United States Constitution.

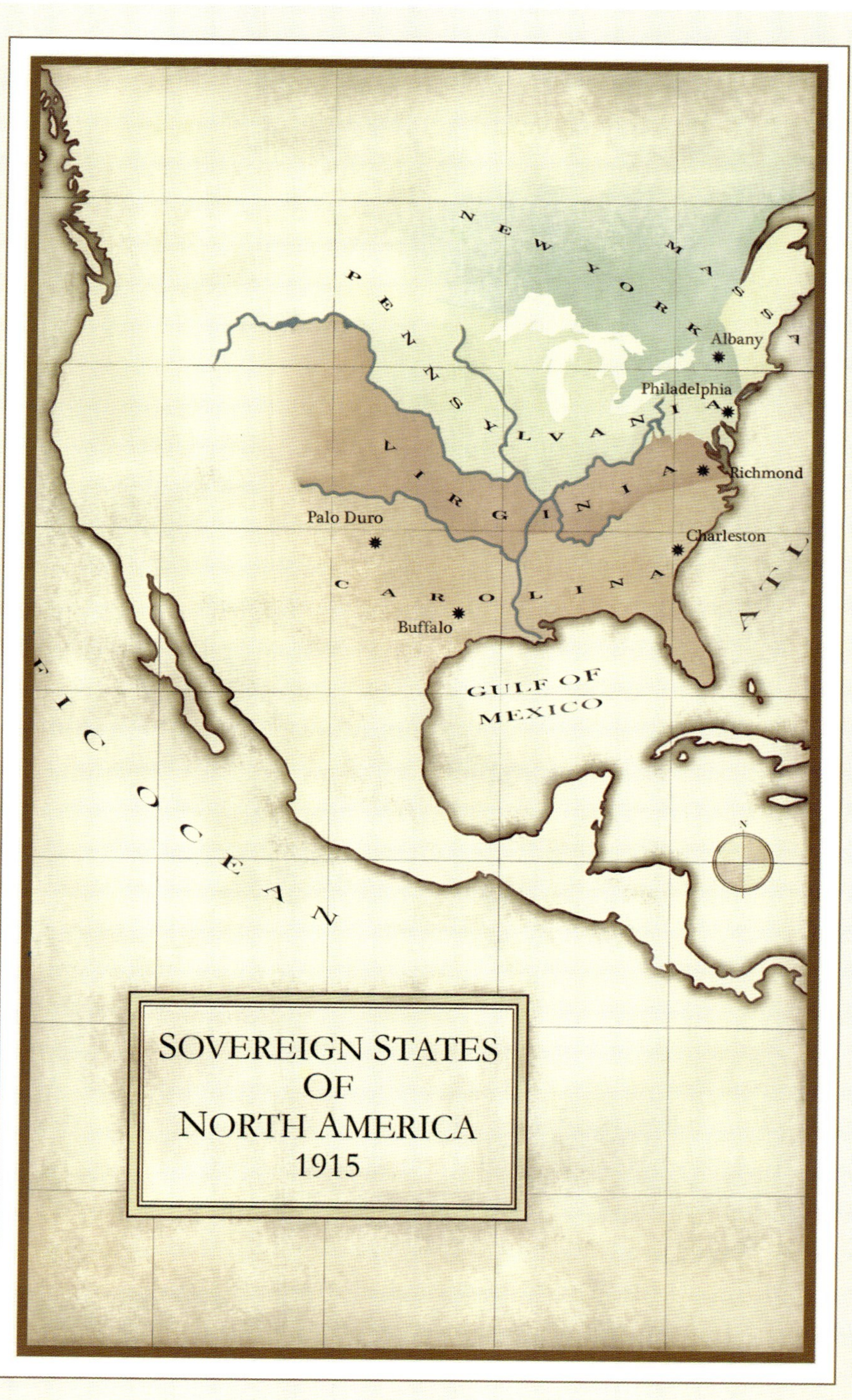
NEW YORK
MASS
PENNSYLVANIA
Albany
Philadelphia
VIRGINIA
Richmond
Palo Duro
Charleston
CAROLINA
Buffalo
GULF OF MEXICO
FIC OCEAN
ATL
SOVEREIGN STATES
OF
NORTH AMERICA
1915

July 26, 1788

New York, another long-standing champion of states' rights, rejects the proposed United States Constitution.

July 31, 1788

Rhode Island votes to reject the proposed United States Constitution. Being the fifth of the thirteen states to do so, Rhode Island eliminates any chance that the required nine-state majority can be achieved. With the premature death of the United States of America, the Sovereign States of North America are born.

June 15, 1802

Massachusetts invades New Hampshire and Vermont and defeats the combined militia of these states at the battle of Hanover.

* * *

The original thirteen American states eventually consolidate into the sovereign nation-states of New York, Massachusetts, Pennsylvania, Virginia, and Carolina.

* * *

PROLOGUE

IN THE YEAR 1915, the state of the world was not all that it *might* have been. Peace reigned, but it was an uncomfortable peace. Britain still ruled the waves, but all of the other nations resented it. France had recovered from her turmoil, from the labor of her liberty, but she had become nervous with time: the might of the Prussians had grown, and France's neighbors to the east had disappeared one by one, devoured by the insatiable desires of the old Kaiser. And across the Atlantic, that great experiment in democratic union—the United States of America—had long ago failed of its purpose. The idealistic attempt at a fresh start in an unspoiled new world had been short-lived; the failure to adapt that highly impractical roadmap to domestic tranquility—the United States Constitution—had left the new world no more perfect than the one from which it had sprung. By the year 1915 the five sovereign nation-states that remained in North America—Massachusetts, New York, Pennsylvania, Virginia, and Carolina—were weary and broken from a century of violence that was unable to boast of a single year in which the future looked brighter than the past.

But with the turn of the twentieth century, the inventors had come! Many believed their rise beckoned a new dawn for mankind and that the recent strife of the new world, as well as the ancient strife of the old, would be washed away by the power of their genius, by the torrent of their creative spirit. Out of their laboratories and factories came miracles that promised to lift man from his unending misery. The invention of steel enabled a revolution in building; the cities of Europe and America began to mount up toward the heavens. Travel between continents shortened from weeks to days by fast and powerful ocean liners, and the distance between cities shortened from days to hours by ever expanding networks of rail. Roads were carved across the landscape in every direction as motorcars became more affordable. Electricity, seeming little less than the power of the gods, now lighted all the major cities. The telegraph, and recently the telephone, enabled great business tycoons to control vast industrial empires without ever having to leave their desks.

Others though, still very much in the minority, saw not the golden rays of a new enlightenment, but the dark clouds of a tremendous storm—the harbinger of some final disaster. They pointed to the fact that each new step toward Eden had been dogged by darker creations: the machine gun, the great artillery gun, the armored battleship, and the submarine boat. The ultimate significance of still other ingenious machines, for good or ill, still hung in the balance. Whether the Prussian airship, barely ten years old, or that recent and most spectacular invention of all, the French aeroplane, would transform man's world into a heaven or a hell, only time would tell.

One particularly stalwart and optimistic champion of progress was a wealthy Englishman from Northamptonshire by the name of Sir Horace Maxim. Sir Maxim's tirades in parliament against the Prussians and the Austrians and the Turks were legendary. But it was his incessant clamoring about flying machines that finally did him in. It all began in 1911, shortly after the channel had been crossed by a lone Frenchman—a hero to some, a fool to many—in a small contraption of wood and fabric. There were boisterous celebrations on both sides of the water at the Frenchman's audacious stunt. And though the real significance of his feat was lost on most, it was not lost on Sir Maxim—England's splendid isolation was over!

It was unthinkable that England should have constructed the world's greatest navy, only to leave its skies open to French aeroplanes and Prussian airships. Sir Maxim particularly abhorred airships! He believed that only the dimmest of fools could fail to see their sinister potential. The fact that these machines had been built for peaceful purposes and had provided the world its first airline, plying back and forth between the cities of Prussia, did not matter—the fact that the craft occasionally blew up was beside the point.

Sir Maxim would see his country defended—regardless of the cost to his reputation or his pocketbook!

And so, after a particularly passionate and infamous outburst that got him ejected from parliament, Sir Maxim decided to take matters into his own hands. Through extraordinary efforts—that is by cajoling his friends, by threatening his enemies, by begging his relatives, especially his cousin, the Prince of Wales—Sir Maxim procured the government's grudging agreement to commission a battalion of fliers. But after having funded the construction of the aircraft himself, as well as the recruitment and training of two dozen fliers, Sir Maxim was disappointed to experience the government's continued neglect. In one last attempt at proving the potential of his ideas, he bullied the prince into posting the entire force—planes, pilots, and mechanics—to the North African desert where they could keep an eye on the Turks, who were being prodded by the Kaiser to join in his designs on the other European nations. Sir Maxim had made the most of the rumors circulating about the Turks in Tripoli; many feared they might try to snap up the Egyptian Canal and thus precipitate a great war between the competing European alliances. He intended that his battalion of fliers should provide early warning of any advance on Her Majesty's forces in Cairo.

And there in the North African desert his battalion remained, unnoticed and forgotten by all. The fliers had never gotten the opportunity to prove their worth, the Turks having never gotten the nerve to make a move. Sir Maxim retired from public life and wasted away, a broken man. And there in the desert his battalion remained, guarding against an event that was never to happen, baking in the hot sun day after day.

Chapter 1

CAUGHT IN THE DESERT

Another dawn broke on Africa's great Western Desert. It broke on Sir Maxim's private army, adrift in the Egyptian sand, not far from the Cyrnacean border. His men slept in bleached tents pitched on the sand in orderly rows and columns, the space between any one tent and its neighbor so small that from a distance the camp seemed a single mass, like a wart on the otherwise smooth surface of the surrounding plain. Later, the sun would hammer the plain much like Sir Maxim's walking stick had hammered the lectern at parliament just before they threw him out for bad conduct.

The sun hung just below the pink horizon, and as the temperature inched up, a gust swept over the vacant dunes to the east. It hugged the undulating hills and sent up tendrils of dust as it scraped each crest before settling onto the plain and twisting through the passages of Sir Maxim's sleepy camp. As if frustrated at being delayed, the breeze pushed and pulled on every loose piece of canvas it found. One drooping tent near the center of camp billowed and flapped and sagged sadly to one side.

Within, an empty bottle fell from its perch and rolled across the wooden planks; it dribbled whiskey from its open mouth. Each drop quickly disappeared, vaporized by the harsh dry air. Due either to the sound of the toppled bottle, or from the odor of the whiskey itself, a pair of eyelids shot open to expose questioning brown eyes that searched through the dimness.

Satisfied that all was safe and sound, Lieutenant William Hastings took a moment to search around within his own head; he hoped to find everything *there* safe and sound. Although he didn't feel completely normal—a result of the copious amount of liquor consumed a few hours prior—he eventually reached the conclusion that he would get by without too much discomfort. He pushed his flannel blanket to one side, pulled himself upright, and roughly rubbed his face and scalp. As he waited for his head to clear, he stared at the vague, snoring figures that lay like lead weights at the other end of the tent, each man wrapped in his own filthy blanket. He contemplated his tent mates as he ran his fingers over his knuckles; the cuts on them were still open and the bruises still tender, and he was disappointed to realize that the fight had not been a dream. Reluctantly, his gaze shifted to the cot next to his own. It was empty. He had bidden farewell to its owner, now resting in a sandy grave just outside camp, by cracking open his precious last bottle. From that point it hadn't taken long for him to start a small private war with his fellow camp mates.

Aware that his thoughts would soon turn dark and dreary, Lieutenant William Hastings forced himself to his feet. He took an unsteady step forward and grasped at the leathery objects dangling about the wooden pole at the center of their Spartan home. He removed his flying cap from the tangle, pushed his way through the flaps, and stepped out into the cold morning air.

William's gaunt form loped between the silent tents. Had any of his fellow soldiers been awake, and had they been waiting in the darkness to take their revenge—as they sometimes did—all they would have seen was his gangly silhouette moving across the walls of pale canvas. He walked in a characteristic way that others found odd, with his head and jaw thrust forward so that he appeared a bit hunched. His eyes were constantly on the move as if searching and hunting and trying to peer around the distant corners ahead. He carried his arms straight at his sides, stiff, unbending, and his hands hung in balled fists. Whenever he approached one of the camp's inhabitants, no matter his mood—joyous or angry or drunk—William gave off the impression, almost an odor as it were, that violence was imminent, as if he were a boxer stumbling back into the ring for the final round. William, of course, was completely unaware of this aspect of his character; he was always too preoccupied with his own thoughts to spare any for the impressions of others.

He counted off the rows to mark his progress and executed overly precise military turns to the left or the right according to a well-practiced formula. Although he would occasionally rebel against the monotony of his current life by choosing a new route through camp, he tended to favor one in particular that led past a miniature oasis of stunted shrubs and dried grass where an old lizard had made itself at home. The creature was reclusive and irascible and preferred to show itself during the quieter times of day; the men for the most part had left it alone. As William passed by, the creature let out an irritated hiss. William thrust out his jaw and hissed back and, without slowing his stride, kicked a small stone that sent the thing darting back through the scrub.

William paused when he arrived at the broad tent that served as the battalion's mess. The morning air was silent and calm. The disturbed ground surrounding the mess was the only remnant of the previous night's violence. He bent down and searched carefully through the sand; he scooped up handfuls and let it sift through his fingers. The morning light had grown but it was still too dim to make this an easy task. He searched among the tangled footprints, impatient, unable to find what he was looking for. Then just as he decided to postpone his search until later, he sucked in his breath; he reached down for two strangely shaped pebbles with the appearance of ivory and slipped them into his pocket.

William carried on, working his way through the remainder of the camp's silent passages. When he reached the last row of tents he halted, balanced on an invisible edge that seemed to separate mankind and all of its turbulence from the empty wasteland around him. Today as he waited he sensed an intruder, and after glancing to one side, he caught the flare of a match being held carefully to a cigarette not far away. The odor of sulfur and tobacco reached out to him and enticed him to remain in the world of men.

The smoker, Major French, was a restless man who frequently held vigils at odd places and odd hours. He could be seen at times gazing up at the stars or kicking in the dust, usually mumbling to himself. Now he stood between two tents and waited for the sun. William gave him a salute, not much more than a wave; the major responded with a silent nod of acknowledgement, due more to the presence of another human being than to any martial formality. The glowing ember at the end of his cigarette pulsed while William waited.

William felt as if he were trapped—trapped between a world in which he didn't belong and the lonely sands before him. The wilderness whispered to him; it beckoned him. But he was well aware that if he succumbed to its temptation, that if he gave it half a chance, it would snuff the life out of him. And so he hesitated as if steeling himself for a journey of forty days and forty nights.

Usually he departed early for his morning patrol, before the other men rose. His life here had become difficult, his fights with them more frequent—and more violent. Most now avoided him, as much as this was possible within the confines of their little village. He knew they were elated by the rumors that he might return home to England, but he tried to not let this bother him. They didn't understand that he could never really go home.

He took one deliberate step out onto the stretch of sand that served as their landing strip—then another and another. He didn't travel far, only about a hundred yards, until he reached an aeroplane so dilapidated and abused by sun and sand that its faded brown paint blended perfectly with the dunes not far behind. William leaned his head back and stared up at the slab-sided radiator mounted on the front; he let out a discontented sigh.

He circled the craft, bending to peek under its wings and under its tail. He pulled on wires and struts, eventually working his way back to the propeller to complete his inspection. William put on his flying cap; tufts of red hair poked from its edges and gave the appearance that he had not had first choice of flying gear and was left with a cap a size or two too small.

Startled by the sound of footsteps in the sand, William turned to find the major wandering over to lend him a hand. The other men had been quite content to let him struggle on his own each morning, and he had overheard them more than once speculating as to how he managed to start the aeroplane's motor all by himself. Their perplexity gave him some small satisfaction.

'It's against regulations to do this on your own,' muttered the major, smoke drifting from his nose. 'Besides, Willy, it's not safe. Go ahead and climb aboard. I'll get it for you.'

William grimaced at the nickname but let it pass; he had been taunted with it the night before. The cuts on his knuckles seemed to throb as the images of the fight flowed back into his head. *Willy huff, Willy blow. Will he stay or will he go?* The fool had had it coming—astonishing how easily his teeth had popped out.

'I suppose they'll use this against me,' said William. 'Just another reason to cancel my leave home!'

'They might,' shrugged the major. 'We can't really afford for you to go—there aren't enough fliers left as it is. I wish you hadn't kicked up such a ruckus last night. You're your own worst enemy.'

'Well, it's just that I hate this rotten place!'

'It's only rotten because you make it so.'

William opened his mouth to argue but shut it without uttering a word. He turned and gazed back at the camp, the wellspring of all his troubles. 'Do you suppose they would even bother if I went missing?'

William had said this to himself, but the major looked

startled and, mistaking his meaning, responded sharply, 'Don't be a fool, Willy! They would shoot you the second you arrived in Old Blighty.'

Again William opened his mouth to object, but shut it, expecting whatever he might say would only make matters worse. It seemed to be the regular pattern of things here in his desert prison—not so different from the pattern of things back home in England. He couldn't do or say anything without someone taking it the wrong way.

'Would it help if I found Martin's teeth?' asked William.

'Well,' chuckled the major, 'I suppose it couldn't hurt.'

William reached into his pocket and produced the ivory pebbles he had discovered in the sand. He handed them to the major, who needed a moment to recognize them for what they were. The major quickly slid them into his breast pocket and wiped his fingers on his sleeve.

'I wouldn't worry too much. They won't have forgotten about all you did to find poor Simon. Let's see what happens today.'

William nodded and turned toward his aeroplane. The machine protested his climbing aboard with a series of creaks, groans, and sloshes that would have indicated to any unknowing observer that it was not as solidly constructed as first implied by its massive steel engine. It was in every other respect hollow and frail.

The major placed a shoulder against the nearest blade of the propeller and pushed with his entire weight. The engine resisted every inch of motion as if it had had as rough a night as its pilot. The wings wobbled and dipped as the engine clinked and gasped before discharging a drop or two of pungent gasoline from its exhaust.

Either from some telltale sign that the engine had been sufficiently 'loosened up,' or simply because the officer had exhausted himself, he backed away to one side, where he had direct sight of William's eyes, and shouted, 'ALL RIGHT!'

William gave a feeble salute, flicked a switch, and the major cautiously returned to the propeller. He grabbed a blade firmly in both hands, positioned his feet at a safe distance, and pulled with a sharp jerk, simultaneously jumping away as if the machine were about to spring forward and devour him. But after an anemic cough and a puff of black smoke, an insolent stillness poured from the reluctant motor.

The major repeated the procedure, and on this second attempt the engine caught, ripping the silence from the morning air. The machine lunged forward against its chocks—rattling, quivering, vibrating as if it would shake itself apart. Major French crouched down and yanked out the submerging chocks, then bolted from the restive machine. Glancing over his shoulder so as not to lose sight of the grumbling monster, he marched smartly back to camp.

William opened the throttle and the engine surged; the craft pulled away and fled down the rutted strip. He kicked the rudder back and forth to keep the machine straight as it bounced its way into the air and climbed into a cloudless sky. The effort needed to get the aeroplane safely airborne cleared William's head, and though this flight was but one of thousands, his spirit surged as he left the earth's surface and all its troubles far below.

He followed the rocky ravine that led away from camp and wandered off to the north. Confident in his track, he settled down in his seat, allowing the windscreen to better protect him from the stream of steadily cooling air. Now he could think in peace. What was he to do? His situation here had become intolerable.

Suddenly, and at the very moment William began to let his mind wander, the machine shuddered; the engine misfired; its rocker arms slowed at their task and the engine gave up completely. After a few seconds of shocking silence, with the propeller wind-milling lazily in the rush of morning air, and before William could lean over the side of his cockpit to look for a place to land, the engine just as suddenly roared back to life. It was a similar sort of spasm that had killed Simon Rawlings during his approach to the airstrip the day before. They hadn't pulled much of him from the fire, barely enough to bury. Now the only sign of Simon ever having existed was that sandy grave just outside camp.

William shook his head in disgust, disgust at the engine's poor design and at the mechanics' inability to improve it. He had made several suggestions of his own for their benefit, but they had all gone unheeded. Eyebrows had been raised shortly after his arrival when he began hanging strands of safety pins from his tunic buttons, rubber bands from his belt loops, and paperclips from his shoelaces. The explanation that a paperclip would be invaluable should he need to make an emergency repair aloft had not made a bit of difference. And the fact that others were eventually observed with their own supply of 'unapproved' paperclips tucked carefully away in their pockets to avoid ridicule, or perhaps to avoid giving him satisfaction, failed to make William's novel innovation any more acceptable. Finally, he had been unofficially branded an *enthusiast* after having approached a mechanic about mounting a rifle on each side of his aeroplane—just in case he ran across any stray Turks in the desert.

William cursed himself for having been too intoxicated the night before to perform the maintenance on his craft; the mechanics had gone on without him. He was certain that the slavish discipline of performing his own repair work had saved his life on more than one occasion—once when he found a grain of sand wedged in the jet of the carburetor and the other when he discovered a small crack in the engine's crankcase. God forbid there should ever be a war—he didn't need an enemy to make his life more dangerous than it already was!

He had been in the desert two years now—one of the first to arrive. Sir Maxim's recruiting posters had appeared on Bedford's High Street just before his sister's wedding day

Sir Maxim,
Member of Parliament
Would Have
YOU
Defend the Empire
From the
AIR!

Many of the High Street pedestrians had been forced to step out of their way to avoid him as he gazed up at that poster, mesmerized. Machines of all sorts fascinated him. He had even incurred the wrath of his brother Hubert, the earl, by completely disassembling the family's first motorcar the very day of its purchase. His mother had called him a guttersnipe for the foul language he had picked up while lingering around Bedford's only automobile repair shop. At that time, William had but once seen an aeroplane; it had thrilled him and left him feverish with excitement. He desperately wanted to ride in one. But the family would never approve of such a course—only lunatics experimented with flying machines, and there would be no lunatics in the family!

His mother would have scowled at the idea, and his brother would have laughed. If his father were still alive, William would have been subjected to another of those humiliating rebukes that the man had so frequently doled out. Perhaps William could have shared his thoughts with his sister if she hadn't been so preoccupied with her wedding. He had continued to study Sir Maxim's poster in idle fascination, even going so far as to take one down to keep folded up tightly in his pocket. He perused Sir Maxim's advertisement in his leisure (which was pretty much whenever he wanted, and whenever no one happened to be looking). This surreptitious dreaming continued right up to his sister's wedding day, right up to the day he had made that awful mistake of interfering with her engagement.

He had tried to do the right thing. But because of his meddling, the fellow had left her standing at the altar, standing in tears at first, then in a shaking rage.

William would never forget that day—the day his home had erupted. He would never forget all those eyes glaring at him—his mother's eyes, his brother's eyes, accusing eyes. None of them understood. Had he been the only one to see it? The fellow was a toffer!

His sister Emily had divined instantly what had happened and turned on him in fury. 'How could you, William! You of all people! I'll never forgive you for this.' Then William had become angry, and he had said things that he eventually came to regret, which of course had only enraged her further. 'I don't want to speak to you ever again, William! I never want to see you again! You must go away and never come back!'

So that's just what he'd done!

He stomped from the wedding, down the road to Bedford, and straight into the recruiting hall, where he had burst in on two ancient army officers at their game of draughts. Once recovered, they seemed quite happy to have him; they completely empathized with the plight of a second-born son. What did one need with ten thousand acres and a seat in the House? Sir Maxim didn't mind that he wasn't to be an earl. They would ship him off to Sussex that very day. The old men, ignoring the fact that William was underage, signed him up on the spot.

The flurry of activity that followed as the battalion assembled and its fliers were trained proved a welcome distraction. All the while William received not a word from home, the family apparently satisfied with his banishment. For his part, he refused to return to Bedford and rejected any leave that came his way. Eventually though, his temper cooled and he came to regret his angry words, only to discover he lacked the nerve to face his sister.

Then, with no warning, the battalion had been packed up and shipped off to the North African desert. And there he continued to receive no word from home—not until this very week. A curt note had arrived from his brother informing him that their sister had become ill, that she was asking for him, and that he should come home at once. But after having provided William with a convenient means of escape, and having provided him his own private purgatory to expunge his guilt, Sir Maxim's army was undecided as to whether it could afford to let him go home. He was one of their most experienced fliers.

William had determined that his staying or going didn't make a bit of difference, one way or the other. Over the past two years he had watched their orderly campsite erode, its white tents and bright aeroplanes worn down by the elements, and the eager step and crisp salutes of its volunteers decayed by an unexpected monotony. During their tour in the desert no enemy had emerged, yet fifteen crewmen had been killed for one reason or another: engine failures, landing accidents, dust storms and, of course, those occasions when fliers simply disappeared, very likely lost in the featureless landscape. He acknowledged aerial horseplay as the likely cause in some instances, but this was completely understandable given the dreary routine of their existence.

Frustration at his predicament swelled inside him. That Major French would imply he might disappear of his own accord was insulting and infuriating. Never for a moment had he ever considered deserting. But now, the further he flew along beneath the rising sun, the more he warmed to the idea. He had certainly paid his dues; he had more flight time by far than anyone else in the battalion. Besides, they didn't really want him. They made that clear each and every day. So he pulled out his navigation chart—unused until now, being virtually worthless in the desert—and located Burdyah; it was less than a hundred miles away, just barely within range. If he were to stow some tins of fuel aboard before his next flight, it would greatly increase his margin for error. It would be easy to do so in the early morning dark, and it would be easy to avoid the major; the officer's nocturnal wanderings always took him to a different part of the camp. The likelihood that the major would show up in the same spot two mornings in a row was a statistical impossibility.

No! It was too late for proper preparations. His sister could be in immediate peril for all he knew. He had decided! He leaned to the left, peered over the side, and spotted the fork in the ravine below, a well-known landmark to all the fliers assigned to the northern patrol. It was generally agreed that this point represented the maximum distance one could expect to hike back to camp. Those who had been forced down anywhere beyond it had for the most part failed to survive. Simon Rawlings had been the one exception, and only because William had continued searching long after the others had given up. But he had rescued the poor boy, dehydrated and seared to a crisp by the devilish sun, only to see him burn up in a crash a few weeks later. The fork below now took on a much greater significance; it marked William's decision to start for home, regardless of the consequences. He banked sharply to the left and headed further into the wasteland. A course of 320 degrees would send him into a disorienting sea of unremarkable dunes beyond which lay the coast and hopefully a steamer bound for England.

Suddenly, though, the geometry in front of his eyes changed. A strut just in front of the cockpit that ran between the upper wing and the fuselage, completely disappeared; one second ago it had been there and now it was not. The aeroplane's frame shook so violently that his teeth chattered in his head. Sparks burst from the engine and a chunk of metal shot from the left cylinder head.

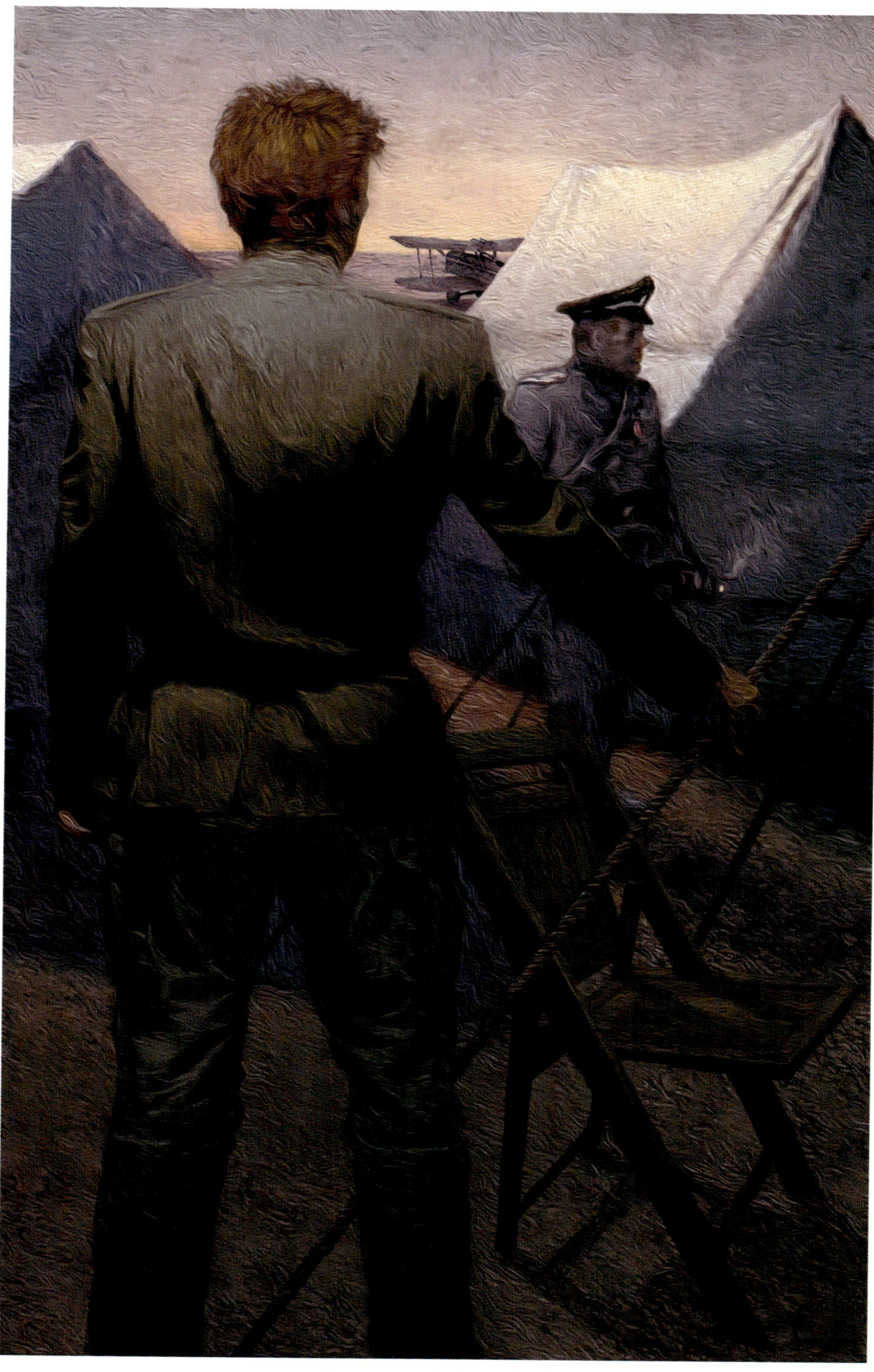

The startling failures made no sense; William couldn't tie them together. As his mind raced to decipher their cause, a piece of fabric tore itself loose from the underside of the upper wing just in front of the cockpit; ragged remnants fluttered in the slipstream.

Then suddenly, from somewhere deep in his soul, from the same place that the crazy idea of mounting a rifle on his aeroplane had come, William understood. He rolled the machine onto its side and yanked on the control stick. He strained to get a glimpse of his attacker, but without success. Despite his maneuvering, bullets pelted the craft around him. They shredded the fabric of the wings, ricocheted off the engine block, shattered the windscreen. Even the seemingly sheltered contents of his cockpit were quickly transformed into a tangled disarray of cables, splintered glass, and burning wood. Just as his instinctive movements cleared him for the moment, fuel began streaming into the cockpit; it poured into his flying boots; it splashed into his open mouth. The fumes began to overwhelm him.

William intentionally kicked the machine into a spin; he hoped that the violent spiral would take him to the ground in time; he wondered if the sacrifice in control was worth the gamble. The risk of exploding fuel now seemed greater than the threat of an invisible enemy somewhere above.

As the craft's rotation accelerated, the desert landscape dissolved into a swirling smear of ochre. Unconsciousness tugged at him. The image of his sister appeared before him, just for a moment—she frowned at him and then was gone.

Chapter 2

THE LEVIATHAN

William labored to pierce the fog of a concussion. A wave of nausea rippled through his gut. He was quite certain there was a pistol pointed at his face, but he was unsure whether it was the pistol that quivered or the inside of his head. Forcing himself to ignore the deadly black dot at the barrel's tip, he let his gaze travel along a trembling arm, up to a rumpled shock of blond hair, and then down to his attacker's eyes—eyes of blue paler than the sky above, eyes that squinted against the brightness reflecting off the desert sand. William concentrated on those blue eyes; he hunted for a sign as to what the stranger would do next.

The man lowered his weapon, but he neither loosened his grip nor removed his finger from the trigger. A thin trickle of blood fell from a laceration that extended from the corner of the man's mouth, back almost to his right ear. It was clear from his flying suit that this fellow must be the flier who had attacked him, but William wondered whether the bloody cut meant the man had crashed as well. A quick glance to one side proved that this was not the case; the stranger's aircraft, a bright red monoplane, sputtered some distance behind him, perfectly intact, its motor idling roughly. William's aircraft, however, popped and crackled a few yards away, its twisted wreckage burning furiously on the side of a tall dune.

'You sneaking, loose-bowelled latrine rat!' croaked William, his throat parched and tight. 'Why the hell did you do that?'

'*Sie sind hier*,' said the man with a shrug. Then, switching to a lightly accented English, he repeated, 'Because you are here.'

'Because I'm here? What the bloody hell is that supposed to mean? Who the hell are you?' William examined the flier's uniform: Prussian!

'*Ich heisse Heinrich!* Who are you?'

William winced as a spasm shot through his injured leg. He twisted to find a less painful position. 'I am Lieutenant William Hastings, First Air Battalion,' he responded, then continued angrily, 'of Her Majesty's North African Expeditionary Force! What gives you the right to shoot at me? What the hell are you up to, you bastard? And just what do you think you're going to do now, Herr Heinrich?'

The air between them grew tense and seemed to increase the uncertainty of the Prussian flier. His blue eyes vacillated back and forth between the man at his feet and his burning machine. Heinrich's shoulders seemed to bunch up around his ears as some internal struggle played itself out. Then, with a distinct slumping in his frame, his will collapsed. He let out a resigned, '*Nein!*' A faint smile formed on his lips and he threw back his head, exhausting his tension with a strange and guttural laugh. When he returned his attention to William, he seemed to have regained his composure. William was baffled by the Prussian's behavior.

'So what are we to do now, English?' pondered the flier out loud.

Before William could respond, the noises of the fire and the idling motor were drowned out by a strange throbbing drone. The sky darkened as if a thundercloud were approaching—an event all but impossible in the surrounding region. He leaned his head back to find the sun blotted out by the dark form of a dirigible as it thrust itself over them like a breaching whale. It barely cleared the crest of the dune and sent currents of sand whipping about them, into their eyes, into their mouths, and into their bleeding wounds. William's heart skipped a beat; the giant machine overwhelmed him.

The Prussian, being least surprised of the two, gathered his wits quickly. After spitting the sand from his mouth, he shouted at William in an effort to be heard over the racket, 'I am expected to shoot you! They will be angry when they see that I haven't. I suggest you pretend to already be dead.'

'What?' snarled William; it was a ridiculous suggestion.

'*Speil wie kindern!* Play act! Play act like you are dead!'

William rolled his eyes in exasperation.

'Now!' gestured the Prussian, pointing at the ground with his pistol for emphasis. 'There is no time—they will see you moving. Trust me!'

Unable to devise a plan of his own, William growled and threw himself on his back; he fought to still his heaving chest. The Prussian cast a quick glance over his shoulder to ensure that the airship was indeed continuing its course downwind before eventually turning toward the open space to the west, the logical place to approach and land.

'Not like that!' said the Prussian with disapproval. 'On your belly, as if you died crawling from your aeroplane.'

William cursed under his breath, rolled over, and spread himself out in as convincing a manner as possible. With these minimal theatrical preparations complete, the two men remained in their respective positions, silent, tense, unsure how to pass the several minutes it would take for the lumbering machine to safely come to rest. William's mind raced; he struggled to come up with a better way to extricate himself, but an idea wouldn't come.

If William had been less preoccupied with his own thoughts, and had he taken the opportunity to look up, he would have noticed an unusual transformation in the Prussian as he stared down at his captive. It would have been obvious that the Prussian was beginning to reconsider his decision; it was as if being released from the gaze of his foe was enough to harden his will and recall him to his duty. But the Prussian remained motionless and waited.

The ponderous ship expended its momentum and slowed to a stop a few feet above the firm desert surface. A dozen men in gray uniforms burst from hatches and slid down ropes suspended from the aluminum gondola protruding under its bow; they were like so many Jonas coughed up from the jaws of the leviathan. A startling boom echoed between the dunes as a steel shaft shot out from beneath the craft and, like a harpoon, instantly shackled it to the ground. The craft wallowed in currents of its own making as the crew rushed about and heaved on ropes released from several points along its length. Some men dangled on the ends of the ropes while others, frantic, hammered long iron stakes into the ground on which to tie them. A couple of men were yanked roughly about, a result of the creature's unwillingness to be restrained.

Three men, black booted, dressed in gray like the others but with caps that marked them as officers, marched across the sand and up to the blue-eyed flier, who now stood above William in a pose strikingly devoid of triumph. William fought against the growing impulse to get up and run.

'*Ist ihn tot?*' asked the first officer to approach.

'*Ich denke so*,' said the blue-eyed flier.

'*Was mienen sie—ich denke so? Desen sicher! Schiess ihn!*'

'*Meine pistole verstopft.*'

'*Trett ihn mit dem fuss!*'

'*Was gibst hier?*' interrupted a new voice, deeper, older, more demanding, a voice that had been issuing commands for many years. It belonged to the pair of boots that planted themselves near William's waist.

The tone of the conversation thus far convinced William he had made a mistake by agreeing to such a foolish plan.

'*Wir wollen ihn mit dem fuss tretten*,' said the first voice. '*Wenn ihn lebst, wir wollen ihn schiessen.*'

'*Idiot!*' barked the commander. '*Gibst es einen rundfunk-sender?*' There was a moment of uncomfortable silence, some shuffling feet, '*Ausfinden!*'

As the first pair of boots trotted off in the direction of the burning wreck, William felt the toe of another bury itself under his ribs and lift him a few inches. Pain shot through his chest and he couldn't help the escape of a soft groan.

The owner of the boot hesitated, surprised, and then pushed him over onto his back. William shaded his eyes from the glaring rays of sun that seemed to transmute the ramrod-straight officer towering over him into the silhouette of some Teutonic Jehovah. The officer rested his hand on the butt of his holstered pistol, a pistol that surely never had, and never would, jam. But the officer waited—not hesitating, but calculating. The scrutiny lasted less than a minute, after which he muttered, '*Nicht jetzt*!' He raised an arm and snapped his fingers at the other men waiting in the distance. '*Nehmt ihn zur dem schiff.*' After giving the blue-eyed flier a fierce and penetrating glare, he stomped back toward the airship.

The flier turned and watched the officer's back with a frown, shrugged, and whispered to William, 'See, I told you to trust me.'

Two foul-smelling crewmen hoisted William to his feet. When he lifted his eyes to examine the waiting machine, they pushed his head down with a gruff, '*Nein!*' and then immediately covered him with an oily smelling jacket.

Although William received only the briefest glimpse of the majestic craft, the sudden imposition of darkness seemed to burn its image into his mind, as if it had been exposed onto a photographic plate. The dirigible's shape was roughly that of a long cylinder formed by a series of flat strakes that extended for several hundred feet. The front end was somewhat flattened and seemed to emphasize its similarity to a great sperm whale. The other end tapered to a point amid a set of box-kite-like structures that were obviously intended to provide steerage.

The dirigible's hide was gray, worn, mottled, and stained. It reflected little of the surrounding brightness. The occasional glint of glass set in a row under the bow seemed to hint at teeth not quite exposed to view.

William gasped from the painful knocks and scrapes as

his captors pushed him through a hatch and roughly guided him down a narrow passage. His only sight was that of his own blood as it dripped from his wounds onto his boots. Deeper inside he was struck by odors that reminded him of his tent at the airstrip after a day of flying: sweat, grease, oil, fuel, exhaust, possibly boiled cabbage, and perhaps even vomit. He began to feel sick. Eventually he came to rest on a scratchy blanket atop a hard cot. His nostrils grew accustomed to the new surroundings; the smells of the hallway faded, only to be replaced by the faint scents of alcohol and chloroform that identified his place of confinement as the ship's infirmary. His escorts securely restrained his hands and legs with leather straps and steel buckles. They yanked the covering off his head and locked the door behind them, leaving him in virtual darkness. A thin strip of light squeezed into the windowless cabin through a gap at the bottom of the door.

He lay quietly as each injury took its turn clamoring for attention. The fright of the crash had begun to fade, only to be replaced by desperation as he realized these men were going to thwart his return home in a much more significant way than his commanding officer could ever have done. And back in a corner of his mind, not clearly identifiable, covered up by the pain and the panic, a cold fury began to grow—a personal rage at the unwarranted violence that had been perpetrated against him.

There was little to distract him, only the thumps and thuds of heavy mechanical work somewhere nearby, accompanied at times by hurried, strained, and often angry voices. Though by the time the voices had worked their way through the labyrinth of aluminum, canvas, and wood, they consisted only of muffled emotions, devoid of meaning or information. Eventually the noise subsided, and then many heavy feet tromped past the door of the infirmary. A single pair of boots lagged behind. A hand fumbled unsuccessfully at the lock, and a familiar voice asked, 'Are you all right, English?'

*

William woke with a start. His surroundings appeared unchanged. However, a steady vibration had replaced the earlier stillness. The various utensils arranged on the metal counter across from him rattled and jingled. They were underway.

*

The click of a key in the lock of the cabin door interrupted another doze of uncertain length. A silent visitor slid inside the dark cabin. William could hear him open and shut cabinet doors and handle obscure objects. The visitor was apparently satisfied with the weak illumination provided by the hallway lamps. Then came the sound of a cap being screwed off the top of a glass bottle. Suddenly the room filled with fumes reminding William of visits to his own camp infirmary, usually after the crash of another flier, or to hospitals back home in England. A moment later he was struggling against his bindings as the stranger pressed a chloroform-soaked rag to his face. He fought against the fog and the gray night that gave way to bad dreams, stern faces, and unending questions—questions to which there never seemed to be a satisfactory answer.

*

William regained consciousness as if he were climbing from the narrow depths of a deep well. A smile on the face of the blue-eyed Prussian flier greeted him. William slowly recognized him as the man responsible for his predicament.

'*Guten morgen*, William Hastings,' said the Prussian pleasantly.

William nodded and gazed stiffly about at his surroundings;

he was no longer in the infirmary. The small cabin to which he had been transferred was barely large enough to hold the two cots running its length. It was relatively well lit by sunlight streaming in through a small, egg-shaped porthole in the wall opposite the door. The Prussian's flying suit and helmet hung from a hook on the wall above the foot of his cot. A folding metal table had been placed in the space between them; on it, steam rose from two tin cups filled with pungent coffee. The Prussian, who had been resting with his back against the far wall, reached down and gently lifted a cup to his lips, drinking with noisy slurps.

'Morning is it?' asked William hoarsely. Then gazing about, he asked, 'Yours?'

'*Ja!* My home,' the Prussian chuckled, 'even smaller than my room in Berlin.'

William reached up and rubbed his face, forcing himself into coherence. He now noticed that his limbs were no longer bound. He touched his forehead and discovered a neatly trimmed bandage. Lifting his blanket and peering underneath, he observed a pair of wooden splints along his right calf, held securely in place by canvas strips.

'It is only . . . ' the Prussian hunted for the words to express himself, 'sorry, how do you say it?' With his free hand he twisted the corner of his blanket. 'You know, like this.'

William stared, confused, and then understood, 'Sprained?'

The Prussian thought for a moment, 'Yes, that's it, sprained. Herr Doktor said it is only sprained and will heal nicely and quickly. You may find it a bit difficult to get around for a while, but that will not matter as you have nowhere to go.' The Prussian chuckled.

William pushed his elbows back into the cot and tried to pull himself into a sitting position. He gasped as pain shot through his right side.

'Oh yes, and you have two broken ribs as well. Sorry again. You are in rather pathetic shape, my friend. Please let me assist you.'

The Prussian crossed the space between them and stretched out a helping hand, but stopped short, halted by the ferocity in William's eyes. 'Very well, suit yourself,' the Prussian responded and eased himself back into his former position. He then took obvious satisfaction in watching William struggle, the pain accompanying each shift in his body clearly evident. Eventually, William managed to get himself upright and began sipping from his own tin cup.

'Let me introduce myself again,' continued the Prussian. 'My name is Count Heinrich von Gotha, or rather Oberleutnant zur Luft von Gotha, though most everyone calls me Heinrich. You may call me Heinrich.' He again extended his hand with a smile.

William stared at it resentfully, his first inclination being to punch the man. But eventually, reluctantly, he reached out and took it, wincing as they shook. 'I hope you're not expecting me to thank you,' said William, 'for preventing your friends from murdering me.'

'Not at all, but you are, of course, quite welcome. Though you should not get too comfortable yet. Last night I had to argue with them again. They wanted to throw you out.'

William's eyes widened slightly. 'Charming company you keep. Not very officer-like.'

'*Ja*, some of them are animals. They're from the army.'

Each took a moment to swallow more coffee.

'A count, eh? You're awfully young. A real one?'

'Of course, a real one,' exclaimed Heinrich with a wounded expression, 'although being a count today is not what it used to be.'

'Instead of murdering unarmed fliers, why aren't you shooting grouse back at your castle in Bavaria?'

'Firstly, Gotha is not in Bavaria. Secondly, while you may have been unarmed, you still have eyes in your head. Thirdly, it's not a very nice castle: holes in the roof, cracks in the walls, and no money to fix them, like many of the castles back home these days. It is strange though, how even crumbling castles still attract the attention of the tax man.' Heinrich stared vacantly after making this remark, momentarily consumed by other thoughts. 'However, the Kaiser has kindly provided me an aeroplane in return. And as I like to fly, it is not so bad.'

'I didn't get a good look at your machine,' said William. 'How did you do it . . . all by yourself . . . shoot up my aeroplane?' He was fairly sure that he now owned the unfortunate distinction of being the first man ever to be shot out of the skies.

'Ah,' said Heinrich, hesitating. He fingered the cut on his cheek, absently, and his good-natured smile faded momentarily. 'If you did not notice, better for you not to know.' Then after a brief pause, with a gleam in his eyes, he added, 'So tell me about Emily.'

'What?' coughed William as he choked on a mouthful of coffee.

'You talked about her quite a bit last night.'

'Last night? What happened last night?' Disturbing images skittered about inside William's head, and the scent of chloroform seemed to return to his nostrils.

'You were interrogated. I was there.'

'Interrogated? Why?'

'We do not want anyone to know that we are here. We needed to know where your friends are located so we could avoid them.'

'And I cooperated?'

'Oh yes, your performance was excellent. The admiral seemed very happy. Perhaps that is why he did not throw you out.'

'Admiral? An admiral in command of a lone airship? You must be up to something particularly unpleasant.'

The smile faded from Heinrich's face for a second time, but his concern quickly passed. 'You didn't answer my question. Who is Emily? A picture of a very pretty girl was in your pocket.' Heinrich reached into his tunic pocket and produced the photo.

'This must be Emily. Is she your girlfriend?'

William frowned. 'She's my sister,' he muttered.

'Your sister!' said Heinrich in surprise. 'She doesn't look a bit like you. Is she married? I don't have a girlfriend.'

'Give me that photo!' growled William, and for the second time during their conversation his eyes filled with a venomous animosity.

Startled by such passion, a surprised look spread across the Prussian's face. 'We do not have to be enemies.' Heinrich extended the photo toward William, who snatched it from his hand.

After a couple of minutes of uncomfortable silence, the emotion on each side drained away. Heinrich emptied his cup and jumped up from his cot. William could feel the flooring sag under his weight; even the walls seemed to bow slightly.

'Wait a minute!' cried William. 'Where are you going?'

'I must join the others for breakfast in the mess. Would you like me to bring you something to eat?'

'Just hold on. What's going to happen to me? Where are we going?'

'The answer to both questions is . . . *I* . . . *don't* . . . *know*. There seem to be fewer and fewer answers to important questions these days. But we will have plenty of time to talk later. My duties are rather light now—unless another flying Englishman should appear on the horizon. Not likely though, this deep in the desert.'

Heinrich left the cabin and locked the door behind him. William could hear him chuckling through the thin wall as he disappeared into the ship.

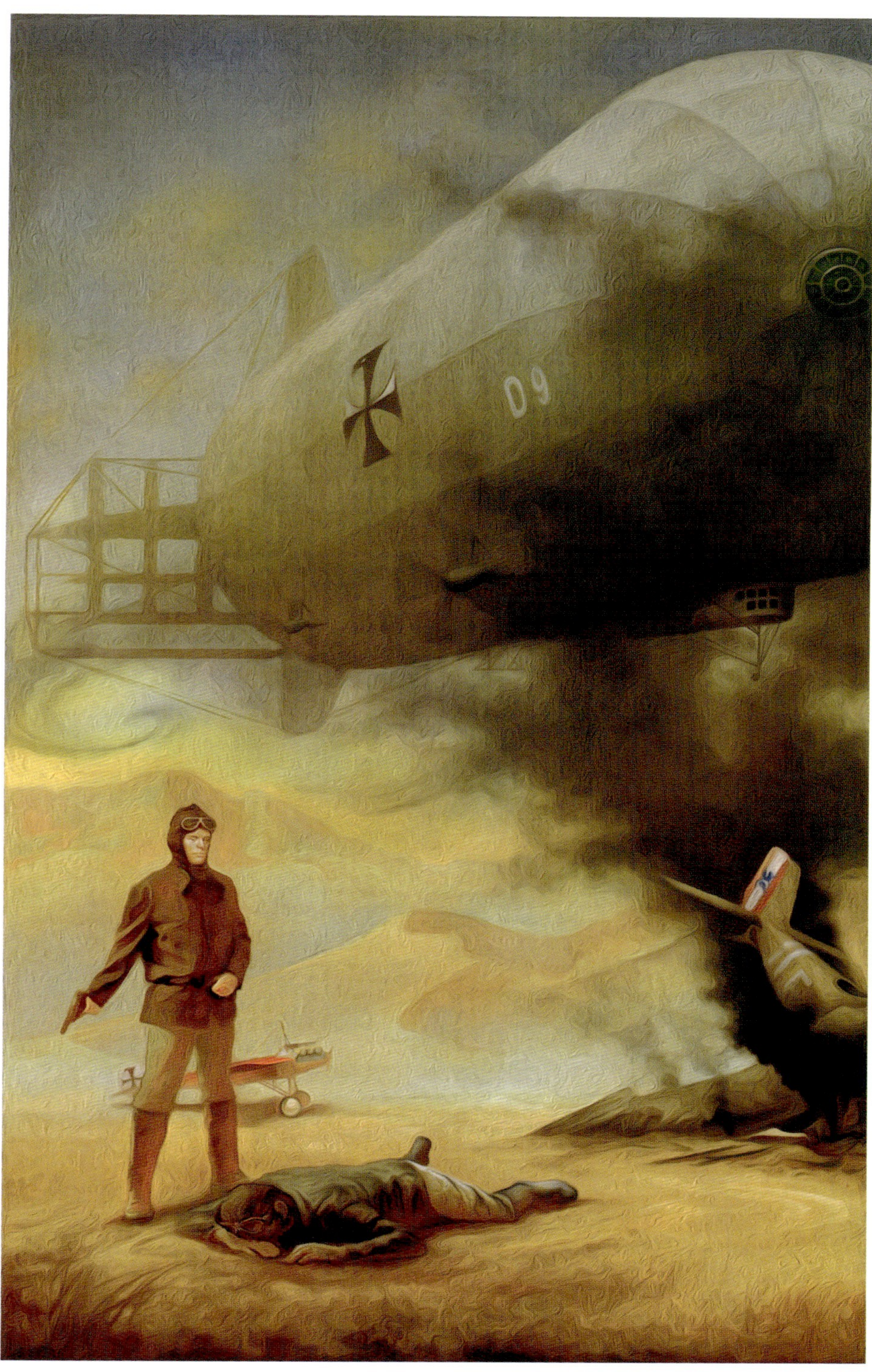

Chapter 3

Von Krupp's Uhlan

Heinrich strolled along the narrow corridor of the officers' deck with his head bent; he mulled over his impressions of the Englishman. He found William's charged display of animosity disturbing and a bit ridiculous. How long would that silly Englishman stay angry with him? He ought to be happy just to be alive, given the circumstances. After a little time to heal he would be none the worse for wear.

Heinrich hoped the same could be said about him. His reluctance to shoot his adversary the day before had come as a surprise, and now it bothered him. The admiral's orders had been precise, and the attack well executed—a complete validation of this particular method of downing a hostile aircraft, albeit a docile and unsuspecting aircraft. But to shoot a man in the face with a pistol had somehow been beyond him. And now, instead of basking in the pride of his unique accomplishment, the first in the short history of aviation, he felt ashamed. Thank God he hadn't gone for the cavalry. The only thing worse than shooting a man up close would be chopping him in half with a sword. Still, there was no room for the squeamish anywhere in the Prussian military, not even in the navy where one didn't usually get too close a look at one's enemy before killing him.

He blamed his weak nerves on the startling and unexpected side effects that had accompanied his aerial attack. He reached up and gently stroked the gash on his cheek; he hoped he wouldn't be left with an ugly scar.

From the first moment of his enlistment he had been concerned about how he would behave in a fight. He didn't like admitting that he had been experiencing an increasing sense of relief, as this bizarre mission seemed to take him further and further from the potential scene of any battle. Europe had become a powder keg, and none could say when or where war might erupt.

As luck would have it, within days of their departure, he had been faced with the very event he had dreaded. He had been forced to fight with dozens of eyes watching his every move from the portholes of the airship, and he had then failed to completely vanquish his foe. If his father had been looking down from heaven, he would have shaken his head in disappointment. His grandfather, a cavalryman, the very first Count von Gotha, would have called him *eine kleine maus*—a little mouse.

Eventually the corridor opened onto a wardroom with a metal table at its center. Six uniformed men had squeezed around it; they rested on small metal chairs that all but disappeared beneath their collective mass, chairs so flimsy that each man sat in his own distinctive and awkward position, as if anticipating some structural failure during the course of the meal. Heinrich had found the scene more and more amusing with each passing day and hoped eventually to capture it with the chief engineer's camera. The only concession to decorum was a blotched white cloth draped across the table; multi-tinted stains shared space with the navy service spread upon it: dull aluminum plates, dented cups, and twisted mess ware. The stains could never be completely removed given the limited washing facilities aboard; there was insufficient water even to redress the officers' soiled uniforms, or to let them shave the prickly growth of their new whiskers.

Most of the officers were present:

Oberleutnant zur Luft Peter Dürr, the ship's executive officer
Steuerman Karl Nebel, the navigator
Unteroffizier Klaus Schmitt, the wireless operator
Oberingenieur Franz Bach, the chief engineer
Herr Doktor, Emil Dreckmesser

Also, they had a guest at their table that morning: Flieger Erste Klasse Hugo Klimt, the sail maker.

Noisy conversation ricocheted off the close walls as Heinrich entered; his heart lifted and he smiled.

'There you are, Heinrich,' smiled Karl, the navigator. 'We are so happy to see you.'

'Actually, we are *surprised* to see you,' said Ober Dürr.

'Why?' asked Heinrich as he took an open seat at the end of the table; this left two seats free at the other end: one reserved for the captain, in charge of the ship's operation, and the other for the admiral, in charge of their mission. The admiral had been a last-minute addition to the crew—a disturbing event given that admirals didn't typically stoop to the command of a solitary ship.

'Well,' explained Ober Dürr, 'you shoot this poor English fellow's aeroplane out from under him, break his leg, crack his ribs, practically scalp him in the crash, threaten to shoot him with your pistol, and then let Herr Doktor experiment on him.' The doctor, a pale and jelly-faced man, grinned with pride that his amateur talents as an interrogator had not gone unnoticed. 'And after all that, you invite him into your own cabin. It's a wonder he didn't strangle you in your sleep.'

Everyone laughed. Heinrich nodded in mute submission. He liked Dürr, whose authority aboard ship in no way interfered with his good nature. Even though Heinrich had known him for only a couple of weeks, he recognized the man's competence and admired the gentle manner that had earned him the respect of most everyone on board.

Dürr's jests were meant in good fun, but they had a point. Heinrich hadn't invited the Englishman into his cabin; the admiral had insisted, as punishment for Heinrich's timidity the day before. Now, having become fully aware of the English flier's antipathy toward him, the jests only added to his growing discomfort. He did not share with them the fact that he had not slept well that night.

Heinrich also could sense the ill will, barely held in check, from some of the others at the table. Although none would openly admit it, he was sure that they were wishing he had been more thorough in his aerial ambush, and that they resented the foreign flier's presence aboard. They were all apprehensive about where their journey would take them, as their destination was still a secret held closely by the captain and the admiral; they didn't want any further complications.

With the intention of diverting the conversation from himself and his Englishman, Heinrich blurted out loudly, 'Franz, has anyone looked at my aeroplane?'

The chief engineer looked up; he was a small, downcast man who rarely participated in their conversations and was surprised at being directly addressed. 'You mean your little oil leak?' he asked.

'It does not seem such a little leak when flying all by oneself at three thousand meters—and with only one engine. Little leaks have a way of turning into big ones.'

'No, your motor has not yet been looked at,' responded the engineer morosely as he turned back to his food. 'All machinists are busy with engine No. 4.'

'Still not fixed?' blurted the navigator, whose concerns had been growing with every delay in their journey.

'No, Karl,' interjected the wireless operator, irritated, 'you're thinking of engine No. 3. It's been fixed. He's talking about No. 4—it stopped running a little while ago. It just quit, like one of those guild strikers back home.'

'We haven't been under full power for more than a single hour since we left Bulgaria,' muttered the navigator. 'We're going to be late.'

'Indeed, Karl, I'm sure we will,' said Heinrich, who was at times guilty of encouraging the navigator's neurotic tendencies.

'Machines aren't perfect!' cried the engineer, looking up fiercely. 'But they can be fixed, which is more than can be said for some of you!' Grins spread around the table.

'Well, at least we haven't caught fire yet,' chuckled Heinrich, happy that the conversation had been successfully redirected.

Everyone turned to stare at him. None laughed. The chief engineer frowned.

'It's easy to joke about fire when you've been aboard for only a short while,' growled the navigator. 'We'll see how you joke after a few months.'

'Karl's right,' said the wireless officer. 'I've been in the naval air service for two years now. Over a thousand hours of flight time on airships since I left the army, and I've never been on a ship more plagued with problems than this one. No wonder it was a year late out of the Dusseldorf sheds.'

'And what about those workmen at Dusseldorf?' chimed in Hugo Klimt. Some of the others rolled their eyes in irritation at the ancient sail maker's comment.

'What, Hugo?' asked Dürr. 'You mean those silly rumors about men falling from the frame, getting crushed by motors, being set on fire by welding torches? Soon you'll be whispering about ghosts!' Dürr laughed derisively, effectively shutting the sail maker's mouth.

'*Schiesse!*' shouted the engineer, throwing down his napkin. 'You're all a bunch of clowns. I'm going back to the motors.' The engineer jumped up, grabbed the remaining chop from his plate, and stormed out of the wardroom.

During the commotion the sail maker quickly took the opportunity to pass something under the table to the wireless officer and inadvertently bumped Heinrich's leg. With an impish expression on his face, Heinrich reached under the table, grabbed the object from the sail maker's hands, and pulled it into view—a heavy, rectangular shape covered by a wrinkled paper bag.

'What are you up to, gentlemen?' laughed Heinrich loudly. 'Passing love notes at school? Is it candy?' A couple of men laughed and gazed on in curiosity; all had left their personal effects back in Prussia in reluctant compliance with the maniacal effort to save weight for precious goods such as fuel, food, and water. Others did not laugh, and from the irritation on their faces, it was clear that they were already familiar with the bag's contents.

Heinrich reached in and pulled out a thick bundle of papers that at one time had formed the vital part of a fine, hardbound volume. Its cover had been removed, probably to reduce its weight—a ludicrous notion in light of the flagrant disregard of orders forbidding such personal effects. Even the title page had been removed as nonessential.

'What have we here?' asked Heinrich as he leafed through the pages. 'Where did you get this, Herr Klimt?'

'I have friends,' mumbled the sail maker.

'I'm sure you do,' chuckled Heinrich. 'What is its title?'

'It's called *Von Krupp's Uhlan*,' said the wireless officer as he wrenched it out of Heinrich's hands and shoved it under his thigh out of sight.

'*Von Krupp's Uhlan* . . . I believe I've heard of such a book. What is it about?'

'It's about a creature,' said Hugo. 'You know, about a monster.'

'It's not about a monster, you dolt,' shot back Klaus, the wireless officer. 'It's about a lunatic general.'

No sooner had Klaus let fly this comment, than the admiral stepped into the wardroom. All conversation stopped, and through involuntary reflex from his years in the army, the wireless officer started to rise from his seat. Before his mind could reassert control over his limbs, he was in a half crouching position that exposed the illegal literature. All eyes in the room not already riveted to *Von Krupp's Uhlan* shot over to the admiral; all searched for signs of an impending eruption. None came. After a casual glance at the contraband clutched in Klaus's hands, the admiral eased himself down onto his post at the head of the table, opened his neatly folded napkin, and laid it across his lap, while the steward, who also served as both cook and second wireless operator, brought in his meal.

'I happened to pass the chief in the corridor,' said the admiral, as he examined his plate and gathered his utensils. 'He was muttering something about ghosts. To what was he referring?' The admiral's eyes shot up and scanned the officers around him; he scrutinized each in a random manner. Those with food still on their plates busied themselves with it, thus avoiding the informal interrogation, while those less fortunate gazed at each other mutely.

'School children!' thought Heinrich.

'You must all take care with your bearing,' the admiral calmly lectured. 'Kapitanleutnant Timmer would be very disappointed. By the way, where is the kapitan?'

'In his cabin,' responded Dürr.

'He's been locked in his cabin for most of the last three days,' said the admiral. 'Who, may I ask, is commanding the ship?'

'I am,' said Dürr, in a matter-of-fact tone. 'The kapitan is available should I need him.'

Exasperated by the news, the admiral simply shrugged his shoulders before continuing. 'If all of you begin fueling this ridiculous talk of a bad luck ship—.' The men opened their mouths to object but were immediately cut off. 'No, no, I have heard such talk—gossip expected of army privates, not officers on one of our Kaiser's airships. I am ashamed of you. You must do better. Indeed, I appreciate that this is a complicated machine. Like any complex ship it acquires its own personality—its own *mechanical* personality—but it is not alive! My last flagship, the battleship *Gurtherstein*, would behave in a most peculiar manner during heavy seas. There is nothing in this airship that cannot be remedied or improved with sufficient effort on your part.'

Other than the recent episode with the Englishman, Heinrich had had little interaction with the admiral, their journey having only just begun. Nevertheless, Heinrich had taken a quick dislike to the officer. There he sat on his little aluminum throne; he deftly buttered a chunk of glistening black bread while his eyes moved about in their deep purple sockets under a heavy protruding brow. The man didn't hesitate to award himself special privileges; he alone among those around the table presented a clean-shaven face. But it was more than that. Heinrich could not exactly put his finger on it—something to do with the man upsetting the proper order of their life aboard. He would lecture the captain's subordinates indiscriminately, as if they were privates fresh from the recruiting halls. It reminded Heinrich of those times as a child when he was punished by his grandfather rather than by his father. It was inappropriate.

Heinrich's last conversation with his grandfather had started with a lecture by the old man about Heinrich's duty to the family and the importance of maintaining the Von Gotha estate. It had ended in shouts. Now, years later, after his father's recent death, Heinrich was left with nothing but crumbling stones and mounds of debt. Frantic to shepherd the small inheritance passed on to him by his mother before she returned to her family home in England, and to gain favor at court, Heinrich had been one of the first to join the Kaiser's fledgling air service. Some had speculated that it would someday make the cavalry obsolete. The old man, a great cavalry officer in his day, would have choked on that. Heinrich liked the idea of his grandfather choking and wished the old man had lived long enough to see the new order of things.

Heinrich's thoughts were interrupted by the sudden appearance of a panicked machinist's mate. 'Sir!' the mate shouted, not addressing any one officer in particular; he seemed overwhelmed by the bundle of authority gathered around the table. He was a cherubic young man, a boy really, sprouting light blond hair atop a bloodless face.

'Yes, Ernst?' said Dürr, looking up from his meal. 'What is it?'

'There's a leak in the hull!' the boy shouted.

'A leak in the hull?' said Dürr with concern, a hint of a smile forming around his eyes.

'Yes, sir, a leak!' repeated the boy, a little less loudly. Doubt flitted across his face. This was clearly not the reaction he had expected; no officers bolted from the table, some had not even looked up from their meals. The admiral gazed at him as if he were mad.

'A leak is it? What kind of leak, Airman Halterman?'

The boy flushed. Then, with his confidence crushed, he muttered, 'An air leak, sir.'

'An air leak . . . in the hull?' asked Dürr, now openly grinning. 'I see.' He then reached behind him to open a small porthole in the side of the wardroom, letting in a blast of hot desert air. 'You mean like this, Herr Halterman?'

The boy locked his jaws, dropped his arms stiffly to his sides and blurted out, 'Sorry, sir. They said . . . '

'All right, Airman,' said Dürr, 'I am glad you are so concerned about the safety of our ship, but you should learn to trust your own judgment. To do that, you must learn everything there is to learn about the ship. Tell the others we will perform a thorough inspection of the hydrogen bags this afternoon. And you will accompany me. You may go now.' The boy relaxed slightly, but appeared to receive little satisfaction that those who had practiced on his ignorance would suffer.

'Yes, sir,' said the boy glumly, before disappearing back into the ship. After his departure there was a pause, followed by a few chuckles. Dürr closed the porthole, shutting out the rushing noise.

'You especially, Herr Klimt,' said the admiral, picking up where he had left off. He pointed at the sail maker with his knife and shook it like a conductor's baton for emphasis; a small dab of butter dropped from its tip into the bowl of gravy beneath. 'You have much influence over the rest of the crew. You must help to keep this nonsense under control.' The sail maker choked on his bread. Heinrich had no doubt the poor man would have preferred taking his meal in his usual location, in the crew's mess, with the crew, where his years of experience secured him a throne of his own.

During this harangue, Heinrich was momentarily distracted by a soft bump transmitted to him through his creaking chair.

Actually, he couldn't quite call it a bump; the water in his cup didn't spill. It was more like a tremor, a twisting motion that appeared to contort the orthogonal geometry of the wardroom. Apparently he was not the only one to notice this strange perturbation; others raised their eyes to make contact with those opposite them at the table. Eating utensils hung in the space between plate and mouth.

The admiral opened his mouth to share another shard of advice when suddenly all were thrust up from their seats and found themselves flailing about in midair. The entire volume of the cabin—all eighteen hundred cubic feet of it—became evenly distributed with sauerkraut and admirals, pork chops and sail makers, turnips and doctors. Slices of bread scattered. The navigator did a somersault. Potatoes bounced off the walls. The intervening spaces were filled with droplets of water, globules of gravy, and dollops of applesauce.

This liberated period of free flight and democratic sharing of the cabin's entire volume lasted only four or five seconds. Then, just as suddenly, all the contents of the room, animate and not, came crashing down, flattening the aluminum table and its attending chairs. One ulna, two clavicles, and three ribs were instantly snapped in two.

The men, once having regained contact with the wardroom floor, found it at a very different angle from when they had left it. Those not groaning in agony amongst the stew collecting to one side immediately realized the ship was now diving toward the earth at a precipitous angle. While shouts of panic filled the air, and as Herr Doktor giggled hysterically, the admiral clawed over the bodies and made his way to the door. 'Get to your posts!' he shouted.

The urgency of the vibration traveling through the ship's frame grew with its building momentum. But just as the officers began to disentangle themselves from each other, the ship began to right itself. Its aluminum skeleton groaned and a rapid series of metallurgical pops and pings shot about over their heads. Once level, the officers bolted for their duty stations; they cleaned scraps of food from their faces as they ran. The steward assisted those still rolling around in the muck.

Heinrich managed to keep his composure, though his heart beat violently. He took off after those officers headed to the control cabin located at the most forward point of the officers' deck, but halted at the door to his cabin. After searching through his pockets for the key and then wrestling with the finicky lock, he managed to push the flimsy door open halfway. Something resisted from the inside; this turned out to be William, who had been thrown to the floor and lay there in a disheveled heap.

'All in order?' asked Heinrich, forcing himself to maintain an even tone of voice.

'What the hell just happened!' yelled William. 'Do you fellows really know how to fly this thing?'

'Just the desert air, you know. A little bump.'

William began to shout obscenities, and so Heinrich pulled the door closed. As he tried to relock it, he discovered something jammed in the keyhole from the inside that hindered him from turning his key. Pushing the door back open, he reached in and felt around for the other side of the keyhole; he found the twisted end of a paperclip protruding from it. Exasperated by William's behavior, he yanked the wire out and threw it at William's head, then quickly finished his duty as jailer.

Although he had made light of the ship's tumble, Heinrich was actually quite shaken. Had such a turbulent fit engulfed him in his small aeroplane, he would have been greatly concerned for its structural integrity. He could only imagine the effect on such a large and ungainly craft as their airship.

Finding the control cabin crammed tight with worried officers, Heinrich turned about and retraced his steps, heading toward that part of the ship from which his aeroplane was suspended. He trod through the wardroom, now an empty swamp, but paused when he noticed the gilt-edged pages of

Von Krupp's Uhlan lying in the debris. He picked up the bundle, already swelling with moisture, and brushed it off, flinging its crust of sludge to one side. He slipped it inside his tunic, so he could peruse it later in the privacy of his cabin; he carried on toward his destination.

The aft-facing door of the wardroom connected with a narrow, inclined ramp that provided Heinrich access to the ship's keel, a long cage-like structure of interconnecting girders. The keel ran the entire length of the ship and provided both structural support for the hull as well as an important corridor for the crew. From this point one could travel in either of two directions—forward for approximately two hundred feet as the keel ran above the officers' deck where it followed the gentle curve of the ship's bow, or aft for over five hundred feet to the stern.

From the first time he had climbed aboard, Heinrich had found the keel to have an Aladdin's cave feel to it. Much of the ship's important mechanical gear was mounted along its length, like so much sparkling treasure amongst the walls of drab canvas: oil tanks with their new silver paint spoiled by black drippings, gasoline tanks now half-full and sloshing at each bump, bulging sacks of leather that jiggled with ballast water, dented spare-parts bins painted dull black, toilets of polished aluminum that no longer sparkled, and a wide assortment of ladders. Ladders appeared at regular intervals all along the keel; they led to gangways that gave access to the motor gondolas; they led to the aeroplane bay; and they led up between the gas cells to the axial corridor fifty feet above, and then on to even loftier heights.

Heinrich arrived at one of these ladders just as Ober Dürr dropped to the floor before him like a monkey swinging from a tree.

'Peter, has my aeroplane survived?' asked Heinrich.

'How should I know,' said Dürr impatiently. 'Who cares about your aeroplane right now. The whole ship could fall apart after a tumble like that. If the thing happens to still be there, maybe you ought to climb in and fly away.'

'Ok, ok, Peter, no need to be so nasty. So how bad are things, really?' Heinrich probed Dürr's face. Having no direct responsibility for the ship's operation and living a life somewhat apart from the crew's normal routine, Heinrich was left with a very superficial understanding of the dirigible's construction. It was only by the emotion evident on his fellow officer's face that he could gauge the seriousness of their condition. Dürr's face left him anxious.

'I don't know yet, Heinrich,' said Dürr, looking carefully about, continuing his inspection as he spoke. 'So far I haven't found anything too bad. This beast is tougher than it looks. We lost three mechanics, though.'

'What do you mean *lost*?'

'I mean *lost*—over the side.' Heinrich's eyes widened in shock. 'Franz and three off-duty machinists were helping out on engine No. 4. Most weren't wearing their safety cables. Now they're scattered all over the desert, poor fools.'

'What about Franz?' asked Heinrich in dismay.

'They're hauling him in right now. We'll be lucky if he lives though. The safety cables are so long there's not much difference between reaching the end of the tether and hitting the ground. I'm surprised he wasn't ripped in half.'

'And what about the kapitan? What's he doing about all of this?'

'Calm down, Heinrich. He's in the control cabin. He got there before I did. Everything is being managed. Now, you must get out of my way. I must finish my inspection!'

Heinrich left Dürr to his work and headed further down the dimly lit keel. He balanced himself on the narrow plank flooring by reaching up with both arms and clasping the keel's aluminum beams; they ran parallel to his path a couple feet above his head—wires, cables, copper tubing, black rubber hoses, all snaked around these beams and their interconnected bracing like tendons and ligaments around bone. The shadows cast by the small electric lamps hanging in their explosion-proof mountings and pulsing with yellow light made for ghoulish companions. The subterranean feel of his surroundings grew as he traveled deeper into the ship; there were no portholes in this section of the hull, and the only clue that they were actually airborne came from the random knocks of turbulent air; the only clue that it was daylight outside came from the suffocating heat.

Eventually Heinrich arrived at a small ladder and climbed down onto a metal platform suspended beneath the keel. He knelt to unlock a hatch at its center and, as he opened it, let in a blast of hot air and searing light. He recoiled into the relative gloom with his eyes tightly shut.

Once acclimated to the light, Heinrich leaned forward, grasped the hatchway frame firmly with both hands, and thrust his head outside the confines of the ship. The slipstream rippled against his scalp and rushed into his nostrils; the dry air brought tears to his eyes. When he could again see clearly he noticed the landscape below and his heart jumped into his throat; they had plunged from five thousand feet to less than one thousand—dangerously low. Another turbulent gust, half the magnitude of the last, must surely send them crashing into the sand below, where those lucky enough not to be crushed by the wreckage, or roasted by the burning hydrogen, stood no chance of reaching civilization before succumbing to a slow, thirsty death. Peter Dürr's suggestion of flying away, ridiculous as it was, nagged at Heinrich.

Heinrich turned his attention to the tube-frame device, much like a trapeze, from which his brilliant red monoplane hung suspended—wobbling gently and contentedly in its captivity—undamaged by the recent tumult. However, Heinrich observed that the paint on his aircraft's wings was steadily wearing away. Apparently there was enough sand swept airborne, even at altitude, to erode the resin and paint from the

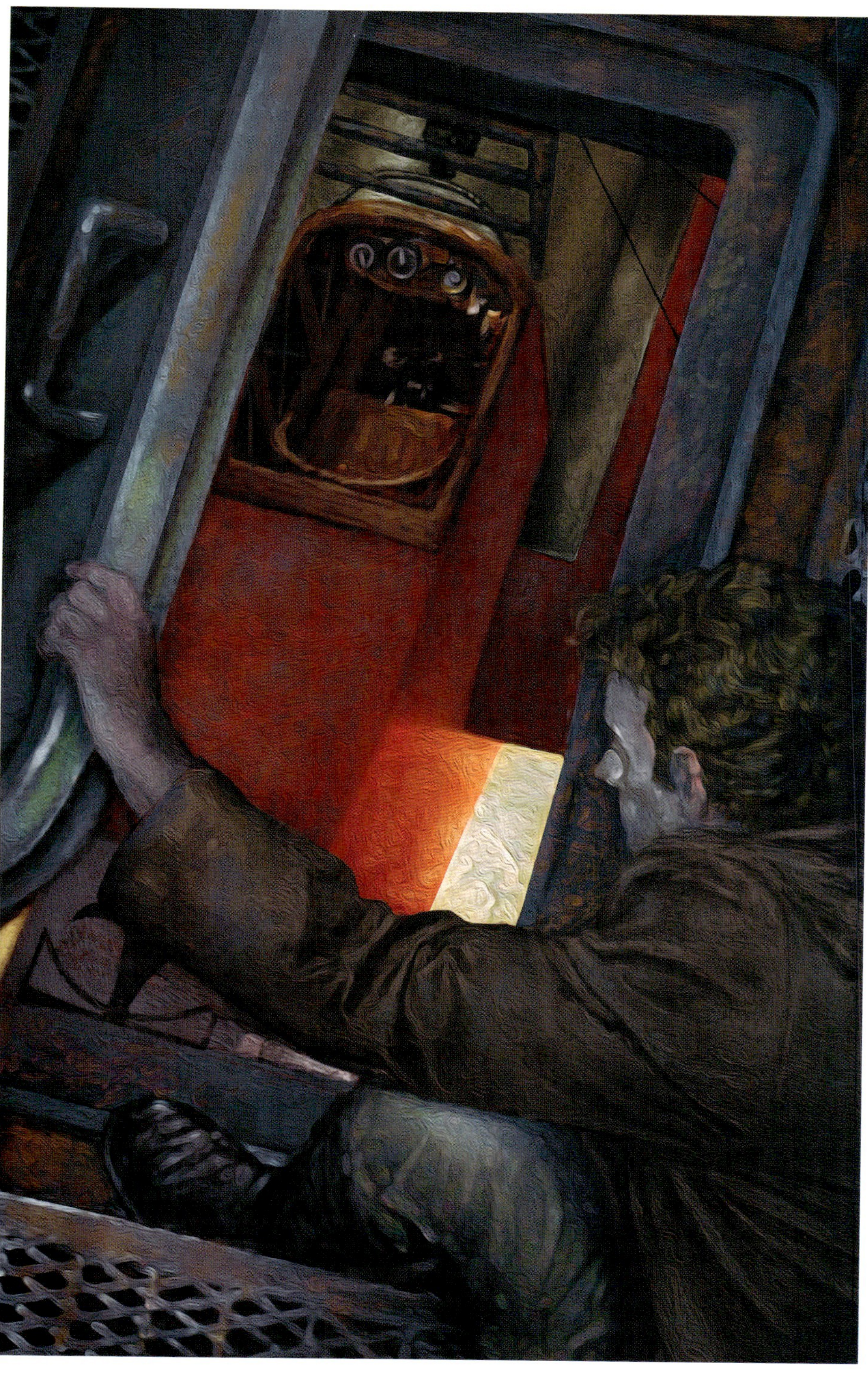

leading edge and expose a long, even strip of pale cotton cloth. The craft could not withstand such abuse indefinitely, and the realization that he might be forced to fly, regardless of the machine's condition, renewed his sense of dread.

'How did I get myself into such a situation?' he mumbled to himself.

Satisfied that his aeroplane was relatively intact for the time being, he couldn't resist a closer examination of the propeller. In particular, he focused on the small steel plates imbedded in the backside of each blade and held securely in place by large counter-sunk screws. The plates were pitted, and small spots of exposed metal glinted against the dark paint. The plates were intended to protect the propeller from the stream of bullets coming from the machine gun mounted atop the fuselage—the secret weapon Heinrich had been so reluctant to disclose to William. The engineers in Dusseldorf had assured him that the angle of the plates was such that any bullets coming in contact with them would be deflected safely to one side. But Heinrich's experience had proven otherwise. Within a few seconds of his squeezing the trigger, with William's aeroplane squarely in his sights, a jagged bullet had shot back and sliced open his cheek. Heinrich had been forced to break off his attack early, before his foe had been destroyed, for fear of inadvertently killing himself. He still hadn't determined which emotion had the upper hand—his anger at the engineers for having lied to him, or the dread at having to pull that deadly trigger again. Heinrich turned from the sickening view and slammed the hatch down. He fumbled with the padlock in the blackness while he forced himself to ignore these depressing thoughts.

Chapter 4

THE GARGOYLE

William darted after the twisted paper clip he had been using as an improvised lock pick and was soon back on his knees boring at the uncooperative tumblers. It was tedious business, and after several minutes of unproductive effort, his mind began to wander. The more he thought, the angrier he got; the angrier he got, the harder he jammed the paperclip into the keyhole. But this was only making things more difficult. Experience had taught him that picking a lock was a delicate task, or so it had been when breaking into his brother's study back home to rifle through his desk. Nevertheless, William couldn't restrain this boiling over within himself. He grew more and more ashamed at having been so easily shot out of the sky, and more and more furious at having been kidnapped. The realization that this ship was no safer than Sir Maxim's flimsy flying machines made him more impatient to escape, even if it were only from the confines of Heinrich's cabin.

William stopped for a moment, closed his eyes, and deliberately calmed himself. It was necessary to consider his position logically and to devise a plan to extricate himself; but the anger and frustration kept swirling up and toppling every attempt at rational thought. As he pounded his fist against the door, the pain from the cuts on his hand only infuriated him further. Think! Think! How was he going to get out of this mess? Where were they taking him? What could have justified their attack? There was no war—not yet anyway. The whole thing was outrageous!

Then it dawned on him. Perhaps war *had* started, and perhaps he had been its first casualty—the very first prisoner, trapped inside this bloated gasbag of a prison. But no, that idea didn't quite measure up. If war had indeed begun, Heinrich's manner toward him would have been altogether different; there would have been no question of them being enemies. Still, as far as William was concerned, Count Heinrich had certainly declared war on him through his sneaking, cowardly ambush!

Perhaps this was the beginning of the move old Maxim had crowed about. William, along with everyone else, had considered the old man a bit daft; he had certainly looked it during his visit to their camp, well over a year ago, while he puttered around in the sand in his top hat and spats. He looked like a lost penguin! But maybe the old coot was right!

William jumped to his feet; he could sit still no longer. He tottered uncomfortably on one leg for a moment. When he observed the fall of the shadows and the rays of the morning light pouring in through the cabin's porthole, he hopped over to peer out the small oval of glass. Down below he picked out the dirigible's shadow as it shot across the monotonous surface of the desert, the only sharp feature in the barren ochre sea. As best he could, judge they were headed in a southwesterly direction, in exactly the opposite direction of the Egyptian Canal. 'Guess old Maxim was wrong,' he muttered to himself. The ship seemed to be traveling deeper into an unpopulated wasteland of little military value. Even the Prussian colonies, somewhere on Africa's eastern coast as best he remembered from his geography lessons, seemed unlikely to be their destination.

After a few more minutes of unproductive and increasingly painful pacing about the cabin, William sank back to the floor and crawled over to the uncooperative lock. He exhaled deeply, then resumed his work with a self-imposed patience; he was prepared to stay at the task until he succeeded, however long that might take. After only a few minutes, however, there came a liberating click, and the door popped open. William let out a grunt, somewhat disappointed that the harsh discipline he had screwed up within himself had not been required after all.

William poked his head out the doorway with a smirk on his face to bestow on anyone who might be standing around to discover him, but finding the corridor vacant, he crawled cautiously out of his cell. He climbed to his feet, hesitated a moment or two—still half expecting someone to sound an alarm—before he hobbled off on the same path that Heinrich had taken earlier. The pain in his leg prevented him from progressing in anything but short spurts, and he paused momentarily at the ship's galley where he was able to snatch up a loose apple. As he took a greedy bite, he noticed a pile of mess ware waiting to be cleaned; the handle of a soiled dinner knife poked out from the pile in a tempting manner. 'A knife is always handy to a prisoner,' he mumbled to himself. He snatched it up and slipped it into his boot.

William carried on with his excursion and eventually found his way up to the keel and into the bowels of the ship. He gazed about in amazement at the tangled ingenuity surrounding him. He had often daydreamed in school about what a motor might look like from the inside, and now here he was, not inside a motor, but certainly inside the next best thing—absolutely marvelous! He poked and prodded the strange mechanisms and ran his fingers over the complex framework. He couldn't resist jabbing the large, bulging bags that he thought must certainly be full of hydrogen gas; they felt like giant punching bags. Once this initial examination was finished, he immediately began snooping around for a nook or crevice in which to hide should one of the crew happen to appear. This proved more difficult than he first imagined—every bit of space seemed filled to overflowing with bizarre shapes of formed aluminum, wood, canvas, and rubber.

Limping further and further along the ship's keel, it wasn't long before he felt a prickling sense of claustrophobia—there were no windows, no doors, only dim light and shadows. He eventually hobbled to a point so far from the bow of the ship, and yet so short of the stern, that his only view in either direction was an unending series of triangular structures dwindling into obscurity. Where was everyone? How had he managed to get so far without being accosted by one of the crew? Who was flying this absurd machine anyway?

Carrying on in the same direction for a few more steps, unsure whether there was any point in continuing, he suddenly noticed movement in the distance ahead. At first it seemed only a faint flashing of light, but soon he realized he was observing the intermittent reflection of the long string of lamps off the head and shoulders of some crewman coming his way. Panicked by his precarious situation and unable to outrun anyone with his injured leg, he began frantically casting about for a crevice to hide in. It was then he noticed a small ladder tucked between two aluminum girders where it stretched up at an awkward angle. He scrambled onto it and with difficulty pulled himself along its length using only his arms and his one good leg. He backed himself against the inside surface of the ship's hull.

William waited, still and silent. The crewman (Heinrich as it turned out) eventually passed without looking up or noticing William as he sat crumpled on his uncomfortable perch. William remained still for several more minutes, giving the preoccupied Prussian plenty of time to move away. While he waited for Heinrich's footsteps to fade, William noticed that he had all the time been leaning against a small hatch in the siding behind him. He turned around and opened it.

If he had thought twice, he might have expected what awaited him on the other side, but instead he received a shock that almost toppled him over and sent him tumbling down the ladder that he had mounted with such difficulty. Brilliant light and a maelstrom of noisy air burst around him. It took time for his eyes to grow accustomed to the brilliance and for him to notice a small gangway, about ten feet long, that led out across the dizzy, turbulent atmosphere to one of the motor gondolas.

William crawled out on the catwalk. He ignored the long cables suspended at waist height; he felt safer on his hands and knees and clutched tightly to the small wooden treads. Not once had he experienced vertigo during his aeroplane flights, but as he crawled along such a flimsy and vibrating support, and as he made his way across the dangerous open space, he shut his eyes more than once.

At the end of this trial he found another hatch; he opened it and climbed into a dim chamber. Inside, William found himself facing an imposing behemoth of a motor. He stared at it aghast. It was enormous—a heavy, leaden beast that sat silent as a tomb and was suspended in a spindly framework that looked incapable of supporting its weight; it was tangled in a nest of dull gray wiring and sprouted contorted exhaust manifolds scorched to the color of sweet potato skins. William suspected the noise and vibration must be absolutely frightening when it was in operation. That their recent plunge toward earth hadn't wrenched it loose seemed miraculous. Indeed the surrounding gondola had not survived entirely unscathed. Twisted pieces of aluminum tubing stuck out at weird angles, bits of torn fabric fluttered in the vicious slipstream, and blood was spattered all over the place—wreckage, unbeknownst to William, left by the three machinist's mates who had been catapulted through the gondola's sides.

William had just begun to examine the impressive motor, reaching out to touch it, when a man's head popped up from the other side of the engine block—a most unusual head, with a blank expression on its face. It was ghostly pale, with sunken cheeks, a grossly protruding jaw, and eyes so deeply set that the shadow of the stranger's brow prevented William from discerning the color of his eyes. Atop this face was a patchwork of stubbly hair that gave the man the appearance of a mangy dog.

William started at this unexpected appearance and braced himself for screams and shouts of alarm at the escape of the British prisoner. But nothing of the sort occurred. The man simply observed him for a moment, calmly, and then turned back to whatever had been occupying him prior to William's arrival.

The fellow disappeared behind the far side of the motor

for a few seconds, then popped back into view, his face contorted to the point of grotesqueness by the strain and effort involved in lifting a heavy object up to the top of the engine block—a large piston, as William soon discovered. The fellow was so intent on his repairs that he had little attention to spare. William wondered if the poor creature had even heard of the British prisoner. Without a moment's consideration, William worked his way around the cramped spaces to help the poor struggling mechanic as he lifted the piston the last few inches into its hole. With the engine block no longer interposed between them, William was able to get a good look at his companion. The mechanic's frame was so twisted and contorted that William wondered whether he had perhaps been injured during the ship's tumble. But once the piston was in place and William had returned to an upright position, he observed that the mechanic did not follow suit; in fact, it quickly became apparent that the strange fellow was severely and permanently deformed. He had a hunched back with a knotted spine that protruded visibly through his uniform, and an arm and a leg so much shorter than their mates that he had a lopsided, keeled-over aspect. William tried not to stare, but it seemed hardly worth the effort—the fellow paid no attention to William and there seemed little risk of offence. How on earth this poor fellow could have been drafted into the military, William could not fathom.

The mechanic reached up to begin extracting the next piston in line, but it appeared to be an impossible task. The piston lay in such an awkward position relative to the man's stunted frame that it prevented him from getting a good grip. Then, having failed in his first attempt and without any display of frustration—actually without the hint of any emotion at all—the fellow grasped part of the motor's frame and braced himself as if to climb on top. Before the fellow's feet left the floor though, William shouted, 'Wait!' and reached over to lend a hand. In doing so, he accidentally let his hand brush against the mechanic's arm. The inadvertent contact resulted in a sudden, almost explosive, response. The stranger yanked his hand away and spasms of emotion passed violently over his face—surprise and fear and anger, all in quick succession and so intense that William's heart skipped a beat. But then the emotion disappeared as suddenly as it had erupted and was replaced with a stony, unflinching stare. It was as if a valve had been shut off so tightly and so completely that not a single drop of emotion dripped out.

'Sorry,' said William, 'just trying to help, you know!' He then realized that the Prussian probably didn't understand a word of English, so William pointed at the piston and gestured with a pulling motion to convey that his intentions had been to be helpful. Still, though, there was no reaction forthcoming, just that steady, cold gaze. Unsure how to remedy this awkward situation, and unsure how to communicate with the bizarre creature, William decided to press on with his original intention. He reached over and started to extract the piston on his own. It was heavy and tightly wedged in the cylinder, and he had no more luck than his strange companion. But William refused to quit and he tugged with all his might; beads of sweat formed on his brow, and all the while the stranger, unmoving, silent, continued to stare at him.

Just at the moment when William's grip was beginning to fail, the stranger's hands slowly made their way back over the exposed motor block, and the pale, bony fingers slid around the piston; he took obvious care to avoid any physical contact with William. The combined effort of the two men eventually started the recalcitrant hunk inching its way out, easier and easier, quicker and quicker, and then suddenly it popped free—a gleaming billet of polished steel resting comfortably in their combined hands, much like a newborn babe.

William let out a triumphant 'hurray' as the stranger lowered the piston gently to the floor. William turned his attention to the next cylinder when, for the second time in as many days, he suddenly found himself staring into the black opening of a pistol pointed at his face. This time, however, it was not held in the quivering hand of a young flier, but in the grip of a weather-beaten old man wearing the ragged cap of a naval officer. William could only assume he was now face-to-face with the airship's captain.

All three—William, the twisted mechanic, and the gnarled old captain—stared at each other from their various positions in the noisy, windswept space surrounding the mute, granite behemoth; they looked back and forth at each other as if they needed some decisive reaction, some spark for one of them to make time start flowing again, to ignite the conflagration that was sure to follow. But none came, and no one flinched. They remained in this suspended state until the tension, the uncomfortable balance, was disturbed by the entrance of a flustered Heinrich. He was out of breath from his scramble up the ladder and had a panicked look on his face. Ober Dürr followed immediately, looking unhappy as well.

'What on earth is going on here?' asked Dürr, his question articulated in William's direction before he became aware of the captain's presence.

'English! What have you done!' yelled Heinrich, clearly hoping that such an accusatory tone might place him on the proper and safe side of this unpleasant affair.

William said nothing, his attention, like Ober Dürr's, fixed on the old man with the pistol.

'Get him out of here!' shouted the captain. Heinrich reached for William's arm and began to pull him away; Heinrich was intent on dragging William, if need be, all the way back to their cabin. William, not clearly understanding the captain's command, planted his feet firmly on the floor, despite the pain. Heinrich's first tug was completely ineffective.

Before Heinrich could make another more forceful attempt, Dürr cried out, 'Wait!'

William sensed some type of invisible communication

passing between the oberleutnant and the twisted mechanic. William thought he could discern something in the expression of the pale fellow's face that prompted Dürr to propose an alternative to further incarceration. 'Kapitan,' said the oberleutnant in a softer, almost beseeching tone, 'Lothar needs help here. The Englishman seems to have had mechanical training. I suggest we leave him here . . . under Heinrich's supervision, of course.'

The captain lowered his pistol, but the dark expression on his face indicated he considered the idea ridiculous. He cast a withering glance in Heinrich's direction; it was clear he had little faith in Heinrich's capacity to execute such a role. Dürr continued, 'We have two motors inoperative and not enough men to work on them. We don't have much to lose.' Dürr paused for a moment, then grinned as if he had suddenly come upon an unassailable argument. 'Think of it as slave labor!'

Heinrich let out a soft chuckle but swallowed it as soon as he realized the captain wasn't laughing.

The captain turned his attention to the mechanic, 'Lothar?'

Again, there was no clear reaction. There was perhaps the hint of a nod.

The captain turned away and holstered his weapon. He whispered something into Heinrich's ear and then left the motor gondola, but not before he shot an icy stare in William's direction; the captain patted his holster for emphasis, and William could not mistake his meaning. Despite the fact that he hadn't understood a word of their conversation, he gathered now that he was being left there to assist the silent mechanic; this was much better than being locked up in Heinrich's cabin. He breathed a sigh of relief as Dürr whispered something of his own into Heinrich's ear and then departed as well.

Once the officers had gone and the tension had faded, Heinrich let out a disgusted sigh, and an expression of deep irritation spread across his face. 'You will get yourself killed before this is all over! Probably me too!' Heinrich vented his frustration by pulling out his own pistol and removing its clip.

He examined it with an exaggerated manner, while he nodded and grunted in satisfaction; he tilted it in William's direction so he might observe the neatly packed bullets. Confident he had made his point, Heinrich slapped the clip back into the butt of the pistol and then found a comfortable perch; he threw his head back in a manner that challenged William to test his resolve. 'Go ahead and get back to work! Or else I will indeed shoot you this time . . . with pleasure.'

William rolled his eyes and turned abruptly toward the mechanic. 'So, it's Lothar is it?'

Lothar stared back at William without expression, though William thought he detected defiance seeping out of the man's eyes. Again this quickly faded to indifference as Lothar turned back to the behemoth, the commotion of the past few moments apparently not worth any more attention. The crippled airship continued its way across the vacant expanse of western Africa.

Chapter 5

DAWN ABOARD

Dawn on the third day of William's aerial captivity found the airship's crew scattered about the vessel. The men were exhausted from their efforts to control the wayward creature on its journey across the treacherous desert, and they each rested in whatever manner permitted by the local geometry of the ship's construction.

Second rudder-man Otto Rass, airman second class, stood with his eyes closed and slouched against a girder. His clean-shaven face had an unhealthy malleability to it, and its pliable folds softened, then sagged each time he dozed. As sleep took hold, his knees would buckle and then collapse, striking a sturdy aluminum pedestal in front of him; each time his knees hit the pedestal he would open his eyes, give his compartment a cursory inspection, and then drift off again. After one particularly deep slumber, followed by a particularly painful impact against the uncompromising metal pedestal, his eyes opened wide, and he tipped back onto his sore and swollen feet.

Otto Rass stared down with contempt at a small brass wheel the size of a dinner plate, mounted vertically on the pedestal; it seemed to rotate of its own accord, randomly, inching back and forth every few seconds as if defying him to prevent its freedom of motion. The platform under his feet, suspended within the structure of the ship's tail, served as an emergency steering station for those occasions when the controls became disabled on the officers' deck at the bow; the brass wheel permitted the rudder-man to directly control the position of the ship's giant rudder only a few feet away.

Earlier, while at his station in the main control cabin, the rudder cable had jammed. He had tried his best to dislodge it, but then a pulley had torn loose somewhere in the bowels of this infernal ship; as it shot from its mounting, it had sliced a ten-inch opening in gas cell No. 6.

Ober Dürr, turning a deaf ear to all of Rass's well-considered explanations, had immediately banished him to this closet at the aft end of the ship—he had been ordered, in a none too gentle tone, to remain at his post until repairs were made, however long that might take. From this windowless platform he had continued to steer for hours, all the while receiving commands through a mechanical enunciator; its red tin arrow pointed left or right every few minutes as necessary to keep the ship on course.

Unsure of the length of his slumber, Otto Rass had completely lost track of the time. The main rudder controls had apparently been repaired and seemed to be functioning properly, so he debated whether to leave his post. He suspected that he had been forgotten.

Unable to immediately resolve this debate, Rass decided to occupy himself with other business. He directed his gaze up into the empty space above, and after assuring himself that he was alone, knelt down and reached under the metal platform on which he had been standing. He retrieved a small cloth sack sealed by a white drawstring. He opened the sack, peered inside, and mumbled numbers to himself while he inspected its contents and ran through the list in his head. Assured that the contents accurately matched his list, he retrieved a small bar, wrapped in silver foil, and slipped it into his pocket before returning the sack to its hiding place.

Otto Rass groaned as he stood, then glanced upward again to confirm there were no other crewmen skulking about. Although it was unlikely his actions would be observed in such a rarely visited region of the ship, he couldn't be too careful. He had no illusions about how the others would react, officers and crewmen alike, should they discover the sack and its contents. And then there was that nasty little hunchback who always seemed to show up at the most inconvenient of times.

Suddenly, Rass let out a harsh cough that surprised him by

its violence. He screwed up his face, which increased threefold the number of lines and wrinkles on its rumpled surface. Then leaning forward, he sent a globule of spit down into the well beneath him; a click echoed as the wad hit a metal rib in the darkness below.

As if perturbed by this petty act of insolence, the dirigible shuddered, and the bracing cables surrounding him rattled in their guides as the ship met the first turbulent jolt of a new day. The steering wheel seemed to respond automatically, first with a gentle sweep to the left, and then with a longer sweep to the right, before it returned to its original position. Otto Rass clambered up the ladder and disappeared down the keel toward the mess.

*

Airman First Class Thomas Schilling, who had been laid out as if dead on the floor of the keel, sat bolt upright in fright; an unusually violent vibration woke him from his fitful slumber; he woke to observe Otto Rass's shrinking hindquarters as they continued along the keel toward the distant mess. The rudder-man's leap across the airman's sleeping form had jolted the plank flooring and disturbed Schilling in a way that the morning's first atmospheric bump had not. Airman Schilling rose stiffly to his feet and stared at the dwindling figure of Otto Rass. As the distance between them grew, the sense of panic gave way to resentment.

It was a rare occurrence that Rass would pass up such an opportunity to harass Airman Schilling; this persecution usually took the form of a derogatory comment, paired with insulting physical abuse: a slap to the back of the head, a poke in the eye, or a ridiculous, but painful wrestling hold that Rass had learned somewhere in basic training. Airman Schilling wasn't the sole recipient of this treatment, but that did nothing to lessen its unpleasant nature. That Rass had passed up an opportunity to torture him in his sleep was nothing short of miraculous.

With Rass swallowed up by the ship, Schilling pulled from his pocket a neatly folded slip of gasoline-soiled paper; he examined the sequence of numbers penciled across it and then looked up to choose a bright red valve among several others. He twisted it open. After rechecking his figures, he reached down and began rapidly working the handle of a fuel pump; his motions slowed as the device primed and then resisted from the increasing backpressure.

He repeated this sequence of actions and moved from one valve to the next, until each of the gravity tanks suspended above the distant motor gondolas was topped off with one hundred liters of gasoline. Airman Schilling then waited nervously. If he had miscalculated and inadvertently sent a surplus of fuel to an already full gravity tank, he would be informed in short order. He had already done this once and there would be no forgiveness from his mates if he doused them with gasoline a second time. No angry crewmen appeared and so he tromped off toward the mess, his growling stomach overpowering his dread of running into Rass.

*

Three of the seven machinist's mates who had not fallen overboard—Kurt, Friedrich, and Albert, with eyes shut and limbs twitching—could hardly be said to be sleeping. Each sat on a small wooden stool; each was confined to his beetle-shaped motor gondola; and each rested his fume-filled head directly against the exposed surface of an engine block. This intimate nestling with the motor was intended to provide a point of instant penetration into their dreaming skulls should the pounding pistons and whirling gears begin to change their tone. Oily red rags, compactly folded, provided modest insulation from the motor's searing heat and numbing vibration.

As the surge and bump of the morning's first turbulent shock hit the ship, the head inside each gondola clunked against hard steel. The three wads of cloth dropped in turn and blossomed between their feet; this certainly was the closest thing to a potted flower that ever would be found aboard the ship. Waking, the young men gazed up at their mechanical altars and thanked the Lord that their repairs had held and that they might live just one more day. They glanced expectantly behind them, hoping that breakfast would soon arrive.

Airman First Class Albert Doring, machinist's mate, waited with special anticipation. His stomach ached from an unusual emptiness, and his head throbbed from the noise and smell of the great screaming beast that cohabitated the small space; his mouth began to water. Earlier in his shift he had begun to suffer from feelings of regret—his bargain with Rass had been foolish; he had given up two weeks' pay in return for satisfying a childish desire—but now, as he waited for Rass, those regrets faded.

Once more he checked the various gauges, oiled the rocker arms, and confirmed the quantity of gasoline in the gravity tank. Just as he sat back down on his stool, Otto Rass poked his head into the chamber. Neither man spoke a word. Rass carefully scanned the small space to ensure no one else was present and then tossed the small silver bar he had retrieved from his hidden sack into Albert Doring's lap. He disappeared before Albert could offer a word of thanks.

Pausing, controlling his desire, and hoping to make the moment last long enough to justify its cost, Albert slowly and gently peeled back the silver wrapper to expose a small bar of chocolate. It was absolutely mesmerizing in its darkness, absolutely intoxicating in its aroma, absolutely perfect but for the crescent shaped line of teeth marks left from the vicious bite taken out of it by Otto Rass. For one fleeting instant Albert considered darting after Rass to cancel the deal; he had bargained for a whole bar of chocolate, not two-thirds of a bar. But the aroma of the dark, luscious cocoa was too much for him, and he swallowed his anger as quickly as he swallowed the bar. A few seconds later he was again leaning forward with his head vibrating against the growling behemoth; his soul sank into a regret as viscous as the saliva in his mouth.

*

During his trek down the narrow keel, Airman Rass could not easily avoid passing Oberleutnant Dürr, who was still alert despite his lack of sleep and active despite the pain from his broken rib. The officer concentrated on the transfer of water from one ballast tank to another; his calculations were detailed and accurate; his whole mind was focused on carefully trimming the ship in order to avoid the need to vent any of the precious hydrogen gas. Ober Dürr looked up and acknowledged the rudder-man with a nod. The junior man passed quickly with his gaze glued to the floor. Dürr scrutinized Rass's back as he continued on his way.

Dürr was not entirely happy with the composition of his crew. He had not had complete freedom in choosing them and some ne'er-do-wells had crept in; Airman Rass was one of them. Dürr suspected that any antagonism that existed within the ranks emanated from this man. Nevertheless, the rudder-man's skills were needed; the airship's crew was limited—only twenty-six at the journey's start, not counting the admiral. At this point the oberleutnant could take none for granted.

*

Airman First Class Hugo Klimt, the sail maker, hung in a hammock along the keel like a caterpillar in its sack, the turbulent bumps inducing in it a lazy oscillation. Airman Rass seemed surprised to find the sail maker strung up in such a conspicuous spot and expressed no small irritation when he noticed the hammock's identification tag; it read O. Rass A2K.

He gave the hammock a violent shove and continued on his way.

The disturbance woke the drooling sail maker who punched his face out of his cocoon and gazed dumbly about at his surroundings. It was several more minutes before he extricated himself. After stretching his arms by pulling them roughly behind his back, and after giving each of his legs a good shake, Klimt shot up a nearby ladder to examine his handiwork on gas cell No. 6. The awkward location of the gasbag's wound, and the pain from his broken collarbone, had made the repair a difficult one.

The sail maker stared at the patched-up gash and admired his handiwork. He didn't understand how someone like Otto Rass could get away with such flagrant incompetence. In his day the sail maker had seen shocking brutalities dished out on young and ignorant recruits for much less significant infractions. He wasn't so young that he couldn't describe from personal experience the sight of a man being keelhauled; it was an interesting thought though: How do you keelhaul someone on an airship? He considered this for a moment, but couldn't devise a suitable equivalent. Well, it would come to him later no doubt. He would mention it to some of the others over supper.

Hugo Klimt had learned one thing during his long years in the service; individuals like Otto Rass eventually got their just deserts—though they frequently shared these deserts with an innocent bystander or two.

*

Airman Second Class Wilhelm Bauer reached out and caught one of his eggs as it rolled off the counter with the surging dawn air. His duties alternated between that of ship's cook, officers' steward, and second wireless operator. The crew's meals were Spartan and usually cold, consisting primarily of brown bread, sausages, hardboiled eggs, and a small supply of fruit. The officers were somewhat luckier in that the admiral, with little argument from anyone, had stowed aboard a crate of salted chops; Airman Bauer could fry these chops on a small electric stove that was powered by a wind-operated generator mounted on the ship's port side, just outside the galley wall; Bauer spent much of his time repairing this generator, as well as its twin mounted on the ship's starboard side outside the wireless room.

Had Airman Bauer been consulted during the original design of the airship, he would have explained the practical value of locating the wireless room directly across from the galley; this would have enabled him to more easily alternate between his disparate duties. Instead, the designers had placed the wireless room further forward, where it had the seemingly minor benefit of providing quick access to the control cabin. Airman Bauer's proposal also would have prevented the nauseating experience of preparing meals in direct view of Herr Doktor as he stitched up dripping wounds, set compound fractures, and slathered nasty smelling ointment on oozing burns. But no one ever consulted with Wilhelm Bauer.

He hoped that Airman Rass might soon wander by. Bauer had discovered that one of the officers desperately wanted a drink; Airman Bauer had said it might be possible and offered to check around. Now he had an opportunity to partner in Airman Rass's entrepreneurial operation, and hopefully gain some favor in the eyes of that unusually clever businessman. At the very least, this referral might provide him some small luxury at a time when he might desperately want it. More importantly though, it could be the opportunity he long had been looking for—to embark on an alternative career, one more profitable than capering about on this floating stick of dynamite for ten marks a month. What's more, the ship's destination had remained a tightly held secret—a bad sign. Bauer suspected that his willingness to risk his neck for the Kaiser and these ridiculous political adventures might be coming to an end. Rumor had it that Otto Rass had done so well in Dusseldorf that he would be able to turn the Kaiser down come his next enlistment date.

Otto Rass did stop by, but only long enough to learn that the crew's meal would not be served out for another thirty minutes. Bauer had started to explain his new opportunity, but by mid-sentence he was speaking to empty air.

*

Petty Officer Klaus Schmitt, the wireless officer, leaned back in his wooden swivel chair, his pencil having long ago slipped from his hand; it rolled about on the floor of the wireless cabin. The morning's first turbulent tremor articulating through the ship passed him by without so much as shifting the course of his dreams. Shortly after its passage, the wireless receiver began its frantic tapping.

Schmitt jerked himself up and spun around as he chased down his errant pencil. He hunched over his desk and scribbled onto a small pad of yellow paper; it was a struggle to keep up with the annoying little machine. At this particular moment though, communication from the outside world was reassuring. He had found the broad expanse of desert deeply disconcerting, just as he had found the broad expanse of the ocean disconcerting earlier in his career. He had not anticipated this dread of empty, open spaces when he transferred from the army to the navy several years ago. His last transfer, from the surface fleet to the airship division, had done nothing to improve things. He now frequently questioned his decision and thought perhaps he should have gone to the new submarine flotilla.

Suddenly, almost as if the man had been skulking outside the cabin door in wait of just such communication, Otto Rass stuck his face through the partially opened door. 'Any news?'

'Piss off, you piece of shit. Get back to your post!'

'I'm off-duty, Herr Wireless Operator.' The wireless machine started clattering again, viciously, and Schmitt turned his back and scribbled frantically. Rass waited for another pause. 'I'm not asking for any state secrets, nothing of any military concern. But you know how it is; everyone wants to hear a little about the outside world. It calms them down and makes for a happier ship.'

Schmitt ignored him and continued writing as the wireless started up for a third time. Rass frowned for a moment, then shrugged his shoulders. He retreated from the cabin, but a moment later returned and tossed a small object onto the wireless operator's desk, 'Here you go. It's just a taste of possibilities.' Rass then disappeared for good.

As soon as Schmitt received the code sequence that indicated the transmission was now at an end, he looked up to learn what Rass had left for him. It was a tiny tin box, about the size of his thumbnail. Scribbled in pencil on the lid was the word ASPIRIN; inside were four small round tablets. Schmitt couldn't believe his eyes. He had been fully prepared to chuck Rass's little bribe down the toilet, but this item had been completely unexpected. Schmitt invariably ended his shift with a splitting headache, either from the altitude, or the noise, or the fumes, or who knows why. He debated the appropriateness of accepting the bribe, for about a minute, and then slipped the packet into his shirt pocket; he was dissatisfied with himself for succumbing so easily. Nevertheless, Rass would get nothing from him, not so much as a weather forecast. Rass could offer him anything he wanted from his illicit little treasure trove; it would do him no good. Schmitt wasn't about to get himself shot over that miserable little dung rat.

*

Herr Doktor, exhausted but awake, rested on a small stool in his infirmary. He rubbed the swollen sacks under his eyes. His legs and those of the stool were covered with brown splatters of dried blood. His metal coffee cup was smeared with the same stuff; it had formed into thick streaks and was spotted with fingerprints. Surrounding him were his sleeping patients. They would require his uninterrupted supervision for some time to come: a compound fracture in the femur of a machinist's mate who had slipped down a ladder well, and of course the engineer who had failed to regain consciousness and was unlikely to see the noonday sun. The ship's medical facilities were rudimentary and incapable of supporting surgeries. The doctor's own skill was questionable; he could admit that to himself. A betting man by nature, Dr. Emil Dreckmesser jotted down a short comment in his spattered notebook: Engineering Officer Franz Brock, odds one in ten.

As the doctor returned the notebook to his pocket he was startled by the abrupt appearance of Otto Rass. 'How's everyone doing in here?' asked the airman enthusiastically.

'Shhh!' whispered the doctor, putting his finger to his lips. 'Don't wake them.'

'Ah yes,' whispered Rass with a slow nod. 'Need any help? I'm off-duty now, but not at all tired. If you need a nap, I'm happy to stand guard.'

'No, Airman, thank you for the offer, but I'll be fine. Things are a bit critical right now. It wouldn't look good if one of these poor fellows were to die on you.'

A frown flitted across Rass's face. Clearly he hadn't considered this possibility and quickly agreed with the doctor's diagnosis. He disappeared with no further comment. This was exactly the response the doctor had hoped for. The previous day, before the big tumble, he had taken Rass up on a similar offer, asking him to keep an eye on the English prisoner until he woke from the chloroform. The doctor had been concerned that he might have used a bit too much of the substance during the man's interrogation.

It had been a mistake to leave Rass alone in the infirmary—a carboy of methyl alcohol had disappeared. He had no proof that Rass had taken it, and the man had denied any wrongdoing, but the doctor was suspicious nevertheless. His only fear now was that Rass might be fool enough to pawn the stuff off as drinking alcohol. The doctor now had the added worry that crewmen might soon be showing up in his infirmary with acute alcohol poisoning. He had toyed with the idea of speaking to Dürr, but despite that officer's good nature, the doctor was pretty certain he could not escape without reprimand. He kept the incident to himself.

*

Kapitanleutnant Herman Timmer was awake; all of his attempts at sleep had failed. He sat hunched over his desk in his black leather coat with his gloved hands supporting his head at its brow. Pinned on the wall above his desk was a child's drawing of a contorted dwarf; the drawing had been titled *Rumpelstiltskin.* On the desk's wooden surface rested a small mound of technical diagrams and drawings. Atop them lay a worn slide rule and the stubs of several used up pencils.

The morning's first articulating tremor struck the cabin; after the vibration faded, the captain's arms began to quiver. Several drawings slid from his desk into a sea of blueprints and calculations that lay inches deep across the floor of his cabin. Then his entire body shuddered, and a single tear dropped to the desk with a delicate plop. He was tired; he missed his beautiful granddaughter, and he was mortally afraid that he would never see her again.

Startled and ashamed and a little confused at his loss of composure, the captain jumped to his feet, violently, sending the chair flying back against his cot. He snatched up the drawing on which he had been jotting notes, rolled it up tightly, and secured it with an elastic band. He yanked open his cabin door with the intention of stepping across the hallway to share his calculations with the admiral. Now, as he stood staring at his superior's cabin door, he found he had a sudden aversion to speaking with the man, especially in his current and vulnerable state of mind. And so he stood there, hesitating—an experience not all that familiar to him. It was then that Otto Rass happened to stroll by, while he rambled aimlessly about the officers' deck and waited for his breakfast.

The captain failed to remember this particular crewman's name—another shameful performance, tempered only by an instinctive realization that this particular man was trouble. He could see it plain as day; one look at that corpulent face and those shifty eyes was enough. Nevertheless, he would not permit himself to retreat, and he refused to speak to the admiral. The captain's only alternative was to trust this insipid crewman.

'Airman!' the captain barked.

'Yes, sir!' returned Otto Rass, stopping in his tracks, the blood draining from his face. He had been dreading a formal reprimand for the incident with the rudder cable, but to receive it from the ship's captain was going to be particularly unpleasant.

'Hand this to the admiral!'

'The admiral?' responded Otto Rass, confused. Was the captain insane? The admiral's cabin lay directly across the corridor. It took Rass a moment to come to his senses. He indicated the cabin at his back by gesturing, uncertainly, over his shoulder with his thumb.

'Yes, Airman. Exactly!' The captain thrust the drawing into Rass's gut and slammed the door in his face.

Rass stood for a moment facing the door; he examined it ever so closely; the surface of the gray plywood had come to a stop only an inch from his nose. He turned 180 degrees and knocked on the duplicate sheet of gray plywood.

*

Admiral Baron Helmut von Ramstein lay stretched out on his cot, his boots standing at attention on the floor near the door. His delicate spectacles rested precariously on the end of his hooked nose. His eyes shot back and forth across the report in his hands. He had been at this activity for several hours now, and the reports he had consumed formed a small unkempt stack in his lap; they leaned dangerously to one side.

A deep grumble of dissatisfaction bubbled up from his chest as he dropped the report onto the mound with disgust. Typed on its red cover was the title, *Opinions on the Use of Airships for Long-Range Bombing — Top Secret.* He bent forward and selected another from the neat stack resting at the edge of his desk; it was titled *Experiments with Sub-Cloud Car — Secret.* He already had read this one and did not wish to read it again. He placed it on the growing mound and reached for another report, *Investigation: Crash of Charlotte 3 During Experiments with In-flight Retrieval of Aeroplane – Top Secret.*

The crash of Charlotte 3 had been a horrific accident. The aeroplane pilot had misjudged his approach and had careened into the belly of the airship. Of course this had instantly caused a fire, and while the crew fought to smother it with whatever material they had at hand, Captain Schoner had pushed the ship over into a precipitous dive in order to reach the ground before the fire reached the hydrogen-filled gasbags. He had not succeeded. The first bag began burning at an altitude of one thousand feet, and the remainder caught fire by the time the ship slammed into the ground. Most of the crew had died from ghastly burns while en route to the hospital.

It was at this exact moment that Rass knocked on the cabin door; the admiral jerked in surprise and sent his pile of reports spilling onto the floor. '*Verdammt*!' He disentangled himself from his reading material; he was distinctly perturbed by the time he pulled open the door.

'Yes, what is it?' he growled at the airman standing before him.

Airman Rass snapped to attention. It was as if a bolt of lightning had shot through his frame; he presented a perfect salute—respectful, submissive, crisp. 'Herr Admiral, sir, technical documents for your immediate review.'

The admiral reached out and absently took the drawing; his gaze was riveted on the visage of Otto Rass. The airman dropped his eyes in a thoroughly subordinate demeanor. If only such exemplary military bearing could be spread to the rest of the ship's crew. This junior man put every one of the ship's officers to shame. 'Thank you, Airman. You may continue with your duties.' The admiral returned the salute, intending it as a small but sincere reward for such an outstanding demonstration. He then returned to the privacy of his cabin.

As soon as the door was shut, Otto Rass's entire frame slumped. He rolled his eyes and continued on his way.

*

William sat before his oily adversary in quiet frustration; he alternated his attention between Lothar and the silent motor. The two men were exhausted and waited for their strength to return. Pieces of the machine's insides were scattered about the floor of the gondola. The pieces had once been organized, but this organization had been spoiled some time ago, first by gradual movement across the vibrating floor and then by kicks of frustration as William struggled to repair this hulking, overly complex beast. For the moment he had forgotten about home and about his need for revenge; his desire to overcome the contrary machine consumed him entirely.

Although William and his silent partner had not communicated in any normal linguistic sense, a sympathetic bond, nevertheless, had formed between them. The Prussian mechanic seemed to read the ebb and flow of frustration on William's face as one approach failed and another took its place. The Prussian would acknowledge this frustration with a slight curl of his lips, whether in amusement or contempt or empathy William could never quite tell. One thing was evident though; the Prussian never lost his composure; he never let out so much as a discontented sigh. And he was clever. Once William began acting on some idea, the Prussian would decipher his intentions and either assent to it, with a curt nod, or he would give an equally curt shake of his head indicating a contrary opinion. As William became more and more familiar with the inner workings of the machine, he began to recognize that the Prussian's intuitions were always correct.

After rubbing his hands together to warm them, William reached down for the single remaining piston. He was surprised by the golden sheen on its polished surface—a reflection of the morning light that had squeezed into the gondola through a gap in its canvas envelope. He gingerly lifted the piston with both hands, concerned that it might slip from his fingers and plunge through the floor to be lost forever.

The two men coaxed the piston into the block and attached it to the crankshaft without injury or mishap. They silently agreed to take another short rest before reinstalling the cylinder head, another heavy task. It was during this period of inactivity that Heinrich poked his head into the gondola. The flier had been absent for some time, having become bored hours ago and given up his duty as guard in order to get some sleep; now he was back.

'*Guten morgen*!' shouted Heinrich in a voice loud enough to startle them. Lothar rose to his feet. William remained inert.

'Morning,' responded William dourly.

'I have something to show you,' shouted Heinrich with a grin.

William shrugged his shoulders and nodded toward the motor; he was not yet finished and had little time for games.

'Come!' Heinrich encouraged him. 'You can see from the gangway here.' Heinrich backed himself out of the gondola and beckoned William to follow.

William stood up stiffly and followed him out. He found Heinrich sitting directly on the gangway, with his chest against the cable that served as a handrail; Heinrich's feet dangled in the slipstream below. He had donned a pair of goggles and reached into his tunic pocket to extend a set to William.

William squinted at them for a moment before recognizing them as his own and then joined Heinrich on his unnerving perch.

The sun showered the desert with golden light. It was still low in the sky and imparted on the dunes below a harsh pattern of stripes. As William peered down between his boots, Heinrich elbowed him in the ribs and pointed into the distance ahead. William realized that what he had mistaken for early morning haze was, in fact, the gray hue of an ocean spreading out into the blurry horizon to the west, the wandering coastline ten to fifteen miles distant.

Although William nodded in appreciation, he had apparently missed the point of Heinrich's gesture and received another elbow in his ribs, followed by more insistent pointing toward one particular point on the ocean. William concentrated his gaze in the indicated direction and eventually noticed a fleck of white floating on the surface not far from shore. William was unable to tear his gaze from this spot. It was like a fleck of plaster that had fallen from the ceiling of his childhood home and come to rest on the soft blue quilt that had blanketed his bed.

The dirigible maintained its course, heading directly toward the distant fleck. William now realized he was gazing at a ship resting at anchor less than a mile from shore. And, at a point on the shore near the ship, a sharp line interrupted the otherwise desolate beach—a camp. William's heart plunged, and as the pleasant expression drained from his face, Heinrich also became more serious.

William tightened his grip on the cable stretched across his chest. The airship made a sudden shift in attitude and pointed its nose downward so that its course would converge on the distant vessel. Though the change in angle could not have been more than a few degrees, it nevertheless filled both men with the uncomfortable sensation that they were about to topple into the empty space below. Both glanced back at the motor gondola; the unused safety cables lay neatly coiled on the floor inside.

The airship's speed increased, and the slipstream buffeted them as they descended into the humid coastal air. As the airship approached the encampment, the two fliers gazed at the scores of white tents organized in two straight rows and at a black metal tower planted at an isolated spot on the beach several hundred yards from the camp. As the elliptical shadow of the dirigible engulfed the tents below, dozens of soldiers poured from them like bees from a disturbed hive. The swarm grew and organized itself into a teardrop-shaped mass that ran across the sand toward the black tower.

The dirigible made a sweeping turn to the south to circle the sea vessel; the vessel displayed no markings, no flags, no cannons, nothing to give away its purpose, other than an unusual number of aerials shooting up like the whiskers of an old rat. Sailors burst from hatches and doorways, crowded around rails, and pointed up at the airship; they waved at the airship idiotically. Heinrich, caught up in the excitement, waved back vigorously.

As the ship slid behind them, they shifted their gaze forward to the limitless sea of royal blue ahead. William wished they would keep going and thus avoid the unpleasantness that awaited him below. A pit grew in his stomach.

'We must go now!' shouted Heinrich. 'You understand?'

William became agitated. He had realized all along that his voyage would eventually come to an end, but he had not expected this. The outpost below them was as far from civilization as one could get. There would be no communication with Cairo, no train to Alexandria, and practically no means of escape through the vast surrounding desert. They could keep him here until the end of time and nobody would ever know about it. His mind began to race, but short of leaping to his death, he saw no way out.

Heinrich stared at his companion with discomfort. Although William nodded in comprehension, his eyes glowed with a desperation that made Heinrich nervous. He hoped he wouldn't be forced to wrestle William back to their cabin, or even worse, that he might suddenly find himself plummeting to the water below. He would be glad to be rid of this volatile and unpredictable Englishman.

'I will do what I can!' shouted Heinrich, trying to reassure his unsettled companion. 'Come, we must go now, back to the cabin.'

Chapter 6

MISSING

The soldiers jumped up at ropes that dropped from the airship above. A steel cable descended through an open hatch from a reel in the airship's bow. Oberleutnant Dürr leaned out of the hatch and shouted directions to the soldiers below. Two men wearing thick gloves grabbed the cable and hauled it over to the black tower—a mooring derrick that eventually would keep the airship chained to one spot, but free to rotate around that spot as the prevailing winds might dictate, like a dog tied to a stake.

The soldiers bolted the free end of the cable to a chain made of heavy links that wound from the bottom of the derrick between two iron guides and up to the top where it meshed with a large, greasy gear. There the chain disappeared inside, only to reappear at the bottom to begin the entire revolution again.

A diesel motor chugged to life; belches of oily smoke hung in the calm air and gradually spread, obscuring the distant camp from view. The motor strained as the operator eased out the clutch; the chain clattered in its guides; the slack in the cable tightened in spasms. The cable rose higher and higher, forming a graceful curve between the top of the derrick and the bow of the airship. As the curve became more shallow, the airship nudged forward; the men at the ropes resisted the hungry tower by firmly planting their feet in the sand, thus they maintained tension on the cable and prevented the airship from lunging forward and crashing into the tower. The men were dragged along despite their resistance, their boots leaving deep furrows in the sand as they went. After several minutes of slow progress the cable was eventually consumed, and a heavy iron clamp at the derrick's summit closed on the airship's mooring ring; a loud clang signaled to all that the job was complete.

Dora Nine's crew alighted by a rope ladder thrown out from the door of the control cabin. In the ship's shadow, the men gathered and waited for the captain and the admiral to descend. It hadn't taken more than a few minutes for the men to begin wishing they were still aloft; all had failed to appreciate the modest currents of cool air that always had been present while the ship was airborne. They began to bake in the heat—and might soon be fainting.

Once the senior officers had alighted, they examined their subordinates one at a time; they inspected each for any glaring embarrassments and ignored only the soiled uniforms and scruffy jowls. Heinrich had squeezed into line next to Ober Dürr and waited impatiently for the admiral to stroll by. As he waited, he scanned the surrounding landscape. The sky dominated all with its brilliant blue. The ocean to one side was heavy and dark, and its smoky horizon seemed to hint at strange secrets beyond the grasp of ordinary man. To the other side lay jagged, rocky bluffs sprouting occasional tufts of anemic scrub—the bluffs had not been apparent during the airship's arrival, but from the low perspective of the beach, the bluffs held a menacing appearance. The panorama was beautiful in its contrasting textures, but at the same time intimidating in its expansiveness. Heinrich wondered if these feelings were generated by something inherent in the strange surroundings, or were only the result of being cooped up in the close confines of their ship. He was brought back to matters at hand when Dürr nudged him and whispered, 'Be still, Heinrich.'

An army officer approached them. He wore a clean uniform, the color of the desert sand, and was accompanied by two of his own subordinates who maintained themselves in a somewhat less unblemished state. 'Welcome, Admiral von Ramstein!' barked the officer. He saluted sharply, but the deep sand muffled the click of his heels. 'I am Colonel Wilhelm Strasser. We have been eagerly awaiting you. As you can see, we were ready to receive your ship. It is absolutely magnificent—an overwhelming creation.'

'Thank you,' the admiral responded with an equally sharp salute. 'Your men executed the mooring perfectly. We have had a rough time of it though. I have men who are injured and in need of immediate medical attention. Do you have a surgeon with you?'

'Of course, on the ship!' Strasser pointed out to sea and then snapped his fingers; one of his two subordinates bolted toward the camp in search of a stretcher. 'Please, Admiral, you and your men shall come with me. You must be exhausted, and it is not good to remain in the sun. It will become hot soon.'

Not waiting for a response, Colonel Strasser turned sharply and, without looking back, marched off toward camp. The admiral remained in place, his eyes following the officer with amused curiosity. Heinrich shook his head in contempt. This martinet was like so many of the officers who strutted about back home, anxious to throw their weight around and chomping at the bit for war. These were the men that would tarnish Prussia's honor, perhaps destroy Prussia itself. It was bad enough that they were taxing the country's citizens beyond all endurance, all for an army, the greatest in Europe, and for a High Seas Fleet second only to one.

During this brief pause, Heinrich approached the captain. 'Sir, I would like to fly. I may not have an opportunity to practice for some time.'

'Could this not wait until later, Leutnant?' responded the captain.

'We have all of these men about,' argued Heinrich, nodding toward the dozens of soldiers circulating about the dirigible behind them. 'And the weather is quite good.' The captain stared into Heinrich's eyes and seemed to test Heinrich's resolve. Heinrich held his ground.

'Very well, you may fly if you can find men to help you with the aeroplane. Use the opportunity to inspect the harness mechanism carefully.'

Colonel Strasser had returned by now, having discovered that he had no admiral in tow. He had overheard Heinrich's request and bowed curtly toward the admiral and the captain and said, 'My men are at the flier's service.'

'And what should I do with the Englishman?' asked Heinrich innocently. The captain winced. The admiral flushed. The soldiers nearby murmured amongst themselves. The colonel raised an eyebrow.

'An Englishman?' gasped Colonel Strasser, in a tone that matched the astonished expression on his face.

'Yes, a captive,' explained the admiral. 'We came across him in the desert and must transfer him to your care. This is not the time to discuss it though.'

'I would be happy to drop him in one of the ship's empty holds. He will be at home there with the rats.' This was spoken with such venom that even the admiral seemed startled. 'As soon as your men are transferred to our infirmary, we will take possession of the prisoner. I will be fascinated to hear the details.'

'We will discuss it later, Colonel Strasser. For now, two guards will be sufficient'

'Of course, Admiral, as you wish.'

Heinrich easily recruited ten soldiers who were willing to assist him in lowering the aeroplane from the underside of the dirigible. All seemed enthused by any distraction from the routine of their isolated existence. He instructed them carefully on the design and operation of the trapeze from which the aeroplane dangled, before he released the locking mechanism and let the craft's full weight fall into the men's outstretched arms.

It proved a simple and uneventful task to lower the craft to the ground as they supported it by its wings. However, it was a much more onerous task to tow it toward the beach through the pliable sand under the already broiling sun. The ebbing tide had left a strip of compact sand that would serve perfectly as a landing strip.

It was during these exertions that William was escorted from the airship. He was backed down the airship's rope ladder, with a rifle pointed at his head from above and another pointed at his back from below, with many curious eyes looking on. As William's feet touched ground, Heinrich temporarily abandoned the men pushing against his aeroplane's wings. He stood up, shielding his eyes from the sun, and gazed over at his Englishman. William stared back—visibly defiant even at a distance. Heinrich threw up a hand, but William remained expressionless; the Englishman turned without a word and was led off, limping through the soft yielding sand, toward the camp. Heinrich continued to follow their progress until his thoughts were interrupted by the soldier to his right—a beefy private with a florid complexion glistening with sweat.

'Who was that?' asked the private.

'An English flier,' said Heinrich. Then adding under his breath, 'A real powder keg, that one.'

'Poor fellow! Old Strasser will use him for target practice.'

'Sure he will,' said another, 'right after the *bloke* cleans out the latrines.'

Heinrich grunted and returned to his aeroplane. He had decided this was not an opportune time to intercede on William's behalf; Heinrich was unsure the man was worth it. William had rebuffed him on every attempt at making amends and had rejected every friendly advance. So Heinrich put his head down and pushed.

An hour later Heinrich roared down the beach and scratched his way into the moist air. He flew around the camp in lazy circles as he climbed for more altitude, and the buzz of the aeroplane's motor echoed off the rocky bluffs. Then, to everyone's surprise and enjoyment, came an exhilarating aerobatic display; it more than compensated those who had struggled to move the ungainly aeroplane to the water's edge.

Heinrich executed several low-level rolls in succession, none exceeding an altitude greater than one hundred feet. Then came three elegant and perfectly circular loops, all flown with a precision that even the most ignorant could not fail to appreciate. For his finale, he kicked the red monoplane into a violent spin and, from an altitude of one thousand feet, twirled it down toward the water. The trick was so convincing that even the most hardened of his audience gasped when they realized some critical component must surely have failed and that the flier would pay for his exuberance with a very public death.

But Heinrich surprised them all by pulling out of his death spin at the very last moment. The engine screamed as he wrenched the machine upward. They thought it magnificent. He made a sharp 180-degree turn, pulled the throttle, and coasted onto the beach near camp; the noise of his sputtering motor mingled with sporadic applause.

However, it was now Heinrich's turn to be surprised. As he glanced back at the camp, he noticed trails of dust being kicked up by a line of horses galloping down from the heights beyond. The riders stood in their saddles with rifles pointed into the air and announced themselves with shrill screams and random shots. Heinrich sat in his cockpit and let the motor idle; he was uncertain what to make of this advance; he was intent on discovering its outcome before dismounting a ready means of escape.

It was soon apparent that the visitors, robed in bright colors and flowing headgear, were not there to pillage and burn as they swirled amongst the tents and between the soldiers like so many horseflies. They laughed and shouted, chasing each other and causing no small amount of mayhem. Heinrich would later learn that their spirited sweep from the hills was a regular event. The nomads frequently visited the camp for news, commerce, and entertainment—a pleasant diversion from their regular and tiring treks up and down the African coast.

Today, however, it had been Heinrich's performance that had attracted them. They formed an aggressive line abreast and slowly approached his aircraft. The line bent into a shallow crescent of whispering men and jumpy horses as they inched closer and closer. A most unusual spectacle thought Heinrich, as he smiled uncertainly and waved at them. They pointed at him and laughed.

Behind the horsemen, Colonel Strasser gesticulated with wide looping motions of his arms, indicating that Heinrich should repeat his performance. Heinrich gracefully complied, this time finishing his aerobatic demonstration with a low pass over the nomads' heads. The pack of startled horses burst apart and galloped toward every point of the compass. Their riders soon brought them under control, regrouped not far from the airship, then tore through the center of camp; happy and excited, they disappeared up the beach to the north in a cloud of dust.

Heinrich landed a second time and cut the motor. He then spent an hour in a vain search for help; he hoped to hoist his craft into its sling under the airship before nightfall. Colonel Strasser eventually provided the necessary assistance, only too willing to order his men back to work; he explained to Heinrich that the performance was of great value to him in improving his strained relations with the desert folk.

*

As the sun sank into the ocean, Heinrich washed himself in its drowning light under streams of fresh water. It fell like rain from a perforated rubber sack that had been filled from a barrel out of the sea vessel's copious stores. He shaved; he greased his hair and did his best to remove the stains from his uniform. He was in good spirits by the time Dürr joined him and they strolled together toward the mess tent.

'He's gone!' said Dürr.

'Who's gone?' asked Heinrich.

'Your Englishman—he's missing!' Heinrich stopped in his

tracks, astonished; his first thought was that he was being teased. Dürr smiled back, then grabbed him by the arm and pulled him toward the waiting food. 'I'm serious, probably during your show this morning. It was very nice, by the way. During all the confusion with those Arabs, it seems the colonel's men lost track of him. He slipped out through a hole he cut in the back of his tent. It ought to make for interesting dinner conversation tonight, don't you think?'

Heinrich chuckled, but continued to contemplate the news; it was one thing to escape from a tent, but after that, where does one escape *to*? He tried to envision his own actions in such circumstances, but he could only imagine a thirsty death in the desert or a bloody one at the hands of an excitable nomad. 'I don't imagine he'll get far.'

'Well, he's gone now,' said Dürr. 'Who cares; let's eat!'

Their dinner was naturally strained at its start. The airship's crew was distributed randomly among Colonel Strasser's staff around makeshift dinner tables of plywood mounted on saw-horses. At first the men followed the stiff example set by the two senior officers; the Englishman's escape was an embarrassment to both. But after pledges by the colonel that his armed patrols, now teeming about the area, would recapture the escaped flier before morning, and after reassurances by the admiral that the loss was of only limited concern, the conversation turned pleasant. Encouragement from several crates of thin red wine soon turned it positively uproarious—for everyone that is, except Captain Timmer, who sat morose and silent.

Conversation had broken into small groups, each bursting into laughter at random moments from some humorous anecdote or bawdy joke. It was after one such outburst, when the surrounding discussions had succumbed to a momentary lull, that the word 'exploded' seemed to carry quite clearly throughout the tent. The word was attached to the end of an otherwise unintelligible and quiet discussion between two army lieutenants. Everyone was alert and attentive when the conversation continued: 'Well, you know, sometimes the gas just burns without exploding.'

'Really?' interrupted the doctor, who had been sitting near the two junior officers and had been listening somewhat unobserved. 'How did you discover this?' The junior officers became uncomfortably aware that at least part of their conversation had been overheard; after receiving cold stares from the admiral and the colonel, they straightened in their seats and closed their mouths for the remainder of their dinner.

This disruption in the flow of the evening's festivities seemed to provide the admiral the opportunity he had been waiting for. He slid his seat back across the rough noisy planks, rose to his full height, and from there glared down at his minions. He took his time; he scanned every man individually. Wordlessly, he assured each that now was the time to muster any remaining discipline not yet consumed by the wine, for what he had to share was of great significance.

The room became quiet and within a moment or two the last chuckle died out and the last belch had been swallowed. The only challenge to the admiral's authority was the soft sound of the ocean patiently washing against the shore, clearly the only entity with a right to such a challenge.

'Soldiers! Officers! Airmen! I am proud to be standing before you on such a grand occasion.'

Heinrich suppressed the desire to roll his eyes; his contempt for the officer rose like gorge within him. The desire to avoid eye contact with the man had caused Heinrich to glance around the tent and at its occupants. He quickly realized that the audience was composed of two very distinct groups. Of course the army soldiers were visibly distinct from the navy airmen, but there was another division, only slightly less obvious—those who had no idea what the admiral was about to say and those who clearly did. Smug grins formed on many of the army faces; they whispered amongst themselves; they wore a knowing and disconcerting expression. One particularly inebriated sergeant caught Heinrich's eye and exposed his yellow teeth in a vicious and mischievous smile.

'I must again commend the crew of Dora Nine for their heroic efforts in bringing the ship thus far. And, of course, heart-felt thanks to Colonel Strasser and the soldiers of the Kaiser's grand army for making our mission possible, for the competent manner in which you received the Dora Nine, and for the warm welcome you are showing us tonight. I'm sorry to say, though, that we cannot tarry here long. As much as we would like to partake of your continued hospitality, we must be moving on!'

Instantly every man of Dora Nine's crew sat up in his seat. The answer to the question they had been most eager to learn seemed but a few short words away. Their worst fears hung in the balance, much like a dream that suddenly reveals itself to the dreamer—perhaps pleasant, sometimes innocuous, often nightmarish.

'I know all of you have been most curious, if not anxious, about our ultimate destination. Many of you have questioned me privately—requests that I have been obliged to ignore, for the Fatherland's security as well as your own. But now the time has come for such secrets to be secret no longer.' If possible, the gathering of drunken men had become more silent—even the ocean seemed to hesitate, and the surf to momentarily abate. 'America! We are going to America!'

Twenty jaws, in perfect unison, dropped to their full and unbelieving length. Twenty pairs of lungs momentarily ceased the function for which hundreds of thousands of years of natural selection had made essential. One drunken airman vomited on the spot.

The admiral continued to beam at his men, as if he could will them into seeing things as he saw them. But Heinrich discerned a flicker of doubt in the officer's bearing—perhaps disappointment that his carefully orchestrated evening hadn't worked out. Instead of righteous and heroic cries for the Fatherland, the admiral saw a collage of naked fear.

Heinrich shared such feelings with his comrades. After the first shock of the admiral's announcement had passed, however, he wondered if he hadn't jumped to a premature conclusion. The admiral had said America, but he had not been specific; he had said nothing of the Sovereign States. Perhaps their journey would take them to South America: sunshine! palm trees! white beaches! But the more Heinrich tried to overrule the pit in his stomach, the worse he felt.

'Where in America?' asked Ober Dürr, breaking the silence in a hoarse, strained voice.

The admiral seemed relieved that conversation, and time itself, had begun to flow again. But before he could open his mouth to respond, others blurted out a torrent of angry questions: 'You mean crossing the ocean? You can't mean North America? How can our ship perform such a feat? When? Why?' Some men reached for wine bottles and began drinking; they didn't bother with the glasses that decorum dictated. Others simply got up and stormed out.

The admiral raised his arms and shouted, 'QUIET!' The mob reluctantly returned to its seats.

'I know you have many questions, some of which I can answer—others will have to wait. We will be crossing the South Atlantic in a day or two, as soon as our ships have confirmed that the weather along our route is acceptable. I realize the South Atlantic has an ominous sound, but you must realize that the distance across the ocean is significantly shorter than the distance across the desert that you have already so skillfully traversed. And, unlike the desert, our ships will be positioned at predefined intervals to assist us should we run into any trouble.' Few seemed assured by these arguments.

'Now as to your most pressing concern—yes, our final destination is North America—to be more exact, the Sovereign State of Carolina. As to the reason why . . . well, I am not at liberty to say. It is not my secret to share.'

Carolina? Heinrich thought silently to himself. Why in the world are we traveling to Carolina? Carolina is British . . . well, indistinguishable from British. It's inconceivable that Prussia would participate in anything with Carolina—except to . . . then it hit him. The full realization of the calamity bore down on him. All along he had been worried about being caught up in an ugly European war. Now it was perfectly clear that he would be caught up in an even uglier American war, thousands of miles from home, in a strange land that was so inhospitable to mankind that William Hastings' dash into the desert now seemed a reasonable option. 'Lord, how did I get into this mess?'

The admiral had continued his lecture, trying to explain away the concerns of the crew, but the excited voices and their varied emotions soon became unintelligible. Heinrich disappeared into his own thoughts. The details of water and balance, hydrogen and venting, wireless messages and convoy ships, Kaiser and Fatherland, all faded away. He glanced at a nearby bottle of wine, but the thought of it turned his stomach and he looked away. He cast a glance in the direction of Captain Timmer; his dour visage was unchanged, unmoving. Now Heinrich had a clear understanding as to the source of the man's displeasure.

Although Heinrich had found the captain to be an odd man from the start, he sensed capability and compassion in him, despite his intimidating manner. Heinrich's interview with him for the posting had consisted of short questions, each fired off before the prior could be completely answered: *Where were you born?* In Goth—; *How did you do at flying school?* Well, but—; *Do you suffer from seasickness?* Not since—; *Are you willing to be away from home for a long time?* How long will—; *Where did you learn to speak such good English?* From my mother who—. The interview had ended with, '*I've read your fitness report. You'll do.*'

Heinrich had not even been given leave to return to his home; he was forced to make the necessary arrangements for the upkeep of the family home by proxy, through a lawyer named Varmin in Berlin. Even worse, it was only after he had accepted the assignment that he discovered his home for the foreseeable future was to be a dirigible identified as Dora Nine, a bad luck ship—Destination Secret. He quickly learned that when construction first started, it was intended that the ship would be christened Dora One, but by the time she was finally completed, the designation had to be changed to Dora Nine. Heinrich had once seen the scorched ground, outside Berlin, from where the wreckage of a passenger ship had been removed. He would never forget the sight. And it was foremost in his mind when he was first taken aboard for a flight on Dora Nine.

Immediately after joining the crew, the ship had been moved forward to a base in Bulgaria. It was there that he was informed he had precisely one week to become comfortable with his aeroplane's aerial release, while the airship continued its shake-down cruise by sailing in circles each day around the new base. The captain had been present for all of this. He drilled the crew by repeated lift-offs and landings, each representing an opportunity for the aeroplane to be re-attached and for Heinrich to experience the disorienting drop. The captain had seemed satisfied by Heinrich's methodical approach and actually complimented him on his flying. 'Graceful' the captain had said. Heinrich had found compliments to be scarce in the service. Then the admiral had joined them, and the captain had all but disappeared.

The close confines of the army tent had become stifling. Heinrich was sweating profusely. He wanted to get up and leave, though he didn't want to be observed doing so. Just then, several soldiers jumped up after having received a silent signal from Colonel Strasser. They cleared chairs away to create an open space at one end of the tent. Heinrich assumed this was all part of the admiral's pre-arranged plan. The colonel stood and shouted to interrupt the heated dialogue; he explained that it was now time for his soldiers to perform a short skit they had prepared on their own and had been practicing for a while—a skit that some might find a bit bawdy for their tastes, but nevertheless was guaranteed to lighten the atmosphere. Heinrich took the opportunity to slip out amidst the confusion.

He strolled along the beach; the cooling air, the gentle breeze, and the soft surf all soothed his nerves, and he began to relax and think more clearly. He was no less concerned, but he accepted that his early and violent death was not imminent, and that there was time for him to weigh his options and steer his fate as he would.

Suddenly though, his thoughts were interrupted by a strange sound. It was the cry of some strange nocturnal animal, some lonely creature of the desert complaining about his lot on God's earth. As the strident cry came again, Heinrich realized it was coming from a nearby bonfire a bit further down the beach in the direction of the moored airship. Heinrich picked up his pace and headed in that direction.

As he moved closer, he could make out strange gyrating forms in the flickering light, silhouettes of three or four men dancing around and making excited gesticulations. The flames would leap up momentarily, usually accompanied by another agonizing cry, and then both would die down. Heinrich sensed that something was amiss and he moved along more quickly. When he arrived at the bonfire, he was shocked to discover that Otto Rass and a couple of drunken soldiers had erected a thick wooden pole on the beach and had surrounded it with a ring of wood scraps and dried scrub; it was this material that fueled the conflagration. And lashed to the pole at its center was Lothar—his eyes bulging, desperate, panicked. The flames weren't actually close enough to do the man any real harm, but the nature of the whole thing was no less terrifying. His mouth was stretched wide; panic gurgled out of the gaping hole like some primordial birth. Up close the sound was horrific, worse than the death agony of some trapped and wounded game animal. Around the ring Otto Rass and his comrades danced an American Indian war dance; they made strange whooping noises and patted their hands against their mouths for effect—they had even gone so far as to paint war stripes on their faces with soot from already charred wood.

Heinrich bolted from where he stood. He rushed through the ring of fire. It flared up as his motions disturbed the air and the flames singed the hair on his arms. He kicked at the wood, sending it out and away from the pole. Swirling clouds of sparks and ash shot up and stung his eyes. He covered his ears to keep out the shrieks of the captive, the Indian whoops, the complaints of Otto Rass.

Heinrich picked up a branch, still burning at one end, and threw it at Rass and the soldiers; they all jumped out of the way, unscathed. Rass let out a dramatic Indian shriek and then ran laughing into the night. The other soldiers followed Rass as soon as Heinrich turned his attention back to Lothar. The poor man was panting like a dog, as he struggled against his bindings; he was no more in control of himself than when the flames had been licking at him. Heinrich got behind him and loosened the heavy knots. As soon as the bindings began to give, Lothar tore himself loose and bolted away. Heinrich cried after him, 'Wait! Sit and calm yourself! Everything is all right now!' Lothar ignored him and tore down the beach as quickly as his twisted form would allow; he disappeared into the night in the direction of his airship.

After regaining his own composure, Heinrich continued his stroll along the beach. He was unsure what he should do about the incident. Maybe it was best to leave the poor fellow alone. Heinrich had little confidence he could find him anyway; at the best of times the ship was a confusing maze of passages. He was sure that if Lothar did not want to be found, then there would be no finding him. This first evening in the desert had turned out to be a tumultuous one. His only objective now was to get a good night's sleep.

A few steps further, as he picked his way through the furrows ploughed up by the African horsemen, Heinrich's boot caught on something buried beneath the surface. Reaching down, scraping the sand away, he uncovered two thin strips of wood tangled in pieces of cloth. He pulled the fragments out of the earth, held them closer to his face, and immediately recognized them as William Hastings' discarded splints.

Chapter 7

THE CROSSING

Dora Nine and her crew departed the African continent on a heading of 210 degrees. The control cabin was packed with anxious crewmen: the rudder-man, the elevator-man, the navigator, Ober Dürr, Heinrich, and a few others. The ship glided through the homogenous blue haze as it climbed to its cruising altitude of four thousand feet. The troublesome motors had been repaired and droned on at a steady and comforting pace.

There was nothing of specificity visible through the spotless glass panels that enclosed the men, not a single object on which to focus. Nothing but a smooth gradation of marine color lay before them—murky blue-green of the sea below, turning to gray where the horizon ought to have been, fading to white from the thin morning overcast. The scene did not vary in the slightest as the ship cruised onward at fifty-two knots. It was as if they were standing still, floating in a tranquil amniotic void; even the airspeed indicator mounted in the framework overhead remained frozen in place, the delicate needle pinned to the first notch beyond the number fifty.

The peaceful expression on Heinrich's face belied the dread growing inside him. The start of this new phase of their journey left him disoriented and uncertain. His mood was similar, perhaps, to that on board the sailing ships of old at the start of a voyage in search of the end of the world. Throughout the airship's flight over the treacherous African desert, Heinrich had recognized that if the ship had fallen from the sky, he would have likely suffered a fiery death or, if not that, then an agonizing desiccation under the merciless sun. Nevertheless, he had taken comfort in the fact that there was solid earth beneath him, and he harbored the faint hope, however small, that he might survive a crash. If he had indeed been lucky enough to survive, he would have had time to gather his thoughts, to plan, to scheme, and to eventually devise a way to escape death—not so now. There was no such irrational hope to buoy him up as they sailed out across the South Atlantic. There were no lifeboats—much too heavy; there were not even life jackets. He could not deny that their willful craft floated above a sea of cold death like a coffin suspended above a well-dug grave.

Heinrich twisted around to peer through a window that gave a somewhat aft facing view. The narrow, white string of beach, their last sight of land for the past thirty minutes, had now disappeared into the haze. He turned back to gaze about the control cabin; he sought comfort in the intricate machinery. At first glance he couldn't help but appreciate the complexity of the mechanisms, strung about like Christmas tree ornaments; all were fabricated to a merciless precision.

There were several instruments housed in cylindrical casings of gleaming brass; beneath their crystal bezels lay dials etched with delicate numerals. Each of these varied gauges measured some critical aspect of the ship's operation: attitude, altitude, airspeed, heading, voltage, gas pressure, as well as a myriad of other functions. There were just as many wheels, levers, and buttons, all connected to the rest of the ship by bundles of black wiring, row upon row of copper tubing, and dull steel control cables. Heinrich pitied the men who were expected to manage all this complexity during an emergency.

He then looked past the well-crafted controls to the framework that carried the weight of the control cabin and its occupants. The skeleton upon which everything rested was stamped from thin-gauge aluminum. He had no doubt that if he grabbed and shook any one member, it would buckle without hesitation. Most of this structure lay hidden behind panels of drab-colored canvas; the floor supports were hidden beneath painted plywood that already showed signs of wear; a crack was forming beneath the heels of the elevator-man's boots.

The control cabin's external covering was a light sheet of corrugated aluminum, riveted to the metal framework so as to streamline the structure and insulate its occupants from the blast outside. None of it would withstand a good punch.

'God is not forgiving of fools,' Heinrich mumbled to himself, shaking his head in consternation.

'What is that you say, Heinrich?' asked Ober Dürr, turning toward him.

'Nothing. Just enjoying the view.'

The wardroom echoed with its usual raucous chatter as Heinrich and Dürr entered. The admiral was devouring the freshly cooked eggs that Colonel Strasser had provided as a parting gift; the senior officer seemed content to let the other officers' conversation run free. Even the pale captain had joined them and sat quietly picking at his food under the casual but curious eye of the admiral.

'I've inspected the steering deck,' announced Heinrich with mock formality, followed by a quiet chuckle, 'and am happy to report that everything is in order. I can guarantee no drownings before breakfast.' Nobody laughed. The steward dropped a steaming hot plate in front of him. 'What, no applesauce?' griped Heinrich.

'No applesauce!' responded the steward.

'Did you forget it?'

'I didn't forget,' blurted the steward as he worked his way back around the table. 'Someone stole it!'

'Did those army pigs take our applesauce?'

'Someone did,' said the steward. 'So you must be content with what you have!'

'Maybe it was your ghost,' suggested the admiral with a shallow grin, but his rare attempt at humor fell flat. Heinrich suspected the others didn't consider that a joking matter. The comment did, however, remind Heinrich of a complaint he had intended to make; his volume of *Von Krupp's Uhlan*, after having grown surprisingly precious to him, had gone missing, and he suspected the wireless officer of invading his cabin to retrieve it.

Heinrich was finding the story far more engrossing than he had originally expected. A cavalry general, Herbert von Krupp, had been filled with despair at the loss of his troop of Uhlans—slaughtered in a fictional battle against the French. Standing amongst the dying and the dead on the gore-soaked battlefield, Von Krupp had decided he could not accept this particular reality. Out of his moral and professional agony he decided to challenge God's order of things. By pooling the skill and experience of the army's very best surgeons—along with some vague and mystical religious incantations by a crazed army chaplain—he brought to life a great monstrous creature that was stitched together from the various undamaged limbs and intact organs retrieved from the field of a subsequent battle. Heinrich had progressed to the point in the story where General Von Krupp loses control of his creation and it begins wreaking havoc upon the world.

In Heinrich's view, the fact that the illegal volume had been in the wireless officer's possession before the tumble over the desert did not legally entitle him to it afterwards.

'Those poor fellows back there can have my applesauce for all I care,' said the doctor, interrupting Heinrich's thoughts. 'I don't know how they can stand it. Did you know they've been stuck there for over a year?'

'A year?' cried the navigator. 'No booze, no women, just fishing for sharks in the sea and trading shots with those crazy horsemen.'

'You know what that means!' stated the wireless officer, nodding his head in a knowing manner. 'We're not the first. I've often wondered what happened to all the other Doras.'

'That's enough, officer,' said the captain. 'You'll learn more than you want in due time.' The captain's presence in the wardroom was a rare thing, his voice rarer still; it startled the others into silence, and each man quietly pursued his thoughts in private. The admiral coughed and the captain changed the subject. 'Oberleutnant Dürr, have any mechanical issues developed since our departure?'

'No, nothing new, just the small things we weren't able to repair.'

'Fine. Keep me informed. Losing the engineer was unfortunate. You'll need to compensate for his loss by staying ahead of the ship.' Dürr nodded. 'Also, avoid venting hydrogen at all costs—we have a long voyage ahead. As the ship lightens, maintain a negative angle of attack rather than vent. Understand?'

'Yes, Kapitan . . . ' responded Dürr, 'but the operations manual states four degrees as the maximum down angle.'

'You may go as far as six with no problem,' returned the captain. Then seeing the doubt in Dürr's eyes, he added with just the hint of a smile, 'Herr Dürr, don't be overly concerned. The operations manual was written by me.'

The other officers grinned; Dürr was not usually caught off guard.

Unable to discuss the things uppermost in their minds, the officers continued with their meal in silence. The admiral, upon swallowing his last mouthful, gazed about and then with a nod took his leave; he wished the men a good day. The captain departed a short while later, leaving the others a few minutes to chat before they were obliged to pursue their various duties. It was then that Heinrich made his move.

'Herr Schmitt, have you finished with that book about the monster? I would like to borrow it for a few days as I have little to occupy me until we reach our destination . . . no flying, for the present.'

'I don't have the book,' growled the wireless officer. 'I didn't get to read a single page. I lost it over the desert. Or, someone took it!'

'Oh, come now,' interjected Dürr, 'it probably got swept overboard with the filth from the tumble. No need to accuse.'

'Who would throw *Von Krupp's Uhlan* overboard? It's a masterpiece. I'm sure someone took it. It was probably that rat

Otto . . . got it hidden in his cubby hole of treasures.'

'What's this?' asked Heinrich, perking up, his curiosity piqued.

'Oh, did you not know? He hoards all kinds of merchandise, each available for an exorbitant price,' said Schmitt. 'Surely you've noticed that Airman Rass never displays so much as a patch of stubble on that flabby face of his.'

'Really?' said Heinrich. 'I hadn't noticed.'

'Why don't you just pay the man?' asked Karl.

'Bah!' growled Schmitt. 'I'm not going to pay for it. It doesn't matter anyway; there's no time to read. I can't get enough sleep as it is. I'll bet the count, here, could afford it though.'

Heinrich frowned, but ignored the jab. His irritation grew as he became more confident in his suspicion that someone had entered his cabin. This violation of private space, a rare commodity aboard the vessel, broke every rule of naval conduct, formal and not. It was a gross transgression and set him firmly against the man who had perpetrated it. He decided that odds were against a single ship carrying two people of such low moral standing as Otto Rass; Heinrich's suspicion now concentrated entirely on this man.

'Well, maybe you're right,' said Dürr. 'This might be just the opportunity to put Herr Rass in his place. Heinrich, you haven't much to occupy yourself these days; why not endeavor to locate this hidden cargo of razors and monster stories? Just tell everyone the captain has chastised you for not knowing enough about our ship—that should be entirely believable. I can assign Airman Halterman as your guide if you feel the need for one.' This last jest managed to produce a few chuckles around the table, the closest thing to mirth since their departure.

That day, the very first of the three days allotted for their transatlantic crossing, Heinrich displayed a dramatic increase of interest in the workings of the ship. This aroused considerable comment among the crew, his vast ignorance to date having been quite conspicuous. While some chalked this behavior up to boredom, most, as Dürr hoped, thought it a result of the captain's displeasure. As Heinrich wandered about the ship, he was subjected to a bewildering flow of helpful suggestions (and behind his back to a wide variety of grins and gestures). The sail maker proposed he spend time in the control cabin with the elevator-man; the elevator-man encouraged him to visit the motor gondolas; the machinists suggested he travel to the rear of the ship, or even better, that he help at the water ballast pumps—the ship's trim being of the utmost importance to their continued survival. He took all of this assistance, good-natured and not, with a patient and pleasant smile.

Heinrich quietly ignored the suggestions and explored the ship in a manner of his own choosing. During this first day of the crossing he focused his attention on the ship's keel. He began by inspecting every device along its length; he peered into every crevice and probed every hole. Once satisfied that a given section had been thoroughly examined, and having found no sign of the missing *Uhlan*, he would move on to the next. In this manner he progressed quite slowly down the keel's seven-hundred-foot length. He happened to reach the ship's midpoint just as the off-duty crewmen were sitting down to their midday meal, and he paused in the shadows just within earshot of their conversation.

'Not our numerous selves these days, are we?' commented the sail maker to the four men gathered about him. The duty shifts had been revised by Ober Dürr in order to make the best use of the reduced crew. The men sat on bunks to each side of the keel; they hunched over dirty napkins laid across their laps; on these soiled surfaces they spread their sausages and brown slices of apple.

'So what!' snarled Otto. 'That just means we get the best pickings. We'll send whatever's left to the motor gondolas.' The off-duty machinist's mate glanced at him with irritation. Ernst Halterman glared at him with hatred.

'You'll want to be careful there, Herr Rass,' said the sail maker.

'Disrespectful deeds have a way of coming back to haunt you.'

Rass bit ferociously into the side of his sausage. He had scooped up the fattest one for himself while transporting the rations from the galley. Particles of white gristle clung to his lips. 'You just worry about your gasbags, old man.'

'That would be easier if someone wouldn't make such silly mistakes . . . like you did with No. 6. I don't like wasting goldbeater's skin. It's precious stuff. The kapitan keeps warning me to use it sparingly.'

'The kapitan?' snorted Otto. 'We could use *him* sparingly! Probably could do without him altogether now that we got ourselves an admiral.' The surrounding crewmen grew tense; the rudder-man was on dangerous ground; they concentrated on their food and ignored him. But Otto Rass didn't like being ignored. 'You know, yesterday, I opened the door to the head, and there he was, just sitting there with his trousers still up—forgot to lock the door. I'm thinking he's half cracked—probably inhaled more hydrogen than's good for him.'

'You can say whatever you like, Otto Rass,' retorted the sail maker. 'He's the most experienced captain in the fleet and none too patient with troublemakers. I once personally saw him throw a man out of the control cabin for sassing him. Of course the ship was still on the ground, so it didn't hurt him, only scared him. Point is, you'd best be careful around the captain. You hear me! And don't be doing any more stupid things that use up more of the goldbeater's skin. I'm sure our Dora's gonna need her bowels patched up sooner or later, whenever we get to wherever it is we're going . . . she being the dainty cow that she is.' The sail maker gazed up lovingly as he spoke about the ship.

'You don't mean she's lined with gold?' asked Airman Halterman, hesitantly. The question had been nagging at him, but he had been afraid to ask; his confidence had been so undermined by the other men's practical jokes that he expected a drubbing after any question.

'Of course it ain't lined with gold, you idiot,' snapped Rass. 'Don't you know that gold's heavier than lead!'

'I tell you what, boy,' said Hugo, coming to the rescue, 'it cost about like gold. I heard tell, a hundred thousand marks to line her gasbags.' The sail maker let this figure sink in for a minute. 'Amazing that cow innards could cost more than a baron's castle.'

'Cow innards?' laughed the elevator-man. 'What nonsense is this, Hugo?'

'I'm talking about cow innards! Every one of these gasbags is lined with goldbeater's skin to keep the gas in. It comes from the guts of cows. Why do you think I call our dear old Dora a cow? It ain't because of her shapely figure. They slaughtered a million of 'em to make our Dora. A regular Von Krupp's monster she is.' The crew around him snickered, unsure whether to believe him. 'So you better do what the captain tells you and don't go doing stupid things as use up the goldbeater's skin. And another thing, you stop irritating the other officers as well. The wireless-man was asking about that book. Asked if I took it. I told him it was you.'

Rass devoured the last of his sausage before he responded, 'I never got paid. No one sees the monster until I see the gold. I'm taking a nap now. What did you do with my hammock, old man?'

Heinrich left the messing crew behind, as irritated by the rudder-man as his mates, but having little authority to confront him. His resolve to discover the rudder-man's vault hardened as he continued his inspection. He also wondered whether the old man had been pulling everyone's leg about the gasbags. By the time Heinrich finished his tedious tour of the keel, late in the afternoon, he had discovered no sign of *Von Krupp's Uhlan*.

The evening of that same day found Heinrich standing on a narrow platform in the ship's nose. He was wedged between two drum-shaped reels that were used during moorings; each was five feet in diameter and wrapped with hundreds of feet of braided steel cable. During a mooring this platform was a busy place, with Ober Dürr directing everything by thrusting his head out the small hatch, or by peering through one of several large glass panels that formed a transparent circle in front of the platform. Now, over the South Atlantic at four thousand feet, with the nearest mooring mast five hundred miles behind them, this was a quiet spot to enjoy the serene vista ahead.

Heinrich eventually tore himself away from the vista to examine the platform. He poked around in the crawl spaces behind and under each reel. Satisfied that the object of his search was not hidden there, he turned his back to the window and its panoramic view. He peered into the dark hole of the axial corridor.

Dora Nine's gasbags were doughnut shaped and were confined between circular rings of aluminum girders that supported the cylindrical form of the ship; each ring was braced by a web of strong cables. If the ship were observed with the gasbags deflated, these rings would look like fifteen Ferris wheels lined up side by side. Through the exact center of these rings, and through the center of the gasbags as well, ran the axial corridor, the central spine of the ship—unobtrusive, uncomplicated, but under great tension as it maintained the integrity of the ship's form. The axial corridor had a very different feel from that of the keel. Its atmosphere lent itself more to the womb than the cave. The gasbags, pregnant with hydrogen gas, seemed intent on smothering the small tunnel, bulging through the large nets designed to gently but firmly confine them. The corridor was a quiet place, relished by any crewman desiring a momentary hiatus from the relatively crowded areas below.

Heinrich's inspection of the axial corridor was as painstaking as that of the keel, only much more tedious due to the unvarying nature of the scenery—an unending repetition of bulging canvas bags. At one point during his search, while his back was turned, Captain Timmer descended silently from a nearby ladder; he held a folding ruler in one hand and a roll of blueprints in the other. Descending after him came Lothar, slowly, awkwardly.

'Leutnant von Gotha!' cried the captain, halting his descent. 'What are you doing up here?'

Heinrich spun around, startled. Then, just as he mouthed the words 'Yes, Kapitan,' his left foot slid out from under him, the floorboards slick from a pool of some slippery substance. He fell with a thud onto his backside and then sat there, astonished. He hesitated, considering his response, and then answered the captain's question while trying to ignore the embarrassing position in which he found himself. 'I'm exploring the ship, sir . . . using my free time to learn about it.'

The captain's eyes brightened. 'I'm impressed, Leutnant. I must admit I hadn't noticed your interest in such technical matters.' Then, a slight smile of suspicious amusement flitted across the captain's face. Heinrich sensed that this had less to do with his awkward physical predicament, and more with his explanation. 'Perhaps you would care to assist us in our work?'

Heinrich was momentarily taken aback by the suggestion. 'Yes, of course, Kapitan, what would you have me do?' It was then that Heinrich first noticed Lothar as he stepped off the ladder and approached the captain from behind. Heinrich hadn't seen the man since the horrible incident on the beach. Once Heinrich had climbed back onto his feet, he searched Lothar's face for any sign as to his current state of mind, sympathetic to what that awful experience must have been like; but there was nothing, just the usual stony, distant expression.

'Very well,' said the captain. 'Our ship will require certain modifications once we reach our final destination. I need to document the necessary design changes. Lothar has discovered that the dimensions on the drawings provided by the ship's original manufacturer are inaccurate. We are now taking the necessary measurements to correct them. However, we are falling behind schedule and the task needs to be finished before we make landfall—there will be no time for it afterwards. Perhaps you could take one of the drawings. Do you feel competent for such a task?'

Without waiting for Heinrich's considered response, the captain knelt down on the floorboards and unrolled his drawings. While waiting for the captain to separate the intended drawing from the rest, Heinrich moved to clean himself up; he wiped the slippery and mysterious substance from his trousers and flung it to one side. The pulpy fluid had a disgusting texture to it, a texture that Heinrich found familiar in some way, but could not immediately identify. He raised his fingers to his nose and then immediately understood. Applesauce! He had to suppress a chuckle as the captain stood and rolled up his drawings.

'So, what do you think?' asked the captain as he handed Heinrich the drawing. 'Are you up for a bit of engineering work?'

Heinrich gazed at the drawing; he was perplexed and bewildered by the tangle of intricate lines. At first he could decipher nothing; he turned the paper upside down but this made it no more comprehensible. He returned it to its original orientation and studied it further, all under the amused eyes of his commander.

The captain quickly explained the meaning of the various symbols that represented the braces, fittings, and cables surrounding them. 'Look, Leutnant, just continue along the corridor as you were, but while doing so, measure the distances between all of these fixtures and mark them down here. Bring the drawing to my cabin when you are finished.'

Captain Timmer gave Heinrich an encouraging pat on the shoulder and disappeared down the ladder; Lothar followed without a word. They left Heinrich dazed, standing there with a pencil, a folding rule, and the drawing; he spent the remainder of the day doing his best to fulfill the captain's request. At one point Heinrich abandoned his task long enough to seek out Ober Dürr. He didn't want to disappoint the captain, and so he persuaded the ober to come upstairs and check his work. At first, Dürr had laughed at the request, but then willingly assisted, taking the opportunity to explain a few more details about the drawings and the ship's design. In the end they had finished the task by working together; Dürr called off the measurements and Heinrich jotted them down.

Heinrich knocked on the captain's door late that evening with confidence, and no small amount of pride. He was disappointed when the captain yanked the door open—just far enough to extend a ghostly hand—and then snatched the drawing from his grip. The captain uttered a hoarse '*Danke*' before he slammed the door shut with a thump.

On the second day of the crossing, Heinrich ventured along still another route through the dirigible's interior. This third pathway barely justified the label of corridor; it existed in those gas-permeated spaces at the very top of the ship. The path was nothing more than a series of narrow wooden planks hung from the upper edges of the great aluminum rings. In an upside down manner, this area formed the ship's true netherworld. Heinrich crawled along its claustrophobic length and lit his way with a special explosion-proof flashlight he had taken from the engineer's empty cabin.

The wooden gangway jiggled under his weight. The strong odors of rubber, gasoline, and engine exhaust were concentrated in the confined space, and he quickly became nauseated. He pointed the flashlight ahead of him, but its weak beam penetrated no further than twenty feet. Moving slowly, he directed the feeble light to each side and closely examined the exposed surfaces of the gasbags. They were like the hides of old, dusty elephants packed contentedly together, side by side, inside a bizarre Noah's ark. Whenever the ship passed through a turbulent patch of air, they wobbled and pressed against each other in a manner that Heinrich found disturbingly lifelike. It took Heinrich three very unpleasant hours to work his way to the tunnel's midpoint. There he arrived at another small platform; a hatch was inserted into the low hanging ceiling above.

He needed a rest, and so he took a seat on the platform with his back propped against a bulkhead. From his tunic he pulled out a piece of sausage left over from breakfast and munched on it as he sat; he switched off his flashlight to conserve its limited and already fading power. The snack was disappointing, the noxious air having spoiled its taste. Heinrich leaned his head back, closed his eyes, and dozed.

Disturbing dreams of barons and baronesses and their skulking daughters danced through his head; all were vaguely familiar, but distorted and quite unattractive. They laughed at him. They teased him about the fact that he never invited them to his family's estate. Of course they knew why; their eyes said everything. Prussia now contained two very distinct types of nobility—those that could afford their trappings, and those that couldn't. He had just slapped one particularly offensive young girl—one for whom he retained a particularly distasteful memory—when he was awakened from his dream by a different sort of laughter.

'What are you doing up here, Heinrich?' questioned an invisible voice. Heinrich was now back in his aerial sewer and was being interrogated by an indistinct figure who was masked by the glare of another flashlight.

After growling at the intruder and pushing the light from his face, Heinrich recognized the navigator. 'Never mind, Karl,' responded Heinrich acidly, irritated by his dream and from the throbbing headache that had replaced it.

'How can you stand it?' asked Karl. 'It reeks up here. Would you like some fresh air? I have to take the noon sighting.'

Heinrich accepted the offer immediately. He was aware that certain crewmen would climb out on top of the airship for just such activities; he also knew that requests by unauthorized personnel to participate were harshly refused. Karl unlocked the hatch and pushed it open, letting in a hurricane of cool, moist air. Heinrich immediately began to shiver, but he also became more alert.

'Here, put this on!' shouted the navigator, handing him a safety belt.

'This isn't much use, is it? It didn't help Franz!'

'What?' shouted Karl, unable to hear Heinrich over the blast and not waiting for Heinrich to repeat himself. When Karl stood, two-thirds of his body extended above the ship's upper surface. Heinrich attached his safety harness and joined the navigator. The opening was small and the two men consumed most of the available area. They stood with their backs to the gale while the navigator fiddled with his sextant. Heinrich gazed at the distant fin jutting up from the tail of the ship.

Massive cumulus clouds towered over them. The percolating tops extended into the airless heights above, and the dark, heavy bases hung a thousand feet below. Heinrich turned into the oncoming blast and observed that the ship was being steered into a gap between two tumultuous towers of vapor. Once through this pillared gate, the ship would be forced to deviate from its current course or else plunge into another of the faceless giants. Heinrich watched Karl gazing about at the clouds; he seemed disturbed by them.

'Can one climb up and walk around on the outside of the ship?' asked Heinrich, shouting into Karl's ear.

'Yes,' indicated Karl with an exaggerated nod of his head. 'Sometimes they must repair those things,' he shouted, pointing to flat, metal protrusions poking up at regular intervals along the otherwise smooth surface of the ship. 'It is very dangerous. Men can lose their balance and slide over the side. We haul them back in, but they sometimes end up like the engineer.'

After Karl jotted a few figures into a small, worn notebook, the two men knelt down and secured the hatch. The dizzying effects of the wind, accompanied by the pitch-black atmosphere, left Heinrich disoriented. As he fumbled with his flashlight, Karl suddenly cried out, '*Ach*! What's this?' After the light was switched on, they both examined Karl's outstretched hand; they found it covered with a translucent slime.

'Ah!' exclaimed Heinrich as he scraped off a small amount of the offending material. He stared at it for a moment, sniffed it, and then stuck it in his mouth. Karl stared at him in disgust. Heinrich grinned and said, 'It appears that our ghost likes applesauce.'

The navigator growled, clearly not wanting to be bothered with such unimportant matters; he climbed down a ladder between two gasbags and was gone. Heinrich remained behind; he sat in silence while he decided whether he really wanted to continue his exploration of this noxious tunnel. He wiped the remaining bit of slime onto his breeches and contemplated this strange finding. 'Applesauce . . . twice,' he mumbled to himself. 'Odd.'

Applesauce was only for officers; Heinrich could see no motive for one of the officers to indulge in a guilty but innocuous appetite in such a strange place. Heinrich was also coming to the conclusion that Otto Rass would never choose such a foul part of the ship for his lair. That left only Lothar, whose reputation for holing up in strange corners of the ship was pretty widely known. But somehow that didn't feel right either. Heinrich thought it over a bit more. As he got up onto his knees, and just as he decided to follow Karl down into a more pleasant region of the ship, a startling thought came to him. He let out a gasp. He growled into the darkness around him, 'THE ENGLISH!'

Chapter 8

THE STORM

The stolen applesauce churned inside William Hastings' stomach. The ship had been jerking him around in a violent manner for the past hour—all too reminiscent of the frightful plunge he had experienced during the ship's flight over the desert. He shifted a bit in the hope that it might settle his stomach, but there was a limit to how much he could fidget in his awkward burrow. He sat curled up like a gestating embryo; he was tucked into the smothering space between two of the massive gasbags.

The inspiration for his hiding place had been born of panic. Immediately after his escape from the army tent, he had scrambled through the desert scrub looking for cover. At that moment he realized he had little time to decide his course of action, and based on intuition more than a carefully weighed plan, he made his way swiftly to the airship—the ship's ultimate destination surely could offer no worse prospects than this arid wasteland surrounding him. While Heinrich was busy stunting his aeroplane, William had climbed aboard unnoticed.

Once inside the airship he was immediately hampered by the lack of light despite the morning brightness outside; the crew had switched off all power before disembarking, and this had left the ship's passages dark and silent. William had been unwilling to risk a surprise encounter with any of the crew that might be left on board; he had a sneaking suspicion that Lothar might not accompany the others to their desert camp. William remained on the officers' deck only long enough to visit the galley and snatch up the first thing he could lay his hands on; as it turned out, this was a fat tin of applesauce.

With this nutritious cargo tucked under one arm, he had climbed up into the ship as swiftly as his injured leg would allow. He mounted first one ladder, then another; slowly and cautiously, he worked himself through the labyrinth of confusing passages. He wandered aimlessly at first and fumbled in the darkness for anything that might feel familiar. Then, sure enough, his worst fears were realized; he heard the soft tread of footsteps in the darkness ahead. He dove for cover with no clear idea of what lay in the shadows. It had required the frantic energy of panic for him to worm his way between the tightly packed gasbags; the whole time he feared he might only succeed in suffocating himself.

The air was indeed close, just barely sufficient to sustain life, but he didn't pass out. To his relief he discovered that once he burrowed a little way between the bags, the friction of the their covering against the cloth of his uniform was sufficient to counteract gravity's pull, and he simply hung there, suspended in a bizarre maternal limbo. In the beginning he would struggle from his womb every few minutes out of a sense of claustrophobia and the need for fresh air, but as he grew accustomed to it, he could stay hidden for hours at a time, despite his headaches and nausea. His only long-term difficulty was food, boredom, and the need to use the airship's facilities.

The tin of applesauce was large and had lasted him the ship's voyage thus far, although his prolonged exposure to such a monotonous diet was creating its own risks; he had to make more and more frequent visits to the head. He was afraid to venture to the galley below for some other kind of sustenance; he felt he was pressing his luck; he already had been observed during one of his essential trips—perhaps by Lothar—though in his rush to return to the womb he didn't get a clear view of the man. Nevertheless, he had somehow remained unmolested, either because he had been wrong about being seen, or because the observer was not overly concerned with his presence—this was another fact that suggested the man might have been Lothar.

The gurgling in William's gut subsided momentarily, despite the turbulent jostling; he could rest easy a while yet. So he eased back and let his mind wander to thoughts of home and his sister; he wished desperately the airship would land soon—anywhere, even in Prussia. Eventually he drifted off to sleep.

*

As the afternoon progressed, the buffeting grew. By dinner it had become rough and unrelenting—Dora Nine's crew decided to forego formal mess and simply munched on foodstuffs they could manage with one hand, so that the other was left free for maintaining balance. The boiling currents of air tossed the airship about.

By midnight, bolts of pink electricity illuminated the control cabin's interior with frightening regularity. They also illuminated the ship's surroundings. Huge, seething thunderstorms loomed over them, storms of a size and mass much larger than the proud cumulus clouds that had jostled them during the day; it was as if playful cubs had grown into great roaring polar bears.

The captain, the admiral, Ober Dürr, and the navigator crowded into the control cabin. Unobserved and silent, Heinrich pressed himself against the rear bulkhead. Heinrich was no less concerned than the others, and he secretly prayed that none of the bolts would strike the inflammable craft. At the same time though, he desired more of the flashes; it seemed that only the brilliant illuminations enabled Karl to avoid driving the ship blindly into one of the cataracts. Each man seemed to be making a special effort to keep panic from his voice as they exchanged comments; this was wasted effort—Heinrich was sure that each man had eyes and ears only for the frightful forces raging outside their fragile cage.

'We must climb!' ordered the admiral. 'We will travel over the storms.'

'No!' shouted the captain. 'Bow down ten degrees! Drop to five hundred feet! It is safer to drive under the storms. If we climb, we will be forced to vent hydrogen, and if lightning finds the trail and ignites it, the flames could follow the trail back to the ship.' The admiral accepted the rebuff and remained quiet. But before the ship could begin its descent came the very event all had feared. A meandering thread of electricity snaked its way up from the depths ahead. It twisted and turned in the void before them like a thrashing serpent, flailing about, aimlessly at first, but then with a more deliberate and seemingly malevolent purpose. The flickering light turned toward them; the destruction of the ship and its crew seemed to have been its intent all along, as if the momentary delay had only been a feint to play with their fears and magnify their terror. The lightning struck the ship's starboard horizontal fin with a bang! And the fin began to burn.

'Ober Dürr, see to the emergency!' ordered the captain calmly. Dürr scrambled out of the cabin and disappeared into the ship; he raced toward the tail and snatched crewmen as he went.

The initial shock of the strike caused the men in the control cabin to lose their composure momentarily—all except the captain; the admiral let out a long grunt; the navigator produced an odd muffled yelp through his tightly closed mouth; the elevator-man gripped his wheel so tightly that he caused the ship to lurch; the rudder-man completely let go of his wheel and cried out to God until the captain brought him back to his senses with a quick slap on the ear.

Despite the fire, the controls remained effective. The captain fed a steady stream of instructions to the two frightened helmsmen as they drove the ship to a lower altitude where they could avoid the need to release any more hydrogen. Once the initial shock passed, the helmsmen had little more to consume their attention than before the strike—little more than the vision of everything about them transmuting into a hydrogen-fueled fireball.

Heinrich had been standing in stunned silence. Once he came to his senses and realized he was not doing anything to help, he bolted from the cabin and chased after Peter Dürr. The keel was strangely quiet, until Heinrich made it to the relatively open space at the ship's midpoint where the crew messed. There he found Dürr at the center of things, spitting out orders quickly and confidently. Men shot off at intervals to execute his commands—they had been assigned in pairs to extract water from the ballast bags located along the keel and to carry it in whatever containers they could find to various points of the ship. They were to wait there for further instructions.

Dürr ordered the men he trusted most to follow him to the ship's stern where the fire was burning. He pulled Heinrich along behind him. The men filed up the aft-most ladder to the axial corridor, and there they found the conflagration—a raging beast intent on their destruction. Fortunately it was still caged in the metal and fabric structure of the tail. Although the fire had not yet found the hydrogen gasbags, it had made quick inroads; it had spread from the original strike-point out on the starboard horizontal stabilizer and traveled along many separate avenues toward the main body of the ship. Multiple spurts of flame devoured the ship's fabric covering like a pack of jackals ripping the hide off some downed prey. As each man's head emerged from the ladder-way, he hesitated momentarily and let out a gasp at the size and ferocity of the fiery intruder. This was only for a moment; each recognized that they were in a race and that every second was a precious ally in a fight for their lives.

At first, Dürr seemed at a loss as to how best to come to grips with the flames, but only for a moment. 'We will form teams!' he yelled. 'Each team will have three men—two men delivering buckets to the third, who will toss the water on the fire. The lead man will switch positions after every ten buckets so he doesn't get too tired. Hugo, Thomas, and Herr Doktor, you move into the last segment of the axial! Go! Quickly!'

'Heinrich, Otto, and Ernst, go in there!' Dürr pointed at the entrance to the stabilizer access tunnel. The three men hesitated at the command; this narrow tunnel leading into the aluminum framework of the fin was where the fire was the most intense. 'NOW!' screamed Dürr. 'GO!' Heinrich was startled by how swiftly, and how coldly, Dürr ordered him into harm's way. He and the other two men obeyed, automatically. They each squatted down to half their normal height to squeeze into the passageway. They went in single file: Heinrich first, Ernst second, and Otto last.

As the two teams inched themselves toward the hot flames, Dürr organized the remainder of the men into brigades that transported buckets of water up the various ladder-ways from the keel where the ballast water bags were located. Dürr maintained his position at the top of the aft most ladder-way, an intersection of the various pathways and a location where he could keep an eye on both of the firefighting teams, as well as on the aft most gasbag; this was the bag at greatest risk of catching fire and exploding. It quickly became difficult to keep the men organized. The heat was growing; the air was filling with heavy, black smoke, and the noise from the crackling flames and the excited men made it difficult to make himself heard. At his side he had Lothar, who heaved buckets from the men in the nearest ladder-way; he alternated distribution of the buckets between Otto and the doctor.

Heinrich pushed himself as far out in the fin as he dared. This was the hardest moment. The flames were licking at him; the smoke was choking him and burning his throat. His eyes were watering, and it was difficult to see where he could safely step; the aluminum framework was tripping him constantly. And he still did not have his first bucket of water.

'Peter! I need water! Ernst! Tell them I need water. I'm burning up here!' Heinrich could hear Otto Rass shouting at Dürr, passing his message along. It wasn't long before the water arrived in soft canvas buckets; unfortunately the buckets tended to spill with each person's handling. By the time Heinrich had the first one in hand, it already had spilled half its contents. 'More!' screamed Heinrich. 'More water! Faster! We'll never put it out unless I get water faster!' The buckets did come—faster and faster, but not fast enough.

Heinrich was starting to beat his share of the flames back, but the smoke increased and soon he was unable to see any further than a few feet in any direction despite the brilliant illumination of the fire. His uniform was soaked and his boots began to slip on the narrow planks supporting him. And his arms began to tire.

'Faster! You need to work faster!' shouted Otto Rass. 'You're slowing down!'

'Go to hell!' Heinrich shouted back. 'I'm working as fast as I can. You just keep the buckets coming, bigmouth.'

The team continued to fight, but the behavior of the flames changed. As the fabric that covered this part of the fin was consumed, more and more of the outside air rushed into the ship; the air fanned the flames into all sorts of wild and fantastic patterns. At times they circled around and came at Heinrich from behind; they seemed to be attempting to separate him from his teammates and the rest of the crew. He knew he was at the edge of panic.

Suddenly, just as the wind had churned up the flames, some shift in the weather outside caused them to withdraw, and Heinrich was able to see about him. The smoke cleared for a moment and he drew fresh air into his lungs. He could think a bit more clearly now. Otto Rass was right. He was wearing out. It was only now that he remembered Peter's instructions that they should change roles after ten buckets. Heinrich felt as if he had thrown a hundred of buckets already. 'Ernst!' he yelled. 'Take my spot. I must rest.'

Ernst moved up and started to take Heinrich's position. But at that moment several things happened simultaneously. The wind changed direction again and whipped the flames up and the blinding smoke billowed around them. Otto Rass decided to hurry things along by giving Ernst a push from behind. Not realizing that Heinrich had just slipped in a pool of water and fallen to the floor, Rass caused Ernst to trip and fall head first into a burst of flames. Despite the fact that Ernst was soaking wet and that there were pools of water all over the flooring, Ernst's uniform caught fire. Over the noise of the wind and the flames and the men's voices, Ernst's high-pitched screams of panic and pain filled the narrow compartment. Heinrich scrambled to his knees to help the boy, but things were happening too fast. Ernst sprang to his feet and shot past; he had been transformed into a bundle of flames and blood-curdling screams. Heinrich chased after him and knocked Otto Rass out of the way as he went. 'Get out of my way, you bastard.'

Ernst bolted from the access tunnel and burst through the men grouped around Dürr. He knocked Lothar to the floor. 'Heinrich!' shouted Dürr. 'Go after him! Don't let him get near the gasbags.' Heinrich complied without breaking his stride. Once outside the narrow tunnel, he felt a wave of new energy and was now able to make use of his legs instead of his weary arms. Lothar sprang to his feet and followed. But Ernst was already far ahead of them and already amongst the gasbags. 'Stop!' Heinrich shouted after him. But the words were useless.

To Heinrich's shock and horror Ernst slammed against a gasbag; the boy was oblivious to where he was and to what direction he was running; he was consumed only by the searing pain of the flames. But before Ernst could rebound into another gasbag, a third man emerged from the darkness of the axial corridor and knocked the boy down. Both men rolled about the floor, Ernst writhing in agony, the other frantically batting out flames with his hands.

Heinrich dove onto the pile to add to the smothering force. Now it was Heinrich's turn to feel pain—excruciating pain. Panic took over. Instantly he shifted his attention from Ernst's agony to his own. But just when he thought his tormentor might win, he and the others were dowsed with cold water. The flames went out immediately.

The tangled bodies lay wet and slippery on the floor with Lothar stooped above them holding an empty bucket. Ernst whimpered, half-conscious, crying, '*Mutti*.' Heinrich groaned at the searing throbs that were his hands. And the third man swore, 'God this fucking hurts! My hands feel like they've been right up Satan's bloody arse!'

Chapter 9

LANDFALL

Singed and scarred from the storm, Dora Nine shot from a fog bank much like a spent casing ejected from the breech of a cannon. Tendrils of smoky air grasped at her and then reluctantly let go. The terror of the stormy skies receded as the ship sped into clear air—a powder blue sky above, and an aquamarine ocean below. It was the morning of Dora Nine's third day at sea.

Dora Nine's skin was so pocked with fire damage that she seemed to be suffering from some infectious and deadly malady. Even the glass panels surrounding the mooring platform had been shattered and, having not yet been repaired, let in a maelstrom that could be felt virtually everywhere on the vessel. A jagged scar cut across the dirigible's starboard side, a permanent imprint of the storm's savagery and ill will.

The empennage sustained the most damage. The protruding fins and control surfaces had attracted electrical discharges all through the night, and much of their fabric covering had been consumed in one blaze after another. Miraculously, none of the hydrogen-filled gasbags had been ignited. Perhaps the natural powers, for all their seeming malevolence, had been ignorant of the destructive potential held within the bags.

Those members of the crew not involved with the immediate operation of the ship were given the assignment of replacing the fabric on the damaged surfaces. The work was made easier by the solid atmosphere through which the ship glided, and the captain had reduced the ship's speed to an absolute minimum; yet the work remained harrowing and perilous. The men supported themselves as best they could within the fragile skeleton of the fins, two thousand feet above the sea. Two men stapled a sheet of cotton fabric to its supporting structure as the slipstream tried to rip it from their hands, while two others struggled to sew it into place; they used large steel needles. The quality of their workmanship was inferior, but it was sufficient for the surfaces to resume the stabilizing influence for which they had been designed. At one point the sail maker nearly lost his life when he slipped from an awkward perch, his safety cable having been abandoned after interfering with his work.

Heinrich was assigned the simpler task of assisting Airman Schilling in the repair of the windows at the bow. He held small sheets of plywood in place by leaning against them as Thomas secured them with large, metal clamps. For Heinrich this was a mindless task that left him free to think about the events of the day before. His hands were heavily bandaged, and they hurt badly, but the burns were not as severe as he at first feared; the doctor had explained to Heinrich that his hands would be useable and pain free in a couple of weeks despite their ugly appearance. Not so for Airman Halterman, who lay in the infirmary and regained consciousness only at intervals for a few agony-filled moments. The men on the officers' deck plugged their ears with their fingers to block out the high-pitched screams. Not even Otto Rass was tempted to visit the infirmary while the doctor went about his ghastly task of removing the swathes of burned and dead skin from the boy's body.

Although unexpected, Heinrich had not been shocked by William's appearance in the flame-filled region of the ship the day before. Ever since his suspicions had been aroused, he had accepted that it was only a matter of time before their paths crossed again. None but he and Lothar were aware that William had been the deciding factor in preventing an immolated Ernst from setting fire to the gasbags and killing everyone on board. During the confusion, when the conflagration was first brought under control, and as Ernst was carried down to the infirmary, William had slipped back unobserved into the more deserted parts of the ship. This morning, Heinrich had divided in half the small supply of dressings and ointment the doctor had given him for his burns; he set the supplies on the floor of the axial corridor at a point midway along the ship. He had shouted his intentions out loud in the hope that William might hear him and then left to receive his assignment from Ober Dürr. When Heinrich returned to the same spot a couple of hours later, the medical supplies had disappeared. He could only hope that William had retrieved them as intended.

What preoccupied Heinrich most, as he pressed his back against the plywood and watched Thomas Schilling at his task, were his feelings concerning Peter Dürr. Heinrich understood that Peter had been forced to make decisions yesterday in the best interest of the ship and its crew, but in his heart, Heinrich felt betrayed. The cold, ruthless manner in which Peter had ordered Heinrich into that fiery tunnel made him feel lonely and weak and at the mercy of everyone around him. Although Peter had always treated Heinrich as a friend, he now understood that Oberleutnant Dürr, when faced with the choice, would always choose duty over friendship. It was much the same feeling Heinrich had experienced after discovering the engineers had lied to him about their fancy new machine gun—the gun that would spew as many bullets back at him as it did at the enemy aircraft before him. He was discovering that the world was a much harsher place than he imagined while growing to manhood back in Gotha. He was becoming disenchanted with the world at large.

Heinrich let the thought go and looked back over his shoulder through an opening on the framework that had not yet been plugged with plywood. He noticed three small brushstrokes of white on the otherwise monotonous blue surface of the sea. 'Look! Out there! Whales!' He pointed excitedly with his bandaged right hand, and in doing so let his sheet of plywood slip out of place and spoil Schilling's work.

'So what!' cried Schilling, frustrated, forgetting the difference in their rank. 'We'll get to see them up close if this isn't finished before the ober gets back.' He indicated with a jab of his wrench that Heinrich should pay more attention to their task. Heinrich frowned at Thomas's lack of interest, but ignored the lapse in military etiquette.

Once the wooden sheet was in place, Heinrich again gazed out through an undamaged pane of glass and searched for the whales; he was intent on determining which species they might be. But he failed to spot them; they had disappeared. As the ship crossed the point at which Heinrich had last seen them, he carefully scanned the surface. Though he couldn't be certain, he thought he could discern three tapered forms beneath the roiled water. The creatures were quickly left behind.

By noon, the crew's spirits had improved considerably. The weather had remained perfect throughout the morning's repairs, and it now seemed they would succeed in their crossing, though many felt they had exhausted their account with fate in a single throw.

The navigator soon became the most popular, and most irritable, man on board. Throughout the day the crew pestered him with an unending stream of questions: *When would they make landfall? Where would they make landfall? Where would they head after landfall?* By dusk his irritation had boiled over, and he would speak to none but his superiors. Using paperclips, he mounted two paper cards on his cap, one fore and one aft; on these he penciled, for all to see, his estimate of when they would hit the South American coast.

After Heinrich and Airman Schilling had finished their task of sealing up the nose of the airship, Heinrich wandered about the control deck uncertain what to do with himself. His head was still filled with gloomy thoughts from the previous night's disaster. He was tempted to head back up into the ship to continue his hunt for *Von Krupp's Uhlan*, but with Airman Halterman's screams reaching a particular crescendo, he decided that he didn't want to go anywhere near the scene of the fire. So he slipped into the navigator's chart room to poke around and learn what he might. It was empty, Karl having departed some time ago for his noon sighting atop the ship. Heinrich deposited himself in Karl's swiveling wooden chair, the most comfortable seat aboard.

A lacquered oak chart table extended across the width of the cabin, and upon it rested a variety of colorful navigation charts, most having been published in March 1911 by the Brock & Tuttle Marine Company, Hamburg. There were various tools of navigation spread about: straight edge scales, protractors, calipers, compasses, wax pencils, ink pens, notepads, and slide rules. Mounted on the wall ahead were three identical chronometers of superlative quality, each of the same make—Schenk Brothers, Stuttgart.

The uppermost chart on the table was of the east coast of Brazil, and a penciled line ran from an obscure location out in the ocean to a spot on the coast north of Rio de Janeiro. Heinrich rolled the chart back awkwardly with his gauze-wrapped hands to examine some of the other charts lying beneath it. There was a chart of the isthmus connecting South America to North America and one of New Spain; then came several charts depicting the Sovereign States. While Heinrich examined the geography of the areas labeled East and West Carolina, a pencil rolled from the desk and fell to the floor. Just as he bent over to retrieve it, Karl's harsh voice startled him from behind. 'What are you doing in here?'

'I've come to keep you company,' said Heinrich.

'Getting lonely without your English friend?'

'Maybe. A little.'

'Can't you find another? I'm busy. And you're in my way.' Karl entered the room and pushed Heinrich gently to one side.

'Having trouble finding America?'

'No!' growled Karl in irritation, 'But we ought to have hit the coast before now.'

'Well, what does that thing say?' asked Heinrich, indicating the sextant that Karl grasped gingerly in his hands.

'Oh, this is perfectly worthless. It's only accurate to about a hundred miles.'

'Come now, that can't be true.'

'Look, I don't know exactly when we'll arrive. Soon!'

'Relax, Karl,' said Heinrich, rising from the navigator's chair. He then patted Karl on the shoulder. 'Everything will be fine. It's not like we're going to miss South America. It'll turn up.'

Karl grunted, then said, 'I suppose you're right. But still, they expect me to know the exact location of the ship at all times.'

Heinrich tried to take Karl's mind off such matters. 'I looked through your charts. I suppose I've broken some regulation by doing so.'

'I've no orders saying you can't,' said Karl.

'Can you show me where we're headed? I saw the chart of Carolina. Is that really our final destination?'

'Well, now you go too far Heinrich. You'll get me shot.' Nevertheless, Karl rolled back the charts and exposed Carolina in its entirety. It was then that Heinrich noticed a penciled line coming out of the south and ending at a small, black square in the western portion of Carolina, just west of the Mississippi River. As Heinrich reached out a bandaged hand to point at the small, black square, and before he could read the name of the nearest town, Karl said, 'Enough!'

'Do you know what we'll find there?' asked Heinrich.

'Not exactly,' said Karl. 'But I assume you've noticed Lothar going about the ship taking measurements and making drawings of the ship's frame. It has something to do with that. I think they're going to make modifications when we get there. That's all I can say. Now, get out!'

Before Heinrich could object, the airship suddenly reduced power. The nose dropped several degrees. More of the navigator's pencils rolled off the table and onto the floor. Heinrich stuck his head into a bulbous porthole that protruded outward from the side of the cabin; the porthole had been designed to provide the navigator with a slightly better field of view.

'It looks as though we have arrived,' chuckled Heinrich. Karl pushed Heinrich out of the way and leaned over to peer out the porthole. Barely visible on the horizon ahead was an indistinct darkening. Land! Rolling up the chart of the Brazilian coast, Karl stormed out the door and into the control cabin. Heinrich followed.

The little cabin was crowded, but Heinrich managed to squeeze in. The admiral and the captain waited silently as the navigator poured over his chart; the navigator frequently glanced up at the approaching coast; he was frantic to correlate the contours depicted on the abstract Brazil held in his hands with the vague and gently curving coastline of the real Brazil visible through the windows.

'Are we south of the Amazon?' asked the admiral.

'Most definitely,' responded Karl. 'The coast is on a southwest to northeast line.'

'But not as far south as Rio . . . correct?'

'No, we couldn't be so far south.'

'You must be certain. Do not approach the coast unless you *are* certain. Do not approach Rio. We must not be observed.'

Karl concentrated on his task, silently. Heinrich pitied the poor fellow. The navigator's hands gripped the chart so tightly that it was beginning to tear at its edges. Eventually, he said, 'There are few landmarks, only beaches, cliffs, and jungle. I propose we turn northeast now, remaining parallel to the coast until we find the next river; that will help me determine our position exactly.'

'Very well,' responded the captain. 'Make our course zero-four-zero.' The rudder-man immediately executed a slow turn to starboard.

During the next three hours, the dark green coast failed to produce rivers of consequence, the only sight of fresh water being the wispy translucent clouds below their cruising altitude. However, the coast made a gentle shift in direction that required continuous adjustments to the airship's heading, always to port. Thus Karl's confidence grew to certainty; they had made their earlier landfall at a point approximately one hundred and fifty miles south of Recife. It was only a few short minutes later that the aforementioned village came into view through the smoky afternoon humidity.

'Deviate to starboard,' ordered the captain. 'Maintain twenty miles between us and the coast.' The rudder-man complied, and they circumvented the small coastal town.

At dusk, after the town of Fortaleza had been left safely behind, the captain ordered the distance to the coast reduced. Heinrich volunteered to act as steward, retrieving sandwiches and coffee at intervals, thus buying continued admission to the control cabin. Although the helmsmen rotated through their two-hour shifts, the navigator refused to leave his post in the very front of the cabin where he kept his forehead pressed against the glass. At nightfall they stood out to sea where the captain intended to circle until dawn, not wanting to miss any critical landmarks. Heinrich spent the evening in his cabin. He now felt very far away from home indeed. Their ultimate destination was slowly taking shape and it filled him with foreboding. The sense of danger he had been feeling was steadily growing.

The new day presented a landscape unchanged from the last. If anything, the clarity of the air and the visibility of the Brazilian interior had improved. This perturbed the captain and the admiral, but it lifted Heinrich's spirits. His gloomy thoughts from the night before faded in the bright light. He split his attention between the vista ahead and the mountains off the port side. Dangerous mountains, he thought. They were deceptive in their appearance; gentle slopes of dense, green foliage were each capped with small, lenticular clouds that indicated strong updrafts and harsh turbulence. He would not want to fly over those crests.

Karl, refreshed and secure in the knowledge that he had

successfully guided Dora Nine to the New World, requested a course that would bring them closer to the coast; the captain consented. They approached a river that Karl believed to be the Parnaiba; it was not their ultimate destination that day, but it *was* a waypoint that would provide additional confirmation of their position. The coast and the seas that surrounded them were desolate. So, with the captain unconcerned about the Dora Nine being discovered, the helmsmen brought the ship down toward the water. Eventually Dora Nine was cruising over the mouth of the river at three hundred feet; flocks of white birds burst from its surface at the ship's approach.

The rudder-man selected a small white patch, triangular in shape, located on the far bank of the river, as a landmark for maintaining his course as they crossed the river's wide delta. The landmark appeared at first to be a rare patch of rock or cliff that managed to poke its way through the strangling jungle. As the dirigible came closer, an expression of confusion and alarm formed on the rudder-man's face. 'Herr Steuerman,' he whispered to alert Karl, as well as the captain, 'what is that?'

Heinrich noticed the captain's entire frame grow tense. Something was wrong.

'Steer ten degrees to starboard,' ordered the captain.

At the captain's command the ship's speed was reduced as it bore down on the mysterious white patch. Heinrich stepped over to a portside window and was soon joined by other officers. The captain pulled open the sliding door and let in a swirl of exotic smells. The rudder-man divided his attention between his compass and the view out the door to his left.

The whiteness of the triangle had been an illusion created by the contrast with the dark foliage of the jungle. It was, in fact, drab gray and the shape became uncomfortably familiar as they approached. Heinrich suddenly recognized it for what it was—the remnants of a dirigible's stabilizing fin which pointed like a road sign toward a deep gash in the jungle just beyond. Down in this green defile, at its very bottom, lay the charred remains of an airship; its tangled metal structure looked like a nest of wilted spiders. All four men remained silent with shocked looks across their faces as Dora Nine quickly passed the wreckage. It was several seconds before the captain gathered himself sufficiently to bark out a stream of orders. These took the airship out to sea and then along a circular path that eventually brought it back along the river bank, where it cruised twenty yards from shore and only a few feet above the surface of the water, with just enough speed to maintain steerage.

Ober Dürr and Airman Schilling, stripped to their underwear, dropped from the portside door into the brown water below and swam to the muddy bank. Schilling arrived at shore well before his superior, Dürr hampered by his still-healing injuries from the tumble over the desert, Schilling encouraged to swim quickly by cruel jests of alligators and snakes. The ship then departed from the risky confines of the tree-lined river and stood out to sea; Dürr and Schilling were left to scour the site for signs of survivors. Four hours later, each swimmer stood at attention in the center of the control cabin; they dripped black ooze after having hauled themselves up the rope ladder that had been dragged in the water to retrieve them.

'No survivors,' Dürr reported. 'It appears that most of the crew were killed in the fire. The only complete remains were hanging in a tree. The animals have gotten to the rest.' The captain nodded.

'Were you able to identify the ship? Did you find any logs?' asked the admiral, having just joined them for the debriefing.

'I found the kapitan's box, but it only contained this one log,' said Dürr, producing a small rectangular package from his wet trousers; water dripped from the rubbery substance that covered it. The admiral took the volume and slid it into his coat pocket; small stains formed on the outside of his coat as it soaked up the loose moisture.

'How do we recover the body?' Dürr asked quietly. The admiral ignored the question. The captain gave a quick shake of his head and ordered the helmsmen to resume their course up the coast. He dismissed Airman Schilling after demanding that Schilling keep any gruesome stories to himself.

For the next twenty-four hours the airship plied westward along the sparsely populated coast; it kept good distance between itself and the infrequent towns and villages plotted on their charts. By late afternoon of the following day, they had reached their apparent destination—the spidery network of muddy channels that formed the great Amazon Delta. The river's identity was easily confirmed, and the captain ordered the airship back out to sea, where it again circled and waited. While the crew and the officers ate their noon meal, the admiral, the captain, the oberleutnant, the wireless operator, and Karl closeted themselves inside the wireless compartment with a thick roll of charts.

Shortly after midnight the ship left its holding area on a course that carried it directly over the mouth of the Amazon. To Heinrich's surprise the ship did not stop there, but instead proceeded upriver at reduced speed, the broad course of water clearly visible in the moonlight. After traveling several miles upriver, a momentary stab of light shot up from the earth far off in the distance. For several seconds it appeared like some heavenly column, then disappeared and allowed the night sky to close again. This column reappeared every quarter of an hour, for a few seconds at a time. It was toward this pillar of light that the dirigible made its way. All the while Dora Nine sank slowly, illuminated by the setting moon.

Once the ship had descended to five hundred feet, the navigation lights embedded in the fins and beneath the motor gondolas were switched on; they sent out small twinkles of red light. When it seemed that the ship must be directly upon the source of the beacon, the river basin was suddenly flooded with a ghostly yellow light; it came from a string of spotlights positioned somewhere near the river's edge. These powerful lights illuminated the riverbanks for several hundred yards and painted all surfaces—trees, water, and slithering alligators—the same deathly yellow.

The helmsmen, working together, steered the airship down to only a few feet above the river's surface. The motors ran at low revolutions as the airship crept up the river. Soon, though, they were able to determine the source of the floodlights—a ship moored to the riverbank. The airship approached a mooring mast, brilliantly illuminated and extending over the water at an angle of forty-five degrees from the bow of the ship. A motor launch departed from the sea vessel and sped out into the river where it picked up the mooring cable that had reeled down from the dirigible's nose. The mooring proceeded smoothly in the calm night air.

As the dirigible glided alongside the ship, numerous alligators slipped off the muddy banks and distracted Heinrich from the mooring activities. The sight of these creatures made the hairs on the back of Heinrich's neck stand straight.

After the airship was securely lashed in place, and once the motors were stopped and all of the lights extinguished, the river bathed in an inky darkness. The ever-present grumble of the Grimbach motors was replaced by the rhythmic screeches of every jungle creature known to man. It wasn't long before the crew began to miss the clean air above as they fought swarms of mosquitoes that seemed to be abandoning the rusting hulk to infiltrate Dora Nine in search of fresh blood.

The captain gave word that those crewmen not currently on duty were free to descend along a gangway that had been run up from the ship below. They might enjoy a badly needed shower and a hearty meal, compliments of the Prussian merchant marine service. After receiving a favorable weather report from the merchant ship's skipper, the captain decided that Dora Nine would remain birthed along the *Frau Gerber* until the following evening. Karl, momentarily relieved from his taxing navigational duties, became a civil companion and accompanied Heinrich and Ober Dürr as they descended through the hatchway that led to the lower decks of the old supply ship. Their hosts provided a feast of sauerbraten, wiener-schnitzel, dumplings, and good Bavarian wine. Their laughter seeped out the *Frau Gerber*'s portholes, only to be overwhelmed by the nocturnal noises of the Amazon.

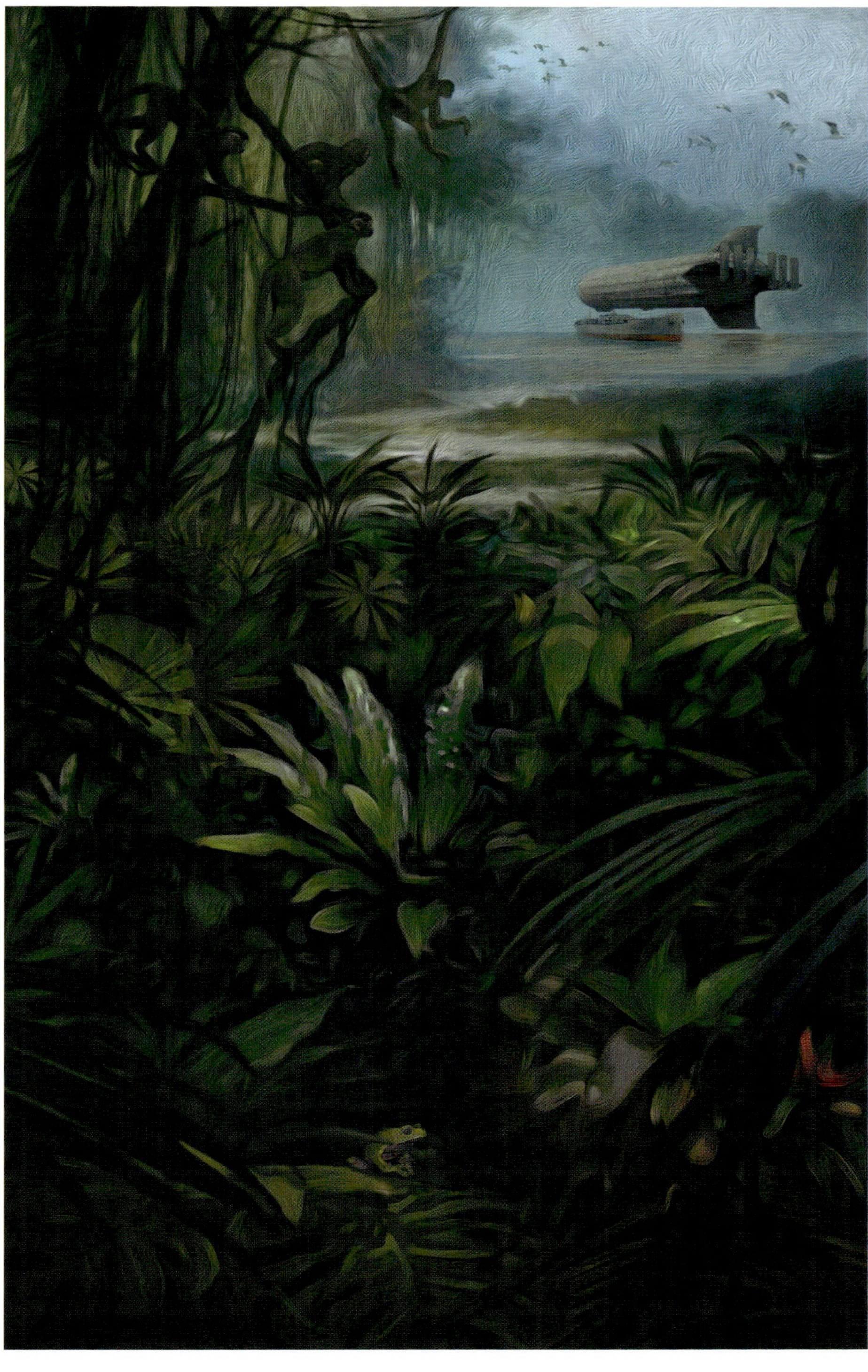

Chapter 10

THE PILOT

Forty thousand cubic feet of hydrogen stored in gas cylinders, eight thousand gallons of eighty-octane gasoline, three thousand gallons of river water ballast, five hundred gallons of lubricating oil, one hundred gallons of drinking water, one thousand pounds of spare motor parts, two thousand square feet of No. 1 grade cotton, one hundred gallons of dope resin, one thousand yards of No. 5 thread, two hundred yards of braided steel control cable, one thousand pounds of fresh and canned foodstuffs, mostly canned, along with an assortment of medical, navigational, and cooking supplies were to be carefully transferred from the *Frau Gerber* to the gently rocking dirigible by noon.

Heinrich woke from a troubled sleep, well after the others; he had been disturbed by the raucous chatter of the birds and the pitter-patter of curious monkeys that swarmed on and off the ship from the gnarled branches that reached out of the jungle; the activities aboard the *Frau Gerber* seemed an endless source of entertainment to the little creatures. Heinrich stumbled out of his cabin in a drowsy fog and wandered through the ship's empty corridors; he looked for a way out into the morning sunshine. He passed the galley, where he secured nothing more than half a cup of coffee from the ship's taciturn cook, and eventually emerged onto the empty stern deck.

Heinrich leaned over the stern rail and sipped the odd tasting coffee from his metal field cup, coffee that he suspected of having been brewed from river water. He tossed over the rail small portions of sauerbraten, surreptitiously pocketed during dinner the night before, to the monsters swirling in the shallow water below. They snapped and barked and seemed to be taking as many bites out of each other as they did of the meat he dropped to them.

'Nasty creatures,' said Karl, walking up behind him.

'Umm,' grunted Heinrich, feeling there was nothing more he could add to such an obvious statement. 'You're up early.'

'How could anyone sleep through those horrible shrieks.'

'The birds certainly didn't keep *me* from sleeping.'

'Don't joke, Heinrich; I wasn't speaking of the birds.'

'What then, those silly monkeys?'

Karl gazed at Heinrich, a quizzical expression on his face. 'Have you not heard?'

Heinrich shrugged his shoulders, indicating that he had not.

'Dear Lord, how could you sleep through all that commotion. It really was horrible. It seems that Otto Rass was stowing a rather large stockpile of contraband aboard the airship before dawn—several bottles of schnapps, amongst other things—stuff he purchased from the *Frau Gerber's* cook. He was hauling them up through that hatch . . . ' Karl pointed to an open hatch in the side of the dirigible, just above the *Frau Gerber's* deck and across a small open space of three feet. 'Well, either Otto Rass lost his footing, or the fabric gave way, and he fell into the river down there. Those brutes gobbled him up.'

Heinrich turned pale as he returned his attention to the creatures. He slid the last scrap of sauerbraten back into his pocket. 'Are you inventing this?'

'Of course not, the cook saw the whole thing! I can't believe you didn't hear the man running through the halls screaming for help. By the time everyone made it topside, there was nothing left.'

Heinrich swallowed hard, then said quietly, 'I find it difficult to take my eyes off them.'

'Oh, and another thing,' said the navigator, ignoring this remark. 'They found Otto's hiding place—your monster book too. Dürr has it . . . said he would give it to you later. God, I'm dying for a smoke. Do you suppose it would be safe to go on shore for a few minutes?'

Heinrich stared at Karl with wide eyes as if to say, 'You idiot!'

'I saw someone smoking back here last night,' continued Karl, 'but I probably wouldn't get away with it. This lovely old barge would make a wonderful brig—can you imagine being locked up here? It would be worse than the desert. I have no doubt the admiral would do it, too. He doesn't smoke.' Heinrich grunted and took another sip of coffee. He grimaced at the taste as he swallowed.

'Do you know where we're heading today?' asked Heinrich after a few minutes of introspective silence.

'No . . . not really . . . we just keep following the coast. We're getting a new pilot, an American; he's to assist us in navigating the rest of the journey.'

'Why?' asked Heinrich. 'You got us to this godforsaken place without any problem.'

'I'm not in trouble,' said Karl, chuckling at Heinrich's concern. 'This fellow knows the ground around here. I met him. He's quite a character.' As if not wanting to continue the discussion, Karl turned away. 'I'm going for a smoke. Stop feeding those brutes!'

It was then that Heinrich looked from the reptiles up to the hatch from which Otto had fallen. As he considered what the horrible scene must have been like, he suddenly noticed a pair of eyes staring back at him. There, just inside the hatch, obscure in the dimness, knelt a shadowy figure. It took Heinrich a few seconds to recognize the man. It was Lothar, and he had been gazing down at the water in much the same way that Heinrich had. Lothar looked up and caught Heinrich's gaze, gave him a curt, emphatic nod, then stood up and disappeared back into the airship—the hair on Heinrich's neck stood straight. He quickly fled the scene of the 'accident.'

Early in the evening, the breeze that had been rippling the surface of the wild river began to fade. The monkeys and the birds continued to shriek, and it seemed that their numbers had continued to swell throughout the day so that virtually every branch in the trees around them was occupied by an expectant, wide-eyed creature.

Heinrich stepped off the gangplank leading up from the *Frau Gerber* and entered the control cabin with much anticipation. The loss of Airman Rass had left the complement of rudder-men reduced, and during dinner the night before, Dürr had asked Heinrich whether he would be willing to take a shift at the rudder wheel; he was expected to have developed some aptitude for the job through his training as a flier. Dürr seemed delighted when Heinrich consented; the ober apparently had some concern that the request might offend Heinrich, the job typically being the duty of an enlisted man.

Heinrich joined the men in the control car to observe the departure and stood just behind the first rudder-man, Adolf Dresser. Of course Heinrich could not be trusted with the wheel until the craft was safely at altitude where the likelihood of something going wrong was minimal.

The command to start the motors began with a tug on each of the four red knobs that hung above Dürr's head; the command was transmitted through cables that snaked their way through the ship to each of the four motor gondolas. The machinists, each sitting refreshed in his own gondola, responded quickly, and the still air churned as the motors began to grind and cough. They started without incident and set the monkeys howling and scurrying for cover. Soon the dirigible's airframe was vibrating in its familiar manner, and its occupants became eager to be off and away from the infested river basin.

A metallic clang echoed across the river as the clamp released Dora Nine and startled the few remaining birds, sending them beating for the skies. The dirigible hovered for a moment as if having second thoughts about leaving the security of its jungle home, until the men along the *Frau Gerber*'s starboard rail released the rope lines. The airship lurched upward and wallowed in the free air, thirty feet above the jungle canopy. The engine revolutions increased, and the craft made headway; it cut a path across the jungle terrain in a northeasterly direction and climbed steeply as it headed toward the coast.

As he observed Airman Dresser's movements, Heinrich kept one eye open for the entrance of the foreign pilot. The mysterious man had been quietly shuttled aboard during the afternoon. But Heinrich was to be disappointed, as the man did not present himself anytime that evening while the ship fled seaward from the coast to resume its normal cruising position twenty miles from land. In fact, the pilot failed to show himself anytime during the following day as the dirigible fought its way up the Brazilian and Venezuelan coastline against an ever-increasing headwind. The choppy air buffeted the craft; it made meals difficult, stomachs queasy, and tempers short.

*

'This is quite enjoyable,' commented Heinrich to his fellow helmsman, Airman Immelman. The air outside had calmed, and the two of them were alone in the control cabin, Heinrich acting as watch officer as well as rudder-man for the moment, while Dürr was occupied with problems further back in the ship. 'It seems to be not so difficult. I suppose one man could even take over both wheels if necessary.'

'Sometimes,' responded Joseph, 'but when the air is rough like yesterday, or during mooring, it would be too much. Besides, it's lonely all by oneself.'

'Indeed it would be,' said Heinrich. 'Am I performing well?'

'You're steering very well,' said the elevator-man, 'although you needn't correct for every bump. Most times the ship will return to its heading without a correction; you must be patient with her.'

Heinrich nodded in understanding. He didn't mention to Airman Immelman that the same was true for aeroplanes, and that he simply enjoyed feeling the ship respond to his inputs, despite the fact that they were unnecessary. But he eventually curbed these desires after he learned that everyone onboard could feel him at the helm, and some complained that he upset their stomachs. Various officers took to standing behind him with smiles on their faces, or in some cases, smirks. At the dinner table they took to calling him Airman.

Toward the end of the next day, with Heinrich at the helm, while they were cruising far from the sight of land through the middle of the Caribbean Sea, the mysterious and long-looked-for pilot suddenly appeared. One moment Heinrich was staring out at the azure sea before him, gently fingering the wheel, lost in a vacant daydream, the next moment he found a tiny figure standing next to him. The man was so short that he failed to rise higher than Heinrich's chest—a wrinkled, brown, weather-beaten fellow who Heinrich guessed to be about sixty, although his crusty appearance might cause one to overestimate his age.

Heinrich greeted the stranger with a friendly, '*Guten Abend*.' The stranger nodded in response. Airman Immelman turned and nodded a welcome as well. The pilot turned toward Heinrich and glanced up at him in a peculiar manner; he rolled his eyes up without moving his head the slightest bit—the stranger seemed intentionally to avoid leaning backward to gaze up at Heinrich's height, as if the man had long ago decided to concede only so much in his interactions with taller folk.

'Mighty fine view,' the stranger blurted out in English. Immelman, not comprehending the stranger's speech, glanced momentarily at Heinrich before returning his attention forward.

'Very pleasant indeed,' responded Heinrich, 'especially when the air is so calm.' Then after a brief pause, 'Have you ever been in such a vessel before?'

'I've been up in balloons. You know what I mean?' the man made a small sphere-like shape with his hands that Heinrich understood to mean captive balloons. Heinrich was quite taken with how the little man spoke. His intonation and pronunciation was like nothing he had heard before—a slow, calm speech that was both languorous and proud. 'This is quite a machine you fellers got here. I can't believe you made it this far.'

Heinrich laughed gently, glanced about the control cabin with fresh eyes, and agreed with the man without articulating it.

'I understand from our navigator,' said Heinrich, 'that you are to be our guide.'

'Yes, starting tomorrow,' said the man, nodding slowly, 'just as soon as we hit the coast of New Spain. I'm just out for a breather, been feelin' a little puny these past couple days. The damn jungle does it to me every time.' Heinrich did not quite grasp *puny*, but assumed it meant unwell.

'Have you been told what is to happen with us when we arrive in America?'

The pilot paused for a moment, but he continued to gaze out the window, unperturbed by the question. 'Yes, indeed,' he said. 'There's gonna be some fireworks. But it wouldn't be right for me to say any more. You and the others will get more information from your admiral in just a little while.'

'Well, I can't say that sounds very encouraging,' responded Heinrich.

'I understand what you mean,' said the pilot with a chuckle. But then in a much more serious tone he added, 'We all do our duty though.' The man cast a casual glance up at Heinrich to observe the impact of his words but only for a moment; then his eyes dropped and came to rest on Heinrich's breast pocket, where his flier's insignia was pinned—a silver eagle with its wings thrust out to each side. 'So you're the feller that flies that little aeroplane?'

'I am,' responded Heinrich. 'It's much more enjoyable than flying this beast. We seem to have run short of helmsmen during our recent adventures. So I've been drafted, so to speak. Still, it's better than sitting around with nothing to do.'

'I don't have much experience with aeroplanes. All my friends back home think they're a waste of time—'bout as useful as a toy kite, they say. But I'm not so sure about that. Big things can come from small beginnings. Only time will tell. I heard about your scrape with the English machine. It didn't take you long to make mincemeat of it—though it might have been better if you had made mincemeat of the man instead.'

Heinrich grunted at the comment, the whole incident still a difficult one for him in many respects; he was surprised that the pilot already had heard of it. But the man seemed to recognize that his comment might have rankled and added, 'Don't mind what I just said. That was a real special accomplishment, if I do say so—and one you should be proud of. I never seen a horse run his first derby without gittin' a little bit skittish.'

Heinrich considered this point. The conversation had turned in a direction that brought back memories of Heinrich's grandfather and the shame that came from all of his barbed criticisms. The pilot had made a point that could easily have come right out of the old man's mouth. But for some reason Heinrich didn't feel upset by it. Though at the moment he felt strangely exposed before this little man, he didn't feel that the pilot was judging him.

The pilot continued, interrupting Heinrich's thoughts. 'Sometimes it can be hard to fight unless you're sure what it is you're fightin' for. Don't you think?' The pilot looked up at Heinrich again, this time keeping him under his gaze for an extended period of time. But before the conversation could go much further, they were suddenly joined by others: Karl, the captain, and the admiral, each out for a final inspection before the admiral retired to his cabin for the night.

'Good evening, Herr Stanton,' said the admiral. 'I see you have found your way to the center of things. I hope you are feeling well.'

'Evenin', Admiral; evenin', Captain. You, too, Lieutenant.' He nodded to each of them in turn, in a friendly but reserved manner. 'Yes, I'm feelin' much better. Thank 'ee.'

'English is spoken by only a few of my crewmen,' said the admiral. 'Whenever you are ready, I can have someone explain the operation of any of the equipment you need to perform your tasks.'

'I'll be just fine, thank 'ee, Admiral. All I need is this compass here. I'll be able to talk to these fellers at the wheel just fine. Suddenly, to the shock of all present, Stanton pulled from his shirt pocket a wrinkled, hand-rolled cigarette, popped it into his mouth, and lit it with the click of an old metal lighter. The admiral's mouth dropped open. Just as Stanton began to inhale his smoke, the captain reached up and snatched the cigarette from the pilot's mouth and extinguished it between his thumb and forefinger.

A stunned look spread across Stanton's face—it quickly transformed into rage; the man seemed on the verge of violence. But as suddenly as the emotion had erupted, with everyone waiting aghast, he bottled it up.

'Kapitan Timmer!' shouted the admiral. 'You forget yourself!'

'No, no, no, Admiral,' said Stanton, shaking his head. 'The captain is right. I forgot. It's a hard habit to break. Captain, please forgive me. No hard feelin's I hope.' The captain nodded, his English sufficient to understand that the pilot was apologizing. The admiral continued to glare at his subordinate, then walked up to the compass for one last look before departing for his cabin; he wished all a good night. Karl shot a glance toward Heinrich, directly over the head of the pilot, a glance wide eyed with concern; then he, too, departed. The captain remained a few more minutes and then departed as well.

'Everyone's kind of touchy about the gas, aren't they,' commented Stanton. Heinrich was unsure how to respond to the strange observation. 'Shoot, I can remember when lightning would strike our balloons back home. Nothin' at all would happen, 'cept burn a hole in the bag.' Then after a long pause, 'Still, I suppose one shouldn't tempt fate.'

Heinrich nodded and smiled faintly at the man, somewhat disconcerted by his casual manner concerning their hazardous cargo. They chatted quietly until sunset, both adamant in their mutual dislike of the teeming jungle behind them.

*

Heinrich returned to his new post at the helm the next morning after an enjoyable breakfast that included fairly fresh fruit, compliments of the *Frau Gerber*, and after copious questioning about the character of their new guest, news having traveled quickly concerning the previous night's incident with the cigarette. He found Stanton standing behind the helmsmen, wearing a light blue shirt with its sleeves rolled up over his biceps, dark blue trousers, and black work boots—all devoid of any military insignia. His appearance seemed that of a factory worker who might have walked off the street of any major city. However, Stanton carried his small frame with a verticality that could only have been bred from long service in the military.

The morning greetings dispensed with, Stanton informed Heinrich that he and the helmsmen had the coast of New Spain in their sights, dead ahead. Heinrich's glance out the window failed to produce such a coast, but he had no doubt that the little man's confidence was justified.

'I am not familiar with this particular corner of the world,' said Heinrich. 'At what part of Spain do you expect us to arrive?'

'We're gonna stop off at the Yucatan.'

'The Yucatan?'

'It's a finger that sticks out into the Caribbean. Gotta stop and get some instructions. You'll like the Yucatan, there's some real interestin' sights there—genuine historical temples and such.' Heinrich raised his eyebrows, indicating sincere curiosity at visiting *genuine* historical temples. He also hoped this would provide an opportunity to brush up on his flying, there having been no opportunities of late.

True to Stanton's promise, the Yucatan proved a fascinating waypoint for the entire crew. Prehistoric pyramids served as quite functional landmarks, assisting Stanton in his navigation. One particular pyramid sat proudly near a clearing that had been hacked out of the dusty jungle by what must have been a virtual army of local inhabitants. The dirigible made an uneventful landing as a few curious natives hung about the eaves of the surrounding jungle. No mooring mast was present, and the ship settled into the gap; it announced its arrival with another thunderous boom of its landing harpoon. The crew poured out and secured the ship to the ground.

The engines were switched off. Beneath the bow of the airship, Stanton, the admiral, and the captain met a party of five scrappy men—three with moustaches, two with beards—all unwashed. They had emerged from the jungle without fanfare, and they did not smile. They were dressed in somber clothing much compromised by the elements, either from a long stay at this remote outpost, or perhaps from a rough time in getting there. Once introductions had been mediated by Stanton, all eight men disappeared into a small hut, crafted from the remains of the trees that had been felled; it rested in the shadows of the thin jungle canopy.

Those crewmen not on duty, including Heinrich and Karl, were drawn toward the ancient structures so entirely out of place in their antediluvian surroundings. Naked children had overcome their fright of the great machine and its passengers, and swarmed around them as they tromped through the foliage. Once the crew's destination became clear, the children pulled and tugged at them; the children laughed and giggled as they herded the men to a path that made their progress easier.

The crew spent hours climbing over the pyramids; they chucked loose stones at each other and chiseled their names into the soft surfaces. Dürr arrived later with the ship's camera and organized a group photograph on the steps of the temple.

*

The airship departed the next day, as easily as it had arrived. Their five dreary hosts had disappeared into the jungle as soon as the craft had climbed above the treetops. Soon the ship was cruising at fifty knots, course 310 degrees, altitude one thousand feet. Before nightfall they had crossed the northern coast of the Yucatan and were headed across the gulf.

It was at this point that the atmosphere aboard the ship began to change. The entire crew sensed that they were approaching the final purpose of their mission. The men paid more attention to their duties, and their dress. The formality of communication between officer and subordinate returned—stiff and efficient in manner. Even Heinrich, who had been disappointed that the terrain of the Yucatan and the time available had prohibited any flying, was now spending more time inspecting his aircraft; he had been required to climb down into it to clean out the debris that included one small but colorful snake.

The next day they crossed the coast of North America and left the sea behind them. As they began to cut across the arid scrubland, the dirigible climbed to ten thousand feet and disappeared into the overcast.

* * *

Chapter 11

THE GAS PLANT

William dangled from a cable like a spider hanging from a silvery web, just for a moment, before letting himself down into the cool night air. The cable extended from the nose of the airship over to a steel mooring derrick, much like the one he had seen at the army camp on the African coast, only larger and more complex. There was a thick rubber hose, suspended just below the cable, that also led to the derrick, and at times William could balance his feet on the hose, giving him momentary relief from the steel braiding that cut painfully into his scorched hands. There was a mist in the air that made the cable slippery, and more than once he almost lost his grip, but he managed to work his way safely along. After several minutes of slow progress he reached the derrick and swung his legs over a steel brace; from there he climbed through the structure, found an access ladder, and climbed down as quickly as his sore and still-healing ankle permitted

Once on firm earth, he flopped down and stretched himself out on the derrick's cement foundation to let his lungs recover from his exertions. He retrieved the knife from the ankle of his boot and gripped it tightly in his right hand while he listened carefully for any signs of detection, for the sound of approaching sentries who certainly would be circulating through the area. William's bowels grumbled, dissatisfied with the monotonous diet of applesauce, unchanged for the past several days. His head ached from fumes and lack of oxygen; the copper tubing he had pilfered for use as a makeshift snorkel had provided only a minimal amount of clean, fresh air to him in his womb-like hiding place. And his hands, though not badly burned, still stung like the blazes.

Slowly, as his breathing became more even, William's curiosity began to overcome his exhaustion. It appeared that he had overestimated the vigilance of the camp's occupants, and so he sat up and looked about. He was at a complete loss as to his current location; he knew only that they had traveled a great distance. He let out a sharp gasp at the scene before him. Spread out to either side of the dirigible—his dirigible, his unwelcome home for so many miles—lurked seven others, all in a neat row, three to the left and four to the right, each, as best he could determine, of roughly similar dimension. All sat deathly still, lit up by the yellow lights of the mooring derricks; the ships glowed like pale ghosts under the silver moon.

William, having had so little human contact over the past several days and having had nothing to occupy himself as he hung in his smothering cocoon, had forced his mind to focus on speculations as to the purpose behind the dirigible's voyage. Although it was obviously of nefarious purpose, he had come to the conclusion that even with the most malevolent of crews the fragile craft could never have much impact and was almost certainly doomed to some calamitous fate. But now, gazing aghast at the imposing mass of the eight giant dirigibles and the vast facility built to support them, he immediately reconsidered this conclusion.

While he contemplated the significance of this new turn of events, he was startled when the still night air was suddenly interrupted by a loud, piercing whine. It was like the wail of some great screech owl, howling its disapproval of the lumbering beasts that had interloped on its hunting grounds. However, William quickly recognized that this was no screech owl; the sound was produced by a machine; it came from a large, two-story building located a short distance in front of the row of airships. The interior of the building was partially exposed to view through a large opening that seemed to have been designed to provide access for wagons and lorries to its interior. An orange glow, pale and unnatural, poured out of the opening and illuminated a small patch of surrounding scrubland; the rocks and stunted brush were painted the same unhealthy hue. It was from this opening that the mechanical whine gushed out into the otherwise silent night.

Though curiosity nudged at him, William controlled it for the moment and continued his examination of the camp. Several hundred yards south of the airships lay a huddled grouping of low buildings, single-story structures that appeared to be personnel barracks. Beyond them were many large and strangely shaped towers, visible in the dim light only as black silhouettes amongst several high derricks with crisscrossing braces. Two massive storage tanks, hundreds of feet high, stood to one side. Barely visible through the gap between these storage tanks lay another large industrial structure, illuminated by yellow floodlights. It was a jungle of pipes, tanks, and steel beams. Small clouds of steam percolated from many of the strange structures and buildings.

William pondered the mysterious scenery for a moment and wondered as to its purpose before his attention was caught by a brief flicker of light as a doorway opened in one of the barracks. Although some distance away, he could discern, just barely, the figure of a man silhouetted against the soft, golden glow of the opening. Once the figure had passed through the doorway, entering or exiting William could not tell, the door was shut and the light extinguished. William was alone again in this bizarre desert landscape.

After several long minutes of close observation, no further activity caught his attention and curiosity gained the upper hand. He left the mooring derrick behind and began working his way toward the opening in the shed behind the airships. When he had reached a point still fifty yards away, he halted and waited. William then noticed several thick hoses snaking their way along the ground. Each hose led to a different airship; one end rose in gentle curves, first up to a mooring derrick and then into an open hatch in the nose of an airship; the other end disappeared into the shed. He guessed that the building and its contents were in some way related to providing gas to the dirigibles. The hazardous nature of the hydrogen seemed the logical explanation for the scarcity of guards.

Just as he was divining the purpose of the machinery before him, his own purpose began to blossom. He had had long moments in the close confinement of his hiding place to relive Count Heinrich's assault on him. His anger had grown; it had evolved into something just short of lunatic rage. One strategy after another for destroying the mechanical monster had consumed him. He had become excited by one idea, only to realize it would be too risky, reckless to the point of foolishness.

It was at one moment during the voyage, when these emotions had gotten the better of him, that he had slid from his hiding place intent on causing mayhem. After only a few steps along the exposed corridor, and after only a few breaths of fresh air, he had been confronted by the fire that had been set off by the storm. He suddenly realized the magnitude of the risk his was taking, and once he had helped to extinguish a flaming Ernst Halterman, he quickly returned to his womb. Now, the situation before him represented a wholly unlooked-for opportunity. Anger still coursed through him, but it had cooled; it had turned frosty, like a river glazed over by a thin and deceiving layer of ice. His better judgment tried to regain its hold, and he recognized that finding a way back home to England should be his only priority. However, this was an opportunity he simply could not pass up.

It was a startling idea, and so frightening that he had to sit back down for a good, long think. The moon still hung high in the sky. Dawn was still distant. 'Bloody hell,' he mumbled to himself, 'one match in the right place and up it all goes. Maybe me, too, though—I'll have to be careful about that.' He reached into each of his pockets, 'Of course, no matches! Probably not a match within ten miles of this place.'

William remained captive to his thoughts; he was frustrated by his inability to make fire exactly when he needed it. He could find no solution. But he would not give up trying. He remained immobile and lay on his back for over two hours; he shivered in the cooling night air. Unable to solve the problem, his mind drifted into other paths: images of his recent voyage flitted through his head; he returned to Sir Maxim's camp in North Africa and then eventually to his personal disaster back home. These waking images merged into dreams and then into nightmares. Unobserved by anyone, William began to twitch, then grunt and groan as the nightmare took hold of him. Just as the twitching turned into thrashing, he was wakened from his nocturnal struggle by a new sound—the motor from an approaching truck. The noise came from the direction of the barracks, the vehicle's exhaust sputtering and gears grinding. Two feeble headlights illuminated the rutted pathway as the vehicle puttered by and bounced along the dirt road toward the entrance of the gas plant.

After coming to a halt fifty feet from the plant's open doorway, a stooped man, dressed in overalls, climbed out and grabbed a toolbox from the open bed behind. He walked the remaining distance and was greeted at the doorway by another mechanic. After exchanging a few brief words, both men disappeared into the orange glow.

William bolted from his hiding spot, and though he stumbled over the uneven ground and tripped on bushes, he eventually reached the dirt road. There he permitted himself the briefest glimpse into the mysterious plant. Not a complete stranger to machinery, he was still startled by the tangled mass of pipes and tall steel tanks and bizarre whirling gears. All was bathed in the orange glow of lamps suspended from the building's rafters. The whole scene was made more eerie by the fingers of white vapor that cascaded off frosty vessels and obscured the deeper recesses of the building.

'Double, double, toil and trouble, fire burn and caldron bubble,' William muttered to himself. He left the weird sight behind, scurried over to the truck, and hid in the shadows behind the headlights.

Before long, the shift mechanic who had been relieved loped from the plant and carried his weary frame toward the truck and toward William. The man had no sooner opened the truck door and placed his right foot onto the running board than William jumped up from behind and put his knife against the startled man's throat and then slipped his belt around the man's neck; William pulled ferociously in anticipation of a violent response. The startled man scratched frantically at his throat and immediately started to choke. William released his grip enough to open the man's windpipe, and as the mechanic gasped at his first desperate breath, William backed into the truck's cab; he pulled the terrified man in behind him.

'Where am I?' growled William into the mechanic's ear.

'*Ich versteh sie nicht?*' cried the panic-stricken man.

'English!' shouted William.

'*Ich spreche kein English! Ich bin Deutscher.*'

William hunted through his brain for any words that might somehow be assembled into a useful question. Language class seemed a distant and useless memory at the moment; German and Spanish and Latin seemed to get all jumbled up in the heat of the moment. Faced with this unexpected linguistic complication, much of the fury left William's voice. The mechanic relaxed slightly. '*Wo bin ich?*' William asked tentatively. '*Versteh?*'

'*Ja, Ich versteh. Ich weiss es nicht.*'

William pulled tighter on his belt.

'*Ich weiss es nicht! America! Carolina!*'

'*Carolina? Wo in Carolina?*'

The man rattled on in German without further enlightening William as to their exact location, so William changed tack. He asked the man about the gas plant and his job.

'What *tun du* here? What is your *beruf?*'

'*Ich bin ein ingineur. Ich arbeit mit machinen.*' Although the mechanic had responded quickly to the questions, the tone of his voice had changed. His initial shock had faded, and this new line of questioning seemed to raise other fears in him, unseen fears.

'What *macht diese* machines?' William continued.

The mechanic did not respond. It was as if he were unsure which would do him most harm, speaking or not. William pulled the belt tight again.

'*Wir machen luftstoff*,' gasped the mechanic.

'*Luftstoff*?' echoed William. 'What in the world is *luftstoff*?' He tried to remember if that was the German word for hydrogen. 'Probably. Sounds right.' Suddenly, William noticed that the other shift mechanic, the one who had recently arrived, was now wandering about the building's entrance; he was busy inspecting various instruments and pieces of machinery.

'Drive!' commanded William. '*Fahren!*'

'*Wo?*' asked the mechanic.

'*Die Strasse*! Now!' William indicated the desired direction by pointing his thumb toward the road behind them, in the direction leading away from the gas plant.

The mechanic complied. He put the vehicle into gear and executed a turn by coaxing the truck off and, then back, onto the dirt road. They had not gone very far before William reached down and flicked off the lights. This action momentarily diverted his attention and he inadvertently loosened his grip on the belt; together with a sudden jolt from a rut in the road, the frightened mechanic decided to make his move. The man jumped from the vehicle with a yelp. No sooner had he left the truck's cab than William thought he heard a sickening crack above the grumble of the motor. He stopped the truck and hopped out only to find that the mechanic had split his head on a sharp rock at the side of the road.

William dragged the mechanic's limp body off the road, out of sight of anyone who might be traveling along it and, after confirming that the poor fellow *had* truly killed himself with his frantic leap, did his best to hide the body in a shallow gully. William covered it haphazardly with brush tugged loose from the surrounding soil.

At this point William's own courage began to fade, and he had to suppress a growing panic. He had never killed a man, accidentally or not, and he found the event deeply disturbing. His hands quivered, but he stilled them by climbing back into the truck and fiercely grabbing the steering wheel. He forced himself to re-engage the gears and drove the truck off the road; he nudged it across the rough terrain in the direction of the dirigibles; he avoided the patch of ground illuminated by the gas plant. The last hundred feet proved the most difficult, and it was on four bare and battered rims that William eventually came to a stop, virtually on top of the black hose lying in the dirt beneath the first dirigible in line.

He switched off the truck's motor, then hopped out and hoisted the heavy rubber tube onto the truck's front bumper; there he dropped to his knees and set to work with his knife, boring a hole in the gas-filled artery. He dug at it frantically for an hour; he shaved away the thick rubber, layer after layer, eventually producing a small hole, half an inch in diameter. Pressurized gas burst out the moment his knife punctured the final layer and a low, fervent whistling followed the gas out into the night air.

This first task complete, William stood and removed the sheet metal hood covering the truck's engine. After a failed attempt at unscrewing one of its four spark plugs with his bare fingers, he managed to pull one free using a wrench from the mechanic's tool bag. He stretched the electric cable to its full length and jammed the spark plug into the hole he had just made in the rubber hose.

He glanced up at the massive airship hovering peacefully above him; it seemed to blot out the stars. 'Now for a bit of Guy Fawkes,' he mumbled to himself. He made a quick decision about the direction he would run, spat on his hands, and gave the engine crank a good turn.

Nothing!

Another crank.

Still nothing.

He pulled the spark plug from its makeshift socket, laid it on the radiator where he could keep it directly before his eyes, and gave the engine a third crank. A bright blue spark snapped in front of him—just as he expected. He tested the plug once more before he returned it to its ragged socket in the hose. Then more cranks. And more cranks. But, no crack—no pop—no flames. No explosion!

William stood up with a groan and rubbed the small of his back. Then, with a manic surge of energy, he jumped at the motor crank, and although there was again no hint of an explosion, the truck's motor managed to start. It coughed and jerked as it sputtered on three cylinders. The air filled with fumes from the gasoline vapors that spewed out of the open cylinder.

He gazed up in utter disbelief and smacked his fist into his palm, the pain this caused him going completely unnoticed. The airship sat quietly above, unperturbed, its seven sisters resting quietly at their tethers. The gas plant glowed patiently. The truck chattered. The smoldering but ineffective spark plug continued to spark. The odor of burnt rubber mixed with that of the vaporized gasoline. William let out a disgusted and desperate laugh and kicked the truck just as a new set of headlights appeared in the distance.

He quickly recovered from this bewildering failure, scanned the countryside around him to get his bearings, identified east, and then abruptly walked out into the empty Carolina landscape, his only companion the pathetic chattering of the wrecked motor truck fading in his wake.

Chapter 12

THE GOVERNOR

Heinrich sat on a wooden bench that ran along an inside wall of a windowless hut. The building was of wood frame construction, crude and unfinished; exposed beams supported a roof of corrugated tin. Heinrich sat hunched over with his elbows resting on his knees. He was uncomfortable; it was very late and he was tired. He gazed about from his social no-man's land—between the morose group of eight airship captains to his left and an equal sized grouping of young aeroplane pilots to his right; a third group, strangers, whispered amongst themselves in the corner of the room furthest from him. Heinrich did not wish to join in conversation with any of them: the captains outranked him, the adolescent exuberance of the pilots irritated him, and the strangers did not conduct themselves in an inviting manner. At times these rough looking men would break into coarse laughter from some private joke.

Anxiety hung in the air. It displayed itself in different ways depending on the age and personality of the given individual. Heinrich fidgeted, his sweating hands repeatedly clasping and unclasping, cracking the scabs that had formed over his burned skin, and his stomach grumbled in a noisy and unpredictable fashion. It did not help that the hut, roughly sixty feet by thirty, had grown stifling from the heat thrown off by a black cast iron stove; *potbellied* the locals had called it, stuffed to bursting with oil-soaked wood. Each group of men had now distanced itself as far as possible from the stinking furnace.

The conversation had not grown much above a murmur and Heinrich was startled when the door burst open and the martial figures of Admiral von Ramstein and Stanton strode in. Stanton's workman's clothes had been replaced by a fresh, olive-colored uniform that was decorated with bright ribbons and glittering metals lined up in rows on one side of his breast. Heinrich was pleasantly surprised to see Stanton's familiar face despite the changed aspect of his dress. He glanced over to Captain Timmer who seemed in no way surprised by the transformation.

'Attention!' shouted Stanton loudly. 'Officers! Your attention please!' Those occupants who were seated jumped to their feet, those who stood snapped their hands up in salute; all remained in their three curiously formal piles. Four Carolinian soldiers of junior rank carried in a large table and placed it in the center of the room; they thrust men out of their way. They placed a large zippered map case on the table, departed, and left the door open behind them. A cool draft of night air crept in to do battle with the potbellied stove. A tall man, a civilian, then strode calmly into the room. He stopped just inside the doorway and scanned the room's occupants; his pale gray eyes seemed to miss nothing. Few of the younger men could withstand this piercing gaze for long. Heinrich, once out from under the penetrating examination, inspected this unusual figure in return.

The civilian wore a gray flannel suit over a pressed, white shirt with a black bow tie, and although the lower part of his trousers had picked up a heavy layer of Carolina dirt, Heinrich's trained eye did not miss the suit's expensive cut; 'Paris!' he thought. In curious contrast with such fine garments, there rested an old, worn hat comfortably on top of the man's head.

'Welcome to Carolina!' the stranger greeted them in a loud but effortless voice. His southern drawl, deep and velvet, was much like Stanton's, but more refined—crisper, and if possible, more commanding. One of the olive-uniformed privates reached in and quickly pulled the door shut, sealing them all inside. The Carolinian approached the table and, by doing so, positioned himself in the center of the three groupings of soldiers. 'I am Mortimous Collier!' After a brief hesitation, during which a vague smile flickered across his otherwise expressionless face, he added, 'I am the governor of West Carolina! I most heartily welcome you to my country.'

He paused again, letting his words hang in the air before he continued. 'In order to save time, we will dispense with the normal pleasantries. I know who you are, and now you know who I am. In a few short days, West Carolina will secede from the Nation of Carolina. Each of you is to play a critical role in ensuring this occurs successfully and with complete surprise.' The governor waited a moment as if gauging their response. There was utter silence. Heinrich's heart sank. He was not surprised by the far-reaching consequence of the announcement—not at this point; but until this moment he had been able to pretend that some other future might be possible—not so, now. 'General Stanton will lead you in this endeavor and he is here tonight to brief you. General Stanton, please proceed.' Heinrich was startled by the reference to Stanton's rank—a general no less. Of course! He should have known! He kicked himself for being so informal with the man. He hoped he hadn't said anything he would regret; he thought back on his time with Stanton and tried to remember every word he had said to the man.

'You all, move in closer,' said Stanton, gesturing them toward the table as he opened the chart case. Unfolding it, he exposed a color-tinted map of North America. 'For those of you who don't already know it, we are right here—at Palo Duro,' indicating with his tobacco-stained forefinger a small, red dot placed in the middle of West Carolina.

'*Polo Doro*,' repeated one of the airship captains.

'That's right, *Palo Duro*,' instructed Stanton, emphasizing the '*a*' with an exaggerated, nasal twang.

One of the pilots attempted to mimic the twang, '*Paalo Duro.*'

Stanton gave up and continued.

'These are the geographical particulars that will be important to you in the near future: the Mississippi River runs from way up north in Pennsylvania, here . . . all the way down to New Orleans,' he traced the river's path with his index finger. 'The

Ohio River breaks off just south of St. Louis and runs back east, right between Pennsylvania and Virginia. The Missouri River breaks off right here . . . and runs northwest, between West Pennsylvania and West Virginia. And these cities are important too.' Stanton pointed to each in turn—St. Louis, Chickasaw Bluffs, Natchez, Baton Rouge, New Orleans, Natchitoches, Buffalo, Galvezton, Corpus Christi, Mobile, Pensacola. He waited a few minutes for the observers to catch up; he let them scan the points of interest. 'Don't worry about rememberin' all the names right now. You'll git your own charts later on.'

During this geographical preamble, with the attention of the room's occupants focused on the map before them, the governor began to closely inspect each man's face, one at a time, unobserved by all but Heinrich, who stole covert glances at him as the man's eyes progressed around the room. It was during this slow study that Heinrich began to suspect, and eventually became certain, that the governor's right eye was false. Heinrich's gaze darted back and forth between the man's gray eyes. Suddenly Heinrich was caught in the grip of the real eye—its power, its will, glowing with an intensity that more than made up for the lifeless one. Heinrich dropped his eyes; he felt naked under that cold stare. When he looked up again, the governor had moved on to another.

'It'll be real important for all of you,' continued Stanton, 'to have a rough understanding of our plan, so you can adapt if somethin' goes wrong; I've never seen an operation as big as this one that didn't have somethin' go wrong somewhere! This information is not intended for your crews. There'll be another briefing jis' for the officers of each ship later on tonight. You can ask whatever questions you like now, but I might choose to hold off answering some of 'em.'

His opening remarks complete, Stanton reached into his uniform pocket and produced one of his hand-rolled cigarettes. He popped it into his mouth and ignited it with a quick click of his lighter. This was the same action, performed in exactly the same manner, that had caused such an uproar aboard Dora Nine shortly after Stanton had first appeared. Heinrich glanced over at the captain, only to find him staring stonily at Stanton. A barely perceptible grin formed on Stanton's lips as he puffed out his first cloud of smoke—a grin that confused Heinrich at first. Noticing the various reactions—surprise, irritation, indignation—on the faces of the other airship captains, Heinrich suddenly grasped what was happening and gained a deeper understanding of Stanton's character. Heinrich realized that the general must have piloted many, if not all, of the other airships on their final leg to West Carolina, and had probably used his cigarette trick on each one of them, testing each captain's character with this ludicrous and hazardous challenge. Acrid smoke settled like a cloud layer onto the chart before them.

'Each airship has two jobs,' continued General Stanton. 'The first—before the fightin' starts—will be to land several units, five men each, at different spots on the eastern side of the Mississippi River, near important railroad junctions and railroad bridges. These will be destroyed to prevent the enemy from moving troops into the Mississippi River region. This will all be done at night.' Concerned expressions spread across the faces of the captains. 'You will each be given a pilot familiar with your assigned area—someone born and raised there. That is the purpose of these gentlemen over here.' Stanton nodded toward the strangers who had been standing quietly out of the way. 'You all can get to know each other after this briefing; I suggest you get to know each other well.

'The troops you will be carrying are all members of the West Carolina Ranger Corps and have been handpicked for this mission. It is your job to get them to the right place at the right time. They are Comanche warriors, some of our fiercest soldiers.' This last comment caught Heinrich's attention. He had seen photographs and heard stories about the various American Indian tribes, and this announcement caused his heavy heart to lighten just a fraction. He very much wanted to see an Indian, though perhaps not under these circumstances.

'As soon as you have dropped off these troops, the second part of your mission begins. This will involve regular patrols up and down the Mississippi River, the Missouri River, and around the gulf coast. You will patrol within specific boundaries, along specific routes, under specific timetables, and you will provide detailed observations as to the enemy's activities—troop movements, train movements, and progress on repairs to the damaged sections of rail.

'And finally, if anything goes wrong with the demolition of the bridges along the Mississippi, you will help in *any* way you can to complete their destruction, either by droppin' off more troops or otherwise.'

'Otherwise?' blurted Heinrich under his breath. Then, as if to emphasize his thoughts, one of the logs burning in the potbellied stove cracked sharply and spewed sparks from its ill-fitting hatch; the embers scattered across the plank flooring, where they glowed for a moment, then expired to specks of ash.

'Otherwise,' responded Stanton, 'you will just have to do whatever it takes to destroy that particular bridge. This is critical to our success. A single intact bridge could spoil the whole shootin' match!'

What are *we* to do?' asked Heinrich. He gestured toward his fellow fliers who had unknowingly concentrated at the top of the table where they were forced to read the strange American names upside down. The fliers had been steadily pushed that way by the airship captains who had crowded around the other side for a better view.

'It won't take long for the enemy to realize his movements are bein' watched,' responded Stanton, 'and he'll figure out real quick he won't be able to mount a river crossing because of it. At the moment, there aren't any aeroplanes in the Mississippi River area. The Carolina Officer Corps back East never put much faith in flying machines—certainly not like you fellows from Europe. What aeroplanes do exist are stationed in the

Tennessee River Valley and are just there for general observation. Eventually, though, the enemy will recognize his mistake and fix it. Some aircraft are gonna make their way here. You must destroy 'em. All of 'em! Without mercy!' This last comment was clearly directed at Heinrich, though none of the other fliers seemed to have understood the meaning behind it.

'Are these aircraft armed?' asked another flier.

'Not at the moment; as I said before, they've jus' been used for observation.'

'How many?' asked another.

'I'm not sure, maybe ten, maybe twenty. I don't expect they'll all be in good operatin' condition.'

'Officers,' interrupted Admiral von Ramstein, 'don't let these numbers lead you to undue optimism. One way or another, more will come—I have been warned against underestimating the passion of our enemy. Now I am warning *you*.'

'When does the operation begin?' asked Captain Timmer.

'Right away!' Stanton responded. 'We have reached a point where it's hard to keep things secret. We might have to advance our timetable so we can maintain the advantage of surprise.'

'What about the *luftstoff*?' asked Captain Rumpel, a heavyset captain with a very disheveled uniform. 'So far, only the airships of Kapitans Lerch and Gross have had their gas exchanged. What of the rest of us?'

Stanton and the admiral exchanged glances. They had clearly been expecting this question.

'Captain von Berkheim's ship is almost finished,' said the admiral, 'and if all goes well, it is possible that a few cells of Captain Timmer's ship will be changed as well. We will begin making the necessary modifications to his ship later tonight. The gas plant produces helium at a very slow rate. For the moment, the stockpile of gas is almost depleted.'

This unexpected and unpleasant news turned the grave gathering into something of a mob. The admiral glanced about with a frown, his face turning red as the captains exchanged excited words. The three captains whose ships were filled with helium—Captain Lerch, a brooding man, Captain Gross, an amiable fellow, and Captain von Berkheim, a strutting cock—seemed slightly less excited than their colleagues. This schism in the behavior of the eight captains seemed to attract the governor's attention and his curiosity. When the admiral began clenching his fists, Stanton quietly indicated with a gesture of his hand that all was well and that the admiral should wait patiently for the general excitement to exhaust itself.

'Officers!' shouted the admiral, patience not being a significant part of his character. 'This is the reality of our situation. We will execute our mission with whatever gas is available.'

'Men. Warriors.' interrupted the governor as he emerged from the shadows, his voice soft and distant. 'We must strive to overcome our fears in this great hazard. The joy of vanquishing an enemy, many of us have known. The exhilaration of defeating one's own fears is boundless. This is the victory that God expects from each of us. And we shall not disappoint Him. Give to Him this victory, and He shall deliver us.' The governor then paused for a moment; his face was sharply illuminated by the lamp hanging above the table. 'Deliver them, who through fear of death, were all their lifetime subject to bondage.' After delivering this brief sermon the governor took a step back into the shadows.

Somewhat taken aback by this speech, and as if desiring to sooth his own conscience on the subject, Stanton added, 'All future helium production will be bottled and transported to the operational bases after your departure. It is likely that by the time the enemy mounts a significant aerial response, each of you will have exchanged your gas for non-explosive helium.'

Captain Timmer, who seemed to recognize that further outrage over the situation was pointless, asked for details regarding their patrol zones.

'Yes, of course' said the admiral, clearly glad to be moving on to a less controversial subject. He handed out small cards to each of the airship captains and to each flier; on them was printed the patrol assignments for the eight airships:

D-1 Rumpel,	Gulf	Mobile-Tampa
D-2 Werner,	Mississippi R.	Chick.Bluffs-north
D-4 Gross,	Mississippi R.	N.Orleans-Natchez
D-5 Lerch,	Gulf	N.Orleans-Mobile
D-6 Thompsen,	Gulf	Corpus Christi-south
D-7 Mueller,	Gulf	N.Orleans-C. Christi
D-9 Timmer,	Mississippi R.	Chick.Bluffs-Natchez
D-8 Von Berkheim,Reserve		

As the admiral explained the assignments, Stanton assisted by tracing the various patrol routes on the chart with the end of his smoking cigarette; a pellet of ash dropped onto New Orleans and burned it up.

'And our bases?' asked Captain von Berkheim sourly.

'Werner, Gross, and Timmer at Natchitoches,' responded the admiral. 'Rumpel, Lerch, and von Berkheim at Opelousas. Thompson and Mueller at Buffalo.'

Suddenly, a sharp knock at the door interrupted what Stanton was about to say next. This was clearly unexpected as Stanton's face flushed with irritation. 'Enter!' he shouted.

A junior officer opened the door, just wide enough to insert his young face, 'A moment with you, sir!' Stanton hesitated briefly, then walked out of the room. Another blast of cool air rushed in to sooth the over-heated soldiers.

A moment later Stanton reappeared, visibly upset. He whispered into the governor's ear, and both turned and left without explanation. The officers, the fliers, and the rangers were left staring at one another with somewhat baffled expressions. Eventually all eyes returned to the chart, the Prussians hunting for the various cities with their strange American names without the assistance of Stanton's tobacco-stained finger.

Chapter 13

THE FORTRESS

Captain Jefferson Porter waited impatiently for his unpleasant, but quite necessary, visitor. He waited just outside the easternmost gate of the old fortress. This particular gate—identified by a large letter 'C' carved into its keystone—was a great arched perforation in the ten-foot-thick brick wall. Through this archway ran a set of railway tracks; the tracks continued through the approximate center of the installation, bisecting it, and exited on the opposite side through an identical archway identified by the letter 'A,' and from there the tracks were carried over the Mississippi River by an old trestle bridge of black steel. Running alongside the rails that led up to C-gate was a narrow dirt road that originally had been intended for horse-drawn traffic running between the fortress and the surrounding town of Natchez; the road now served motorcar traffic, which was becoming more prevalent across the country with each passing day. The overall plan of Fort Natchez was roughly that of a four-pointed crown with its base butting up against the river. C-gate faced east, positioned in the defile between two points of this crown; A-gate faced west at the center of the crown's base. The crown-shaped arrangement of the fortress permitted its defenders to bring enfilade fire on any force assaulting by land from the east.

It was on the dirt road leading to C-gate that Captain Porter stood. While he waited, he gazed across the hazy rooftops of the town and at the folk who approached along the road as it climbed from the streets of Natchez, up a gentle incline that cut across a wide swath of grass. This insulating belt of meadowland, half a mile wide, and named the Greenbelt, had been legislated during the construction of the fortress for defensive purposes; but over the years it had been adopted as a park by the town's residents. On any given Sunday the ladies and gentlemen of

Natchez could be seen, still in their church clothes, strolling along under the fort's massive brick walls. The Greenbelt surrounded these walls on all sides except those abutting the river and separated the old fort from the bustling streets of the growing town.

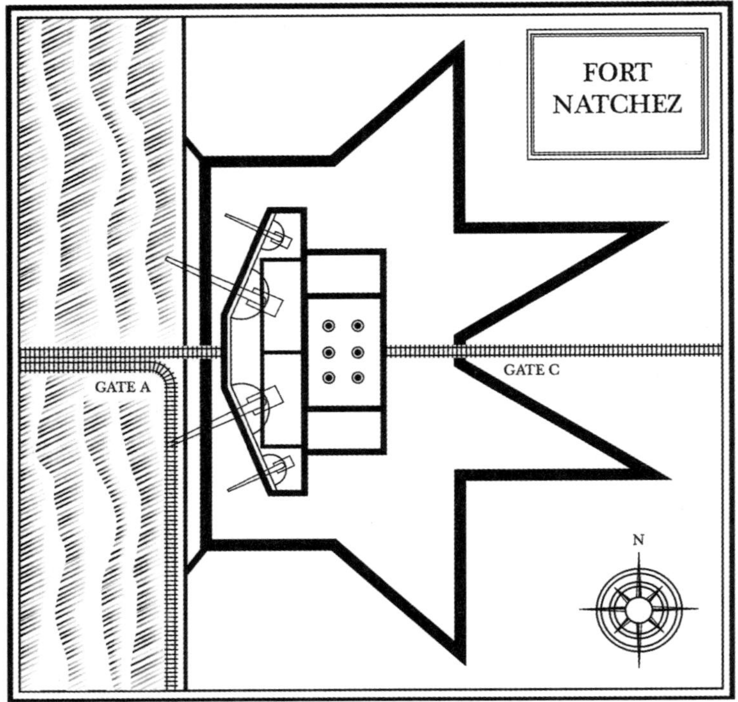

An occasional soldier, usually a private, hastened up the dirt road as he straggled in late from the boarding houses; each would straighten and quicken his step after recognizing the captain in his crisp, bright uniform. Most of the barracks within the fortress had grown leaky and damp from disrepair and required many of the captain's men to take up residence in town.

Captain Porter found the civilians far more interesting, such a wonderful variety of physique, gate, and demeanor.

Sprightly young nurses—not as numerous as his men would have liked—greeted him with a cheerful smile and a pleasant, 'good morning.' The masonry workers, much more numerous, were a glum lot that were sweating profusely by the time they reached the gate; from them there were no cordial greetings; but they were always respectful, cognizant of the captain's rank and the influence he held over their continued employment. If the workers had taken a moment to reflect on the giant mound of crumbling brick that seemed to be sliding down into the river at a rate faster than they could replace it, they would have realized there would be no end to their employment, good manners or not.

It was eight-thirty exactly and by now all the latecomers had gone past, leaving the road empty before him. Just as the captain was about to retire in frustration, he noticed the all-too-familiar form of his visitor as he began his climb, emerging from the shadows of River Street like a bear from its cave. Although he did not like to admit it to himself, Captain Porter received grim satisfaction from the burly man's struggle as he climbed his way up. The captain had explained over the phone that civilian motorcar traffic to the fortress had been temporarily suspended until critical repair work on its interior road surfaces had been completed.

Everything about the visitor exuded roundness: he wore a dusty, round hat atop his smooth round head, and gazed at the world through eyes like black marbles; he contributed his opinions through an oval, gasping mouth. All of this was mounted atop a flabby torso, stuffed tightly into a wrinkled black suit, and loosely wrapped in a stained and billowing raincoat. At one point, roughly half way up the incline the visitor tripped, and Captain Porter had the impression the man might roll helplessly back to the city. But he maintained his footing, regained his balance, and arrived at the gate huffing and puffing like an exhausting steam engine. His face was an unhealthy color.

'Good morning, Mr. Volper,' Captain Porter greeted him. 'Follow me and please watch your step. We have an unusual amount of construction underway.' Then, not waiting for his visitor to catch his breath, the captain turned and marched back into the fortress at a pace that would keep Mr. Volper quiet, but not so fast as to lose him.

Mr. Volper followed Captain Porter; Captain Porter followed the road; the road followed the rail bed through C-gate and into the interior of the fort, its dirt surface immediately giving way to hard, gray stone. They crossed a wide flagstone paddock that was open to the sky, though the overhanging masonry limited the view of the heavens to something like that available at the bottom of a stone-sided well. After traveling a hundred yards, the rail bed and the road disappeared into the dark mouth of a cool tunnel that burrowed under the central keep of the fort. The men followed the rails into the tunnel.

The high structure above them housed the hospital, the enlisted men's barracks, and the officers' quarters. The hospital contained only injured workmen; the enlisted barracks were empty, but the officers' quarters were in acceptable condition, having been the first area to be upgraded. At the very top of the citadel lay the great guns, basking in the sun like obdurate old men who had secured the best space upon their arrival and would relinquish it only after their death.

Directly beneath the monolithic structure of the keep, hidden in the bowels of Carolina rock and dirt, was the arsenal, the ultimate destination of the two men. It required several minutes to reach the approximate midpoint of the tunnel, their progress measured by the shrinking square of light behind them and the growing square of light before them. Damp and musty air filled their lungs as plops of dripping water echoed off the walls. The rhythmic breathing of the heavier-set man seemed amplified in the cave.

'Please watch your step, Mr. Volper. Our eyes are not yet adjusted to the darkness,' said the captain as he steered his visitor through the dim light and onto a wide, concrete ramp that had appeared on their right-hand side. The ramp permitted the unloading of munitions from railway cars onto horse-drawn lorries that could then be transported to the caverns below.

'You needn't be concerned about me,' retorted Mr. Volper. 'I've been here many times.'

'Indeed,' responded the captain, somewhat surprised at Mr. Volper's admission. His visits had always been for the same reason.

The two men progressed cautiously along a series of concrete ramps that spiraled downward; the ramps turned ninety degrees at a time, every fifty feet. The pathway down was lit by dim electric lights that were housed behind moldy globes, mounted on the walls at a height of seven feet; many were cracked or broken. The biggest concern was to avoid slipping on the slick concrete; it had grown moldy over the years. After rounding twenty of these ninety-degree turns, they reached a wide hallway, lined on both sides with massive doors of rusting iron, behind which was housed a large inventory of munitions.

The captain counted his way along these doors and stopped at number eleven. After firmly grabbing the handle and carefully planting his feet, he pulled with his entire weight. The door gave way, quietly sliding open with the assistance of a heavy counterweight suspended in the darkness above.

'This is the most recent delivery of cordite from the Volper Munitions Company,' said the captain, indicating several hundred small drums, four per pallet, grouped together in three layers at the center of the chamber. 'You can imagine our embarrassment during the president's visit last month. Not a single cannon successfully discharged the salute due our nation's leader. I, myself, received a serious reprimand from the colonel for this failure. The whole point of ordering this material was to avoid just such an embarrassment.'

Mr. Volper did not reply. Instead, he waddled into the room and approached a drum that had been pulled to one side.

It had been opened previously and he easily lifted its lid to examine the contents. He plunged his pudgy hand into the acrid powder and held a fistful up to his nose. After making a few grumbling noises that seemed to emanate more from his chest than his mouth, and after gazing about the room in a somewhat contemplative manner, he turned to the captain and said, 'Yes, well, this smells fine to me. I believe you must have let the stuff get wet down here in this damp, moldy crypt. I'm sure if you transfer it to a more suitable location and open the bins, they will dry on their own, and you will be left with superior quality propellant.'

The captain's jaw dropped, only for a second, before he regained his self-control and snapped it shut. 'You know very well that this has nothing to do with dampness.'

'I know nothing of the sort. Look over there!' commanded Mr. Volper, pointing to one of the back corners. 'Look at those stalagmites hanging from the ceiling! This place is as wet as the Mississippi. Let's take it to court and see what happens. We can bring the whole darn jury down here, for all I care.'

The captain, a military man, and purely a military man, stood baffled at this behavior; he had failed to anticipate this situation; he was infuriated by his inability to argue his way out of it—and disgusted by his need to do so.

Mr. Volper observed his adversary's perplexity and took advantage of it, assuming the balance of power would continue to slide his way. 'Now, seeing how you're in such a predicament, I'd be happy to send you an additional shipment, at a slightly reduced price—say ten percent.'

'Mr. Volper, you know very well that I am not authorized to contract for such purchases. That falls within the responsibility of the quarter master general.'

'Oh yes . . . of course, you are right,' said Volper. He then walked away from the drums and began to lead the officer up to the daylight.

Mr. Volper had not taken more than a couple of triumphant

steps, however, before the captain stopped him in his tracks. 'I do not have the authorization to order more cordite from you, or anyone else. But I *do* have control over the transport of our stockpile. And considering my grave responsibilities in the protection of this great nation, I would consider it a dereliction of my duty to leave one ounce of Volper powder in this arsenal. I will load every drum of bad powder, every drum with a red 'V' stamped on it, pretty much every drum in this facility, onto the next train and send it back to your facility in Charleston. Or perhaps I'll ship it directly to the quartermaster general'

Mr. Volper spun around, more deftly than the captain would have thought possible, with a quizzical look on his face, as if to say these threats were absurd. 'Well, I'm sure General Stack would be happy to receive it. He is a very sympathetic man. I've met him several times. In fact, we had dinner just last week.'

'Oh yes, I'm aware of your connections,' continued the captain. 'I may be court-martialed. I may lose my commission. But I will never be accused of failing to perform any task I have set my mind to. I may go down, but you will go down as well. I can see the headlines now—*Porter and Volper!—Accomplices in undermining one of our nation's most venerable fortresses, left defenseless by the incompetence of an obscure captain of artillery and the greed of the Volper Munitions Company.* I have no doubt your connections will defend you in the papers.'

Mr. Volper looked with wonder in his eyes at this maniac before him, unable to fathom the logic behind the threat, but knowing in his gut that the threat was not idle. Mr. Volper grumbled; he deflated. 'Fine. Arrange to have this particular lot, and only this one, mind you, shipped to my factory. I will arrange replacement within two weeks—at no charge to the government, of course.'

'Very good. A troop train is due through tonight. We will find space aboard it. That will have the faulty material back to your factory in a couple of days.'

'Yes, fine!'

'Thank you, Mr. Volper. As always, it has been a pleasure. Now, may I show you the way out.'

Captain Porter left his irritated visitor at C-gate, and after watching the man stomp off toward Natchez, he turned and reentered the fortress. Dealing with a long list of irksome businessmen had become the greater part of his responsibilities of late, and he did not like it. He was beginning to regret the transfer that had been pushed on him by his last commander. Still, having the most unpleasant activity of the day behind him, he was now able to inspect the progress of the numerous masonry crews with a bit more goodwill than usual.

Captain Porter had no doubt whatsoever that the cordite was of inferior quality. However, he could not refute the points made by the munitions dealer as to the dampness of the arsenal. His next task that morning was to examine the construction on the west-facing walls, the walls that mounted from the riverbank at a slight angle, climbing up a hundred feet to the parade level.

He reentered the rail tunnel and continued along its length until he emerged into the daylight of a small courtyard lying just inside A-gate. The guards on duty snapped to attention as he passed through the gate. On the small parapet that extended outward from the gate, perched high above the riverbank, stood a wooden guard shack. Beyond it, sat the railroad trestle, and beyond that, just visible through the kaleidoscopic shadows of the bridge's crisscrossing girders, lay West Carolina. The bridge actually supported two sets of rail track: the aforementioned set that penetrated the fortress, and another set that came up from the south along the riverbank and joined the other before crossing the river to West Carolina.

West Carolina was not Captain Porter's destination. From this elevated point he could gaze directly down onto the riverbank, and onto the heads of the dusty workmen below who were busy replacing brick and mortar in the wall just above the water line. He intentionally ignored those idle workmen leaning over the guardrail smoking. Porter entered the guard shack and shut the door behind him.

'Mornin', Captain,' greeted the duty sergeant. The sergeant and the other non-commissioned officers were responsible for inspecting and clearing those occasional trains destined for the fortress from the west. They maintained an encouragingly organized office, and the captain always enjoyed his interaction with these dependable men.

'Good morning, Sergeant. How are things?'

'Just fine, just fine. They've got fresh ham upstairs this morning. Don't suppose you've had any yet?'

'No, not yet. What time is the troop train due this evening?' asked the captain as he glanced down at a clipboard that held a schedule for all trains that were to cross the bridge, military or not.

'Twenty-three hundred, sir. It's usually late, though. You gonna welcome the men personally? It'll cut your stay short at Miss Clarice's.'

The captain looked up, startled by the comment.

'Oh Captain, Miss Clarice can't hold one of her balls without everyone knowing about it. I hear they're real nice.'

'They are indeed, Sergeant. Though I'm not much for such things. The train will be a good excuse to bow out early.'

'Come now, sir,' laughed the sergeant, 'that's not very sociable.' He then graciously changed the subject. 'You want me to do something after the men are dropped off?'

'Yes, I want to get rid of that last load of powder, if there's room.'

'The president's powder?' asked the sergeant with a serious expression. The captain nodded in response. 'They ought to hang that vulture from the flag pole,' the sergeant added in disgust. 'I'll check for space as soon as it arrives. If there ain't any room, we'll make some. Want me to send word?'

'No need, I'll be here in good time.'

'Right, sir!'

'Now, how are our artisans performing today?'

'Same as usual, sir—'bout a third doin' a good job, 'bout a third doin' a bad job, and the rest doin' nothing at all. I've been tellin' them it's this leaky wall that's caused the powder to go bad. But that don't seem to bother'm too much. They just keep ploddin' along at the same ole pace.'

'Well, I hope they don't waste this opportunity. It's been raining up north and the river's going to rise soon.'

'I'm sure that's just what they're countin' on,' laughed the sergeant.

'I'll see you later tonight,' replied the captain as he exited the shack. He stopped at the guardrail. This time it was devoid of workmen, and he peered down at the men below. They were all busily at work; none looked up. The captain remained at the rail for about ten minutes, before returning to the interior of the fortress.

It required the rest of the morning and most of the afternoon to finish his inspection of all the recently repaired masonry; he took careful notes as to which sections would likely need rework, and then followed up with the various crews spread about the labyrinthine facility. He spent his late afternoon in a tour of the mess; he walked while he ate his lunch, and then visited the infirmary before he finally buried himself in the paperwork that his commanding officer, Colonel Storey, had delegated to him in heaps.

He finished just in time to return to his quarters, exchange his comfortable but trim working uniform for his formal dress uniform, and climb to the top level of the fortress. There he watched the setting sun. From this airy perch, a wide swath of reinforced concrete, Captain Porter could stand in the open space between the two ten-inch rifled guns, one pointed upriver, the other downriver, and enjoy the distant view; the green countryside of West Carolina, the tree-lined fields of cotton were all bathed in a golden haze. The river was placid, reflecting the pink light from above.

Protruding from the embrasures situated directly beneath him were the dull barrels of the great fourteen-inch guns, also aimed up and downriver. And, behind him, housed in a deep pit down on the parade level, like a family of hedgehogs, rested eight batteries of six-inch mortars, each mounted on its own swiveling platform of ancient black iron, placed there to deal with any river craft that might somehow manage to get past the destructive power of their more elegant and far reaching brethren above.

He stood peacefully amidst these heavy instruments of war and contemplated his life. He had experienced little of the adventure he had craved as a youth, little of what he had hoped to find in the military, and it was dawning on him, having just turned thirty, that he would perhaps be destined for one of those quiet and obscure lives that was the usual lot of ordinary men. He was not unhappy—a little lonely, frequently bored. Mostly, he simply wondered why God had placed him where he was. He wondered whether he was a fool for desiring stormy seas over the tranquility of a quiet, country river.

Just as the distant orange disk touched the horizon, his thoughts were interrupted by the steps of Lieutenant Burrows; the lieutenant was the youngest of his subordinates and the most enthusiastic. He had grown up in Natchez under the shadows of the fortress walls and seemed to have already attained his heart's desire by joining the soldiers who manned those very walls. 'Evening, sir. Thought I might find you up here. Me and Clark were thinking about heading over to Miss Clarice's. Thought you might care to join us.'

'I would like nothing better, Lieutenant. Please, lead the way.'

Captain Porter took one last look at the disappearing sun before he turned to follow the young officer. Then, a distant sparkle in the evening sky caught his eye. He blinked and looked again, but it was gone. He thought no more about it and instead concentrated on reviewing the repertoire of banal conversation that would get him through the evening.

Chapter 14

AN UNCOMFORTABLE RECEPTION

Mrs. Clarice Withers lived in what was considered to be the most significant house in all of Natchez. It had been constructed with the proceeds from the liquidation of her husband's business assets, shortly after his accidental death; the man had slipped from the side of one of his many barges while moored at the city docks, had been knocked unconscious during the fall, and then had been pulled under by the unforgiving current, where he had quickly drowned. This accident left his wife a number of riverfront warehouses and a sizeable inventory of cotton and various textiles. Not having much inclination to encumber herself with the management of her husband's thriving concerns, she had quietly sold them to his only competitor, for a reasonable sum, and had taken up entertainment on a regal scale.

All of Mrs. Withers' friends agreed that a suitable stage for her social ambitions was an absolute necessity. Therefore, the construction of a grand home, even grander than the home her husband had been willing to provide during his life, became her all-consuming passion immediately after his death. Through the assistance of her husband's friends, she hired an architect from New Orleans who designed for her a most unusual home, which she built on the outskirts of town.

Knowing Mrs. Withers' proclivities for entertaining both her American brethren and her British cousins, and having just returned from a six-month architectural tour of the palaces and country estates of Europe, this architect, a Mr. Jonathan Stiles, prepared a design for his new commission by assembling a wide variety of architectural styles that had been jostling around inside his brain. One was first introduced to an odd combination of colonial revival and French renaissance revival stonework on the exterior. Proceeding inside, one was then met by two proud Ionic columns, crowned with Scamozzi capitals. From there, one could choose a room to fit one's taste: the ladies' parlor to the left in French renaissance, the gentlemen's parlor to the right in English arts and crafts. Finally, this pleasant jumble of architectural grandness was plopped down on a small mound of earth just south of Magnolia Street, two miles from the city center. It was given the name Hilltop.

Mrs. Withers was herself an assembly of various human architectural elements; she had the liquid brown eyes of a Spanish lady, the rather prominent nose of a Roman patrician, the delicate complexion of an English country maid, and the ramrod straight posture of a *West* Carolinian belle. While all of these features might, individually, be recognized as attractive examples of their type, when assembled into the complete personage of Mrs. Withers they could not really be accused of being beautiful. The real beauty that God had bestowed on her was invisible to the eye. It flowed from her mouth like liquid velvet.

Mrs. Withers could breathe life into any conversation—certainly between two guests of the most disparate background, and almost always into a larger group for which she had had sufficient time to prepare. Mrs. Withers would research her guests as if they were laboratory subjects, down to the smallest detail: their family history, their personal history, their victories, their failures, even their deepest desires and fears, when she could get hold of them. Of great assistance to her in the gathering of this information was her new telephone; four of her dearest friends had followed her lead and together they could create a virtual beehive of social chatter. She would then weave all of this knowledge on the loom of her powerful human insight into a tapestry of conversation of such wondrous color and delightful texture that her reputation as a hostess spread far beyond the provincial confines of the city of Natchez.

From the perspective of Captain Porter, it was this subtle

mastery of those awkward points in conversation, the feeling that she was always nearby, just behind his shoulder, ready to assist in an emergency, that had helped him overcome his natural reservation of such social engagements and enticed him to accept her invitations. Tonight, with his eager subordinates pressing him from the rear, as if he were a reluctant conscript who needed prodding into battle at the point of a bayonet, he was welcomed at the door by Mrs. Withers. He crossed the threshold of Hilltop with little more trepidation than a quickening of his heart.

The golden light, steamy warmth, and vibrating conversation seemed but a grander version of the clattering trolley, with its flickering lights, stifling atmosphere, and crowded seats that had conveyed the three soldiers to the house.

'Oh, wonderful!' cried Mrs. Withers. 'Here is our dependable Captain Porter and, of course, Lieutenants Burrows and Clark. Thank you so much for coming! Please, gentlemen, come right in. You are just in time to save us from another of the colonel's horrible stories.'

Although Captain Porter fully expected his commander to be present, he had hoped that he would not be immediately thrust into his company. While in Mrs. Withers' tow, and still several paces from the reception room where most of the guests had congregated, he could hear the shrill braying of the colonel's laughter. Upon entering the room, it was obvious that his commander had indeed just shared a rather unacceptable anecdote. Those officers under the colonel's command let out forced chuckles through strained smiles. The British officers glanced at each other with raised eyebrows. The women looked down at their shoes; one or two openly scowled.

Mrs. Withers had been keenly aware of the consequences that might result from Colonel Storey's presence. She knew she would be letting the proverbial bull loose in the china shop. But the man had his uses. Applied in small doses, against the reserve of some of her more taciturn guests, like a Washington flung at Yorktown, she could save a reception that teetered on the brink of dullness. But after this, the colonel's mission accomplished and the enemy reduced, he would be whisked off to the library where other military guests were induced to perform a sort of guard duty.

If ever the colonel managed to escape from his pen, she would gently but firmly return him there and then bestow her charming displeasure on his guards; she would hold an imaginary court martial where the accused was invariably convicted on charges of dereliction of duty. After receiving a thorough dressing down by her expressive eyes, the guilty officers would then, in true military fashion, be immediately replaced by a more competent jailor. Captain Porter was convinced that Mrs. Withers' reference to him as being 'dependable' had more to do with his success as jailor than to his competence as a soldier.

But tonight, for some reason, Mrs. Withers had boldly left the bull in the open for an unusually long time. Captain Porter resolved to steer the conversation into polite channels whenever the colonel's tongue began to wag too freely, and thus hoped to avoid compulsory duty in the library.

The reception room held fifty guests: the aforementioned military officers, several of their subordinates, prominent town merchants, civil servants of a certain grade, and many of their wives. At the room's center hung a magnificent chandelier that had been purchased at great expense and shipped at great expense from England. As they conversed, the guests circulated around this chandelier in revolving clusters, like moons orbiting planets that together orbited the bright, hot sun. White-jacketed servants streaked through the room like comets, leaving a trail of refreshments in their wake. Mrs. Withers, the governing force that held this universe together, flitted about the room; she exerted her power here and there and wherever it was needed to maintain cosmic order and social tranquility.

'Ah, Captain Porter, how goes the repairs?' asked Mr. Andrew Wright as the captain passed the outer rim of guests, somewhere near the reaches of Neptune or Pluto. Mr. Wright was the editor of the *Natchez Spectacle*, a liberal, some said radical, local newspaper and was considered by Mrs. Withers to be one of her more controversial guests—hence one who was forced into a somewhat peripheral orbit until his character had been positively validated.

'Slow progress, but steady,' responded the captain. He stopped out of politeness, uncomfortable at having slipped from the wake of his hostess. 'It's hard to undo decades of neglect in just a few months.'

'But she's not likely to crumble to dust before our very eyes is she?'

'No, not hardly. Although I'm afraid the clatter of workmen's hammers is likely to continue for several more months.'

'Well, she is a lovely old thing. Glad to hear she's going to survive. I don't suppose I could send one of the boys around for photographs? I'm sure you've been receiving complaints about the noise. It might help if we were to print a story about resuscitating the old lady—get the town behind the project, so to speak.'

'Yes, of course, a very nice idea. I'll certainly run it by the colonel.'

'I don't want to cause you any trouble though—wouldn't want it to be considered a security risk.'

The captain laughed, but the comment hit home. His request to have the fortress gates closed at all times had been rejected by the colonel, who had acquiesced to complaints of poor access by the contractors. Captain Porter felt the fortress had become more like a museum than a true military installation. Every month, for the past several, he had had to eject local boys from the arsenal. Remarkably, some had been discovered at a game of hide-and-seek at the bottom level of the arsenal; they had been running about amongst the drums of cordite. It had been a complete embarrassment, just short of dereliction of duty. He had resigned himself to restoring the fortress's martial stature in small steps that were less likely to attract the interference of his commander.

Captain Porter could not avoid the imploring glances of Mrs. Withers, waiting impatiently for him to disentangle himself from the usurping editor. The editor, correctly interpreting Mrs. Withers' intentions, patted the captain on his arm and said in a knowing manner, 'I'm sure we'll have a chance to discuss it later, perhaps in the *library*.' Released from the editor's grip, the captain passed through the intermediate planets and was pulled toward the sun.

'So, Captain Porter,' chirped Mrs. Oswald, the petite and mercurial wife of Mr. Oswald, of Oswald Textiles. It was Mr. Oswald who had purchased Mr. Withers' business interests. 'We had just been discussing, prior to Colonel Storey's digression, the state of West Carolina—or rather the state of mind of the West Carolinians. I would like to hear your opinion on the speech the governor made last week during his visit to Charleston. I assume you are aware of it?'

'I'm sorry, ma'am, I am not,' responded the captain. 'I haven't had the opportunity to look at the papers recently.' His heart sunk at the topic being offered him, knowing that it was one perfectly suited to antagonize his commander.

Mrs. Withers blanched, clearly of like mind. She pulled a fresh drink from a passing tray and exchanged it for the colonel's nearly empty glass. Then, as a shot across everyone's bow, she added, 'Yes, I believe I did read about the speech just this morning in the *library*.' The colonel, recognizing the salvo for what it was, shut his mouth and grabbed an hors d'oeuvre from another passing tray.

'I believe it to be nothing but bluster,' continued the captain. 'Oh, I know the papers talk it up, and many politicians of the nervous sort back in Charleston are making much of it. But it would mean the ruin of West Carolina if she left us. It's just the sort of thing that Virginia has been waiting for. Those wolves would gobble her up like one of those delightful looking pastries the colonel is enjoying so much.' The colonel, with his mouth packed full of Stilton layered between thin biscuits of flaky dough, acknowledged the truth of this statement by widening further his naturally popped eyes.

'Yes, and then they'll come looking at us again for the main course,' grumbled Mr. Oswald. With his wife seated before him, he stood behind the sofa; his belly rested comfortably on the sofa's back, just to the right of his wife's head.

'But what about those unionists up North,' speculated Mrs. Oswald. 'They keep gaining seats in their congress, and some say it's only a matter of time before one of them becomes president, and then the whole thing starts over again.'

'Oh come now, my dear Mrs. Oswald,' chided Colonel Storey, after swallowing loudly. 'Those fellows are just a pack of rambunctious radicals. They may gain or lose a few seats, but nobody takes them seriously. You just watch, if any one of them runs in the next election, say even that fellow Morgan, he won't get enough votes to wipe his bottom with. And what's more—'

'I have to agree with the colonel,' interrupted Captain Porter. 'While I do believe the radicals to be just a bit more organized than the colonel gives them credit, I do not think they have enough power to affect the outcome of the election. But, Mrs. Oswald, they do bear watching. They do bear watching!' Mrs. Oswald nodded vigorously at the captain's opinions.

'I think it's unlikely,' said Colonel Caruthers, as he joined the group, his wife at his side, 'no matter what course taken by West Carolina, that the Pennsylvania military would make a move now.' Colonel Caruthers was the ranking British officer in the area and had been given the rather vague assignment of liaison to that portion of the Carolinian army stationed along the Mississippi River.

'Personally, I think this governor of yours is a half-mad dog,' blurted Mrs. Caruthers. 'I heard that he actually assaulted a congressman, or representative, or whatever, from one of the eastern counties during the last session of government; or maybe it was one of the northern counties.'

'You mean physically attacked him?' asked Mrs. Oswald.

'I do indeed! The governor physically beat him; the man ended up in hospital.'

'Whatever did he do that for?' asked Miss Perkins, a spinster who lived in the house next to Hilltop. She attended Mrs. Withers' receptions, whether invited or not. By arriving early, she managed to secure for herself a comfortable seat near the sun and refused to relinquish it.

'Oh, for making some comment about being stuck between a rock and a hard place—meaning the governor was one or the other of them.' At this the guests broke out into laughter.

'Honestly though, Captain,' asked Mrs. Withers, continuing against her better judgment, her emotions as powerful as any other proud Carolinian, 'shouldn't the government take some steps to stop this ruckus. Mr. Oswald says he is handled roughly every time he crosses the river—in just the next county, mind you, where he is a major purchaser of their crops. I wonder if this talk might not end in violence.'

'Please understand, Mrs. Withers,' explained the captain, 'the governor could not start anything violent without significant preparation. He knows we would not let him walk away without a fight. If he were to have any chance of success, he would have to assemble an army and transport it right up to the river. He could never do that without us knowing about it—and without us *doing* something about it. But keep in mind, the government doesn't want to exacerbate the situation either by redeploying troops from the north where they are obviously much needed. Such a move would simply give credence to all of this hysteria.'

'I'm sure you're right, Captain, but it just seems to me that someone ought to nip this in the bud.'

'I think you ought to send a few grenadiers over to Buffalo,' said Colonel Caruthers pompously, 'and snatch this fellow from his bed. Let him rest a while in the Abbey. He'll become sensible.'

'Oh, I'm sure that would set the match to the keg,' responded the captain politely, slightly irritated.

'Perhaps I'm exaggerating a little, but if each of Her Majesty's colonies were to pick up and leave the empire every time there was a decision made in London that didn't suit—well, there would be chaos the world over. Surely the governor could be recalled to Charleston and kept quietly out of the way for a few months. That would certainly cool his inflammatory rhetoric.'

'That always seems to be the way with you *chaps*!' snarled Colonel Storey, whose face, unnoticed by all, had by degrees grown to a bright red; it was a shade of red that Mrs. Withers, who, having just finished decorating her boudoir in various shades of the color and therefore having a finely tuned sense of it, could not help but notice; it clashed with Colonel Caruthers's coat. The bull had indeed seen red and all hope of controlling him went by the board. 'You *chaps* strut around here, throwing out advice like you own the place. You confound our elections; you belittle our troops; you insult our women! And after all that, what have you done for us—not one thing! Not one Virginian shot, not one acre of the Palisade retaken! Perfectly worthless if you ask me. I'd put the whole lot of you on boats and ship you back to England if I didn't think we'd have to build the boats ourselves and provision them with an entire year's harvest.'

'It's all well and good to say you don't need us,' retorted the British officer. 'But I don't imagine the Virginians would sit behind their river for very long if they thought the only thing holding them back were a few pretty guns, stuffed with wet powder and rusting shells.'

The captain's ire was now rising as well, but he checked himself after observing the colonel. His commander shuddered with rage. Even Mrs. Withers seemed at a loss as to how to regain control. In Colonel Storey's current state it would be all but impossible to drive him back to the library. However, to leave him out in public would result in the kind of catastrophe that would be the talk of Natchez before noon the next day.

Colonel Storey opened his mouth, took in a deep breath, and was preparing to eject a molten stream of emotion into his counterpart's face when suddenly, a deep, thunderous thud shook the house at its foundation. The chandelier above them tinkled as it wobbled at the end of its chain. A glass shattered on the hearth; it had dropped from the hand of a startled guest. All conversation stopped. Silence hung in the air as each guest struggled to identify the source of the tremor. Then, again, all too clearly, came the unmistakable roar of a military detonation. It rolled through the streets from the direction of Fort Natchez.

A look of the most profound dejection spread across Mrs. Withers' face. Her reception had just become an irrecoverable failure. Colonel Storey blanched, and he no longer clashed with Colonel Caruthers' coat; instead, he blended harmoniously with the white walls of the reception room. Colonel Caruthers tightened into a catlike stance that would have given any onlooker with attention to spare insight into his alert, battlefield persona.

Captain Porter was nowhere to be seen. He had burst out the front door of Hilltop before the echo of the first detonation had faded.

Chapter 15

THE ASSAULT

Lieutenants Clark and Burrows fell behind, their chests heaving and their lungs burning; they were chagrined that their much older captain had so completely outpaced them. All three men followed the trolley tracks that lay along the center of Magnolia Avenue; they were desperately frustrated by the failure of the electricity plant that left lifeless trolleys scattered along the line; the darkened vehicles were helpless to expedite the soldiers' sprint back to the fortress. The lack of street lighting made the continuing detonations that much more startling and brilliant. Each intermittent flash illuminated the western faces of the buildings surrounding them; all color was leached into a stark and deathly white. By contrast the eastern faces were simultaneously shrouded in such deep shades of black that it chilled the men's hearts.

By the time Captain Porter reached the Greenbelt he had counted six separate detonations. The last two were separated by the scattered volleys of rifle fire that indicated the violence within was not an accidental discharge of explosives, but the result of conflict between two armed forces. It was not much later that he began to hear the faint shouts and screams of confused and sporadic fighting.

Just as his strength began to give way after the three-mile dash from Hilltop, the captain reached the summit of the long roadway leading to C-gate and there received another unexpected shock. The great steel doors, constructed from two-inch-thick steel plates, mated by an intricate pattern of heavy bulbous rivets, were shut and barred his way. He stretched his arms in front of him and leaned against the unyielding barrier to catch his breath; his fingers wrapped around two heavy rivet heads and scratched off the peeling black paint and rough flakes of rust. Then a seventh detonation that caused the steel doors to vibrate on their hinges brought the soldier back to his duty. He turned left and sped down the narrow brick path that followed the southern perimeter of the fortress, running from crown-point to the crown-point along a circular route until it reached the bluff overlooking the river.

He progressed without interruption as far as the first of these two points. But after passing this massive architectural protrusion and as he ran out into the exposed open space between it and the next, bullets began pattering around him; intruding riflemen were positioned on the ramparts above; they had been waiting there for just such an incursion.

Unscathed as he rounded the second and southernmost point, he met with a shower of bullets from a newly exposed rampart. In the distance ahead, at the southwest corner of the fortress, at the intersection of the two walls that formed the side and the base of the crown, he could see the backs of several soldiers, his men, also trapped outside the fort and desperately attempting to find a way inside. They were engaged in a furious firefight with an enemy positioned somewhere around the corner and not yet visible to him. Recognizing that the perimeter was effectively blocked on the south side, and pressed by the need to gain access to the interior of the fort where the critical battle was being decided, the captain turned and retraced his steps across the dangerous space. He was able to proceed safely to the approximate midpoint of the perimeter walk, and was about to jump down into the bed of a stream that trickled through a small culvert beneath, when he was joined by Lieutenants Burrows and Clark.

'What's going on, Captain?' they cried.

'I don't know,' gasped their commander, 'it must be the Westerners.'

'My Lord,' said Burrows. 'They're lunatics!'

Any further speculation was interrupted by a well-placed shot that ricocheted off a brick at their feet; shards of baked clay flew up into their faces.

'Follow me! Down here!' barked Porter.

He led them down into the streambed, then through the culvert and up the shallow gully leading toward the fortress, deeper into the triangular open space between the southern and the southeastern points. The snipers had lost sight of them in the darkness and continued to fire at the spot on the path from which they had dropped. The three men could still hear the patter of brick fragments coming from the impact of the bullets. By the time they reached the apex of the triangular gap, they were soaked and smattered with mud.

'Mind tellin' us what you're up to, Captain?' asked Clark.

'Look, right there!' said the officer, indicating a small, irregular wedge of blackness in the wall ahead.

'What, that crack?' asked Burrows, straining his eyes to decipher his captain's intention.

'Yes, that's how the local urchins have been getting in. I didn't tell anyone about it . . . wanted to repair it quietly, no fuss. Otherwise, before you know it, that editor's boys would have been crawling in with their cameras.'

It was indeed a small crack in the massive brick wall that loomed above them; the crack was perhaps eighteen inches wide and five feet in height—not much impedance to a ten-year-old boy, but an uncomfortable challenge to two twenty-year-old lieutenants and a thirty-year-old captain. What's more, it was not simply a matter of squeezing through a single layer of bricks, as if it were the fractured wall of a house where one could expect to emerge immediately into the open space on its other side. This wall was at least fifteen feet thick, and so the men would be entering a narrow and claustrophobic fissure; they could not be certain the hole wouldn't shrink as they went along or, given the rending explosions, collapse altogether. God forbid they should get stuck inside during the next explosion.

No sooner had this thought flitted through each man's mind than another blast ripped through the night air. 'What in the world are they doing?' asked Burrows, reaching for his ears after the painfully loud detonation.

'Dismounting the big guns,' responded the captain. 'They'll be starting on the mortars soon.'

This last concussion had been so close, and perhaps amplified in some strange way by the converging walls to each side, that at first they failed to notice an odd sound permeating the air around them. It was indeed difficult to separate it from the ringing in their stunned ears. Captain Porter was the first to properly evaluate it, or at least accurately determine its direction, and his eyes darted up, searching the sky above them, just in time to see the dark but clearly discernible silhouette of a dirigible gliding over them. The buzzing noise of its motors reached their highest pitch when it was directly overhead, just before it disappeared beyond the wall above. Each of the lieutenants jumped in childlike fright as the shadow cast by the dirigible whisked past them and scurried up the wall like a Halloween ghoul.

'Let's go!' shouted the captain, and with no further debate, he squirmed his way into the crack; his men quickly disappeared from view after him.

*

It was difficult for Heinrich, or for anyone else in the control cabin, to clearly discern what was happening below. The low-altitude cruise over the fortress seemed a foolish risk, but he kept his mouth shut and tightened his clammy grip on the aluminum girder above him. Sweat dripped from his face even though he was surrounded by a cool blast of night air. His teeth chattered.

General Stanton had assumed a maniacal persona since the start of their mission; at this particular moment he hung out the open doorway on the cabin's starboard side, into the rushing night air. The door had been removed hours ago, before they had crossed the river. The cold air and the additional noise made an already stressful mission that much more fatiguing.

Stanton pulled himself back inside, just long enough to shout a course correction directly to the rudder-man. This new course would bring the ship over the exact center of the fortress below. Stanton leaned out again, supporting himself by one hand on a thin bulkhead, the toe of his left boot wedged under the supporting frame of the elevator wheel. Again he pulled himself in and shouted, 'Cut the motors—let the ship's momentum carry her along.'

A few long seconds later the engine noise faded and Stanton, impatient at even this brief delay in the execution of his commands, threw himself back out into the slipstream like a crazed demon. His windblown hair was permanently twisted into bizarre tongues that gave him the appearance of the devil himself. Heinrich had never felt quite so unnecessary as he did at this moment. Captain Timmer edged his head and shoulders out into the chilly blast and remained perched just a few inches behind Stanton. Heinrich gazed out the opening as best he could without releasing the safety of his grip.

The rising moon illuminated the scene below to a greater degree than Heinrich could have expected, and he now wished that they had had the benefit of this light earlier in the evening when they had been bumbling around the East Carolina countryside while in search of the planned drop sites. It had taken more than an hour to locate one particular spot that lay in the middle of nondescript farmland, and it was at this point that everyone in the control cabin became acutely aware of just how domineering and unforgiving of failure Stanton could be, with himself as much as with others. As the propeller noise faded, Heinrich could overhear the possessed man cursing under his breath, unable to identify the necessary structures below.

Suddenly, a blinding flash burst beneath them, so startling that the captain seemed to momentarily loose his footing. Indeed, if he had been emulating Stanton's entirely exposed position, he would probably at this moment have been hurtling downward through the open space below them. As fantastic as events had been up to this point, Heinrich was filled with a renewed sense of dread by the demonic image of Stanton's illuminated form dangling outside the cabin. Heinrich mumbled the word, 'Lucifer,' to himself as he switched hands on the support above to let the blood descend back into his tingling arm. The man would certainly get them all killed this very night.

Stanton yanked himself back into the cabin; a grin spread across his face, 'I think they got most of the big guns. I can't tell for sure, but I think there's just one still in place. Circle around again and let loose some flares. Quick!'

The captain gave the necessary orders to reengage the motors and speed the airship westward, out over the river and the low-lying fields, where Dora Nine could safely turn in preparation for another pass over the fortress. Visible to all under the moonlight reflecting off the river were the four segments of the bridge, still intact, undisturbed, pristine. That this was as it should be, according to the schedule of the plan laid out, did not reduce Heinrich's discomfort at seeing this absolutely essential target as yet completely undisturbed.

The second pass over the fortress proved to be more eventful than the first. The engines were silenced again, and this had indeed prevented the troops below from anticipating the ship's arrival, but none could now miss the heavenly body gracing the air above them. Stanton had not yet released a flare from its launching tube before a rain of bullets—a most unusual rain as it fell up from the earth rather than down from the heavens—penetrated the control cabin; bullets pierced Ober Dürr's right hand, Stanton's right shoulder, and grazed the captain's left cheek. Sparks and shattered glass flew about the cabin. Heinrich gazed down at his own body in astonishment; it was completely intact. But his hands began to shake uncontrollably.

Stanton, despite his wounds, managed to let go his flares, which had the simultaneous benefit of illuminating the ground beneath them and partially blinding the riflemen below.

There was an immediate reduction in the swarm of deadly little projectiles.

Stanton confirmed that, indeed, the two long-range guns were clearly missing from their disfigured embrasures and were likely buried in the ooze at the river bottom; one of the medium-range guns was missing as well; it dangled precariously over the fortress wall. Men could be seen swarming over it, preparing another explosive charge to dislodge it. Less discernible, down in the dark shadows created by the bright light, was the progress in the mortar pits. After a few seconds of continuous gaze, Heinrich noticed the pinprick sparkles of muzzle flashes; the fight for control of the pits was clearly undecided. What Heinrich, as well as every other officer in the cabin, really yearned to know was the progress in emptying the arsenal's magazine and the preparations for the demolition of the bridge. The ship would be stuck in this uncomfortably exposed position until that task was complete.

Just as the flares faded and the ship carried past the eastern edge of the fort, out over the city of Natchez, the sail maker burst into the control cabin. 'Kapitan Timmer, we have damage everywhere. There are too many leaks in the gasbags, and we've lost most of the ballast water. I can't fix it all!' The sail maker was about to add his opinion on the wisdom of another pass, but held his tongue after getting a good look at the blood-smeared men surrounding him, and at the demonic form of Stanton twisting to get a glimpse at the back of his shoulder.

The captain questioned Stanton with his eyes. After a moment's thought, Stanton nodded in agreement.

'Turn to three-six-zero. Climb to three thousand feet if possible, commanded the captain in a controlled tone. The helmsmen responded with the appropriate actions. The wounded men were then ordered to the infirmary.

'We must give them some more time,' said Stanton. 'They

are doing well. Another thirty minutes, then we'll take another look.'

*

Captain Porter and his lieutenants emerged from the fissure with their uniforms snagged, their hands cut, and their faces bruised. They emerged well after the airship's first pass, but in plenty of time to observe the second. From their perspective, the small arms fire seemed to have little or no impact; anything short of complete immolation of the strange beast was difficult to determine from such a distance.

'What in the world is that thing?' cried Burrows in astonishment.

'An airship,' said the captain. 'A dirigible.'

'I've heard of them,' gasped the lieutenant in undisguised wonder. 'How did the Westerners ever manage to build an airship?'

'I'll bet you one of my bars they didn't build it. I'll bet you its Prussian,' grunted Clark.

'What? Fly that thing all the way from Europe!' said Burrows, entranced, waiting with upturned eyes for another view of the magical ship. 'My Goodness!'

'Come on, you fools,' growled the captain. The men raced toward the firefight in the mortar pit that lay just ahead. Around its eastern brim they encountered a small group of their men. Panicked screams and shouts of hand-to-hand fighting came up from below.

'Sergeant!' shouted the captain, placing his outstretched hand against the back of the burly man leading the riflemen.

'Oh, Captain, I'm sure glad you're here.'

'Tell me as much as you can, quickly.'

'The eleven o'clock arrived early. I should have guessed something was wrong then. The last car was barely inside the gate before they swarmed out like a plague of locusts, sir. Those rotten Westerners! They've knocked three of the old men off their mounts, numbers one, two and four, and number three ain't long for this world. They'll be finishin' him off real soon. There's just too many of 'em. Our boys are about give out down there. And did you see that great big monster up there?'

'Don't worry about it right now. What about the arsenal?'

'I don't know, sir, but I can pretty well guess. We can't get anywhere near it.' The captain nodded as he thought through his options. 'You know, sir, they ain't gonna leave without taking down the bridge.'

'I know,' the captain responded still deep in thought.

*

The crew of Dora Nine used the limited time Stanton had given them to make as many critical repairs as they could. The sail maker ignored the damaged surfaces of the hull and fins and focused his attention on the countless perforations in the gasbags, all whistling together in weird, discordant pitches, like a poorly tuned organ. Ober Dürr sped along the snaking paths of the control cables; he felt for frayed spots; he looked for damaged or weakened pulleys; he hunted for anything that could possibly give out at precisely the wrong moment. He dripped blood everywhere he went.

Heinrich, unable to remain in one spot, distracted himself by inspecting his aircraft. Its wings had been riddled with holes, but as far as he could tell, the vital mechanical components, the engine, the cockpit, were all still in one piece. He wouldn't really know for sure until he had started the engine and had been released into space, should things eventually come to that. It had required all of his self-control to leave the side of his aircraft, a tempting and ready means of escape. In the end, it was the shouts of Peter Dürr that finally persuaded him to return to the control cabin.

The doctor worked as quickly as the others; he stitched

up torn skin in a manner disturbingly similar to that of the sail maker at his gasbags, only with a slightly smaller needle. Neither was too concerned with the quality of his work, or with the ugly scars that would remain as a result of the poor light and trembling hands. So far, two machinists and the cook, Wilhelm Bauer, had been killed; their bodies were stacked up like cordwood in the roomy spaces behind the infirmary. This extra space had been created prior to the start of the mission by removing the walls that formed the sleeping cabins and the officers' mess and had been used to hold the troops and equipment needed for the railway demolition work.

Heinrich had been chilled to the bone when he visited this hold well before they had crossed the river. In addition to the rough-looking Rangers he had been introduced to back at Palo Duro, he had come face-to-face with other men, massive men with dark eyes, dark hair, dark skin, and strange markings of black grease on their faces. Despite the fact that they wore uniforms identical to the other Rangers, Heinrich recognized them for what they were. Indians! Comanche! Heinrich had learned that they formed an integral part of the West Carolina Ranger Corps, but he had not been prepared for the sight of these strange and ferocious looking men in their war paint, and he had embarrassed himself by letting out a small yelp before backing out of the hold and returning to the control cabin.

The doctor took a bit more care in his medical treatment of the captain and Stanton, despite their strong desire to return to their command posts. 'How are we doing?' asked the doctor of the captain. The officer sat on the doctor's stool with his torn cheek turned toward a desk lamp.

'Good enough,' responded the captain. 'We're still airborne, which is no small miracle.'

'Good!'

'It's not over yet, so don't use up all your thread on me, Herr Doktor.'

'Not to worry,' the man giggled nervously. 'I have miles of

the stuff. Enough to sew everyone's arms and legs back on.' The captain did not laugh.

*

'Sergeant, leave the pits! Bring your men!' shouted the captain having decided on his course of action.

'But what about those men down there?' asked the sergeant, surprised at the order.

'Can't be helped. We've got to do everything we can to save the bridge. It's the key.'

The sergeant hesitated for only a moment, fired one more shot with his own rifle, collared as many of his men as possible, and followed the captain. After descending an exposed staircase, mounted on the outside wall of the pit, nineteen of the captain's men gathered in the shadows on the parade level. Around the corner, fifty yards along the rail bed, lay the black, gaping hole of the arsenal tunnel.

The captain explained his plan quickly in a hoarse whisper; it was simple and required no repetition. After reloading their weapons, they stole from their hiding place and raced along the tracks in a loose formation.

They had reached a point just thirty yards from the tunnel when a blinding white flash obliterated their view, and a blast of furnace-like heat threw them back. A storm of shattered brick and mortar rained down on them. Nine men died instantly, two more died thirty seconds later, and the sergeant died one hundred seconds later. Captain Porter, Lieutenant Clark, and Lieutenant Burrows lay unconscious, buried under the smoking remnants of the eighty-year-old masonry.

*

Stanton reached the control cabin in time to observe the flash that accompanied the collapse of the east end of the arsenal tunnel. A red signal flare shot up from below and announced that the blast had effectively sealed the arsenal and the bridge from the remainder of the fortress—and from East Carolina. With the exception of the few men required to lay down fire along the narrow perimeter walkways of the fort, the West Carolina force beneath him was now free to work with little interference from the defending forces. Those West Carolinians left behind to fight their way out of the pit would eventually be overcome by the Eastern forces that had coalesced around the collapsed tunnel entrance. But this appeared to be of no great concern to Stanton. Another red signal flare, fired from below, announced that the ground forces were now shifting their efforts away from the destruction of the fortress guns and turning their attention toward the bridge.

Stanton had exercised much skill in the management of every step of the airship's mission thus far. Now, after six hours of relentless concentration, his strength and judgment began to fail. As soon as the captain returned to his side, Stanton ordered the dirigible down for another pass.

The ship's course carried it across the fort from west to east, and as soon as it approached the western wall abutting the river, Stanton ordered a barrage of flares. They illuminated the ground below like a string of incandescent bulbs strung across a circus tent. Both he and the captain scanned the surface of the fortress; they looked for the movements of both forces that were vying for control. It was Heinrich, however, with his pale face pressed against the single intact pane of glass, who noticed something of concern.

It took several seconds for his waking mind to understand what he was seeing. Down in the mortar pit he observed the two black groupings of artillery—four pieces each. He also noticed an absence of the swarming and pulsing pattern of men in conflict. Instead, he observed the ordered flow of men engaged in concerted enterprise; the men seemed to be working the guns. Then came confirmation of this conjecture—a flash and a small puff of white smoke, directly beneath the airship.

'Kapitan!' shouted the frightened flier at the top of his voice—too late: two more flashes, two more puffs of white smoke. Immediately after the last, came a sharp jolt, and Dora Nine shuddered and groaned. The sickening experience of the ship tumbling over the desert flashed through Heinrich's mind. He braced himself for the catastrophic explosion from the penetrating mortar shell and cursed himself for having placed himself in such an absurdly dangerous position. He let out a scream.

But the explosion never came; the mortar shell had passed cleanly through the bottom of the ship's hull, between rings seven and eight, up through gas cell No. 7, and out the top of the hull, after which it continued its climb for another two hundred yards before detonating in open air. The upper side of the ship was peppered with bits of shrapnel from the relatively harmless blast. Gas cell No.7 contained helium and did not explode.

Although Dora Nine had not been blown from the sky, she could no longer be considered airworthy; she had lost a significant percentage of her buoyancy and was losing gas from the remaining cells at an alarming rate. Stanton realized that fate had been tested beyond that which even the boldest man should attempt and acquiesced to the captain's frantic request to steer for the western side of the river. The likelihood of reaching Natchitoches was debatable.

*

The soldiers of the embattled East Carolina forces below let out a cheer at the small black hole they had made in the underbelly of the monster as it swooped across the sky above them. But just as quickly, they groaned in disappointment when the shell burst brilliantly above it, creating a great black silhouette instead of a roaring inferno. They all stared mutely as the dirigible made a ninety-degree turn to starboard, cruised over the river, and disappeared into the darkness to the west.

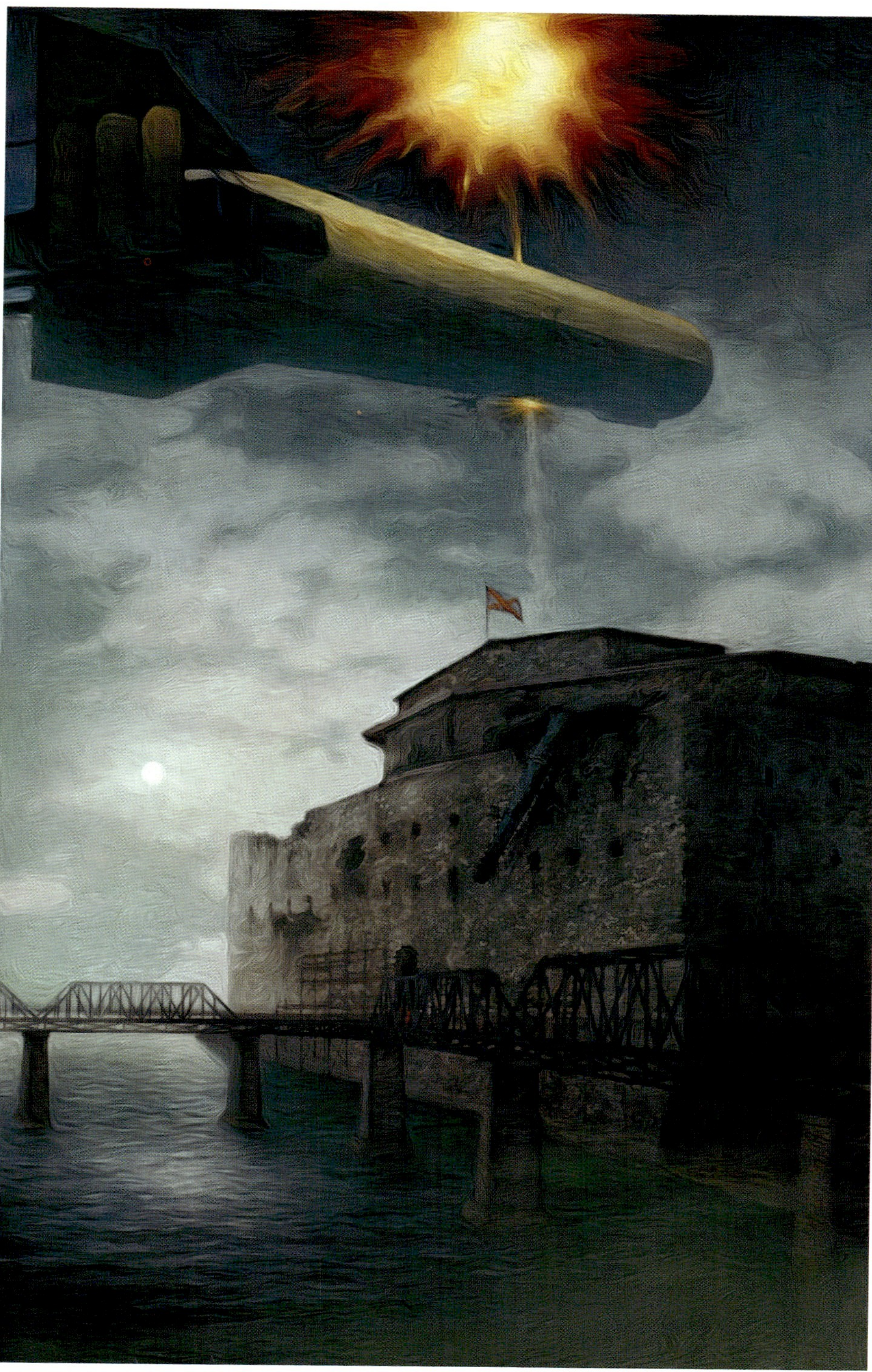

Chapter 16

IN SAFE HANDS

Ignoring the objections of the surgeon, Captain Porter limped from the largest of three tents that formed a makeshift infirmary on the Greenbelt just outside the reopened C-gate. The fortress hospital had been entirely destroyed by the explosive charges that the assaulting forces had ignited to dislodge the recalcitrant gun number three. The local children, mostly boys, incapable of resisting such a temptation, had gathered around the gate; they strained to get a view of the wreckage inside. The gate was an interesting sight in itself, its doors having been dismounted by the demolition charges of East Carolinian engineers tasked with reopening them.

The children did not immediately notice the captain's slow approach as he made his way up the path behind them. When they turned, they discovered a figure that seemed just barely human; the captain's face, neck, forearms, and hands were all entirely covered with white gauze bandages that were already showing red stains from the bloody lacerations beneath. The children were wholly unprepared for such a frightful sight and most fled, shrieking, back down the path toward town. Ignoring the disquieting stares of those who remained, the captain continued to limp his way past the twisted steel doors, each leaning at its own precarious angle against the walls to either side. After traveling another painful twenty yards, he stopped and gazed about, awestruck; the young boys, no less awestruck, huddled a short distance behind him.

The stark linearity of the fortress was gone. Its staircases, its handrails, its parapets, its towers, its tall corners had been rounded and twisted into every conceivable shape other than that formed by straight lines. Tall heaps of brick, mortar, and earth were strewn about the parade ground.

A small, muffled cheer diverted his attention from the

devastation; a group of dusty red men, each covered with a homogeneous layer of powdered brick, had just succeeded in excavating a hole through the dense debris of the collapsed tunnel entrance. Their new tunnel had been burrowed from the inside out, so as the captain looked on, he observed several men, caked with red dust, squirm their way out of the small opening, one at a time, like maggots oozing their way out of a corpse.

The captain continued his awkward march forward, the renewed spirit of these soldiers providing him a small transfusion of hope. They noticed his approach and rushed over to inquire as to his health; they had little trouble penetrating the heavy layer of bandages to discover his true identity.

'We thought you was dead, sir!' shouted one of the younger men.

'Shut up, you fool!' shouted another, smacking him roughly on the back of his head. 'The captain can't be done in by a couple sticks of blasting dynamite. Can you sir?'

The captain responded with a sheepish grin, the truth of the matter being that he indeed felt somewhat *done in*. 'Looks like you boys are pulling things back together this morning. It does me good to see it.'

'Ain't done much, sir, not yet. At least we can get into the tunnel. This here rubble only goes about forty feet. Once you're through it, the rest of the tunnel's in pretty good shape.'

'Lucky as hell, sir,' interrupted another dirty, eager face. 'The last carload of explosives never went off. It's still sitting there. You can see it, fuse burned right up to the barrel. But no boom! Maybe we'll get a chance to send it 'cross the river!' The men laughed.

The captain said he hoped they would have that opportunity, praised them for their efforts, both for having so vigorously defended the fortress the night before and for starting repairs so early that morning. He encouraged them to keep up their spirits and then continued on his way.

The captain's physical condition prevented him from worming his way through the narrow maggot hole, and so he took a longer and much more exhausting route up and down the stairs that led into the mortar pit. Inside the pit he hoped to find an alternate passage into the arsenal, a passage originally intended for the transfer of ordinance to the men working the mortars. Although the wounded and dead bodies had been removed hours before, the pit was still a grizzly site. The lower portion of the walls and the entire floor, approximately one hundred feet wide by fifty feet deep, were so completely stained with brown and congealed blood that the illusion was created of a thick layer of brown paint.

The captain lost his footing at times on the slick surface, but he never went down entirely. He found the aforementioned passage intact and open. After waiting for his eyes to adapt to the darkness, uncertain of the obstacles he might find laying on the floor ahead, he made his way through various right-angle turns until he arrived at the unloading platform from which he and Mr. Volper had begun their descent the day before. But instead of retracing that seemingly long-ago journey, the captain stepped out onto the rail bed. The tunnel was much darker than usual, and the electrical lights were still inoperative; the east side of the tunnel provided only a pinprick of light. He rested a moment, his wheezing breath echoing off the smooth brickwork that arched over him.

He limped toward the light that flowed in from the west end of the tunnel, somewhat dimmer than normal owing to the obstruction of a single railcar resting just within the entrance of the tunnel. Peering into its open freight door, the captain was brought face-to-face with a pile of wooden casks neatly stacked, four wide by three high—plainly visible on the side of each, a large crimson 'V'. A path of scorched wood traced the route of the burning fuse that had failed to ignite the barrels and destroy the tunnel. The captain gasped and then chuckled at the sight. He blessed Mr. Volper and continued on his way.

On the parapet at the tunnel's mouth—the intersection, so to speak, of the tunnel, the bridge, and the perimeter walkway—stood Colonel Storey in a befuddled stupor.

'Morning, sir,' the captain greeted the colonel.

'Ah, Porter is it?' he responded with a weak voice, high in pitch.

Porter could imagine what must be going through his commander's head at the moment. The sight before them was totally suited to unnerve the crustiest of soldiers. The first thing Porter noticed—absolutely could not fail to notice—was the absence of the bridge. The heavy stone piers that had supported each of the bridge's separate spans were the only parts of the original structure still intact—silent stone monuments that now served little purpose other than to mark the graves of the Old Men buried in the river ooze.

Jutting up in random spots from the muddy water coursing somberly between the piers was the smoldering wreckage of the collapsed trestles and the twisted steel of the rails. The wood from the walkways and the rail ties had already floated away; scattered pieces had washed up on the banks downstream.

Glancing behind him, the captain received a shock; he gasped at a sight that was perhaps not quite so overwhelming as the sparse remnants of the bridge, but certainly more bizarre. The massive barrel of Old Man number three was suspended directly above them, precariously, in a canted vertical position, hanging from the wall of the upper keep. It was miraculously held in place by a few strands of corkscrewed steel that snaked over the precipice like an ivy vine. The most disturbing aspect of this sight was the fact that the muzzle of this masterpiece of artillery pointed squarely down at the two officers like a modern day sword of Damocles. The nearness of its dark opening caused the captain's heart to skip a beat. He had to assume that the piece was still loaded.

Once the initial shock of this sight passed, the captain gazed back at his commander; the man was trembling. And by the expression on the his face, Captain Porter imagined his commander was wishing this unique instrument of war was indeed loaded, primed, and just waiting for the hand of God to set it off and so put him out of his misery. But no such absolving event occurred. A warm gust of morning air caused the hollow cylinder to shift its position slightly, not more than an inch or two, but enough to send a grating metallic echo from its mouth.

The captain immediately recognized the fragile nature of the cannon's position and decided his first task would be to cut the Old Man down and, if necessary, let the dangerous mass fall to its grave in the river below. It could always be resurrected whenever its three siblings were dredged up.

As the captain looked upward to evaluate how best to execute this job, he caught sight of red cloth fluttering in the breeze like a flag. But on closer examination, he recognized the crimson coat of Colonel Caruthers, standing dramatically at the summit of the fortress on a relatively untouched pinnacle of masonry. Captain Porter estimated the British officer's position to be roughly at the midpoint between where guns number one and number two had rested, the exact spot at which he himself had so often enjoyed the sunset. Colonel Caruthers was engaged in some act that was difficult to decipher; a couple of brief glints suggested that he might be peering through a telescope, out across the distant plains of West Carolina.

'Look at them over there—those rodents,' mumbled Colonel Storey. He nodded toward a small massing of troops on the opposite side of the river. They were busily engaged in the construction of their own defensive fortifications. 'We're going to pull number three back up and blast them all to hell!'

'Yes, sir,' said the captain patiently, not a little disturbed himself at the sight of the men who had perpetrated this devastation so close at hand. He had not expected to see any sign of them.

'Excuse me, sir,' came a voice from behind. Both officers turned to find a pristine Lieutenant Burrows. He saluted the colonel, but his eyes traveled directly to the captain.

'Yes, Lieutenant,' said the captain, 'what is it?'

'Sir, we have an unusual situation.' The captain waited patiently for Lieutenant Burrows to find the words. 'As you probably know, sir, we've sent patrols up and down the river banks, to pick up all of those . . . ' and here the lieutenant was at a slight loss of words.

'Enemy combatants?' suggested the captain.

'Enemy spies, you mean,' growled the colonel. 'Absolutely can't wait to shoot them!'

'Carry on, Lieutenant,' interrupted the captain.

'Yes, sir, the enemy combatants who seem to be crawling over the countryside since last night. We've already captured twenty-five of them, none wearing uniforms. Well, one of these patrols picked up someone early this morning. He was rowing across the river.'

'What?' chuckled the colonel. 'The patrol went down the river after him? That's just the fighting spirit we need right now.'

'No, sir. Pardon, sir, this fellow was rowing over our way, from the other side. He rowed right up to our patrol and shouted, 'Good morning.'

The colonel seemed a little astonished, but held his tongue.

'And?' said the captain, a little impatiently.

'Sir, he says he's a British flier held captive by the West Carolinians . . . and the Prussians. Not exactly sure where Prussia is . . . but I thought it was somewhere over in Europe.'

'A British flier?' cried the colonel. 'There aren't any British fliers over here. What's he talking about?'

At that moment they were joined suddenly by Colonel Caruthers—fresh, crisp, and sparkling. He had retreated from his perch above and traveled through the fortress to join his fellow officers below, and he had done this with such speed that Captain Porter gazed at the British officer with unfeigned admiration as well as startled dismay. The officer seemed in no way winded or flushed from his journey down, and the morning was already growing hot.

'Good morning, gentlemen,' he greeted them. 'Wonderful. I'm happy to see you all still standing.'

'I'm sure you are,' said Colonel Storey. 'Seems we've captured one of your fliers trying to sneak across the river.'

The British colonel raised a questioning eyebrow and looked over to Captain Porter for an explanation; the captain, in turn, shifted his gaze back to Lieutenant Burrows.

'That's what he says, sir. Says he won't say anymore until he can speak with the fort commander.'

'Where are you keeping him?' asked the captain.

'He's in the infirmary, sir. He looks worse than a drowned rat,' chuckled the lieutenant. Then anticipating Colonel Storey's next comment, he added, 'He *is* under guard, sir.'

'Very well, Lieutenant,' said the captain. 'We'll go have a chat with your prisoner. You get a work crew organized and cut that gun down—without killing anyone, please!'

'Lord Almighty, sir!' said the lieutenant, the blood draining from his face. 'Look!'

All three officers turned and stared out toward the western horizon; they squinted in the direction indicated by the junior officer. Bathed in the bright morning light, cruising directly toward them, but still several miles away, was an airship, glistening like a single drop of reflective dew suspended in the otherwise clear blue sky.

'Bloody hell,' muttered Colonel Caruthers. He had been greatly disappointed at failing to catch sight of the dirigible the night before. It had been much talked about. While the airship had been swooping over the fort, the colonel had been dashing about town rounding up the few British soldiers who might have been lingering about. 'Would you look at that. It looks like a sardine with indigestion.'

The faint echo of welcoming cheers rolled across the river from the soldiers on the far banks, and all four officers looked on with concern until the airship made a sudden turn to the north to follow the course of the river. Once confident that the enemy ship was only conducting a scouting patrol and that it had no other aggressive intentions, the officers split up: the lieutenant darted off to commandeer a crew to deal with the dislodged gun; Colonel Storey returned to his office to begin preparing a defense for his courts marshal; Captain Porter, accompanied by Colonel Caruthers, headed for the infirmary.

*

Caruthers and Porter glanced at each other, wanting some indication of the other's thoughts before speaking; they each faced the simple choice between curious astonishment and complete incredulity. William sat before them, still looking much like a drowned rat despite competent medical treatment. He rested on a stool in the cool, damp storeroom that now served as Captain Porter's temporary office. He glanced back and forth between the two officers looming over him; he wondered which man had more influence over his fate.

'Quite a remarkable story, Lieutenant,' said Porter, not yet committing to any particular reaction.

'Indeed!' added Caruthers. 'So you were part of Sir Maxim's little army?'

'Yes, sir,' responded William, slightly irritated by the colonel's choice of words.

'Sir Maxim's army?' asked Porter. 'What's that?'

'Oh, have you never heard of Sir Maxim? I thought everyone had.'

The captain gave a quick shake of his head.

'It's quite a story . . . a bit of an embarrassment for some in government. A highly enthusiastic MP from Northamptonshire became convinced that Her Majesty's interests in the Middle East were being threatened by any number of belligerents. So he sponsored a battalion of troops and sent them off to the desert.' The colonel then looked William over again, as he sat there disconsolately, hunched over with his elbows resting on his knees, his chin resting in his cupped hands. 'And I believe that in this small army were several of these new flying machines, as well as a few desperate young chaps to fly them. I haven't heard much about it lately. Actually, I thought the whole thing had been abandoned. There has always been a fuss over the legality of it, the whole idea of a privately funded battalion, that is. But it appears I am wrong.'

This last admission succeeded in pricking William's attention and he leaned back in his chair. He gazed complacently up at the colonel. William was undecided in his opinion of the officer; his first impressions were that the man was all bull and bluster, a typical career soldier, not unlike some of the more unpleasant officers of Sir Maxim's battalion. But the more he listened, the more he wondered about the man. He intended to keep his mouth firmly shut for the moment.

'So you believe all of this?' asked Porter, in a manner and tone that indicated some willingness to accept the tale as truth.

'I don't believe we can afford not to. He has accurately named those few officers of the expedition that I happen to be familiar with. And the dirigibles obviously have arrived.'

'We'll have to go through the whole thing again with Colonel Storey. I hope you don't mind, Lieutenant.' William let out a perturbed grunt, but agreed with a nod.

'Might I suggest,' said Caruthers, 'since the matter is of such importance, that there be not a moment lost. To catch today's train for Charleston, I must depart in less than an hour. I believe the proper course of action would be for Lieutenant Hastings to accompany me to the War Office immediately.'

Captain Porter agreed, but gave the pilot a penetrating stare and asked, 'Are you able, Lieutenant? You appear to be in need of rest.'

William gave Captain Porter an exaggerated head-to-foot inspection; William thought the captain didn't appear much better. But he responded respectfully, 'Yes, sir, I'm fine. I agree with the colonel, here. I'm anxious to get moving and to get back home.'

The captain nodded and made the necessary arrangements. He then returned to the infirmary to have his own wounds redressed; his numerous bandages were now so soaked with blood that the colonel had started teasing him about transferring to the redcoats.

*

It was a tedious journey by motorcar along the crowded road from Natchez to Baton Rouge where anyone wishing to travel to Charleston by train was forced to embark. This inconvenience had been due to the nocturnal activities of the Westerners; they had thrown the entire rail network into complete disarray within fifty miles of the river. The confusion had been exacerbated by the crowds of civilians already beginning to evacuate the delta region for safer places in the East Carolina interior, all terrified by the looming conflict. William dozed in the rear seat of the motorcar; he sat behind the colonel and an unfamiliar Carolinian officer who also happened to be traveling to Baton Rouge and from there on to New Orleans. Beyond the Carolinian officer's words of outrage and a dreary monologue about his being stuck at a dead-end post in New Orleans, there were few words spoken between the two men seated up front. Once aboard the closely packed train and seated in a private cabin secured by the colonel, William slept through the remaining afternoon hours.

William woke as the steward, a black man dressed in a white serving jacket, placed a warm meal before them; he already had laid a clean white cloth on the table and covered it with well-polished silver. The two Englishmen quietly devoured the southern dishes that had been prepared for them: catfish, black-eyed peas, and cornbread. They looked up from their plates only when the steward returned to clean up. William had listened carefully to the steward each time he spoke, curious about the unfamiliar manner of speech. However, William's request for more cornbread, a strange spongy substance, dense and dry, had been filled swiftly and without confusion. As his meal digested, his energy returned and his mind began to churn. The colonel's thoughts seemed far away. When both had finished and while partaking of a third cup of coffee, William initiated their discussion.

'What's going to happen to me in Charleston?'

'I couldn't say, exactly,' said the colonel. 'I'm not certain what will happen to *me* in Charleston. Things are always very unpredictable here in America, even when a war isn't erupting.'

'Have you been here long?'

'A lifetime!' responded the officer sourly. 'I arrived four years and two months ago. It was intended that I return to England next month. I don't imagine that's too likely now. Lord Almighty, I can't imagine actually fighting a war alongside these damned Americans!'

'Unpleasant?' asked William, attempting to draw him out.

'That would be an understatement, Lieutenant. You can argue good military sense from dawn to dusk, then they'll go off in some lunatic direction. Take that ridiculous Fort Natchez, for example. It's a monstrosity!'

'Well, it seems they got a fair amount of experience fighting over the past few decades.'

'Sticks and stones, my boy, sticks and stones. That might as well have been the crusades. Warfare is a different animal entirely in these modern days.'

William pondered this point while he sipped at his coffee; the cup was too delicate and too small to handle comfortably; he would have preferred a military issue tin cup. The colonel reached into his coat and pulled out a magnificent cigar, which he then ignited with a large wooden match.

'First,' continued the colonel, 'I expect more than a few questions from the British command about last night's assault . . . and of course there's your story—that will certainly get things buzzing. After that they could very well turn us over to the Americans for more of the same. If I'm lucky my voice will fail, and then they'll have to leave me be for a few days. Rest and recuperation in Bournemouth would be best, but I'll settle for a few days at Mrs. Tabrou's hotel.'

'What about the fighting? What's happening?'

'Oh, impossible to tell. I trust nothing I heard in Natchez. The wires are cut in every direction, train service interrupted, nothing but rumor and gossip. Still, if one considers the perfect execution of yesterday's assault, I would expect that every bridge along the Mississippi has been destroyed and that the West Carolinians have effectively sealed themselves off for now. Those bloody, lumbering airships could be a damned nuisance too. You really saw eight of them?'

'Yes, sir, I stood not a hundred yards from them, lined up like fish at Bournemouth market.'

'And how fast do you suppose those things travel?'

'Sixty, seventy, maybe eighty miles an hour.'

'Amazing! They could afford to lose a couple and still patrol the entire river from St. Louis to New Orleans, as well as the gulf coast. How long can they stay up? Days?

'Yes. Maybe a couple of weeks. But surely they have supply bases nearby. The ship I traveled on was always breaking down.'

'Amazing!' the colonel repeated himself.

'Do you believe the Americans will try to do something about them? I mean the Carolinians . . . I mean the *East* Carolinians. You know, shoot them down?'

'Well, they can't exactly let them go bumbling about the skies, like they're doing now. I imagine they'll have to do something.'

'How would one get involved in that?'

'Whatever do you mean by *get involved*? I don't imagine they'll let you *get involved* in much of anything. Besides, you told me you wanted to be shipped back home. Which is it, Lieutenant, go home, or stay here?'

William sat up, tense, confounded by the colonel's question.

He *did* want to go home. He absolutely *meant* to return home, although the thought of walking in the front door of Woolham Chase made his mouth go dry. Would *she* forgive him? He could handle his mother's tongue lashing. But would she forgive him? And if she did, what then? He simply refused to go to work for his brother. Since Hubert had gotten all the family marbles, he could figure out how to play with them on his own. The only thing William knew how to do was fly an aeroplane, a skill that seemed a rare commodity in America, and one likely to be of much value in the near future.

William made up his mind quickly. 'I want leave to go home! But when my leave is up, I would like to come back. I believe I could bring one of those things down!'

'Well, you're going to have to choose one or the other . . . go home, or stay here. Under the circumstances, it won't look too good your leaving just when the fighting's about to start. You'll be lucky to find someone willing to sign your leave papers.' The colonel paused for a moment to puff on his cigar. 'Are you sure you must go? I could always use a spirited officer in my regiment. But even if you decide to stay, I don't know that you're in a position to do much about those airships.' Then, after another pause, the colonel mumbled to himself, 'How on earth does one get at them? Maybe with crack artillery?' The colonel gazed over at William. 'I suppose you could transfer to the big guns. We have a couple of battalions near the coast, and I have no doubt they'll eventually be shipped out here.'

'No, no, no!' said William, shaking his head. 'That's not what I mean. I need an aeroplane. I want to shoot one down—up close!'

'Well, you don't have an aeroplane,' said the colonel with irritation. '*We* don't have any aeroplanes, and I'm not Sir Maxim!'

'But the Americans must have some,' countered William.

'Yes, I suppose so. Maybe a few here and there. But what are you going to do? Take a pistol up and bang away at it with your six rounds? Or are you planning to land on the damn thing and have a go at it with a bayonet?'

William slumped back into his seat in frustration. He gulped his coffee while the colonel puffed on his cigar. William controlled himself. He didn't want to say anything that might spoil his leave home, but he knew that he was right, and it was always frustrating when officers didn't take him seriously. 'I am absolutely sure that the only way to destroy them is to shoot them out of the sky—with aeroplanes! Did you know that each one of those infernal machines has its own aeroplane slung under its belly? One of those aeroplanes destroyed mine—in midair, mind you. If they can do that, then we can find a way to do it back.'

'We?'

'I mean the Americans.'

The colonel leaned forward, turned his head, and stared into William's eyes for a long moment. After pursing his lips, he eased back into his seat and took another long puff, the tobacco crackling softly. Then shooting the smoke from his lips, he said, 'We'll see, Lieutenant, we'll see.'

Chapter 17

THE CONFERENCE

Colonel Caruthers gathered William from Hotel Tabrou, on Third Street, a few doors down from the British embassy. Actually, it was more of a boarding house than a hotel, replete with its own matriarchal proprietor, Mrs. Tabrou, a swarthy, middle-aged woman who by a circuitous route had managed to find her way to Charleston from her birthplace in Paris. Her roundabout immigration had taken her through Amsterdam, London, and New York, and somewhere along the way she had lost Mr. Tabrou. But she did not seem to mind the loss too badly as the heavy stream of male residents, arriving from all corners of the globe to reside at her establishment for indeterminate durations and intent on indulging in a variety of interactions with the sovereign state of Carolina, provided sufficient canvas for her artistry as a housewife.

Mrs. Tabrou's first sight of William had inspired her to a great degree, and she made the best possible use of the two intervening days; she stuffed him with as many different southern dishes that her cook could create and performed a tolerable job of mending his horribly ill-used uniform. So it was, as they worked their way through Charleston's waking streets, that Colonel Caruthers could not help but cast an occasional sidelong glance at his companion; Caruthers was astonished at the improvement in the boy's appearance. For his part, William could not fail to notice a dramatic improvement in the colonel's own spirits. The officer marched through the streets at a pace that William found difficult to match.

'Now remember, Lieutenant,' instructed the colonel, 'your presence at this discussion is, owing to your rank, highly irregular. It is due entirely to the unusual circumstances that have landed you here. You are to listen, and should they arise, answer any questions directed to you, concisely and respectfully.

And, should these restrictions chafe, just remember that the Americans are much more likely to kick you out than I am. Understood?'

'Yes, sir!' responded William, with good-natured formality. 'Speak only when spoken to, sir. Completely understood, sir!' The colonel glanced over at him again and inspected his face for signs of insincerity. An alert and precise man when faced with a challenging situation, the colonel was nevertheless uncomfortable at introducing such an unpredictable element as William into this particular meeting. The fact that he had been ordered to do so was little consolation.

'Here we are!' said the colonel, as they approached a grand white mansion. It appeared to have been constructed early in the last century as a stately private residence, but as Caruthers explained to William, it had served for some time as the War Office of Carolina, the WOC. The mansion was beginning to show signs of wear, and its lines had begun to sag a bit. 'Not at all like Whitehall,' said the colonel. 'But we will keep any such opinions concerning our insolvent cousins to ourselves. Understood, Lieutenant?' William responded with a crisp, sarcastic salute.

Passing between tall columns that supported a wide balcony above, and between expressionless sentries who mirrored the blank wooden pillars, the British officers were ushered into a large, carpeted foyer by an elderly black man. He asked them to wait and then disappeared into a room off to one side; his gray flannel uniform matched that of the sentries outside, but was devoid of any insignia of rank. A musty odor hung in the air.

While they waited, William examined two portraits hanging on the walls to each side: the first of a dour, cement-block of a man with a long grizzled beard and intelligent eyes; the second of an elderly man with curling white hair and deep warm eyes. The gold-plated tags nailed to each frame were inscribed with the names General James McAfee and General

Nathan P. Harlan. William raised his eyes; he became curious after recognizing the famed names, and gave the portraits a more thorough look. It had been Harlan's movement to the left, around the Georgian right flank, that had been the decisive event. The Georgian troops, who had been glaring down on their enemy from their snug defense on the high ground outside Augusta, had been thoroughly routed from behind. During the ensuing chaos, McAfees's forces had slipped into the Georgian capital, where they had cornered most of the nation's congressmen and captured President Merriweather himself—and then that ignominious photograph of the poor man, hands tied, astride a donkey had been circulated around the globe.

'Would you gentlemen please follow me,' said the aid as he returned. He led them up a curved staircase, wide and sweeping, but tilted a bit to one side, and its warped treads creaked under their boots as they wound their way up the stairs. Upon reaching the second floor they were led through thick oak doors into a large conference room with a set of mullioned doors at the opposite end that gave access to the front balcony and provided a view down onto Fifth Street.

'Colonel Caruthers, sir, your place is here,' said the aid, indicating a specific chair at the long table. There were five empty chairs on each side, and one at each end; the chair indicated by the aid was on the right-hand side, furthest from the balcony. 'And you, sir,' questioned the man, 'mightin' you be the aeroplane lieutenant?' William nodded in response. 'Well, sir, I'm sorry, this table is not large enough to accommodate everyone. If you don't mind, sir, I will have you sit here.' The aid gestured toward a chair placed in the corner to the right of the doorway, but not far from the colonel's place at the table. 'No disrespect intended.'

'None taken,' said William politely. 'This will be fine, thank you.'

'You gentlemen wait here. The others will be arriving shortly,' and with these words the aid left them hovering above a silver urn of hot coffee.

It was indeed only five minutes before the other participants began to arrive. The first, who introduced himself as Mr. Smith, was a man of about forty years in age, dressed in a worn black suit. His grooming was of a neat and trim nature, and his face was covered with a dense beard leaving only his eyes as his main distinguishing feature. He had just finished greeting Caruthers when their conversation was interrupted by the entrance of a second civilian of a strikingly different cast.

This latest arrival was composed of so many straight lines and sharp angles that he seemed much like a skeleton. Although of a height and weight similar to that of Colonel Caruthers, whose lean and wiry frame gave the impression of a coiled spring, this fellow seemed so brittle that he might snap in two if knocked against anything too hard.

'Caruthers!' spat the skeleton, in such a haughty manner that, with this single word, William recognized him as a fellow countryman—a London intonation, he thought. The skeleton spat out another word, 'Smith!' as he nodded toward the nondescript American. And, although not condescending to verbally greet William, he did, after a thorough head-to-toe inspection, curtly nod his skull before turning his back and folding himself into his seat.

The next man to arrive, the last to enter singly and thus afford William the opportunity of close inspection, was a beefy man who overflowed his gray uniform at every opening, like a ham wrapped tightly in its jute netting. His face was red from his climb up the stairs, and he mumbled his greeting to the group, not directing it toward anyone in particular. This solid fellow, Oswald Stack, the Carolinian quartermaster general, took his chair across from the skeleton without direction from the aid. This created a curious imbalance, even to William's moderate aesthetic sense, and he stared at these men for a moment and at the impression created by the stark difference in their appearance.

After a brief period of disjointed conversation the room was suddenly flooded by a rushing stream of uniforms: gray flannel with red linen stripe, generously sprinkled with sparkling medals, row upon row of ribbon, and yards of silk braid. The floorboards creaked and groaned under the hammer blows of their boots. The confident boom of their voices charged the room with the intensity of a thunderstorm. Their ribald conversation continued unabated, as if they had taken no more notice of the room's occupants than if the room had been empty, although more than one of these men cast a quick, questioning glance toward William, who sat slightly amazed at the combined effect of these new powers.

As the volume of their talk began to abate, falling from a level that would have been sufficient for the battlefield to something more fitting for indoors, the last participant quietly pattered in. He was a tiny, hunched figure. Only the top of his head was visible as he walked behind the officers seated on the far side of the table. He made his way to the room's last open seat, just before the balcony windows at the far end of the room—the head of the table. The top of the little man's head was bald and covered with large brown age spots; downy locks of white hung from his temples. He was much older than anyone else in the room, and it appeared that the simple motion of taking his seat and placing his file of notes on the table caused him no little pain. William could not help but notice his curled and arthritic fingers as he fumbled with a small leather case from which he extracted a set of eyeglasses. He placed them carefully and precisely on his small nose that sat like a button in the center of his wrinkled face.

'Welcome, everyone,' he began, without looking up. 'We have a lot to discuss. I hope you have all booked rooms for tonight.' From their reactions, William guessed that not all had done so. The little man then looked up from his notes and surveyed the room, his glance halting almost imperceptibly on Caruthers and on William. 'While most of you are all too familiar with each other, that cannot be said for everyone here. To save time, and knowing some of your individual and narcissistic tendencies, I will make the introductions.'

He paused for a moment before continuing, 'I am Charles Tillock, secretary of war.' Then, starting at his right hand, and from there moving over to his left hand, and thus in an alternating pattern that apparently coincided with the rank and influence of the various participants, he proceeded to introduce the others: 'General Wallace Barton, supreme commander of the Carolinian military forces, Sir Isaac Pinchon, Her Majesty's commander of North American forces, General Wiley Preston, commanding general of the Carolinian forces of the West—*without portfolio*, General Samuel Armstrong, commanding general of the Carolinian forces of the Tennessee Valley, Admiral Maxwell Downey, commander of the Carolinian navy, Sir Martin Henschel, admiral and commander of Her Majesty's Atlantic squadron, General Oswald Stack, quartermaster general, Mr. William Simper, head of Her Majesty's secret service in the Americas, Mr. Edgar Smith of the Carolinian intelligence service and, of course, Colonel Caruthers, or rather *General* Caruthers. Congratulations on your promotion, General.' Caruthers smiled and nodded his head.

The secretary then halted and leaned to one side in order to improve his line of sight, 'You, sir, I do not recognize.'

Every pair of eyes bore down on William. Although startled at being singled out in this way, he maintained his composure, opened his mouth to introduce himself, only to hear Caruthers' voice boom out, 'This is Lieutenant William Hastings, most recently of Her Majesty's North African Expeditionary Forces.' Mr. Simper, the skeleton, let out a muffled snort. Caruthers, obviously hesitant at whether he should continue, eventually added, 'I believe, sir, you have already been informed of the lieutenant's participation today.' At which point Sir Pinchon leaned over and whispered a few words into the secretary's ear.

The secretary nodded, then mumbled, 'I see.' He looked over at William once more and said, 'Welcome, Lieutenant. It is good to have you with us. Please do not let all the feathers and gold braid inhibit you in any way. You weren't asked to attend so you can sit like a lump.'

William did not entirely fathom this comment. He certainly had no desire to be a lump, and responded with a strong, 'Yes, sir, Mister Secretary!'

'A few ground rules before we begin,' said the secretary, bestowing no further attention on William. 'This is not going to be a political discussion. We will leave that to others more qualified. You will restrict your comments solely to the military arena. I know this will be quite difficult for some of you, so please consider this a warning. I will eject any burgeoning politician from the discussion at the first infraction. Now, General Barton, would you care to update everyone on our situation?'

'Not . . . very . . . good, I'm afraid,' said the general, the words falling slowly from his lips, as if he could think of the next only after the previous had been expelled; he seemed to be examining each for any political undertones. 'With the exception of the fighting around New Orleans . . . the Westerns have completely isolated themselves. Every bridge along the Mississippi from Virginia to the gulf has been completely, or partially, destroyed. Fort Natchez is in shambles. Its guns are dismounted and in the river. New Orleans is burning.

'We've got the 122nd Artillery shelling the West Carolinian 32nd from our side of the river . . . of course they're responding in kind and New Orleans is caught in the middle . . . we're bringing down the 98th as we speak . . . and the 5th is still stuck without transportation. But . . . it's fairly quiet now everywhere else along the river.'

'And what of West Carolina?' asked the secretary.

'I don't know for sure . . . had a few stragglers come over. Seems the governor's troops are thick as fleas, over all the western counties.'

'My understanding,' interrupted Mr. Smith softly, 'is that martial law has been effectively imposed over a wide region. As you well know, the populations of the southern counties are sympathetic to the secession. The situation in the northern counties is less clear. That is, the attitude of the general population in the north is less clear. A heavy-handed martial law seems to be in place there.'

'Any new activity by our Virginian friends to the north?' continued the secretary.

'Nothing new that I'm aware of,' said Mr. Smith.

'They don't appear to be fixin' to do anything immediately,' grunted General Armstrong. 'They been transportin' troops up and down their side of the river, and bringin' some more down from further north, sort of showin' off, I think. But no, they ain't ready to start nothin'. Everything is quiet in the Crucible.'

'Sound right to you?' asked the secretary, looking over to Mr. Smith.

'Yes, again, as far as I can tell. It's almost too quiet . . . as if they weren't surprised. As General Barton has stated, they haven't transported any new troops across the river into the Crucible; but there was a noticeable increase in deployments there about six months ago. And those troops are still present. There hasn't been any reaction yet to the destruction of the bridge at Chickasaw Bluffs.'

'What?' shouted General Preston. 'You mean they're in cahoots with those cowboys?'

'I didn't say that, General,' responded Smith mildly. 'I have no proof of that. But with a major military action just down river, and with those dirigibles lurking around, the lack of any major troop mobilization seems odd to me.'

'Those bastards!' yelled Preston, clearly convinced of this new theory.

'May I ask a rather controversial question at this point, Mr. Secretary?' said Sir Isaac Pinchon.

'Controversial questions are welcome, Sir Pinchon, as long

as they are controversial in a truly military sense.'

'How the bloody hell did we get into this mess? Why was there no warning of the attack? How did we get caught with our trousers about our ankles?' Mr. Simper smiled serenely, but his face turned white. Mr. Smith continued to stare straight ahead, as if he were thinking of other things. William found this disconcerting, as Mr. Smith's eyes appeared to be locked onto his own.

'Indeed, a very controversial question, Mr. Pinchon,' said the secretary. 'Let us say there were some failures within the intelligence community and leave it at that. You should now expect Mr. Smith's ongoing participation at our sessions, rather than that of Mr. Rand.'

'Might I ask what your government's intentions are at this point?' asked Sir Martin Henschel. 'Your military intentions that is.'

The secretary paused. He examined a sheet of paper that lay in front of him, then mumbled to himself, 'May as well get into it now.' He lifted his head and addressed the entire group. 'I spent a good portion of last evening in the president's company and his position is inflexible. I am quoting his words exactly when I say, "We are to go and get these prodigal counties back into Carolina. Whatever the cost! There will be no nation of West Carolina!" This should surprise no one here.'

'Yes, sir, but how exactly are we to do that?' asked Sir Pinchon. 'If they're snug as a bug behind the great Mississippi, how are we—as you officers so colorfully put it—how are we to *get at them*?'

The secretary thrust his orb-like head forward, widened his eyes in an exaggerated manner, and blurted out with irritation, 'That's what I want you fellas to tell me!'

'Well, right now, our main problem,' said General Preston, 'is getting the rail lines repaired so we can move troops up close. That's why we can't get the 5th into action. But runnin' a close second to that are those damned whirligigs flyin' up and down the river. One of my officers told me yesterday that he had no sooner put a repair party on the bridge outside Chickasaw Bluffs, than one of those things swooped down and circled the town. Last night they bombarded the bridge, and today we're starting all over. There's not a move we make that's not gonna' be seen by those vultures.'

'And what's the count now?' asked the secretary. 'How many are they using for these patrols?'

'Six!' said General Preston. 'Spread fairly even from the Virginia border down to New Orleans and along the gulf coast.'

Hearing this inaccurate statement, William cleared his throat loudly, and then gently corrected the general's figure. 'Actually, sir, they have eight of them. I saw eight of them outside of . . . well, somewhere west of the Mississippi.' He stopped at this point and looked over at Caruthers.

'Well, then there's eight of 'em,' said General Preston loudly, accepting William's input.

'All of the same design and capability?' asked Smith.

'As far as I can tell, sir,' responded William. Smith smiled and nodded.

'The ship involved in the assault on Natchez is likely out of action,' added Colonel Caruthers. 'I understand from Captain Porter that it was severely damaged. Hit by a mortar shell.'

'It blew up?' asked Preston. 'I didn't hear that.'

'No, no, sir,' said Caruthers. 'In the bottom and out the top, before the shell exploded. There's a new one patrolling the Natchez area now—maybe one of the extras the lieutenant just mentioned.'

'Well, I suppose it's possible,' said Preston. 'From what I understand they all look the same. Anyway it doesn't matter, we're gettin' bogged down in the details. They've got plenty to keep an eye on us. And we're gonna have to get them cleared out of the way before we ever mount a river crossing.'

'Oh, so we're going to cross the river?' asked Pinchon smugly.

'I haven't said anything yet,' cried Preston angrily.

'Come now, men,' said the secretary, 'let's not argue. I would like to leave this conference today with a list of military options, not a final plan. The final decision will rest with individuals outside this room.'

'Well, one thing doesn't change,' continued Preston. 'No matter what we try, whether a river crossing, or in through the gulf, or even around through the North, we can't make a move without getting those airships out of the way. That bastard will see us pilin' up our men with plenty of time to get his guns placed. Guess we know why he made such a fuss about building that rail line all down his side of the river. I knew it was a bad idea.'

'Are we sure his position is so impregnable?' asked Sir Henschel. 'Even if they observe our preparations, that doesn't mean they will interpret them properly. A couple of good demonstrations might do the trick. Keep him spread out thin.'

'That's easy for you to say, Commander. Your men are sittin' in those nice big steel ships where no one can scratch you. No, I know they don't look like much, but those whirligigs are a problem. How come we got no whirligigs of our own?' The general received a scowl from the secretary for this comment; General Barton placed his hand on the man's forearm as a gentle warning.

'General Stack,' said the secretary, startling the quartermaster, who had until now stayed quietly outside the fray, 'how are the repairs to the railways progressing?'

'Fine, sir. Just fine. We have work parties assigned to all the major lines—those to Chickasaw Bluffs, Natchez, and New Orleans.'

'How long until they're ready?' asked General Barton.

'Well, I couldn't say exactly. We lost some big bridges inland of the river. I hope to have those four particular lines open in two weeks, maybe three.' The other Carolinian officers rolled their eyes in exasperation, and William thought he could detect a smirk on Mr. Simper's face, though it was difficult to be certain from his angle.

'Please update me daily, General Stack,' said the secretary

'A pleasure, sir,' said Stack, obviously relieved to be so quickly out of the hot seat.

'In writing, if you don't mind,' the secretary added. The quartermaster's smile faded.

'Now what are we going to do about General Preston's whirligigs?' asked the secretary.

'Get some big guns in there and shoot'm down, sir,' said Barton flatly.

'Like you did at Natchez, General?' quipped Pinchon.

'Well, what else do you suggest, Sir Pinchon?' growled the bear-like man. Pinchon shrugged his shoulders.

'What about aeroplanes, sir?' chimed in Admiral Downey, his first contribution to the day's discussion; it elicited no reaction from the others, although he did manage to halt conversation long enough to elaborate. 'Maybe we could drop a bomb on them from above, or maybe toss a grenade onto them. After all, the things are filled with hydrogen. It ought not be too difficult to blow them up.'

Disrespectful grins spread throughout the room. William leaned forward and whispered into Caruthers' ear, the content of his communication clearly disagreeable to the officer. The colonel frowned and shook his head sharply.

'You have an idea, Lieutenant?' asked the secretary, loudly enough to stop all other conversation.

'No, sir, not an idea. Just something worth mentioning, maybe.'

'Yes, go ahead.'

'Out West, wherever I was, one of the dirigibles was being gassed up after the ocean crossing. I tried to set fire to it, sir, by punching a hole in the filling hose.' This statement created mixed reactions. Sir Pinchon rolled his eyes in disbelief. Admiral Downey became irritated at being interrupted. General Preston grinned.

'That was rather a bold move,' said Mr. Simper, 'considering there had been no hostilities up to that point. What were you trying to do, start a war?'

William boiled over instantly; his face became beet red. 'Those monsters assaulted me, sir! That's good enough reason! Seems to me they started the war there and then!'

'Now, now, Lieutenant,' said the secretary, 'please calm yourself.' Caruthers shut his eyes in frustration at the outburst. 'We are aware of your curious experience and understand that your motives were pure. Let's return to the problem you were just speaking of.'

'The point I'm trying to make, sir,' continued William, his face still flushed, 'is that nothing happened. The gas wouldn't burn. I went at it for almost an hour and nothing happened. I've been thinking a lot about that. I'm no scientist, but I was wondering if they might not be using something other than hydrogen.' With this frank admission, the general opinion in the room, which had up to this point regarded William and his story, at best, in a skeptical light, now quickly fell into incredulity.

'Unexplosive hydrogen?' queried the secretary.

'Yes, sir. Something like that. Maybe.'

'Maybe?'

The room became quiet and uncomfortable, all seemed to consider the suggestion ridiculous.

Mr. Smith came to everyone's rescue. 'I believe there may be a rational explanation for the lieutenant's difficulties,' said Mr. Smith. 'The Carolina Intelligence Service owns several tethered reconnaissance balloons. They are intended for use in much the same way as the Prussian dirigibles, although they are obviously much less effective, not being mobile. I have studied them, having a personal interest in aeronautics. Hydrogen is indeed highly flammable and there have been several tragic accidents. But I have heard on numerous occasions that when some mistake should have resulted in an explosion, nothing at all occurred, much like the story the young lieutenant has related to us.

'Although, like the lieutenant, I am no scientist, my understanding of the chemistry is this: hydrogen becomes explosive only when mixed with the correct portion of oxygen from the atmosphere, and if one holds a match to pure hydrogen, the gas will very likely snuff it out. No doubt, Lieutenant, this is the very phenomenon you experienced. If you had only struck your match a bit further away, you might have succeeded in destroying the airship—and probably yourself as well.'

Everyone gazed at Mr. Smith's dissertation with slack jaws. Even the secretary seemed somewhat overwhelmed by it. Mr. Simper broke the silence and added fuel to the fire, 'It is highly unlikely, Lieutenant, that a new substance of the nature your imagination has conjured up would have remained secret up to this very moment. Nor would it be possible to manufacture such miraculous stuff without anyone hearing of it. Let's do move on!'

The surge of criticism that roiled around him, spoken and unspoken, made William regret ever opening his mouth. He eased himself back into his chair and waited for the storm to subside; he vowed to keep his mouth shut as Caruthers had instructed.

'There is another item worth mentioning, Lieutenant,' continued Mr. Smith, unwilling to let William off the hook so easily. 'One of these machines, in the vicinity of Chickasaw Bluffs, after developing some sort of mechanical problem, settled to the ground, caught fire, and exploded. Clearly a result of its buoyant hydrogen.' William's face remained frozen. 'However, I am aware of the facts concerning your remarkable journey to America, Lieutenant, and believe that this experience places you in an unusual position to provide helpful insights. I believe you may be of assistance in removing this awkward menace. Unless you have some ideas for knocking them out of the sky—other than blasting them from the ground or bombing them from above, as others have suggested, I propose we continue this discussion later.'

William hesitated, worried that he would end up embarrassing himself further. But he took the plunge, 'These ships are fragile, Mr. Smith. The ship I stowed on was damaged numerous times during the crossing. I believe the simplest approach is the best. Mount some machine guns on the biggest aeroplanes available and go up and shoot holes in the gas bags until they can't stay up any longer.'

'Do we have aeroplanes with machine guns on them?' asked the secretary, not addressing his question to any one person in particular. Everyone in the room gazed about at his neighbor with a variety of questioning expressions. 'General Stack, are you aware of such machines?'

'No, sir, I'm not,' he responded smugly.

'Well, Lieutenant,' said the secretary, now becoming irritated himself, 'magic gases and machine gun toting aeroplanes. What are you going to come up with next?'

William grew angry. 'Mister Secretary, I mean no disrespect, but underneath each of those airships, in complete view of anyone with a pair of eyes in his head, is an aeroplane of Prussian construction, with a forward mounted automatic gun. I've been on the receiving end of one of those guns. If you don't believe me, all you have to do is send an unarmed aeroplane anywhere near one of those monsters and I'll have my point proved.'

Before the secretary had decided whether to take offense at William's passionate outburst, Mr. Smith interjected, 'Actually, Mr. Secretary, it is not so uncommon for some of our airmen to take a rifle up in their craft. It wouldn't surprise me if this idea hadn't already been tried once or twice to frighten off those occasional craft sent over spying by the Virginian army.'

'Look, all of you!' burst in Pinchon. 'Surely you're not serious about this. Aeroplanes have been shown to be as dependable as one of my daughter's kites. Surely you haven't forgotten what happened to the son of the president of Virginia. You can't seriously consider them a significant weapon. Oh, I grant you they may eventually have some value in reconnaissance, and perhaps we ought to send one or two out West just to show them they can't have everything their way. But seriously, to think of these machines armed with an automatic weapon is ridiculous. Fiddlesticks! Mr. Stack will repair his railroad, General Preston will move his cannons to the river, and we'll send our divisions across. And after we've expended a goodly amount of ordinance, there just might be a few less dirigibles in the sky. Let's do move on!'

This outburst was supported by nods and grunts from Barton, Simper, and Caruthers. Armstrong and Henschel seemed bored by the discussion, and Stack, too afraid to open his mouth. Mr. Smith said nothing. He simply looked at his hands and carefully smoothed one of his fingernails.

'Now, what I am interested in discussing,' began Mr. Simper, not waiting for the secretary to resume, 'is what the deuce these Prussians are up to. Clearly they have very generously supplied several, perhaps up to eight costly airships to the West Carolinians. What else is on the way? Might they send over their not insignificant navy?'

'None of their capital ships have sailed from Heligoland,' said Henschel. 'The North Atlantic is empty.'

'Yes, but what if they *do*, Lord Henschel? What if they *do*?'

'In that case, if Her Majesty instructs me to sink them, I'll sink them.'

'And how do you suppose they're paying for all this material assistance,' asked Stack rhetorically. 'Oil! That's how. Stop the oil and you stop the weapons.'

'Indeed, General Stack,' said the secretary, 'an excellent suggestion. Admiral Downey, what's the score on that point?'

The young admiral straightened up and cleared his throat before starting. 'We have records for all ships that departed the gulf coast, destined for Prussia, from before the start of hostilities. Currently, there appear to be no merchant tankers underway in the gulf. We have inspected what little commercial traffic we have come across at sea, but nothing of significance has been commandeered. It seems they were anticipating this.'

'Ah, I see, Admiral,' said the secretary. 'Well, General Stack, nice try.'

'Of course,' added Admiral Downey, 'we will continue to blockade the coast, as you previously instructed, Mr. Secretary.'

'Yes, of course. I hope it is lost on no one that this oil we are discussing in so offhand a manner is of great necessity to ourselves. General Stack, you don't say very much, but you certainly hit the nail on the head at times. Oil, gentlemen, makes the world go round and I haven't seen much spouting up between Charleston and the Mississippi. Nor have I heard of many gushers in Sussex.'

Their discussion continued to wind through various topics in a rambling fashion for the remainder of the morning. From William's perspective there were very few concrete actions agreed upon, and he began to wonder how this group of talkers would ever catch up with the events engulfing them.

Just before noon, the secretary dismissed the participants for a two-hour break. As the group rose to their feet and filed out of the room, Captain Jefferson Porter arrived, climbing the stairs stiffly against the descending rush of officers; it was evident that he still felt the pain of his wounds. He approached General Preston at the head of the stairs and made his apologies for being late.

'A day late and a dollar short, Captain. You seem to be making a habit of it,' commented the general as he descended, not stopping to return the captain's salute. He followed his fellow general officers out into the street and left Captain Porter staring vacantly down the empty stairwell. The captain recovered quickly from this cold reception and stepped into the conference room where he joined William, General Caruthers, and Mr. Smith.

'Ah, Porter,' Caruthers greeted him, 'good to see you. Everything all right?'

'We'll see. They've sacked Storey. Appears I'm next in line for the butcher's block. They're going to keep me waiting around a bit though.'

'Never say die, Captain!' said Caruthers, as he departed the room and bounded down the steps; the announcement of his promotion seemed to have filled him with limitless energy. 'We can't afford to throw good men away right now,' he called back loudly. 'Chin up!'

Captain Porter stood awkwardly in front of Mr. Smith and William. He shook hands with William and commented on his improved appearance, and then extended his hand to Mr. Smith.

'Am I addressing Captain Porter of Fort Natchez?' asked Mr. Smith politely and, after receiving assurances of this fact, continued, 'I'm glad you were able to come. I wasn't sure the general would honor my request, given the circumstances. If it isn't too much trouble, I would like to have a few words with both of you. The lieutenant has been expressing some novel ideas concerning aeroplanes—ideas that are somewhat aligned with my own. And if I am not mistaken, you, Captain, through some of your acquaintances, may be in a position to assist in turning them into reality. Please, gentlemen, let's go for a walk in the sunshine.

Chapter 18

THE TOP

'I must beg to disagree with you, sir,' said Charles Tillock, the secretary of war, with all the sincere respect required of a man addressing the president of Carolina.

'They're not dolts, you know,' said the president sourly. 'They'll realize instantly just what they're in for.'

'Look, sir, they have the ships. They've bragged about ruling the waves for hundreds of years. Well, this little piece of work will require just such tyranny over Poseidon. And if they say *no*, well that could play into our favor as well. We've been looking for an excuse to bring things to a head with them.'

'Yes, of course, but not now!' said the president. 'Do you honestly think we can accomplish this without them?'

'Well, sir,' said Tillock, hesitating momentarily, 'what exactly is *this thing* going to be. I've told my staff we're going in, just as you asked. But you haven't shared your final decision with me yet. Are we going all the way?'

'Absolutely! Down to every last man and Jack! All the way! If we're seen to be weak now, it's all over. Can you imagine what it's going to be like begging for money if it looks like we can't rule our own roost?'

'Indeed, sir, I've not had the pleasure of begging, yet.'

Each man sank into his own thoughts; they settled back into the leather chairs in the study of the president's residence on Lording Street. It was a bit early in the season for logs in the fireplace, but both men were comforted by the crackle. Golden light reflected off the oak paneling that stretched from the carpet to the coffered ceilings above where shadows danced about.

The president's home was a grand house, very ornate in its architecture, too ornate; it looked almost like a wedding cake. Of late, its inward nature had turned entirely masculine. The president was a widower, his wife having died of influenza shortly after the inauguration of his first term. This sudden release from an unpleasant matrimony had marked the end of his association with women entirely. His residential staff was composed entirely of men, and as a result, the secretary of war felt quite comfortable extending their discussions until late in the night. He usually departed after the president had slumped over in his chair.

Tillock was well aware of jealousies this intimacy created, but so far, the cabinet's combined efforts against him had amounted to naught, and the current circumstances were likely to affect his relationship with the president in only a beneficial way. Tillock rubbed his painful shoulders, then took another draught from his glass of bourbon. He let out a pent up sigh. 'The generals are not yet in agreement as to the best way of proceeding,' said Tillock. 'I'm sure this doesn't surprise you.' The president responded with a snort. 'However, they all agree on the need for an immediate thrust, even at partial strength, against the gulf coast. I don't know if you've looked at the maps, sir, but the coast is almost perfectly suited to resist a landing. Those breaker islands extend in one continuous line along its entire length, excepting Galvezton and Corpus Christi. They say it is an absolute necessity to secure a beachhead before the Westerners fortify these two areas. And the British are the only ones capable of pulling it off.'

'Is Henschel aware of this?'

'No, not yet.'

'And what about Downey, what's his view?'

'Oh, his feathers are a bit ruffled, but he knows he can't do it. He's just angling for a sliver of authority over some part of the venture.'

'Well, there's no way he's going to get it. Even if they do go along, they're not going to let anyone but Henschel call the shots.'

'Yes, I agree.' This was followed by a long pause that was

filled with clinking of ice cubes.

'What have you heard from the Virginians?' asked the president.

Tillock was startled at the sudden shift in subject, but replied, 'Pretty quiet. Smith says there isn't any significant activity within their military. His agents have been crawling all over Richmond, Baltimore, Pittsburgh, Cincinnati, and Philadelphia. There's nothing of concern so far.'

'I guess that's all the confirmation we need that they were involved.'

'Smith thinks they were indeed informed of the governor's intentions. However, he believes they weren't aware of Prussia's involvement. He doesn't think they're too happy about that. For the life of me, I can't figure out how Smith gets half his information. He did share with me that the Virginians intend to dramatically increase their aeronautical efforts. Says they're getting ready to build aeroplanes like fanatics to make up for lost time.' The secretary paused to take another sip.

'Yes, well, Taylor losing his son like that didn't do much to encourage things.' Tillock only grunted at the president's explanation. 'How important are these dirigibles? Are they really a factor? Oh, I know half the population's quivering in their boots about them. The papers say they're going to bomb all our cities, turn them all into infernos like New Orleans—quite a good circus stunt. But do they really matter?'

'I'm afraid they do, Mr. President. I'll give you an example. We've spent a week repairing the M&M bridge at Chickasaw Bluffs. Yesterday afternoon one of those ships buzzed over on a scouting patrol, then last night some of the governor's troops swam over and blew it to kingdom come. There's not a thing we can do that's not seen and immediately reported back to the governor.'

'So how the hell are we going to mount a coastal landing?' asked president.

'We have to assume the Westerners have as many agents

over here as we have over there, so regardless of the dirigibles, they're going to know we're coming, one way or another. It's pretty obvious where the gulf landings would occur because of the coastal terrain, so in this case the dirigibles probably don't make a huge difference. But whenever we get ready to cross the river, the dirigibles will make a *big* difference—we could cross the river at any number of points, but no matter where, those dirigibles will spoil the element of surprise.'

Suddenly the two men's conversation was interrupted by a knock at the door. A wedge of light poured in through the opening as a thin, elderly black man in a trim white coat leaned in, 'Excuse me, sir, will you be needing anything else tonight? It's gotten quite late.'

'No, Josiah,' responded the president pleasantly, 'nothing more. Mr. Tillock will see himself out. Thank you. Good night.' The black man bowed ever so slightly and backed out of the room, extinguishing the stream of light.

'Back to the gulf operation, Mr. President. What do you think?'

The man continued to hesitate. He emptied his glass with three loud gulps, his sharp Adam's apple bobbing violently. 'Alright, I'll cable the prime minister tomorrow. I hate doing such touchy work over the telegraph. I wish these moneymen would string a telephone line under the Atlantic, but they're obsessed with oil and motor cars—and with trying to fly up there with the birds. You know what happened to old Ic'rus.'

'Yes, sir, I do indeed. You don't want to go straight to Sir Pinchon for the decision? It would be faster.'

'Absolutely not! I could probably wear that priss down, but it would cost me half the treasury, and then he'd change his mind at the last minute anyway. No, I need the prime minister to support this, probably Her Majesty as well. Then everything should fall into place. The difficulty is, I can't fathom the mood over there right now. It's been ten months since I was over, and the ambassador's been ill for the past six. I'd like to know what the answer's going to be before I ask the question. Tell me, would their Caribbean fleet suffice or will they need to reassign part of the Atlantic fleet?'

'I'm not sure. I can ask Downey. It probably depends on the rest of our plan. If we put all our eggs into this basket, we'll need both.' Tillock could see the president's jaw muscles flex as he gritted his teeth in frustration.

'I'm really looking forward to stringing up that Bible thumping, cattle rustler. Gonna pull the rope myself, out there on the lawn, right over there!' The president gestured over his right shoulder with his thumb. 'That way I can look up from my desk during the day and watch the crows pick at him. I'll have ole' Josiah sell rocks to the tourists for a dollar apiece. I'll get months of enjoyment out of it.'

Tillock's own jaw muscles started to twitch as he listened to this vitriolic tirade. They had crossed into unproductive territory, so he finished his glass and stood up to retire. 'Let me know as soon as you hear back from England,' he said, as he headed toward the door. Then, turning back as he pulled it open, 'Oh, and I'll see if I can't do something about those airships.' The president ignored him as he departed.

As the secretary of war wandered home through the deserted streets of Charleston, he followed an indirect course to clear his head of alcoholic fumes. Eventually he arrived at his elegant row house, on the fashionable street of Garnett Crescent. Waiting for him at the wisteria-covered gate that guarded the path to his front door was a lone figure standing in the shadows.

'Hello, Smith,' said the secretary, 'please, come in.'

The secretary led him through a tall foyer dominated by a set of massive doors, one at each end of the foyer like the gates of some medieval castle, both over ten feet high, both greatly exaggerating the secretary's diminutive form. The secretary maintained a tempestuous relationship with his wife, and on many occasions he had had one of these two doors slammed in his face, the polished knobs coming close to knocking out his teeth, and the brass knocker of the outer door suspended at such a distance above his head that he had no hope of demanding reentry.

Smith stepped across the threshold of the doorway onto a checkered floor of black and white marble and followed the secretary to the sitting room. 'My wife is away, visiting friends in Augusta,' the secretary said, 'so we might as well make use of the good furniture. What would you like?'

'Whiskey, please. It certainly is very nice furniture—I don't believe we've had the opportunity of conversing in this particular room. Mrs. Tillock has some flair.'

'Indeed she does,' grumbled the secretary under his breath. 'You know Rand was executed today.'

'Yes, I heard. What have they done with his body?'

'How should I know? They can drop it in the city dump for all I care. Tough nut though. I didn't think he was going to give up anything till right before the end. How in the world did one of those skulking unionists ever manage to climb to the head of Intelligence. My God! I'm glad I wasn't the one that put him there. I expect you to root out any others who might be lurking about. You must investigate everyone's family background. Their sort is the last thing we need gumming up the works right now. Understand?'

'Yes, sir. Of course, sir.'

The secretary finished pouring himself a bourbon and then took a seat across from Mr. Smith. In the process, a couple of drops of liquor fell from his glass onto the fabric of his chair. 'Damn!' he cried as he jumped up and quickly brushed the drops off. 'So what did you think of today?'

'It went as well as could be expected, I suppose. Difficult to get so many strong personalities working together. Competent men though. They'll come together eventually.'

'I hope so. And I hope they don't take too long doing it.'

'What did you think of that English flier?'

'Ho, ho!' said the secretary as he chuckled. 'That's one touchy son of a bitch. He got mad as hell—reminded me of the time when a hornet got tangled up in my wife's new electric fan. Bold young man though. Can you believe he actually tried to blow them up?' The secretary chuckled again. 'I wish he had succeeded.'

'Did you notice that his nose started bleeding when Simper asked him what he thought he was doing?'

'I didn't,' said the secretary, shaking his head. 'I know how he feels though. I'd sure like to set *Simper's* nose bleeding. How that weasel has managed to survive this long I'll never know.'

'Personally, I prefer him to the subtler sort. At least he's predictable.'

The secretary shrugged his shoulders. 'So why did you have this fellow there—the flier? He kind of unsettled everyone, I thought. You going to turn him loose on the Westerners?' The secretary chuckled again.

'I have been considering it. He's got more experience with aeroplanes than anyone else at this point. He certainly has the proper motivation.' The secretary nodded absently. 'He wants to go back home though. He sent a cable to England over the weekend asking about the health of a sister. I've had the response intercepted.' The secretary raised an eyebrow but didn't comment, distracted by other thoughts. 'I'm not sure what I'm going to tell him.' The secretary seemed not to have heard him.

'Smith, I need to know what's going on over on the other side of the river! I need to know what else Collier has up his sleeves—besides those airships. I just finished with the president and his position is unchanged. If we go in, then that eventually means a coastal invasion. They're all telling me we've got to grab at least one, preferably two, beachheads right away. And that means sending Her Majesty's forces in now. Nobody expects it to be pleasant, but if we're sending those Jacks into the furnace, I want to do it knowingly.'

'Sir, the secession has obviously been in planning for years. The expansion of the railway west of the Mississippi over the past several years has been specifically designed to permit the rapid transport of troops and guns to any part of their current borders. All this talk of industrial expansion was only a half-truth. Look, I have all my people out. But when they get back, all they're going to tell me is that he's ready for us.'

'What about an assassination? At this early stage, it might work. Could one of your fellows pull it off?'

'Maybe, if the governor were to stay in one spot long enough. But keep in mind, sir, right now all he wants is to be left alone. If we try to kill him and fail . . . who knows? We could offend his righteous dignity. He just might come over the river at *us*.'

'You know, that would be just like that crazy son of a bitch. That man really frightens me. Do you suppose he really is a genius?'

'I don't know . . . not in the sense of Leonardo or Alexander. But he certainly does show signs of it.'

'Did you ever get a chance to read that letter he sent to the Pope—that one about Catholicism. They published it in the *Gazette* a few months back. I couldn't understand anything past the first paragraph.'

'Yes. Surprising that such a practical man can find the time to write such esoteric things. It was indeed a bit difficult to follow. Though I have to admit, I lost some sleep for a night or two, thinking about his arguments. A real stumper for the Pope, I expect.'

'Don't do anything yet. Just make the basic preparations should we need to go that way. What about the airships?'

'I've already begun executing plans in that direction. I need more money though.'

'Get in line. Downey says he needs five hundred million for ten of these new battleships. Says he needs them to offset those being built by Pennsylvania. Wants some of these submarine boats too. Five hundred million. Shit!'

'Sir, we should rely on the British navy for now.'

'There's a lot of people who don't like that, want them out completely.'

'Perhaps just getting the troops out would satisfy most of our critics.'

'Perhaps.'

'I certainly don't need five hundred million,' said Smith. 'As much as I would like to have dirigibles of our own, we have neither the time nor the skills to construct such complex machines. I believe we should invest in aeroplanes. They're easily built in large numbers, and they're cheap. Men knowledgeable in aeronautics say that their development is just beginning, that they have a much greater potential than airships.'

'The money is still going to be a problem,' said the secretary. 'Maybe not in the short-term, but the loss of oil revenues is going to be disastrous. It'll probably get everyone whispering about going down to the islands again. They would keep us flush for a while—Security of the Caribbean, you know.'

'Well,' said Smith, 'that would allow us to work our way right down to South America. It appears from reports I've seen that Venezuela is brimming with oil. Would be a nice way to hedge our bets, if things don't go well out West.'

'Lord, if the foreign minister could hear us now. Let's talk about something else. Who's going to make all these aeroplanes of yours?'

'Oh, there are three or four manufacturers that could take it on. No problems there.'

'I guess pilots shouldn't be a problem. For the moment we've got more volunteers flowing in than we know what to do with. It's always like that in the beginning. Nobody realizes what they're in for. Do you agree with this young lieutenant's views on shooting them down?'

'Yes, I think so. It's practical and simple. Everyone in the room today was suffering from great ignorance on the subject.'

'I know, me too. That young lieutenant didn't help much

with some of his crazy stories.'

'Oh, that,' said Smith with a chuckle. 'You should know, sir, this isn't the first time I've heard rumors about a special gas.'

'WHAT?'

Chapter 19

THE OCTOPUS

Mrs. Mariana Smith sank back into her husband's worn armchair. She was exhausted—not from the efforts involved in preparing her husband's dinner, which now sat warming in the oven with the gas turned down low—but from doing nothing at all. Several times during the day she had reached for the telephone only to slam it back onto its hook in tearful frustration. She had even gone so far as to wrap her shawl about her shoulders and tie her bonnet around her head, before she halted at the front door with the knob firmly in her grip; she had been shaking from head to foot from the conflicting emotions within her.

Now she was worn out. She waited quietly for her husband's return. It was late. She knew where he was, but there was not a flicker of her usual irritation. This eccentricity, his only eccentricity, seemed insignificant at the moment. Still, she desperately needed to talk, and he was the only person to whom she could speak. So she waited.

'That poor woman!' she thought, as she closed her eyes. The image of Dorothy Rand running frantically about Charleston, trying to save her husband, probably not learning until late in the day that he had been dead for hours. She was now likely involved in an equally frantic search to retrieve his lifeless body. At every door she would have met with the same cold stares and thinly veiled threats. Mariana hoped that Dorothy didn't knock on the wrong door, attract the attention of the wrong person, one of those who might be unsatisfied with punishing the husband alone, desiring to inflict revenge on anyone remotely connected with the affair. Although it was unlikely Dorothy would come to bodily harm, many wives had ended up in the Abbey for lesser offences.

Mariana had visited that place twice in her life, both times ignoring her husband's warnings, unable to abandon an innocent friend who had been caught up in the intrigue of the moment—a well thought out plan that had blown up in the conspirators' faces. The Abbey was a horrible place. Its exterior was made more terrible by the religious architecture that could never be disguised. Those who had been inside could never forget the faint, shadowy patches left by the many crosses that had been removed when it was converted to a prison many years before. Where once the prayers and hymns of reverence rang out, there were now only the cries of desperation, of hunger, and worse. Edgar would prevent her from doing anything about it, if Dorothy Rand did end up there. He wouldn't have to try very hard though. Everything was too close. She feared for him. It was all becoming very dangerous.

*

Mr. Edgar Smith sat on a stool in a small storage room dimly lit by a lantern hanging on the wall, peering into a glass holding tank lit from above by a red colored bulb. His stomach growled. He leaned forward, slowly, gently, not wanting to frighten the languid creature resting on the other side of the glass. The octopus's edges were indistinct, blending almost perfectly with the surrounding bed of rock and gravel. He concentrated, watching closely for the creature's slight movements; one of its tentacles slithered up the side of the tank and attached itself to the glass. At the same time, the tentacles of Mr. Smith's mind slithered over the many problems that faced him.

The study of this still-mysterious animal was his only indulgence outside the duties of his job in the Carolina Intelligence Service. He maintained a close relationship with many of the zoologists sprinkled around the country, some well-known, others not, who through various means might acquire a living octopus. The creatures never survived for long, having a great distaste for captivity, and on more than one occasion he had raced off by train to Pensacola or Mobile or New Orleans, only to find that the specimen had expired just prior to his arrival. However, when he was successful, he would spend an entire day studying it through the panels of a glass holding tank, usually constructed in dimly lit rooms like this one, hoping to see it move, waiting to see it's color change, and even at times, startling it intentionally to elicit an inky shot of subterfuge.

Mr. Smith couldn't help but draw parallels between himself and the obscure sea creature before him. Neither of them could be considered very striking—he could admit that. Both could be so easily overlooked, so easily underestimated, and so easily discounted. Throughout his career he had slowly, inch-by-inch, wrapped one tentacle at a time around the important levers of government, into its dark crevices, into its secrets, into its corruption. He had always been careful, moving slowly, unnoticed, unfelt. And just like the sea creature, he could change his color; he could change the pattern of his very soul as the complexion of the government shifted with the whims of the populace and with the change of each administration. Whenever a problem arose, whenever some politician with aspirations crossed his path, whenever he needed to understand something that was not clear, he would wrap a tentacle around it, quietly pry it open, then suck the meat out of it. But as much as he admired the octopus, he had grown many more tentacles, virtually unlimited in their number.

Every once in a while he could be surprised though, like that sordid affair between Lassier and the Spanish, or like this unfortunate incident with Rand. Whenever caught in a potentially compromising situation, he could instantly send out a jet of disinformation and rippling currents of confusion that made it all but impossible to follow his tracks. The only problematic aspect of these murky escapes was the unpredictability of their final outcome.

Well, he had a big old clam this time, no doubt about it; there was no chance of a pearl in this one, only tough old meat. There were levers moving of their own volition all over the place: panic, reaction, then more panic. He so needed to quickly identify those levers that still responded to his touch, those that would respond predictably. Unfortunately, his biggest concern now was the man at the top, the president, always emotional, always impulsive, but now acting with the fury of a spoiled child who had lost a toy that had never before been of much concern.

He sensed that even Secretary Tillock could see the danger. The president was becoming too difficult to manage, too difficult to predict. An octopus could deal with oysters and clams and crabs, but not a frantic little clown fish darting here and there.

He left the sea creature in its confinement and departed the zoo through a back gate, his own personal entrance to the aquatics building, and then locked it once outside. Strolling through the city center, through the vacant Memorial Park, and between the great marble pillars of the Independence Gate, Smith noticed a vagrant lying on a bench along one of the pathways radiating from the monument, and so he chose another. After fifteen minutes he reached his home in the quiet neighborhood of Amberly.

His home was a three-story row house at the corner of Victory Avenue and Echo Lane, in part chosen for his wife's desire for a home with many windows. It was not a very large home, but its construction was elegant, in a style commodious with the confident and uproarious years immediately following the country's last successful fight for continued independence. The building had aged though, and the country with it. While both were pleasant places to live, they were showing deep cracks and were balanced on a delicate point of disrepair. If action were taken immediately, all could be redressed with little expense, but if not, the decay would become unstoppable.

The location of their home had been carefully chosen. While it was impossible to avoid completely all of the prying eyes that roamed about the city, none of his immediate neighbors were of the sort to take much notice of his clandestine activities. He was surrounded by families of professionals: lawyers, doctors, and mid-level civic clerks, but by none of those influential in government who might recognize one of his unusual guests. Should they happen to observe someone, or something, that Edgar had not intended, they would not have the capacity to properly interpret it.

One could approach the home, like its owner, from quite different directions. Its grand and public entrance was on Victory Street, and a guest climbed to it by wide stairs edged in curling wrought iron. There was a less formal entrance, less well lit, on Echo Street. Lastly, hidden behind an ivy-covered gate, opening onto the dark alley behind, there was a secret entrance. Each of these doors was utilized by very different types of people and under very different sets of circumstances.

Tonight, Mr. Smith stepped slowly up the grand stairs and through the front door. 'Hello, Love!'

'Edgar!' cried his wife, startled from her sleep in the sitting room. 'Are you back already, from visiting with your creature?'

'Yes, dear,' said Edgar, hanging his head in guilt as he hung his hat. He embraced her. The stiffness in her body told him everything he needed to know. The hope that she had not heard about Rand was indeed misguided. 'I'm glad to find you here.'

'It wasn't easy. But I behaved.'

'Good. Did anyone approach you today?'

'No. Why would they?'

'Just checking. I know that Charles broke down, but I don't know how much he gave up. Or whom.'

'If it had been you, we would already have learned of it, don't you think?'

'Probably, but you can never tell for sure. Stay away from Dorothy. I mean it. If she shows up here, don't answer the door. Call me instead.'

'Yes, Edgar, if you insist. Now come into the kitchen and

eat your dinner. I hope it hasn't dried out in the oven by now.'

His wife peeled off his coat, threw it over a chair to one side, and pushed him into his seat. She continued to hover over him as she set his place and finished preparing his meal. Once he began to eat, she took a seat next to him. They talked quietly, he between mouthfuls.

'What does this mean? Are you taking over his position?'

'Yes, I suppose. Nothing formal yet. I had a conversation with Tillock, though. I expect I'll be appointed.'

'That's good! Isn't it?'

'Yes, it's good—and bad—and dangerous. I wasn't prepared for it yet. I get uncomfortable when something this dramatic happens and I wasn't the cause. Rand was too impatient. He took foolish risks.'

'I know. You've said so before. But what's going to happen now? Does this secession make things worse? I suppose it must.'

'I don't know. I haven't made up my mind about that yet. Our biggest difficulty has been inertia. It's hard to change things when everything's stuck in the mud, nothing moving, the minions content. But now . . . now that things are really shifting, opportunities should present themselves. Great change might be possible in a way that it hasn't been for decades. If only I can get rid of all this foreign influence. That's the cancer now. First the British, now the Prussians.'

'Take today, for example. God has placed before me a perfect opportunity. All I have to do is *nothing*, and I'll be sending several divisions of brave young Brits to their death. If I actually try to move it along, say with a few choice intelligence reports, I'm sure I could double or even triple the number. That would just about finish the alliance with Britain. I'm not sure I can live with that though. Love, what if I'm not strong enough to do the things I must? Is union worth the price of so much innocent blood on my hands? Is it?'

'Shhh,' said his wife, putting her finger against his lips. 'Quiet, dear. You will know what to do when the time comes. God

will help you with your decision. For now, just be careful. I know I don't have to say it, but please, dearest, be careful. As you say, there will be many opportunities. Don't rush at the first.' Mariana wrapped her arms around her husband from behind and gave him a gentle kiss on the cheek. He patted her arm and let out a long, deep sigh.

Chapter 20

A HARD PLACE

Sir Isaac Pinchon's home gave him much joy. It had been designed for him by one of the great London architects and had been constructed by the best builder in Charleston. The house was very large, in fact the largest in the city. Sir Isaac beamed with joy every time he overheard it referred to as *The Mansion* because, up to the time of its construction, that had been the informal name applied to the Lording Street residence of the Carolinian president. Sir Pinchon was overcome with pleasure whenever he experienced, first hand, the president's irritation at this shift in architectural preeminence. The house made a statement; it said that Sir Isaac Pinchon was no temporary flash in the pan; it said Sir Isaac Pinchon was here to stay—like it or not. He enjoyed being in his house so much that he would often conduct military business from its library, where audacious dialogues would be conducted between the muffled walls of colorfully bound and neatly organized volumes of military history: *Alexander's Genius* in two volumes, *The Norman Conquest* in three, *Caesar's Triumphs* in four, and *The Campaigns of Corbette* in seven.

Today, however, Sir Isaac Pinchon did not beam with joy. He was unshaven, his uniform was uncharacteristically disheveled, and his tie was pulled loose about his collar. He slouched in his armchair of red velvet, at the head of his long mahogany table; he was surrounded by his military staff: Admiral Sir Martin Henschel, Mr. William Simper, General Caruthers—newly minted—and several others, including General Horatio Crump, commander of the Fifth and Eighth Marine Brigades based in Charleston, and the aging commander of the British Seventh Army, General Clarence Abercrombie. All of them were seated in various postures—Sir Pinchon's rumpled slouch at one extreme and Sir Henschel's disciplined erectness at the other.

All gazed at a slip of yellow paper resting at the center of the vast and polished surface of the table. The color of the note indicated that the message had been translated from code by the embassy telegraph operator and transferred from the embassy to the mahogany table by Sir Pinchon's personal secretary. The note contained a simple message of two lines—but such deadly simple lines, as simple as the lines that define the shape of a dagger.

Sir Isaac sat up, snatched the note from the table, and read it out loud for a second time to his spellbound audience.

HM AND PM APPROVE NAVAL SUPPORT
FOR OPERATION PROPOSED PRESIDENT
CAR.
GOOD LUCK.
WAR MINISTRY COMMUNICATION
341222.

'Any questions?' he growled, as he dropped the note back onto the table.

General Caruthers had been sitting quietly all this time. He had been savoring the odor that rose from the new epaulettes, purchased the day before at Willoughby's on Fifth Street. But the reading of the war ministry's cable upset him; he wasn't exactly certain why. It seemed to come from something other than the pure military challenge it represented; there was something else lurking there, buried deep down in it, something personal. His scalp tingled, as it had so often before when he was poised on a seemingly quiet battlefield just before violence erupted; he had that special sense. Also, he had had the sneaking suspicion, from the start of their discussion, that everybody was averting their eyes from him. At first he thought this standoffish behavior was due entirely to his junior rank and to his relative newness to the commanding general's staff, but now he was not so sure.

It had been his great pleasure to join the general staff of Great Britain's North American Forces the day before; it had been a rosy dawn. He had been pulled to the full height of his career aspirations when he had least expected it. The only downside to his promotion would be his continued posting in America. Still, once this little ruckus was put to bed, he could easily arrange a posting back home.

When he arrived at Sir Pinchon's home that morning, he had not really known what to expect but resolved to keep his head down. The new General Caruthers intended to thoroughly reconnoiter the field before advancing any unsolicited opinions into this rabid group. They had a bad reputation. He knew of more than one general officer who had been ejected from their midst for proposing controversial opinions and then sent back to England, there to be forever blacklisted. Rumor had it that Sir Pinchon did not like to be disagreed with, that he would start his war councils with words that encouraged the candor of his staff and then trounce the first man to do so.

'What exactly is it that we are to do in support of the president?' asked General Clarence Abercrombie.

'First, we're going to flatten Galvezton,' responded Sir Pinchon, 'then we're to land a small expeditionary force to hold a beachhead. Then, we'll land another three divisions as soon as they can be made ready for a move on Buffalo.'

'When?' asked Sir Henschel.

'In a week!' Each officer in the room sat up in his chair and opened his mouth. 'Not the whole thing, mind you—just the first bit.'

'And how many men are to make up this *small force*?' asked General Crump.

'Whatever we can scrape together—the brigade in Pensacola and any loose regiments along the coast. It might make a division when all is said and done.'

'Is there intelligence on what we're likely to run into? Men and guns?' asked General Caruthers, not wanting to seem shy.

'We've been promised a thorough intelligence briefing by the Carolinians in a day or two,' said Pinchon. 'But I think it safe to assume that our landing will be contested by sizable amounts of both. There aren't an infinite number of places suitable for amphibious assault—Galvezton, Corpus Christi, a few others. Strategically though, Galvezton would be the obvious choice from our perspective—and theirs.'

'What about the Carolinians? Are they going to be sticking their heads in the lion's mouth along with us?' asked General Crump.

'The Carolinians are in the early stages of planning an assault across the Mississippi. They, of course, have a bit more time on their hands because they can choose to cross any place they like along its entire length. If the West Carolinians fortify one spot, the crossing can be moved to another. While we, on the other hand, have no such luxury and must move quickly before those few assailable points along the coast become too heavily fortified. Anyone with half a brain can figure out where we're likely to land. If we were to disembark a force on the coastal islands, it would be blown to hell before it ever got organized. No, it must be Galvezton and Corpus Christi.'

General Caruthers' discomfort continued to grow. This was a difficult and delicate operation. He wondered which of these men would become responsible for leading such a hasty and suicidal assault. General Crump would seem the likely candidate, he being responsible for Her Majesty's marines in North America and this type of assault being ostensibly a marine affair. But Crump's men were strung out along the Atlantic coast and would require much more than a week for transport to the gulf coast. Those forces would, by necessity, be available only for the larger assault that was to come later.

'What are your instructions, sir?' asked Henschel calmly.

'Ah, Henschel,' said Sir Isaac with an ingratiating smile. He seemed pleasantly surprised by the naval commander's uncomplaining acceptance of their assignment. 'What do you need to accomplish this truffle of an operation?'

'Could you provide greater detail on the number of troops to be landed? And any intelligence on shore batteries and enemy naval forces?'

'We will transport to Pensacola by ship or rail, whichever happens to be quickest, the Twenty-Second Army Regiment in Tallahassee and the Nineteenth Marine Regiment in Mobile. The Fourth Infantry Regiment is already there, and the Eighth Brigade is on its way from Augusta as we speak. That's about seven thousand men.

'There will be a large mass of West Carolinians to receive us. Mr. Simper estimates fourteen thousand troops—those of the former Carolinian Eighth Army based in Buffalo. I'm sure they are already digging in somewhere between there and Galvezton. I do not expect that they will all be deployed around Galvezton to contest the landing.

'You ask about shore batteries, Sir Henschel. Lots of them! Everywhere! All about Galvezton Bay. Some in permanent installations, most behind temporary field works that are building as we speak.'

'And naval forces?' Henschel reminded him.

'Not much to speak of; most of the Carolinian fleet was safely tucked into Pensacola when all this started. The West Carolinians have grabbed hold of a few destroyers, and maybe a cruiser anchored in Galvezton Bay—the old *Ramiles*, I believe. You should have no difficulty dealing with them.'

'And what about the Kaiser's fleet? asked Henschel.

'Ah, what about the Kaiser's navy? Mr. Simper, any word?'

'Oh yes,' said the man, as he sat up in his seat, 'an infinity of words, but not so many ships. Their heavy cruisers are patrolling the North Sea, not far off the Prussian coast, and the battleships are all tied to their slips at Wilhelmshaven. There's not a single capital vessel this side of the Atlantic.'

'Absolutely sure of this, are we?' prodded Sir Isaac.

'Absolutely!'

'What about submarine boats?' asked Sir Henschel.

'What about them?' responded Simper with irritation.

'Where are their submarines?'

'Where they always are. You can't seriously expect submarine boats to sail all the way across the Atlantic—they're tactical vessels.'

'Unlike dirigibles?' queried Sir Isaac.

Simper frowned and sat in silence for a few seconds before responding. 'You can't deploy submarines and other tactical vessels without support ships. And we have seen no sign of support ships—no oilers, no supply ships, nothing.'

'This is true,' said Sir Henschel, coming to Simper's defense. 'I'll begin expanding our search for them down the coast of Central America.' Simper and Sir Isaac nodded, both supporting this course of action.

'What about the airships, sir?' asked one of Henschel's commanders, a question that temporarily halted conversation.

'The president has assured me that the Carolinians will mount aeronautical operations against them, but his view is that the outcome is in no way guaranteed. So we must plan accordingly. What about a night landing, Henschel? It might mask us from prying eyes if the moon is right.'

'Too risky . . . too much confusion, and I'm not sure it's necessary though. They'll know we're coming regardless of those airships. You can't keep an armada under wraps for long.'

'An armada?' cried Mr. Simper.

'Indeed, sir,' responded Henschel, 'the landing and support force will include most of the Caribbean squadron, plus those ships detached from the Atlantic squadron and en route to the gulf—*Resolute*, *Indomitable*, *Ajax*, *Ulysses*, *Swiftsure*, and their escorts. The first phase will likely involve a severe bombardment of the coastal defenses, followed by whatever raids are necessary to incapacitate their ships. Finally, there will be the landing and its ongoing support. Even this limited first stab will be a major operation. Her Majesty said *support*! By God, that's what we'll do!'

Everyone sat stunned by this patriotic explosion until the silence was broken by General Crump. 'Assuming we do secure a beachhead, we'll have to follow on quickly with the rest of our forces. None of my troops in Charleston have been transported to Pensacola yet, and the railways are in utter chaos. No one can make any commitment whatsoever as to when they will be able to begin their transport.'

'Yes, the rails are indeed in a mess,' said Mr. Simper. 'They get worse the closer you get to the river. And right now all rolling stock is occupied transporting the Carolinian troops from the east and the north. However, I'm sure transportation will become available shortly.'

'I can see it all now!' cried the angry general. 'We'll arrive in Pensacola piecemeal, be loaded onto ships piecemeal, landed piecemeal, and get butchered piecemeal.'

'What about overland transport . . . motorcars and motor-trucks?' suggested Sir Henschel.

'Across these roads?' cried Sir Pinchon. 'I don't think so. One good rain and General Crump's men won't reappear until the whole thing is over. Besides, there aren't enough motorcars or motor-trucks in existence to handle one tenth of General Crump's men. I will have a word with Tillock and that man, Stack. I'll not agree to launch the invasion until they've sorted out our transportation. Will that satisfy you, General?' General Crump nodded quietly, but with a frown.

'What about artillery?' asked General Abercrombie. 'I say, what about artillery! We don't have much, and we're going to need it.'

'We will have more than enough firepower on our ships,' said Sir Henschel defensively. 'What more do you want?'

'Bollocks!' cried General Abercrombie. 'I'm talking about field artillery. You naval chaps do all right pulverizing shore defenses, but you're not so good at placing shots inland along a line of enemy infantry. We'll need artillery, and there ain't none handy. What are you going to do about that, Sir Isaac?'

'You raise an excellent point, General,' said Sir Pinchon, a vicious smile forming on his face—a smile reflected on Mr. Simper's face. 'If you say we need artillery, then we'll *have* to have it. Our Carolinian comrades must spare some of theirs. I've been looking for a way to involve them in this little caper. I believe a cooperative effort is just what is needed to tighten up relations with our cousins.'

'Cousins?' growled General Abercrombie. 'Bah!'

Caruthers had never met General Abercrombie before, but he had heard of him. Drooping eyelids and sagging jowls gave the general the appearance of an old hound dog. His jaundiced eyes were bloodshot, and the milky haze that coated them made him seem more ancient than he actually was. At this point in their acquaintance Caruthers was having difficulty associating the geriatric appearance of the officer with his reputation for vitriol.

'We wouldn't have our bollocks in such a vice right now if we hadn't acted like sweet cousins thirty years ago,' growled Abercrombie. 'We missed our opportunity. If we had started dictating terms then, we wouldn't be in the position of being dictated to now.'

'I don't believe the Carolinians are dictating to us,' responded Pinchon with an exaggerated expression of concern.

'What do you call that!' cried Abercrombie, jabbing his gnarled finger at the yellow slip of paper that had remained undisturbed at the center of the table. 'This situation is ridiculous. If these bloody Carolinians can't mind their own shop, then they'll need somebody to mind it for them. I said exactly *that* the first time they came begging for help. I told Horlick then—either let the Virginians devour them, or take charge completely. Back then, it would have been as simple as kiss my hand.'

'General Abercrombie,' interrupted Sir Pinchon, 'we are all very aware and in great admiration of the role you played in the earliest days of the Crown's defense of Carolina. And if I had been in your shoes *then*, I would likely have proposed the very same views to London that you did—that we should have gotten a piece of the American pie for Britain. However, we can't cry over spilled milk. What's done is done. We must work with the clay we are given. We must be content with the goodwill we have earned in the Lord's eyes for our part in the eradication of slavery in the new world.'

'Pinchon, you sound like one of the dairymaids on my plantation. That's exactly the kind of thinking that landed us in this situation to begin with. Firstly, as for the slavery thing that everyone feels so smug about, I'm pretty sure that had as much to do with the gold we gave the Carolinians as it did with the troops we lost beating back the Virginians. I'm going to be very clear with you right now, and then I'll shut up. We should take all these troops you're moving about in this silly game of Chinese checkers and annex Carolina to the Crown. Once we've got things thoroughly organized on this side of the Mississippi, we can hop over to the other side and settle with those secessionist cowboys, and once we're done with them, we can do something about those Bible thumpers out West.'

'General Abercrombie!' cried Sir Pinchon, aghast, raising his hands in mock defense, apparently for the benefit of those surrounding him. 'I must insist that you keep these radical views to yourself. The distance between Charleston and London is not so great that we can afford to be bandying such thoughts out loud. You may have reached a point in your career where you feel no need for circumspection, but I most certainly have not!'

'Well, perhaps you should be paying closer attention to the views of your supporters back home, Sir Isaac. Perhaps you should speak with them. I hope you realize I am not alone in my thinking!'

'I have not!' said Sir Pinchon sternly. 'And I *will* not!'

Caruthers listened to this interchange in shocked silence. He suspected that Sir Pinchon's antipathy to General Abercromie's fanciful plan had less to do with international politics than with the fact that Sir Pinchon was Britain's top dog in America at the moment and that he had no intention of rocking that particular boat. The fact that Sir Pinchon was so clearly motivated by career interests disgusted Caruthers. But Sir Clarence Abercrombie's aggressiveness disturbed him. For many years the debate had ebbed and flowed in government as to whether Britain should continue supporting Carolina with troops in the field. The arguments were as old as he was: it was too expensive; the troops could be of better use defending the Crown's other and true possessions; the local inhabitants took offence at the foreign presence. Others took the view that *some* foothold in North America was better than no foothold. It assuaged the nation's embarrassment for having lost Canada to New York so long ago. But it had been many a long year since Caruthers had actually heard someone in power seriously push for an extension of the Crown's sovereignty in America. He had little doubt that Abercrombie was speaking the truth when he said others felt as he did. If that particular faction were to grow powerful, things could quickly become disastrously complicated.

'General Abercrombie,' continued Sir Pinchon, 'despite this outburst of radicalism, your views on field artillery are sound, and you have provided me just the idea I was searching for. I'll have a word with Barton about one of their artillery companies; he owes me a favor or two.' One or two officers grinned at their commander's guile. 'Let's return to the business at hand—the initial invasion of West Carolina. We need to consolidate the leadership for this venture. Does anyone have thoughts on the subject?' At this last request a strange silence settled on the group. Surreptitious glances passed between various officers, together with a smug grin or two.

General Caruthers felt a new wave of tingling spread through him. The blood drained from his face. His hands became cold and clammy, and his feet turned into blocks of ice. His vague concerns had crystallized into certainty. Never in his career had he experienced real fear. Oh yes, there were those startling moments when plans went awry on the battlefield—there is nothing quite so disturbing as being outflanked by the enemy. But he had never experienced the chilling realization that he was being happily fed to the wolves by his own superiors. He wondered what conversations had taken place before his arrival. He had no doubt that he would forever associate the pleasant odor of his epaulettes with political ambush, with that of a perfectly laid trap—of sneaking, dastardly, disgusting intrigue. There was nothing he could do now but move forward. He had already been formally promoted; the announcements had been made; his new commission had been handed to him by Sir Pinchon in a public ceremony at the embassy the day before. It was done. He was done!

So, being the bold, go-right-at-them soldier he was, he intentionally tripped the wire that set the trap. 'And who, may I ask, is going to lead the first landing?'

Sir Pinchon turned toward General Caruthers. He pulled his head back with the noble erectness of a cobra and raised his right eyebrow in a self-righteous display of formality. 'Why, General Caruthers, I thought that *you* might like to receive that honor.'

Chapter 21

THE TRAP

General Caruthers gazed up at the *Gorgon* in utter dismay. The general was a man of the open plain, of the dusty battlefield, of the blood-soaked earth. For him, the sinews of war were exactly that: blood, muscle, and bone. He, for one, preferred to see the faces of the men he was about to attack, and he wondered whether he had somehow, unexpectedly, over the past few years become an anachronism.

As the general stood there, overwhelmed, a dirty vagrant limped by; he was cloaked beneath a long beard and a heavy coat that seemed out of place in the southern heat; the vagrant stopped and asked for spare change from the general. No reaction forthcoming, the vagrant turned to follow the general's gaze and cast his own eyes along the cliff of gray steel that loomed above them. The vagrant nodded silently to himself, as if he empathized with the general, then returned his gaze to the pavement and continued on his way.

The general stood as if frozen in the unnatural shadow; he was a curious sight to the occasional passing sailor. It was difficult to believe that this *thing* had been constructed by the frail hands of man. It seemed more like an inorganic chunk broken from some strange island of steel, some volcanic atoll that flung great bolts of molten metal into the surrounding water, where they then cooled into the ready-made form of this giant seagoing monster. Though the ship rolled ever so slightly with the sea's swell, it was so massive and heavy that it appeared the earth was rolling rather than the *Gorgon* itself.

The tapered barrels of the ship's thirteen-inch guns, one pair per turret, were at the moment being trained at different points of the compass and at different angles of elevation; the hum of the multiple electric motors were clearly audible from where Caruthers stood; he assumed they were being tested by the crew. The simultaneous movement of the entire complement of eight barrels created a bristling disorder that seemed odd in the world's most modern battleship, yet quite befitting a creature of her name. It seemed only natural that this modern day Gorgon would sprout a tussle of cannon barrels, just as the head of its namesake sprouted a twisted nest of squirming snakes. And just like the Gorgons of myth, it was not necessary for the HMS *Gorgon* to discharge its guns in order to terrify. Its first appearance off the coast of Scotland had sent ripples of hysteria through every world power.

The HMS *Gorgon* was the first of a new class of battleship that had made every other type obsolete the moment its keel hit water—a monster in every respect, so daunting that sailors had difficulty referring to it as a *she*. The *Gorgon*'s sister-ships were in various stages of construction: the *Medusa* in acceptance trials off the Scottish coast, the *Stheno* afloat but awaiting her guns, and the *Euryale* still on the stocks. All were destined for Sir Henschel's Atlantic squadron.

General Caruthers was required to climb up the gangway and then descend into this creature. He had been invited aboard by Sir Henschel to discuss the details of the invasion of West Carolina. The *Gorgon* was Sir Henschel's flagship; it had arrived at Pensacola only the week before, and the admiral had experienced an unusual impatience while traveling by rail from Charleston; he had literally bolted across the platform the moment the train stopped at the Pensacola station.

General Caruthers straightened his spine, thrust out his chest, and marched off toward the gangway. He was struck by vertigo as he climbed to the gangway's summit and, for a moment, uncertain about protocol, hesitated in front of a marine who stood watch. But a friendly 'Welcome aboard, sir!' followed by a sharp salute, made him feel a bit more at ease, and he placed a boot squarely on deck.

'Marine, would you direct me to the admiral's quarters.'

'Through them doors there, sir,' said the soldier, nodding

his head backward at the open steel hatch, 'then up the stairs. You'll have to ask again up top.'

The general nodded to the sentry, then ducked through the open hatch. He climbed the indicated stairs but, not knowing quite how far he should climb, stopped at the first landing. He asked himself, if he were an admiral, where would he choose to reside. He decided he would want to be located as close to the front of the ship as possible, so as to see where he was going. Caruthers struck off in that direction, marching through several more hatches, up and down several different ladders and stairs, and snaked his way through a maze of passages. Just as he began to doubt his navigational skills, he suddenly reached a startling dead end. Resting before him was a sight not altogether unfamiliar. It was the butt end of a huge cannon, its breach block open, a gaping black hole exposed to view. Now, this was a sight he could appreciate!

'Excuse me, sir!' said a sailor who had come up behind him. 'Can I help you?'

'Ah yes, Seaman,' said the general, 'I appear to be quite lost. How do I find the admiral?'

The sailor started to laugh but instantly bottled it up. He brought his hand to his mouth and stood in pensive thought—apparently not confident in his ability to direct such a high-ranking visitor, one who had somehow, remarkably, found his way into an armored gun turret. The sailor looked back through the hatch and, confirming that his superior was nowhere around, said, 'Please follow me, sir. I would be happy to show you the way.'

The general followed the sailor, but not before gently caressing the breach of the big gun. He muttered under his breath, 'You've my life in your hands, sweet!'

By a long circuitous path, the general was led back to his starting point and, from there, was brought to the ship's bridge where the sailor politely handed him over to the *Gorgon*'s executive officer. Commander Mark Harrow then led him down a flight of stairs and placed him before a lacquered oak door. The exec knocked and, once he heard steps approaching from within, departed with a smile and a, 'Good day.'

'Welcome, General,' said Sir Henschel as he led Caruthers into his stateroom. 'Glad you made it safe and sound. Please come in. I was about to sit down to tea. So what do you think of her?'

'Quite a beast, sir,' said the general. He gazed about the room, its carpets and paneling of such a luxurious nature that they seemed at odds with the remainder of the ship's hard architecture. The general failed to notice the admiral's surprise and disappointment at the word *beast*.

'Please have a seat, General. I was going over the charts still again, as you can imagine. I look forward to hearing your thoughts. Please sit. I have developed a taste for this cold tea they drink over here, and my steward has promised to obtain a bucket of ice each day for me from our new refrigeration plant. You are just in time to partake, General. Would you prefer it sweetened, as the locals do, or not?' A steward appeared from another room with the aforementioned bucket and quickly filled the officers' requests—the admiral's sweetened, the general's not, both putting their war council on hold until their glasses had been sucked half empty. Then the admiral continued, 'So where do they have you billeted?'

'I've dropped my bags at the Sonnesta, though I'm not sure I'll stay there—lots of mosquitoes, mildew, and leaking pipes.'

'Yes, this isn't quite Blackpool by the sea, is it? I would be honored to provide you room aboard the *Gorgon*. It's no cooler than on land, but the food is better.'

'Thank you, sir, but I'll remain on land for now. I'll be moving over to one of the transports as soon as possible. I don't suppose you can tell me which are mine?'

'Of course, General, let's just step over to the starboard side. I would be happy to point them out.'

The general followed Henschel to a large porthole that

looked out across the expansive harbor. The city of Pensacola, resting on the ship's port side, was completely hidden from view behind the bow of the battleship.

'You see that group of merchant vessels?' asked the admiral, pointing toward the bundle of ships in the distance.

'You mean those with the red bottoms?'

'Oh, no, no, General—down there; down there.'

The general lowered his gaze and eventually located four pudgy ships with sides of flaking gray paint, all streaked with years of rust. 'Oh my,' was his only comment.

'Yes, well, they're not quite North Star liners, but they'll do, General, they'll do. My exec, Mr. Harrow, has inspected them personally. They don't look like much, inside or out, but the mechanicals are in good shape. The captain's cabin on the *Partridge* is actually quite nice; it even has a stern balcony. One could certainly enjoy the delightful ocean breeze from there. I suggest you make it your own. The others are named the *Fox*, the *Penguin*, and the *Weasel*, all merchant ships commandeered by the Carolinian government and on loan to us for the invasion. I dare say the owners won't want them back after we've finished with them.' Henschel chuckled.

'Of course . . . delightful ocean breezes, you say,' muttered Caruthers vacantly, distracted by his thoughts.

'Indeed. Now, how about a look at those charts? I assume by now you are already acquainted with the field of battle?'

'Yes, I've been over the charts made available to me. Your charts seem to be slightly more up-to-date.'

'Sir Isaac has passed these on to me. They have been annotated by that American, Mr. Smith—quite a capable fellow, I would say. As you can see, virtually the entire gulf coast is protected by these barrier islands. They are, of course, not defended. But if troops were landed on them, there is no good way to get across the intervening channel. In such an exposed position, the West Carolinians could just bring up their mainland artillery and pound us to dust.

'Nor, for the same reason, do I wish to get my ships trapped in these damned channels. Therefore, the only way is by direct frontal assault through these large gaps around Galvezton Bay, Corpus Christi, and down here around the border with New Spain. I suppose there might be some decent spots near the Mississippi Delta.'

'Well, it might seem easier to land around the Delta,' said Caruthers, 'but slogging it through this swampland would be impossible. Besides, it's too far from the major cities. Sir Pinchon's plan is to go for the throat—Buffalo and San Antonio. I don't see any other way than that which we've already discussed. Steam right in the front door, come what may.'

'Right!' said the admiral, nodding. 'Let me share my thoughts—all of them subject to your approval, of course. The marine brigade goes into the *Partridge*, the army infantry, including cavalry, into the *Weasel* and the *Fox*, and the Carolinian artillery company into the *Penguin*—roughly two thousand men per ship. By the way, who have you got leading these local artillery chaps?'

'I'm not certain yet. I've put in a request for someone . . . have to wait and see.' Caruthers decided not to elaborate further, and so the admiral carried on.

'We'll land the marine brigade at Galvezton, here. I'm afraid there won't be much of the town left after we've finished with the bombardment, but God willing, the bridge to the mainland will remain intact and lightly defended. If it should inadvertently be destroyed, then we'll have to land you at Tejas City. What do you think of these defensive positions that Mr. Smith has indicated? These red marks depict the new gun emplacements as of two days ago, all the way around the bay.'

'That's quite a fellow they have there in Mr. Smith,' said the general under his breath. 'I've never had this sort of detail at my disposal before a battle. I hope it's correct. It certainly looks right. However, there are so many batteries, it doesn't really matter exactly where they're positioned. Every promontory and embankment seems to have field works and artillery already placed on it. If we are forced to enter the bay and land at Tejas City, we'll be taking fire from every point of the compass.'

'Now remember,' said Sir Henschel, 'much of these defenses will be reduced by my battleships. Have you ever seen a major naval bombardment?' The general indicated that he hadn't. 'It's quite impressive—these big guns all going off at the same time. It's quite remarkable. You never forget your first time. It's a pity you won't be aboard the *Gorgon* to experience it, and I almost pity those boys entrenched around the bay.'

The general had his doubts. 'I hope you're right.'

'Our intention is to transfer approximately half your men into small boats—you probably saw them tied up along the quay. We'll tow them in behind the *Partridge* and the *Weasel*. Once they're within a few hundred yards, they'll be cut loose so they can motor onto the beach under their own power. Then we'll run *Partridge* and *Weasel* right up onto the beach as well.'

'Really?' said the general, surprised. 'By what means do we get out if things don't go well?'

'The *Fox* and the *Penguin* will remain close by. I assume, under the conditions of a retreat, two ships would provide sufficient space for survivors.' The general nodded at this assumption.

The two stood in silence, both pairs of eyes darting back and forth across the charts.

'I say,' said Sir Henschel as he looked over at the general, 'this looks damned difficult. Do you really think you can do it?'

Before the general decided how to answer this awkward question, both men's thoughts were interrupted by the bangs of the *Gorgon*'s small-caliber guns, the four-inch cannons. The two officers jolted upright and spilled their tea. They shot from the admiral's stateroom, down the corridor, and up the stairwell leading to the ship's bridge. There they found Commander Harrow perched on the starboard catwalk; he was peering up into the sky through a pair of binoculars.

'Well, I'll be,' said Lieutenant Harrow. 'Would you look at

that, sir! It's one of those dirigibles. I've been waiting to see one. Wish I had my camera. I'll probably never see one ever again.'

'I don't know if I would go so far as to say that,' said Caruthers. 'I think you might get a belly full before we're done.'

'Oh, I sure hope you're right, sir!'

Caruthers rolled his eyes and gave the man a curious stare. All three officers continued to watch the airship's progress as it made a lazy circle around the bay, the whole time descending, apparently unconcerned by the poorly aimed gunfire from the ships in the harbor. It eventually made a pass directly over the *Gorgon*, the ship's guns falling silent, unable to elevate their muzzles toward a target directly above them. Caruthers got a splendid view of the dirigible's underside as it passed overhead at five hundred feet, a bright red aeroplane slung beneath it in clear view.

After the dirigible completed its pass over them, it headed across town, and now the *Gorgon*'s portside guns opened up and dotted the sky above Pensacola with small black puffs of smoke, none having any apparent effect on the airship, but riddling many rooftops about town with falling bits of shrapnel.

'Would you believe the nerve of those people,' said a fourth voice. All turned to find Admiral Downey standing behind them.

'Ah! Admiral Downey, welcome aboard,' said Sir Henschel. 'Yes, quite vexing isn't it. One would have thought them easier to hit. No doubt, with a little more practice, the Prussians will be encouraged to take more care. Come, let's return to my cabin and continue our discussion.'

Returning to the stateroom, the officers found that their overturned glasses had been refilled, the charts blotted dry, and a new glass procured for the recently arrived Carolinian admiral.

'Admiral Downey, I have just been going over the landing plan with the general here, and I believe our thoughts are aligned. Any news of import?'

'Nothing new,' responded Downey. 'I just want to make sure

you're happy with the transports. They don't look like much, but I promise they are seaworthy. My men have inspected them. Also, I believe the idea we've been discussing, Sir Henschel, just might work.' Admiral Downey turned toward Caruthers to explain. 'Since we're planning on running the *Partridge* and the *Weasel* right up on the beach, we thought we might cut holes in her hull near the bow, a bit above the water line, just prior to landing. That way, General, your men will be able to disembark more quickly, with less exposure than if they were forced to climb down the ship's sides by ropes. What do you think?'

'A rather novel idea,' remarked the general, 'as long as the ships don't sink before we get there.'

'Not to worry, General,' said Admiral Downey with a smile. 'Now, Sir Henschel, about our participation in the coastal invasion—I'm happy to inform you that I can provide whatever assistance you would like from our destroyer fleet. I propose that the *Cheever*, the *Rappahannock*, the *Red*, and the *Arkansas* join your squadron. Use them as you will, either for shore bombardment or pickets. Although, I can't imagine there will be any interference by sea.'

With matters becoming purely naval in nature, General Caruthers stood to take his leave; he desired to spend the rest of his afternoon inspecting the troopships and meeting his new officers. Just as he made for the door, he was stopped by Admiral Downey.

'Oh, General Caruthers, I almost forgot. There is one more thing. I was handed a note for you while up on the bridge just now. It's from the WOC. It appears your request has been granted.'

*

Heinrich peered down into the water below. The surface was still, and the shallow bottom was visible through the transparent layer of blue. Beneath its still surface lay a long, dark shape, a shadow really, its edges indistinct in the mud. It appeared as if it had been buried there since the dawn of time, as if it required some recent storm to sweep away the layers of mud and ooze that had been hiding it. At first glance, Heinrich had taken it for a living form, for a creature, for one of the whales that kept surfacing in his dreaming mind while he slept. But it lay there like a dead thing, perfectly still, inanimate. Now, as he looked at the shape more closely it became obvious to him what it really was. It lacked those gracefully imperfect lines of a giant fish of the deep. And it was too dark, too black, too still. It was not a whale. It was a machine.

Dora Nine circled above the shape and waited patiently for the sun to set. She continued to circle, and circle. Then, just as the red sun dropped onto the horizon, the surface of the water below became disturbed, first by eddies, then by foam, then by an upheaval. The machine grew out of the water's surface until its entire length was exposed to the air, and there its upper deck rocked gently from side to side. It dripped water and was streaked with mud. The surface of the water became calm again while the dirigible continued to circle above.

Heinrich did not speak of his impressions to the men to each side of him, Captain Timmer and Ober Dürr. Had he done so, he might have discovered that their thoughts were not so different from his. Each of them had been existing a thousand feet above the earth's surface for weeks, existing in a machine that seemed nothing less than a mechanical marvel to most of the world. Yet, after their adventures and trials against turbulence, storms, and arms, this existence had become, if not commonplace, at least usual. Gazing down at this black machine of corroding steel, each of them began to consider just where they were, and just what they were doing, and whether they might not be at the mercy of these strange and cold machines, both awesome and grotesque. Heinrich turned his eyes from the scene below and glanced at the men beside him.

The admiral was no longer aboard; the officer had taken up

quarters in Natchitoches from where he directed the operations of the several airships, juggling their routes and their schedules whenever one ship or another became damaged or needed maintenance. The continuous service required by the Carolinians pushed the airships beyond their limits, and at times it seemed there were more of them hiding in their pits than plying about the Carolinian skies. The admiral communicated with his subordinates via the wireless on a regular basis, changing their courses, their altitudes, and their missions. It was from Natchitoches that he had reassigned Dora Nine to patrol duty along the coast. Despite the frenetic nature of these instructions, the captain of Dora Nine seemed relieved that his superior was absent, and the captain was found in the control cabin almost continuously now.

'UB-37 has checked in, Kapitan,' said the wireless officer, leaning into the control cabin. 'Everything is in order. They intend to recharge batteries, refresh their air, and return to the bottom. Shall I send them the message?'

'Yes, transmit.'

Schmitt returned to his wireless cabin, from which he sent a signal to the submarine below:

```
UB37 D09 CONFD SURF FORCE
ASSMBLG PENS STOP
ANTIC DEPARTR TWO DAYS STOP
CONTIN DAWN DUSK
COMM D09 STOP REMAIN CURRENT POS
STOP
```

Once the wireless officer confirmed that this prearranged message had been received and was understood by the commander of UB-37, the captain ordered the dirigible to steer a heading of 210 degrees and to proceed at slow speed. All three officers remained in the control cabin, behind the helmsmen. The sky turned pink as the sun sank.

Thirty minutes later, after cruising only twenty miles, another submarine, UB-21, was spotted, and the entire sequence of sending and receiving messages repeated itself while the dirigible circled. The only difference between this contact and the last was the news that a sailor who had been suffering from appendicitis aboard UB-21 had died.

The dirigible carried on, along the same heading. The sun was swallowed by the sea, and the sky became dark. But again, after cruising for thirty minutes, they approached a flashing white beacon floating below on the dark sea, another surfaced submarine boat, UB-10. They continued on through the night; they approached, then circled, then signaled ten separate submarine boats in all; each had risen from its muddy hole to send and receive news.

UB-35 had sprung several leaks and some of her batteries had been damaged as a result; she had been rushed to sea several weeks prior. UB-30 had had one crewman go mad from the long weeks buried in the gulf mud. He was under sedation in the submarine's infirmary. UB-22 was having problems with one of its new compression engines. Some of the wireless operators had broken from standard signaling protocol, desperate for news of the outside world; one asked Dora Nine's wireless officer whether he had been to America and what it was like; another called him obscene names. For most of them, it had been three weeks since their last visit from the supply ship that darted up from New Spain at intervals; it quickly provisioned them at night, then shot back for cover before dawn. Sitting on the bottom required little fuel though, no ammunition, no torpedoes, only food and water, which Heinrich imagined they must have packed into every cranny and crevice. Their air was refreshed once each night under the cover of darkness.

'How many more?' asked Heinrich.

'This is the last,' said Dürr. 'The boats are where they are supposed to be. All except that one that was never heard from.'

'What next?'

'We head back toward New Orleans, then cruise over Pensacola again, at dawn.'

Heinrich gulped heavily. Dürr noticed. 'Don't worry, Heinrich. If the guns begin to get too close, we'll fly at a higher altitude.'

Dürr's reassurances didn't help him much. They had passed directly over Pensacola's harbor twice now. Both times the great battleship that was docked there had opened fire on them, both times failing to hit Dora Nine. There was some small comfort in the fact that the airship's hydrogen had finally been entirely replaced with helium, but still, the shell bursts that had popped up around them seemed capable of destroying their dirigible, hydrogen or no.

The shocking consequences of their flight over the fortress at Natchez seemed permanently lodged in Heinrich's mind; he thought about it through all his waking hours; he even had bad dreams about it at night. If a lucky mortar shot could pierce the ship, then it was only a matter of time before the battleship's guns did the same, or somebody else's guns. Ever since that night, strange feelings had grabbed hold of him—powerful feelings that he was unable to control.

Heinrich felt trapped inside the airship. At times he was possessed with an intense desire to run and hide, but there was no place to run. He felt powerless to protect himself. He knew he was afraid, but he'd been afraid before; somehow this was different. The panic showed up at the strangest times. Sometimes it struck during meals in the wardroom, and he was forced to leave early, his meal half eaten; he would invent some excuse for returning to his cabin. Sometimes it struck when he was alone wandering through the ship's empty passageways. These feelings seemed to have a mind of their own and he could not predict when or where they would attack. It happened frequently in the early morning hours when he was alone in his small cabin. It was a horrible, suffocating feeling. He thought perhaps he was going mad. He did discover, however, that these feelings seemed to subside whenever he had a direct view outside of Dora Nine. It was as if his fears were themselves afraid of the sunlight.

The sunniest place on the ship was the control cabin where Heinrich was surrounded on all sides by windows; so for most of his waking hours he remained there, no matter how fatigued he became. It was fortunate that the captain and Ober Dürr did not question him about this. He wondered if they had suspicions about the turmoil swirling inside him; he wondered if this horrible feeling of exposure was as visible to others as it felt to him.

He frequently fantasized about being off in his aeroplane where he could be alone with nobody watching him and free to control his course, free to run or to fight, however the mood struck him. He desperately wanted to be in a machine that would respond instantly to his immediate desires—unlike this lumbering tub of an airship; it didn't deserve the name *flying machine*; it was more like a *floating machine*. But thinking of his maneuverable little aeroplane brought its own terror. He wondered if he would ever be able to climb into its cockpit without the nightmare vision of being shot in the face by his own guns. He was indeed trapped. Horribly trapped! There were nightmares in every direction.

Heinrich, again, started to sweat. His breath became short. He curled his hands into fists as he fought to keep control. He fought to keep the others from discovering this secret. His knees went weak. He wanted to hide, to run. He had to distract himself somehow. Despite the fact that he could barely control the tone of his voice, he blurted out, 'So how is all this going to work, Peter? With the submarine boats?'

Dürr looked over to the captain, who, with a shrug of his shoulders, indicated that a certain amount of information would be acceptable. He seemed unconcerned with secrecy at this point.

'The submarine boats are strung out in a line two hundred

miles long, extending from the coast at New Orleans out into the gulf. The Carolinian naval force assembling in Pensacola will set sail soon—perhaps for Galvezton, perhaps further south for New Spain. In either case they'll cross this line. Our Dora simply keeps track of them. Once their course is set, once they approach this line, we determine which ships are carrying the troops and direct the submarine boats to them.'

'What do they need us for though? I thought submarine boats have some device through which they can see the ships on the surface. Can't they sort this out for themselves?'

'No, they can't see far through their periscopes, and to use them they must be close to the surface where they might be seen by enemy warships, and where they must burn fuel to maintain their position. Our field of view is much greater than theirs. It's better if they stay submerged until we know exactly when the targets are nearby. From the air we can make an estimate of the enemy's course and then help the submarine boats concentrate their attack.'

'And how are we supposed to talk to them when they're under water? Our telegraph signals don't go through water.'

'No, you're right, Heinrich. For now we transmit messages to them when they surface at dawn and dusk. Once the enemy ships get ready to sail, we will change their schedule and make them surface at shorter intervals, or at whatever time we want them to surface.'

'You don't seriously think this will work, do you? It seems very complicated.'

'I don't know . . . it does sound a bit like a fantasy. But who would have thought these little boats could have traveled this far. Who would have thought *we* could travel so far. We'll find out soon enough.'

'Maybe they'll sink that great big battleship! Then I would sleep better at night. Then we would be safe.'

'No, no, Heinrich,' said Dürr, whispering now. 'The kapitan told me our orders are to sink troop ships above all else.'

'But why? We should sink the ships with guns—the ones that can kill.'

'Don't you understand, Heinrich? We're supposed to create human carnage—British carnage. And we're supposed to do it out in the gulf, not in port. I think everyone is hoping that the British will then leave America. If they do, it's all over, and we can go home. Look, I'm sure the submarine boats have enough torpedoes to sink lots of ships, the big ones as well. So stop worrying.' Dürr gazed at Heinrich with a concerned look on his face. 'Heinrich, are you alright? You haven't looked right these past few days.'

'Yes, of course . . . I just don't like those big guns. I don't like them shooting up at us.' Heinrich then paused for a moment; he contemplated what Dürr had told him. He desperately wanted someone to talk to, someone who could help him decipher these odd feelings. But he knew he wouldn't be able to explain it properly. No, he must deal with this thing, whatever it was, by himself—like a man. Dürr continued to observe him discreetly. Heinrich looked up and said, 'Do you think this makes us murderers? All those soldiers we're to drown. Will God forgive us?'

This comment caught the captain's attention. 'Leutnant von Gotha, your duty is to follow my orders! You let me worry about God! Is that understood?'

'Yes, sir, Herr Kapitanleutant!' Heinrich turned away. 'Peter, when do we return to Natchitoches?'

'Not for a while—we have enough fuel for another three days. As long as the weather holds, we're fine. I don't get it, Heinrich. I thought you would be relieved to be out here over the ocean. We're hanging from helium now. There has been no sign of aeroplanes, and there certainly won't be any way out here—just a joy ride for you!'

Heinrich glared at Peter and tightened his fists.

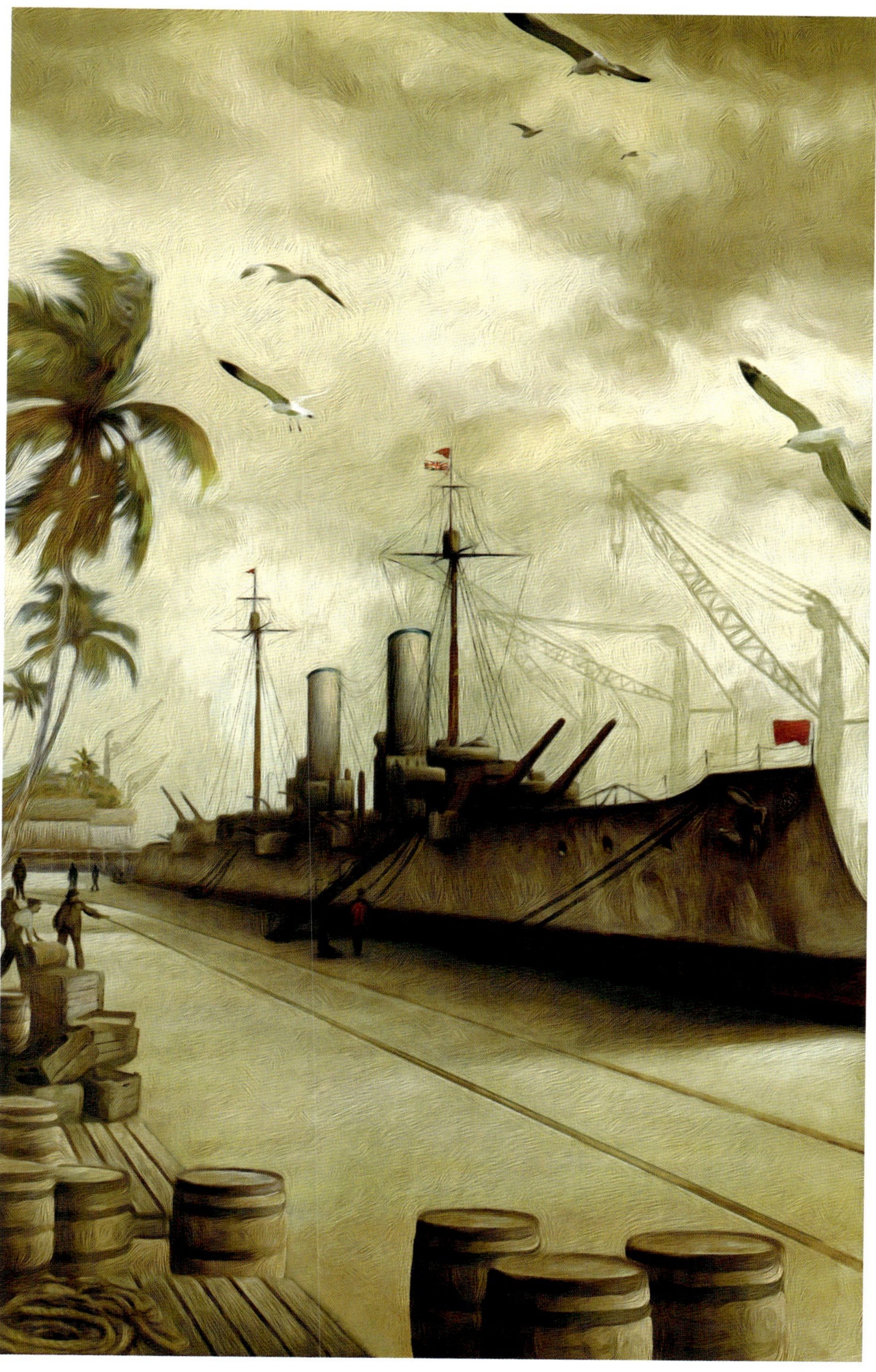

Chapter 22

THE SIBLINGS

William journeyed by motorcar from Charleston. His route took him northwest through the desolate woodlands of the low country and then up into foothills leading to the Appalachian Mountains. Rain began to fall and the steep valleys filled with mist; his progress slowed to a crawl as the road began to twist and turn and as the Humbolt's narrow tires cut into the deepening mud. More than once he had come close to skidding off the side of a steep hill that would have sent him tumbling down into the wild and lonely forests below. But despite his slowing progress, William relished his new-found liberty—finally free from the worry of capture and confinement that had plagued him ever since his departure from Sir Maxim's camp so long ago.

William, also, was free from the incessant probing of the military men in Charleston, both British and Carolinian. Their questions—about Governor Collier's plans, about the Prussians, about the airships, about the location of the gas plant—had been relentless. Eventually he had become irritated with them and refused to cooperate, especially since they seemed to believe only half of what he told them. They, in turn, had become frustrated with him and in the end were only too happy to hand him over to Mr. Smith. He had been conveyed to Mr. Smith's office, located in a nondescript government building in the center of town, and immediately presented with a proposal. If William would accept a mission on behalf of the government of Carolina—a critical mission, a most urgent mission, one perfectly tailored to his skills—then upon its successful conclusion, Mr. Smith would immediately clear the way for his leave home; if not, then William could take his chances with his British superiors and attempt to secure his leave through them. Mr. Smith reminded William that the British were deeply involved here, that they needed every man they could get, and would have little sympathy for his personal plight.

Mr. Smith then shared a startling piece of information that left William contemplating the true nature of his strange benefactor. Mr. Smith informed William that his sister was suffering from scarlet fever, that her condition was serious, but that she was not likely to die.

William had sat stunned for a moment, first by the nature of his sister's malady—the very act of naming it filled him with an overwhelming sense of dread—and secondly by Mr. Smith's proposal; it was not a pleasant choice. His experience with the British army did not leave him hopeful that he would get a better deal with them. Mr. Smith's manner was cool, but not cruel; he seemed intent on some purpose from which he would let nothing divert him, and he indicated that William must make up his mind then and there. If William said *no*, then Mr. Smith would begin searching for another volunteer right away.

William had said *yes*. His mind told him it was the only practical choice, but his heart was filled with misgiving. Mr. Smith showed little emotion. He supplied William a motorcar that through hard use had become prematurely aged; it was dented and rusted, and William suspected that two small perforations in the passenger side door could very easily have been produced by bullets. And of course Mr. Smith provided him the mission.

As the Humbolt chugged through each successive mountain town it seemed to attract more and more attention. William wondered if these people had ever before seen a motorcar—every farmer, every field hand, every man on horseback stopped, stood, and stared. William waved, usually receiving a wave in return, and carried on his way. The fact that the motorcar had become covered by a lumpy coat of mud, with only a small space in the smattered windscreen through which to see, only increased the novelty of his appearance.

Most of the villages were derelict and poverty stricken, consisting of a few tilted shanties huddled around a crossroads or clinging to the outskirts of the towns that were in no better condition for being larger. Each village was populated entirely either by Negroes or by whites, never a mix, and despite the general pervasiveness of poverty in the region, the Negroes were clearly not fairing as well as their white neighbors—but neither failed to look up and wave as he passed. It was with some curiosity at what would befall him that he climbed from his vehicle at one of these crossings after hitting a rut in the road that stopped the Humbolt cold; it was a deep rut, disguised by a pool of muddy water.

William had just begun to inspect the damage when he was approached by an elderly Negro with short, white hair, and a scruffy beard. The man wore a pair of frayed overalls that were rolled up to his shins and his feet were bare. 'Is it busted, mister?' the man inquired, maintaining a safe distance from both man and machine.

'I'm afraid it is,' said William, turning to him with a smile.

'These roads ain't no good for nothin' but a mule,' said the old man.

'Yes, I think you're right. It appears that I've broken something or other. Not much chance I'll find a mechanic out here.'

'Mechanic?' mumbled the man. 'What's that?'

William, amused by the question, gazed at him and chuckled. 'Somebody who knows how to fix a motorcar like this one.'

'Oh, my Lord,' said the old man, concerned, 'they ain't no moto'cars around here, so they can't be no mechanics. What's the matter with it?'

William knelt down and ran his hands along the circumference of the wheel, down into the muddy water. 'Ah yes, the wheel is cracked here at the bottom. I can't drive it like that. I believe I am stuck.'

'Tee-hee-hee,' snickered the fellow, his face becoming a sea of shiny wrinkles, his eyes filled with mirth. He held up his arms and flashed his hands back and forth before William's face, exposing scars and old burns. 'I's a blacksmith. That is once 'pon time. I bet I can fix that old moto-car.' William grinned back and nodded, sharing in the man's friendly mirth.

'I think it might take more than an anvil, my friend. But I am certainly willing to let you try. It's either that, or the mule you spoke of.'

The old man disappeared for half an hour. He returned with a stout rope and an equally stout mule that easily, if reluctantly, pulled the Humbolt out of the rut and towed it a quarter mile further down the road—with occasional rests for grass and berries—to a dilapidated barn smothered in ivy and surrounded by tall weeds. With the vehicle safely out of the rain, the old man, whose name was Arthur, started a fire in his makeshift furnace of loose bricks and stones that rested under a roof of corrugated tin jutting out from the back of the barn. While Arthur was thus occupied, William removed the broken wheel with tools that he carried in a small sack and carefully inspected the damage.

When both had finished these immediate tasks, and while the furnace was heating up, Arthur began examining William with quick and furtive glances; William looked up and inadvertently caught the old man. Arthur averted his eyes in embarrassment.

'What kinda suit is that you got on?' asked Arthur. 'Ain't like t'other army fellas.'

'It's my uniform,' said William, peering down at himself, 'at least what's left of it. I'm a British officer, not Carolinian.' Arthur's eyes widened. He straightened himself up and pressed his large hands across the bib of his overalls, smoothing the material.

'You from England?' he asked, staring at William with his head thrust forward.

'I am.'

'Do you know the Queen?'

'No,' said William with a chuckle, 'I'm sorry, I don't.' At this the man looked crestfallen, but he perked up after a moment. His right hand began to skitter about the front of his overalls; he buttoned and then unbuttoned his pocket in a nervous manner. He reached up and pulled at his beard, only to let his hand drop back to his side. He struggled with himself.

William gave Arthur an encouraging smile—the man clearly had something on his mind—and the smile was just enough to put an end to this strange internal debate. Arthur thrust out his hand, intent on shaking William's. William, astonished by the gesture, took it.

'It was your old King who got us free. I just wanted to shake your hand.' William received a solid pumping—the blacksmith's grip undiminished by his age. The fellow then turned away and attended to his fire.

Working together they mended the cracked wheel; they returned it to a shape that, if not perfectly round, would still permit William to continue his journey. Once the wheel had been mounted on its axle, William handed the man a silver dollar, one of ten he had been given by Mr. Smith, and then departed. William left the blacksmith standing in the road; the old man waved, fading into the deepening gloom of dusk.

*

William parked the Humbolt alongside three others, outside a hotel near the center of the city of Asheville. His bones ached from the vibration of the damaged wheel. He had decided to spend the night in a comfortable bed, after he had a good meal and a pint of ale. He entered the lobby of the Crockett, where he was bathed in welcoming golden light; to the left was the front desk, attended by a slip of a girl in a blue cotton dress, and to the right was a doorway leading to the saloon, from which issued occasional bursts of laughter.

William approached the girl and was greeted politely but coldly, and his brief attempts at conversation were gently rejected. After he received his key and stowed his few belongings in a second floor room, he returned to the saloon for his meal, the hotel restaurant having closed an hour before.

His entrance precipitated a drop in the conversation between the various customers, both travelers and locals. More than one turned on his stool to examine William in a manner that was neither threatening nor welcoming. William took a table along the wall opposite the bar. The barmaid took his order and provided him the large mug of beer that he craved, ice cold. While he sipped, and waited, he listened to the various conversations, all focused on the sketchy news from out West, the information printed in the local paper apparently at odds with that brought by the various travelers.

One old drunk, hunched over the end of the bar, leaned toward William and said, 'You come from out West?'

William shook his head and, after swallowing his first cold mouthful, responded, 'Charleston.'

'This fella over here come from Louisville,' said the drunk, nodding toward the man next to him. 'Says the thing's pretty much over. Westerners knocked down all the bridges, so the whole thing's finished. That what you heard?'

'Well, I hear a lot of things. I couldn't say whether any of them are true,' responded William, taking an immediate dislike to the man.

'Hee-hee,' giggled the drunk, 'that's jis' what I told this fella. What's a book salesman from Louisville know about fightin', anyway.' At this point the traveler from Louisville pushed his stool back, drained the beer from his mug, and walked out of the bar. The glass in the picture frame hanging above William's table rattled from the man's steps reverberating through the wall as he climbed the stairs. 'I don't imagine it makes much difference to you anyway,' continued the drunk.

William ignored him; he didn't want any local boozer spoiling his beer. The man turned to those seated around the bar but continued to comment loudly, 'never seemed to me these

Jacks was worth much. Can't rightly figure out what they're doin' here these days. That old badger Barton'll make'em fight. He won't put up with no prissy ways.' William glanced over at the man, but again held his tongue.

The barmaid brought William his meal. He devoured the food: fried chicken, green beans, and cornbread. The dry bread caught in his throat, requiring frequent slugs of cool beer to clear it. The flavors were strange to him, but the food was hearty and flavorful, not long from the farm.

'Says here in the paper,' said the drunk, again turning toward William, 'all yer friends over in Charleston is bein' redaployed to Pensacola.' This caught William's attention and he looked up from his meal. 'Yeah, that's right! Says all five hundred Jacks of the Twenty-Sixth Fusslers, whatever a Fussler is, is being shipped to Pensacola right away. Guess they're gettin' ready to put you boys to work. Hee-hee.' William frowned at this comment, and his irritation began to swell. It was becoming difficult to ignore the fool. The old man seemed to sense this and quickly added, 'Well, boy, you Jacks ain't the only ones. They're already talkin' about forced enlistments for our boys. Looks like some of you salesmen here better git home real quick and settle your personal affairs, 'fore yir number gits called.'

*

The morning air was clean, and the sky was clear with no signs remaining of the showers from the day before. William's progress remained slow as the paths of drying mud gradually transformed back into roads. The towns and villages that were nestled in the nooks and crannies of the steep hills reminded him of Scotland, not just from a similarity in landscape, but from the way in which the local residents shared space with the land around them. Rocks poked through the grassy surfaces of the hillsides, and the road cut through chasms that exposed plate upon plate of crumbling slate; the rocky layers looked like stony flapjacks. The road weaved between the hills and the rocks. Occasionally a rocky outcrop could be seen hanging precariously over a house or a country store, and William wondered how the people who lived there managed to sleep through the night without fears of being squashed.

By three in the afternoon he had reached his destination, the village of Greeneville, Carolina, resting peacefully on the floor of a wide valley just west of the mountains. The receding peaks were tinted in differing shades of purple. He debated whether to spend the night in town, it already being late in the afternoon, or head straight to his final destination. In the end he chose to carry on.

After receiving well-intentioned but inaccurate directions from a variety of the town's inhabitants, William eventually reached the home of Perry Porter and his sister, Esther. The home was a simple farmhouse of whitewashed wood, located on a tract of grassy farmland between the town and the nearest mountain. When William switched off the Humbolt's motor, solitude washed over him, thick and warm, as the motor's ringing faded from his ears. He then began to notice the rhythmic throbs of the insects in the fields, the chirping of swallows flitting around the oak trees, and the cackles of ravens in the branches up near the top. Other than the animals, there was no motion anywhere, just a blanket of languorous, humid air. William groaned as he climbed from the motorcar. He stretched his aching limbs and looked about at the lush landscape. The afternoon air was so dense that it was difficult to breath.

His noisy arrival had apparently been unnoticed by the Porters. So he mounted the steps of warped gray wood and climbed onto the uneven porch. He knocked on the door, but there was no response, just the heavy throbbing of the insects. After another try he backed away and was about to descend the steps to explore in the back, when he noticed a fluttering of the curtains in the window near the door. He stepped in that direction and was startled as the curtain was yanked back.

Staring at him through the dusty glass was a most unusual face with sunken cheeks and heavy brow; a tussle of dark hair and a shaggy beard surrounded the face and served as an inadequate frame for a pair of black eyes that exhibited such intensity that they caused William to take a step back.

No sooner had William's beating heart begun to recover from the surprise than the curtains dropped back and the face disappeared. He thought he heard a voice bark out something in monosyllables, deep and rumbling. Soon these vague sounds disappeared, and William was again left in the company of the locusts and grasshoppers.

William returned to the window and gently rapped his knuckles on the glass. For a second time, his heart shot in his throat as the curtains were yanked back; he stared into the face of the dark figure, who this time opened his mouth widely and shouted at the top of his voice, 'Cricket!' The strange man then disappeared again.

After a few more minutes of waiting, the front door opened and William was greeted by a young woman, perhaps thirty, with black hair and warm green eyes—smiling eyes. The combined effect was one of both happiness and piercing awareness—an intensity that caused him to easily recognize her as the dark man's sister; however, her expression lacked the crazed look that William had caught in her brother's eyes. She was so astonishingly pretty that William had difficulty catching his already short breath.

'May I help you, sir?' she asked quietly, obviously taken aback by a British soldier knocking on her sitting room window. Before William could answer, she turned away momentarily, distracted by something in the house, and said sternly to someone behind her, 'Quiet, Perry! Just wait in the kitchen.'

As William began to fumble through an introduction, having expected the residents of the house to be forewarned of his visit, a large horse galloped up the lane toward the farmhouse; mounted on top was a gawky adolescent.

'Miss Porter! Miss Porter!' he shouted, while still some distance away. The boy galloped into the yard, stared at the parked motorcar, then glanced at William suspiciously as he trotted up to the porch. 'Here, Miss Perry . . . a telegram from your cousin. I forgot to bring it out last night. I'm sorry!'

'That's alright, Elwood, thank you. It appears that you're just in time.' The gentle compliment made the young man blush momentarily, before he again eyed William. When it appeared that Elwood was not going to depart as swiftly as he had arrived, Miss Perry said, 'Thank you again, Elwood, we'll be fine here. You go on back to Mr. Lawson's.' Elwood nodded, unhappy, and trotted back up the road in the direction from which he had just come, casting several glances back over his shoulder.

Miss Perry opened the envelope. As she scanned its contents, gentle waves of curiosity, confusion, and concern flitted across her face before she looked up and said, 'You must be Lieutenant Hastings,' and then chuckling lightly, 'well, my cousin's telegram did get here in time, just barely.' William grinned in response. 'I'm Esther Porter, Jefferson's cousin. Please come in.' She led him into the sitting room where she offered him a seat on the sofa; she seated herself on the edge of a chair, uncertain where to begin.

'May I see the telegram, Miss Perry? It might help us get started.'

'Oh yes, of course,' she said, slightly flustered, handing it to him. As he read it, she gazed at his face.

'Not very enlightening, I'm afraid,' commented William.

Suddenly, a voice boomed from further back in the house. 'Cricket! Who is that man?' William jumped at the explosive voice.

'Perry, it's a friend of Jefferson's. His name is Lieutenant Hastings. We'll be with you in a moment.' This explanation appeared to be satisfactory, and the booming voice remained silent.

'My brother Perry takes time getting used to strangers.

Perhaps you could tell me a little about yourself before I introduce you to him. The sound of your voice will help.'

William was startled by the request but happily complied, sharing with her a few details about his home and upbringing in England, in a village not so different from Greeneville, and of his service in North Africa. It was when sharing the fact that he was a flier and had mentioned the word aeroplane that her face flushed with emotion. William remained uncertain which emotion in particular he had elicited.

Suddenly, her brother Perry burst into the room. He extended his large hand and clasped William's with such ferocity that it made the blacksmith's handshake seem like that of a child. With soothing words, Miss Porter peeled her brother away from William and coaxed him into the remaining free chair, where he sat rocking back and forth, apparently anxious for the conversation to continue.

'Jefferson knows full well that I don't support Perry's passion for flying machines, so I guess your being here is important and, no doubt, connected with this horrible attack out West.'

'Yes, Miss Porter.'

'Please call me Esther.'

'Yes, Esther. Captain Porter believes your brother might help me with an assignment that I have been given. I've driven from Charleston to discuss it with him.' William's first impression of Perry remained somewhat doubtful.

Unfortunately, Esther read this in an instant and she frowned. 'Perry is a gifted man. Once he has grown accustomed to you, I'm sure your problem will turn out to be nothing.' Then deliberately smoothing her ruffled emotions, she continued, 'Perhaps we can talk about this tomorrow. I believe you'll find you will make better progress after you each get to know one another. Why don't we have dinner? I'll set another plate for you, in the kitchen if you don't mind.'

'Wonderful idea! Dinner!' boomed Perry.

'Yes, wonderful,' added William, with a pleasant smile. As

he caught Esther's reflection in the mirror over the mantel, he noticed that she, too, was smiling.

During the course of their simple meal, fried chicken again, with tomatoes and green beans from the garden, Perry's behavior began to soften. The volume of his voice reduced and his mode of speaking in short bursts lessened.

As the sunlight faded and the room filled with the golden light of an oil-burning lamp, William shared with his hosts the details of his adventure. Its exotic nature helped to overcome Esther's restraint, and he held her spellbound right up to his arrival in Charleston. However, the only word fit to describe Perry's reaction was *rapture*. This seemed to be due more to the details concerning the dirigible than to William's exploits per se.

'I have never seen one,' Perry gasped, 'only photographs in the newspaper.' He jumped up, rushed from the kitchen, and stomped up the stairs. His sister shook her head.

'You're quite an adventurer,' she said. 'Perry is a bit of a local hero himself, though he doesn't know it. But that's nothing compared to all this. It must have been quite frightening. Why on earth did you ever get back in that thing when you had a chance to escape and go back home?'

'Ah,' said William, hesitating in his explanation. 'I was in the middle of the desert; I doubt I could have made it home from there.' William noticed a strange look on Esther's face, as if she didn't believe him.

'I see,' was all she said. 'And what do you think of America?'

'I've not made up my mind yet. It's big and wild and rough, just like in all the books. That part appeals to me. I can't say I've felt all that welcome though. It seems that we, meaning the British army, aren't all that appreciated. I don't mean you, of course. I feel very welcome here.'

'Well, I don't know much about those things. I've never met anyone from England. Jefferson never says much. I like the way you talk though. It's very pretty.'

William raised an eyebrow at this, not quite sure how to react to the word *pretty*. Perry returned and interrupted whatever Esther was going to say next.

'You see,' he said, 'I knew I had a picture. Lookee here.'

Perry laid out an old newspaper, *The Whitfort Gazette*. On page four was a photograph of a Prussian dirigible, moored in Berlin. The local reporter who had written the article had visited the city on his holiday a few years back.

'Yes, they are quite a bag of bolts,' said William.

'And how do they manage lateral control?'

'Lateral control—what's that? Steering?'

'Exactly!' said Perry. 'You know . . . up and down. How do they make it go up and down?'

'Ah,' said William, 'there are vertical and horizontal fins on the back end, like on an aeroplane, and a rudder and an elevator, both controlled from this cabin under the bow. But I gathered that the craft had to be balanced internally as well. There seemed to be a fair amount of water pumped back and forth.'

'Yes, that makes sense,' said Perry, nodding his head. 'How do they manage the buoyancy?'

'I'm not sure,' said William, uncomfortably. 'There are some large, flat valves in the top of each gasbag.'

'Um!'

Perry was not able to ask any further questions. His sister expelled them from the kitchen, Perry to complete a few remaining chores, William to retrieve his bag from the motorcar before being shown his room for the night. Lulled by the breeze that pushed through the curtains of his room, he descended into such a deep sleep that he failed to wake at first light. If he had done so, he might have overheard an interesting conversation between the siblings pertaining to himself.

'So, Perry, what do you think about our lieutenant?' his sister began after filling his chipped cup with coffee.

'A fantastic story.'

'Do you think he's telling the truth?'

'Yes, the mechanical details ring true. He doesn't seem like a liar. He seems to be a serious young man.'

'I think I agree with both your comments. There's a lot hidden in him though—he doesn't say much about himself.'

'He's only been here a few hours, Cricket.'

'I know, I know. But talking with him is like lookin' into the water at the bottom of a well. I can't help but feel there's something broken about him. It's a bit like you and those machines. You take one look at them and you just know there's something wrong there.'

Perry nodded at this, then asked, 'Am I broken?'

'No, of course not, Perry. You're special! Unique!' Her brother smiled at the compliment.

'You do like him though, Cricket? Don't you?' Perry asked with a grin.

'I can't say as yet,' she said quietly, then adding sternly, 'you don't mean in that way do you?'

Her brother laughed at her embarrassment. 'But he is handsome looking?'

'Oh, Perry, stop!' Then after a pause, during which her brother continued to gaze at her with wide, mocking eyes, 'yes, he is handsome, in a way.' Her brother's grin expanded to cover his whole face. 'Stop fooling around, Perry. This is serious. I wish he had never come here. Truly!'

Chapter 23

THE BARN

A rumpled rooster marched triumphantly across the yard and trumpeted the start of a new day. William and Perry burst from the back door of the farmhouse with breakfast still warm in their bellies. The screen door slapped with a crack against its frame, and Perry winced as his sister shouted her disapproval through the kitchen window. William's curiosity was at a high pitch; he had been unable to reconcile his impression of the Porters with what Mr. Smith and their cousin Jefferson had shared with him. The siblings' simple country life seemed at odds with the passions ascribed to Perry by the men in Charleston.

Perry led William along a dirt path that had been so heavily trodden for so many years, by so many generations, that it lay several inches below the grade of the surrounding grass. They walked in single file through a copse of trees, then over a knoll, and headed toward a large tobacco barn that slowly came into view—first its roof, painted green, then its plank siding, charcoal black, and finally, the faded advertisement painted on its side: *Express Tobacco, The Harlan Chew.*

At the knoll's crest William halted and let out a gasp. Stretching out from the barn across the middle of a scraggly tobacco field was a narrow swath of low-cut grassland. William instantly recognized it as a landing strip, albeit much narrower than the fields on which he had learned to fly back in England. Then William's attention was caught by something that gave him an inkling of the true depth of Perry's aeronautical passion. There, resting on the grass next to the barn, tied down with what might have been some of his sister's clothesline, was an aeroplane.

William sprinted to catch up with Perry, who had not waited for him and was now nearing the barn. William whipped past him and raced toward the machine; he circled it as he caught his breath; he inspected its construction and ran his fingers over its surfaces.

It was of an older configuration, a biplane with its engine and propeller behind the wings—a pusher instead of a puller. A pod extended from its front and had an opening for a pilot and a small space for a passenger; the pod's shape reminded William of a giant baby shoe. Mounted on the rear of the pod was the motor; William counted eight cylinders, two banks of four each. Frail trusses of varnished wood extended backward from the wings to which the empennage was attached; everything was braced with copious amounts of wire. At first glance, William found the craft's appearance a bit toy-like, but this in no way dampened his excitement. Back in the African desert he had begun to take flying for granted, but now, with some time away from it, his enthusiasm had revived. He continued to gently run his fingers over the fabric that covered the wings and the pod, and he noticed the many patches and scars that indicated either frequent damage or frequent modification.

'What is it?' asked William, catching his breath.

'What do you mean, *what is it*? It's an aeroplane!' responded Perry, perturbed by the question.

'No, no! What is it called?

'Oh, well,' said Perry, relaxing, 'I suppose it's called a Porter . . . model number three. No, I take that back, model number four.' William grinned at Perry. Captain Porter had clearly not communicated all that he could have about his cousin.

'A Porter,' William repeated with satisfaction, 'Wonderful! How fast is it?'

'In level flight it will go at seventy-two.' But Perry frowned after he said this. 'I suppose the European machines are faster.'

'Yes, a bit. It's respectable though.'

'Come on. I'll show you the barn.'

As strange as his introduction to the Porter household had been the day before, it could in no way have prepared William for what he found inside the old tobacco barn. Perry unfastened a large padlock with a key he kept in his vest pocket, and after he pulled a clattering chain through two rusted metal clasps bolted to the wood, he threw open the doors like a pirate opening his treasure chest.

'Have you ever been in a tobacco barn?' asked Perry. William indicated he hadn't. 'Well, they are made special, to cure tobacco. You stick fifty leaves on one of these wooden stakes and you hang the stakes up there.' Perry pointed up at the long poles, similar in girth to telegraph poles, mounted horizontally across the barn at intervals of ten feet. Layer upon layer of these poles continued upward through the barn, each layer separated by a vertical distance of about five feet. 'The sheaves are hung there to dry.' And while the pungent aroma of tobacco still hung in the air, it was apparent to William that it had been a long while since this particular barn had been used for curing tobacco.

Perry had constructed layers of flooring, one above the other, through an ingenious and intricate network of planking that skirted the perimeter of the building. A tall gallery remained in the center, open to the very rafters. Chains and pulleys dangled from the heights above to the dirt floor and were obviously used to convey heavy items to the upper levels. The whole thing was constructed like some rural opera hall. And crowded onto each of these floors was a wondrous pile of objects: pieces of motorcars, farm tractors, and aeroplanes. Strewn about were engine parts of all sorts: pistons, engine blocks, and crankshafts. Stacks of every imaginable type of container were piled high: boxes, crates, cages, shelves, bags, and bottles. There were electrical devices too, and wires hung over the wooden cliffs like vines. On the ground level stood various machines: lathes, drills, presses, and welding carts. It seemed to William that Perry, like a modern day Noah, had accumulated two of every kind of machine ever created by man.

The atmosphere was filled with the competing odors of oil,

gasoline, and a hundred other noxious chemicals, all intermingling with the faint odor of tobacco. William's stomach began to churn, partly from excitement and partly from the intensity of the assault on his nostrils. He laughed a deep, wondrous laugh. 'Amazing!'

'Cricket doesn't think so. Come in.'

Perry climbed the makeshift stairs; dust fell from the treads in soft clouds. William followed as Perry spewed a torrent of names and explanations while they wound their way through the mechanical labyrinth, sharp edges catching and snagging William's uniform as he squirmed his way through the dim, tight spaces. As Perry's excitement increased, so did the rate of his speech, and William soon lost track of what the man was saying. It wasn't until they had crept through every level of the barn and had returned to the dirt floor below that Perry seemed to have exhausted himself.

'So what's your problem?' asked Perry. William stared back, confused. 'Last night, you said that you had a problem for me—something you needed help with. What is it?'

'Ah yes,' said William, now understanding. 'I am to shoot down one of those dirigibles!'

Perry's eyes widened and he opened his mouth for a moment before shutting it. William suspected Perry was about to ask, 'What for?' Instead, he asked, 'With what?'

'With bullets, of course.'

Perry thought about this for a minute. 'It's going to take a lot of bullets. I don't suppose they'll like it much either. It'll probably just climb away from you.'

'Yes, that's what I imagine they'll do. And don't forget about that aeroplane I told you about, the one they keep tucked under its belly—it has a machine gun mounted on it. I need something that works fast, so I can get in and get out, quick!'

'You could explode the hydrogen.'

'Yes. But how?'

Perry didn't answer immediately. His eyes glazed over, and

his face went blank as he disappeared into himself. He pulled absently at his lower lip and emitted a curious series of grunts and gurgles from his throat. William waved his hand in front of the man's face to no effect. So William sat down on a bench to one side and waited. For ten minutes he dug in the dirt with a stick, until the word 'Match!' burst out of Perry's mouth with a boom.

William jumped to his feet as Perry dashed away from him, back into the barn where he rummaged around on a workbench. Perry returned with a crazed grin spread across his face. He held up a single wooden match. His eyes began to twitch and blink as they focused on William. 'A match, William! It's so simple!' Perry leaned over and struck it against the rusty block of a disassembled motorcar engine. It flared with a rush, and Perry held it at arm's length as it burned itself out. 'Problem solved!'

William stood there slack jawed. 'I don't understand, Perry.'

'Ah! This match is coated with phosphorus sesquisulfide. If we coat bullets with it, they ought to ignite upon discharge from a gun barrel, and hopefully the flame will last until they make contact with the hydrogen in your target. You might have to get close though.'

Before William had a chance to respond, Perry bolted up the stairs and disappeared into his mechanical jungle. William listened to the sound of drawers opening and drawers shutting, of small items dropping to the floor, of grunts and whispers. After an hour, William became bored; he left the barn and wandered about the Porter farm as the morning sun mounted in the clear blue sky.

It was late morning when William returned to the barn. Poking his head in the doorway he found things unchanged; Perry could be heard rustling about in the spaces above, unseen, still busy with whatever it was that had so totally consumed him. So William puttered around the Porter aeroplane outside;

he climbed in and out of the cockpit a couple of times; he tested the controls and imagined how the craft would feel in flight. Eventually he became bored with this as well; he climbed out and was about to head off in search of Esther, when suddenly a shot rang out. Sprinting back through the barn door, William found Perry standing at the top of the first flight of stairs with a bolt-action hunting rifle in his grip; its barrel was pointed at the dirt floor below. And there on the floor, a few feet from William's boots, flickering in the dirt, was a small flame that lasted for a second or two before fizzling out—a strong odor of sulfur hung in the air.

'See! It works!' cried Perry triumphantly.

Before William could comment, the men were interrupted by Esther's appearance at the doorway. She stared down at the smoking hole in the floor, then up at the rifle in Perry's hand, frowned, and said, 'Lunch!' She turned and retraced her steps without another word.

*

William and Perry finished off the cold fried chicken and split a bottle of milk between them. They spoke little while they ate; each man was consumed with his own thoughts. William stole furtive glances at Esther's back as she worked over the sink; she had been strangely present in his mind all morning. At one point, Esther turned and their eyes met, only for a second, before she turned back to her work. In that brief moment she had glared at him in anger. This upset him, though he wasn't entirely sure why.

William turned back to his own thoughts, began to take a sip of milk, but hesitated, and then lowered his glass.

'Perry, have you ever heard of something called luftgas?' Perry shook his head. 'How about a gas that doesn't burn like hydrogen?' Perry again shook his head, not seeming to hear him, still distracted by his thoughts. Suddenly, Perry rose and rushed from the kitchen. Esther and William looked at one another, puzzled. Once Perry was out of earshot, the young woman took a hesitant step toward William and began to wring her hands.

'Please, Lieutenant, don't get him hurt,' pleaded Esther softly.

Before he realized it, the words 'I promise' popped out of William's mouth. 'Besides, I'm the one more likely to get hurt. Don't worry, I don't intend to take Perry along when I leave.' He gently touched the girl's hand, then rose and followed Perry out of the kitchen.

Once outside, just before Perry had disappeared over the knoll near his barn, William shouted after him and waved, encouraging him to come back. Perry retraced his steps and followed William as he disappeared around the front of the house. There he found William standing by the trunk of the Humbolt. William pulled the latch and the lid popped open; there before them lay an ugly looking machine gun. It was like some scepter of the netherworld; it had a dull sheen and appeared as if it had been carved from a single block of graphite. The thing was so heavy that it had dented the metal floor of the trunk, and it looked as though it might burst through the bottom at any moment.

'Lord!' said Perry. Then, after examining it closely, 'Where's the water jacket?'

'It doesn't have one. It's French. It's an air-cooled Hugo.'

'Got any bullets?'

'Lots'

The gun, though lighter in fact than its water-cooled progenitor, required both men to carry it back to the barn. It was impossible to arrive at their destination without traipsing past the kitchen window, and William glanced up only to see a panicked expression spread across Esther's face as she looked up from her dishes. William turned away.

The two men spent the remainder of the afternoon scraping the heads off every match that Perry could lay his hands on; they crushed the matches carefully with Esther's rolling pin and then mixed the resulting powder with an equal amount of red sulfur from a bottle that Perry kept in an old safe. They then mixed the pungent powder with a goodly amount of casein glue in an old metal bucket.

William emptied the bullets from the canisters and Perry bored small holes into the tips, carefully, one at a time, and filled each with the sloppy paste. The bullets were then placed on an old sheet in the hot sun to dry. Later, the bullets would be reloaded into the canisters in preparation for the test that the two men had devised.

While they waited, Perry led William to another barn, an older and more dilapidated structure, not far beyond the one in which they had been working. This older barn had been Perry's first workshop and was now used for storage; from it they removed several old wing panels, leftovers from Perry's first aeronautical experiments. They placed the first wing panel perpendicular to the ground, lengthwise, with its leading edge buried in the dirt and hammered tobacco stakes into the ground for support. The remaining panels were placed behind this first in a series of parallel layers four feet apart. Planted thus, the panels made a lifelike target for the experiment.

The men mounted the gun on a small stand and positioned the stand so that when the gun was aimed at the target, the bullets would be caught in the plank wall of the old barn. Later, the spent bullets were to be carved from the wood and inspected. Perry brushed aside William's concern about fire, explaining that the sulfur would be expended or worn off well before the bullets reached the barn. Perry did, on second thought, place a bucket of water next to the barn door in case of an emergency.

William attached a canister of the experimental ammunition.

'Who's going to pull the trigger?' asked Perry.

'I'll do the first one,' offered William, to which Perry quickly agreed.

William hunched down, pulled the stock of the gun against

his shoulder, and nudged the trigger. Staccato cracks echoed off the hills around them, sending crows shooting up from the fields. Brilliant yellow sparks shot from the gun's muzzle, and glowing bullets zipped through the air like fireflies from hell. Their target disintegrated in an explosion of wood splinters and tattered fabric. A cloud of dust billowed out of the open barn door behind, the slugs having penetrated the wooden siding, shattering the items stored inside.

The gunshots echoed for a second or two after William removed his finger from the trigger. When the commotion had ceased, and the two men's hearts slowed, they jumped up and rushed toward the wreckage. They shouted in excitement as they ran.

'Damn!' cried Perry, examining the fabric in each of the successive wings, 'Look . . . no scorching . . . it didn't work. The paste must have fallen off immediately after discharge.'

'Why don't we try it again, only closer?' suggested William.

'We can try, but I'm not hopeful.'

The men lugged the gun to a position only fifty yards from their target. They stacked the remnants of shattered wing panels into an unkempt pile before returning to the safe side of the gun. This time Perry took hold and immediately yanked the trigger, sending a stream of flashing bullets all around the countryside; none hit the target.

'Pull gently, Perry. Don't jerk it. Hold the stock to your shoulder and be careful not to rest your cheek on it.'

Perry followed William's instructions and tried again. This time the pile of shattered wing panels again exploded into a cloud of fine fragments, and after the stream of bullets stopped, a couple of wisps of smoke could be seen floating up from the remains.

After a few more seconds, flames erupted from the target, and both men cheered and slapped each other on the back. However, at this particular moment, if an observer had been standing before the muzzle of the gun and was looking back to get a clear view of the expression on each man's face, he would have had a difficult time determining which face first flickered with doubt. Then, turning around, the observer would have noticed orange tongues of flame licking up the side of the distant barn.

The men bolted from behind the gun and raced for the tiny bucket of water. But well before they reached it, a roaring gush of flame shot sideways out the door of the structure. Varnished wood, resin-covered wings, and cans of gasoline fueled the conflagration. Within five minutes the entire structure had turned into an inferno.

Trepidation and guilt hung in the humid Carolina air as both men glanced back at the distant farmhouse. It wasn't long before they saw Esther rushing toward them from the copse of trees. The meek girl had transformed into a demented fury; her black hair was flying, and her face was noticeably flushed. Both men were afraid. Soon they could hear her crying out, 'What have you hellions done!' Perry started to tremble. He then gazed over at a pale William and said, 'That gas you were asking about is called helium.'

*

The blaze eventually subsided, and the three, recognizing there was little they could do other than to let it burn out on its own, returned to the back porch of the house where they could keep an eye on the new barn, lest any stray cinders find a way over to it through the still air. Esther's unbundled hair hung down from her head in disheveled lumps. She refused to speak. The billowing black smoke hung in bunches above the farm.

After sitting there in awkward silence for a while, a soft buzzing sound grew in the afternoon air. At first William attributed it to just another sort of American insect—there seemed to be an unending number of them. But the buzzing continued to grow and grow, well beyond anything that nature could have created. 'It's the fellas,' announced Perry.

Esther stood and turned toward her brother, 'Perry, don't invite them to dinner. I don't have enough food for all of them.'

'Don't worry, Cricket. I'm sure the army feeds them just fine.'

Several aeroplanes came into view above the treetops at the far end of the farm. Even at a distance William could easily determine they were each of the same design; they were of Porter design. Perry pulled Esther off the porch, and brother and sister headed off hand-in-hand toward the airstrip; William followed. By the time they reached the knoll overlooking the tobacco field, all but one of the aeroplanes had landed and were in the process of taxiing toward the barn; the last machine settled onto the earth with a couple of sprightly bounces and then hurried after the others. William counted five aeroplanes in all. They were a mismatched looking bunch of machines. While the overall configuration of each was similar, clearly Porter in nature, they differed one from another much as one snowflake differs from another. The shape of the wings varied slightly, as well as the shape of the cockpit pods. And each was covered with its own distinctive pattern of oil stains and fabric patches.

By the time the brother and sister reached the aircraft, the motors had been switched off, and silence flowed back over the countryside. The first flier to climb from his machine, the leader, pulled off his flying cap and let a toothy grin spread across his face. 'Good afternoon, Miss Esther. Afternoon, Perry.'

'Hello, Cletus,' responded Ester with a smile. 'It's real nice to see you boys again.'

Cletus then glanced back over his shoulder and said, 'What happened to your barn?' Esther rolled her eyes; Perry looked down at his shoes; William smirked. 'We saw the smoke from way over by Whitfort—thought Perry might have crashed a new aeroplane or something.'

'No, no,' said Perry, 'no crashes.'

Perry seemed just about to explain further when his sister interrupted, 'Cletus, this is William. He's here visiting us from Charleston on government business. He's a flier too, from England.'

'Well, I'm real pleased to meet you, Lieutenant. It's just fine to meet another flier.' The toothy grin emerged again as he reached out and shook William's hand. By now the rest of the fliers had come up; Esther and Perry welcomed each man warmly and then introduced each to William.

'How are those modifications working out?' asked Perry.

'They've been working real good, Mr. Perry,' said Cletus. 'I can take my hands off the stick for at least thirty seconds before she wants to flip over. That gives me just enough time to write down some notes in my book. I keep a stack of 'em here in my flying suit. I can fly back over our camp, drop one of these little books down to the fellas on the ground, then go back out flying some more. That way, if it ever comes to it, I can report on troop movements or train movements and things like that. It's way better than those silly hot air balloons.

'Cletus, what makes you think hot air balloons are any sillier than these aeroplanes?' blurted Esther. Cletus let his mouth fall open in mock offense. He glanced back at the smoldering barn again and nodded faintly.

Esther invited them up to the house for a glass of iced tea. And there, William listened to the American fliers talk and joke about their life in the nascent Carolinian air service. Their commander knew little about aeronautics, apparently assigned to his post as punishment for some minor offence or political blunder. But despite his lack of warmth for aeroplanes, he oversaw the regiment with a light hand and let the fliers pursue their passion as freely as the group's limited funds would permit—the source of these funds, William was intrigued to learn, was a drab, taciturn civilian who occasionally visited their camp and seemed to bear a striking resemblance to his own Mr. Smith. At the moment, the fliers were experimenting with the communication of aerial messages from their aircraft down to their camp: hand signals, written messages, signal lights, and so on. Though William was tempted to share the details of his own adventures with them, something held him back; he thought Mr. Smith might not want his mission publicized at this stage. And much to his relief, the fliers seemed to intentionally avoid asking the obvious questions about his presence on the Porter farm.

At one point William was shocked to learn that for fun this rough and tumble group of fliers would cross the river border between Carolina and Virginia and intentionally fly above the heavily fortified towns of Whitfort or Salt Lick; they would bait the soldiers below into firing their rifles at them. More than one of the patches on their aeroplanes had been from a well-placed shot.

'Well, we best be going,' said Cletus after they had finished their tea and spent an hour talking. 'It'll be getting toward dark by the time we get back. We just wanted to make sure you all was alright when we saw the smoke.'

'No need to run off,' said Perry. 'Maybe I should give your machines a quick look. Why don't you boys stay for dinner?'

'Naw, Mr. Perry,' said Cletus, noticing the look in Esther's eyes. 'Thank you, though. That was a fine meal Miss Esther cooked for us last time, but we're expected back at camp tonight. I don't know what Captain Prentice would do if we didn't turn up. Probably shoot himself.' The other fliers laughed.

'Well, come over again when you get a chance. William and I might have a surprise or two for you the next time you stop by.' Cletus raised an eyebrow and nodded; he glanced one last time in the direction of the barn and then turned to his men.

'Ok, boys, let's mount up. We gotta git goin'.' The men rose in unison and followed their chief back to the field. The motors sputtered to life again, and one by one the machines sped down the strip and hopped into the air. Cletus made one low pass, rocking his wings as the Porters waved back, then headed north. As the sound of the aeroplanes faded, and just as he turned to head back up to the house, William noticed a lone soldier standing at the top of the knoll. He seemed strangely familiar, but out of place here in this pastoral setting.

'It's Jefferson,' squealed Esther as she took off at a run. She raced up the hill. When she reached the soldier she crushed him in a big hug. Perry and William came up behind her.

'What happened to the old barn?' Jefferson asked. Esther cast an accusing glance toward her brother and William, but her expression remained bright and happy.

'One of Perry's experiments gone wrong,' she said.

'Actually, Cricket, the experiment was a success,' countered Perry; his sister ignored him. 'Hello, Jefferson, happy to see you.'

'It's so wonderful that you could visit us,' said Esther. 'I was so afraid when I first heard the news about Natchez. I thought you might have been killed. I could never have borne it. But you are hurt, Jefferson! My goodness, look at your hands . . . and your face—you look awful. Come into the house and rest.'

Captain Porter resigned himself to his cousin's care and was gently dragged into the house. William and Perry shot relieved looks at each other. They followed the Carolinian officer into the house. A little while later the three Porters and William were seated at Esther's dining table cutting into tender beefsteaks that Jefferson had brought as a gift. The food and conversation did much to sooth Esther's anger and Perry's guilty conscience.

'So tell me, Jefferson,' said Esther, 'how is it that you could come visit? I thought the army would be keeping you very busy right now.'

Jefferson glanced over at Perry, who seemed to grow slightly panicked at the question. 'We are a bit *behind the news* here, Jefferson. I don't know why Elwood has been so bad at delivering our newspapers lately.' Perry then gave Jefferson an exaggerated wink that Esther, somehow, miraculously, failed to notice.

'Well, Esther,' said Jefferson, 'I must come right out and tell you . . . I have been relieved of my command at Fort Natchez.'

'Oh, Jefferson! No! But why?'

'I'm afraid so. Please don't worry, dear. I was a bit concerned for a while—I thought there was going to be a court martial. But a fellow in the government, a friend, helped to get the proceedings suspended—the same fellow who sent this young man here.' Esther glanced suspiciously, back and forth, at both men. 'I'm being transferred to Pensacola. I'm to help the Brits with a naval operation.'

'I don't like the sound of the word *operation*. What does that mean? Is there going to be more fighting? You men and your fighting!'

'Come now, Esther, everyone will be involved in fighting before long. There is no way around it. I'm a soldier. Soldiers fight.' Esther looked down at her food and wouldn't respond. 'I promise to write you often!'

During the entire course of this conversation William sat mutely staring at the family around him. Strong feelings swelled up inside him; he enjoyed participating in the Porter family's life. It made him think of home. He missed his own sister. He hoped she was all right; he had not received a reply to his telegraph and had only Mr. Smith's word to rely on. As Esther rose and cleared their plates, William's eyes followed her.

The men, in unspoken agreement, had tried to restrict their conversation to innocuous and nonmilitary matters. But on those occasions when Esther returned to the kitchen to prepare more coffee or fruit for their dessert, the captain would furtively ask about the day's activities and about the plans for the next day. Now that Esther was occupied with the dishes, Perry and William shared with the captain the details of their experiments with the machine gun. Perry explained his ideas on how to mount the gun onto the aeroplane. William proposed how he might use it to attack the dirigibles and described his experience of being shot down. They all speculated on how the Prussians had managed to fire a machine gun through the arc of a propeller without destroying it.

'Perry keeps trying to talk me into going up,' said Jefferson. 'I was sorely tempted during my last visit when those fliers came down from the river. They bring their planes down every once in a while for Perry to look over. He suggests improvements, and they make them before they leave. Seems the government doesn't take their efforts too seriously. It's about all they can do to get fuel and their pay. How many are there now, Perry?'

'Not as many as before . . . I'd say maybe half a dozen with enough experience not to get themselves killed and about as many usable machines.' He then added with visible pride, 'They're all my design. The others crashed—the ones made by Hemmel down South.'

'Yes, whenever Perry works up an improved design,' said Jefferson 'this man, Kemper, comes over from Charleston and draws them up on paper. He gives Perry a few coins—a very few coins, I think—and then takes the drawings down to his motorcar factory where his mechanics build a new aeroplane whenever these fliers crack up one of theirs. I'm not certain Perry is getting the best end of the bargain.' Perry waved his hand at his cousin's concern. 'So, Lieutenant, what kind of a bargain have *you* struck with Mr. Smith? I hope it was a good one. What did he promise you?'

'He said that if I could shoot down a dirigible, if I could show everyone it can be done, and if I then show others how to do it, he would arrange my leave home. I really had no choice.'

'Well, I'm in much the same position, if that makes you feel any better. I was asked to choose between a court martial and joining General Caruthers' command in Pensacola.' William stared at the captain in surprise. 'Now I must go get Esther's present.'

By this time Esther's mood had plummeted again; the clink of dishes had grown steadily louder as she tried to block out the men's conversation. Jefferson got up from the table and shouted in to her, 'Esther, dear, I have a present for you.' To

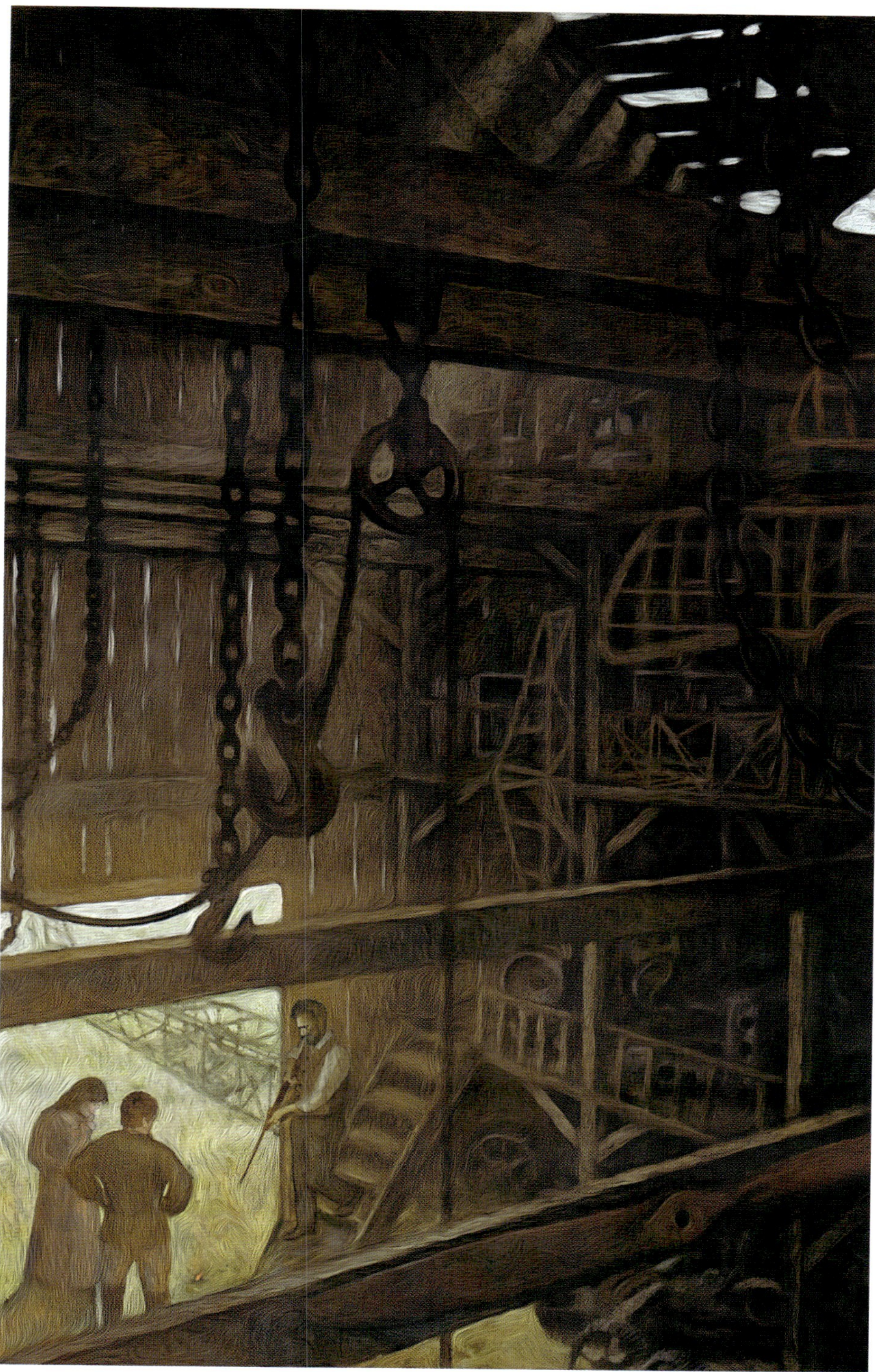

which announcement there was no response other than the clink of more dishes. The captain disappeared out the front door and returned with a large crate that he barely managed to fit through the door.

'Please, Esther, won't you come in and see what I bought for you.'

The three men gathered in the sitting room and waited. A few minutes later she joined them as she dried her hands on a towel, and although she wasn't actually smiling, her frown had certainly faded.

'Alright, Jefferson, what is it?'

Jefferson pulled off the lid, slid his arms into the box, and pulled out a new radio, housed in a polished walnut cabinet, trimmed with gold leaf, and set off with several crystal knobs. An ecstatic wave flashed across Esther's face. 'This is for me? Really?'

'Absolutely, my dear, this will keep you company on those nights when you can't pry Perry out of his barn.'

'Doesn't this need electricity to work?' she asked shrewdly.

'Ah yes, Cricket, it does,' said Perry. 'But I am prepared for that.' He walked out onto the front porch and returned with a heavy metal cube, a battery, which he placed behind the radio and, after fiddling with its wires for a few minutes, stood back and said, 'There!'

Jefferson switched the set on. At first it produced only crackles and pops, as both men twisted the various knobs. 'There's only one station,' said Jefferson, 'the one from Whitfort. But we ought to be just in time for the broadcast.' A second later, a tinny trumpet blared out of the speaker.

'This is Walter Donahugh, over in Whitfort. Welcome to the Donahugh radio broadcast, folks! Well, it's war! This morning the Sovereign State of Carolina and the Commonwealth of Great Britain declared war on Prussia!'

Chapter 24

THE DUEL

Esther, Perry, and Jefferson waved farewell from the platform as the train pulled away from the Asheville railway station. William found himself waving back from a window seat in a second-class car; he was reluctant to leave. A partially disassembled, highly modified Porter, model No. 4, aeroplane was in tow, carefully hidden from view under heavy canvas tarps and lashed to a flatbed railcar that followed along at the very end of the train.

After William's departure, the Porter family remained together just long enough to enjoy lunch in the station's café. Captain Porter experienced a melancholy farewell of his own as he boarded a train departing to the south for Pensacola and the fleet that was gathering there. The two remaining Porters, brother and sister, climbed into Perry's homebuilt motorcar for their journey home. The ride home turned out to be both quiet and a little solemn; the commotion created by the two visiting soldiers had been an unusual and lively event in their somewhat isolated daily routine, and the departures left them both feeling a bit blue. Perry distracted himself by worrying over the implications of the weapon he had just placed in William's eager hands; he eventually decided that he would need to take the matter up with Brother Jack, the town preacher. Esther tried to avoid confronting the strange emotions that had gripped her concerning William. His departure affected her in a confusing and unexpected way; she was eventually forced to admit that her own particular sense of blueness had mighty strong feelings at the bottom of it. As is frequently the case with siblings, each had a pretty good idea what was on the mind of the other, and brother and sister kept glancing over at each other, with care and concern.

*

William's train steamed into the winding mountain passes, through the dark tumbled woods, and then out across the plains of central Carolina. It stopped frequently at quiet rural towns sprinkled across the countryside, and each time it seemed that the number of passengers stepping off was greater than the number stepping on. William's car slowly emptied the further west it traveled.

He had become accustomed to the frequent glances, some surreptitious, others not, of the ever-changing strangers—looking first at his uniform and then at his still scarred hands. He couldn't really blame them for their curiosity; he hadn't encountered a single British soldier since his departure from Charleston, and he realized he must be a rare sight in this region of Carolina. His few attempts at conversation were unsuccessful. The Virginian motorcar dealer heading for home in Nashville looked up from his pamphlets and responded with little more than a grunt; a young mother glanced away when William caught her eye, though her daughter had continued to stare; the train conductor had been the friendliest, but this did not go very far—not beyond a few questions about England and insults flung at the governor of West Carolina.

As William gazed out across the countryside, at the dark summer hues that were changing to autumn russets, he contemplated his situation. He seemed to be always trapped in some machine heading west, heading in the exact opposite direction from that which he wanted. He now debated whether he had made the right choice in accepting Smith's offer. Perhaps he should have run for home; he could have caught passage on a ship and sorted it all out from England. It still wasn't too late, and he could deal with the consequences back home. Surely his mother would know someone who could help—if she were willing.

A child's voice, growling, disturbed William's thoughts; the boy was seated with his mother on the other side of the aisle. He gripped a toy aeroplane shaped much like a Porter and was putting it through its paces, in and out of violent maneuvers, unconcerned with the fact that physics had ruled them impossible. William's eyes followed the gyrations, and a smile formed on his lips. Then the boy, noticing he had secured the attention of the strange man in uniform, suddenly plunged the aeroplane into his mother's lap and announced the craft's destruction with a loud, slobbery crashing noise that left spittle dangling from his mouth. William's smile faded.

*

Lieutenants Burrows and Clark welcomed William on his return to Natchez; they had received a wire from Captain Porter asking them to assist William in any way they could. They arranged for the mysterious railcar to be shuttled onto an empty siding just outside town, two miles to the north, near a wide, open pasture. Then, through much patriotic wrangling and after the application of much Carolina paper, the lieutenants managed to convince the owner of the pasture—a farmer named Druther—to transfer his few underfed horses to the farm of a neighbor and to allow William to operate from the field. It was, perhaps, not the most ideal location for an airfield as the nearest automobile garage was a long walk into town, but its surface was flat and the grass was evenly clipped. So far, their only onlookers had been two grimy urchins from another nearby farm.

'Will you really be able to operate both the machine gun and the aeroplane at the same time?' asked Clark while leaning down into the cockpit and tugging on the bolt of the gun; the bolt failed to move so much as an inch.

'Oh yes, that was the whole purpose of Porter's efforts. By securing the gun on this fixed mount beneath the cockpit, all I have to do is point the aeroplane in the correct direction and pull the trigger. If the gun should jam, the breach is close enough, right here between my feet, for me to clear it. Reloading should be straightforward as well.' Both officers looked a little skeptical, but remained enthused.

'There's not much room for a passenger,' said Clark.

'Actually, there is *no* room. Don't let the extra seat deceive you; the machine couldn't handle the weight,' said William—the lieutenant looked crestfallen. 'It took a fair bit of time to align the gun, so I don't want to remove it right now. But if we succeed, I'll take you both up in the machine afterwards.' This promise energized the two lieutenants to such a degree that they started off on a new tour around the aeroplane, each pointing out interesting and before unnoticed aspects of the craft.

'When do you take off?' asked Burrows.

William stood up and frowned; it was a very good question. The airframe had been assembled, the rigging had been measured and re-measured, the engine and propeller had been carefully inspected, and the controls had been tested; all that remained was a test flight to ensure the handling was correct. William looked about him, held his arms outward as if attempting to divine the answer to the lieutenant's question—in fact feeling for the direction of the wind—then quickly scanned the sky above. 'I'll take her up for a bit right now.' His new squires beamed with enthusiasm.

William strapped himself into the cockpit after lecturing the lieutenants on the proper procedure for starting the engine; this was one of the trickier aspects of the Porter. The individual was required to do this while standing inside the tight space formed by the wooden trusses and wire bracing of the aeroplane's tail section, like a lion tamer locked in a cage with his beast. The two farm boys who had been hanging about on the distant fence, now aware that their patience was about to be rewarded, began to jump up and down. 'Are you going to go up in the flying machine, mister? Can we come along? I sure hope you don't crash! Ole' Druther's gonna get real mad if you smash up his fence!'

The two lieutenants argued briefly about who got the honor of starting the motor, eventually agreeing by some invisible means that it would be Lieutenant Clark. Clark slid under the rear frame of the aircraft and then stood in the position that William had indicated in his instructions. He gripped the prop with both hands, planted his feet firmly a few inches behind, and leaned backwards so that his weight would naturally cause him to fall away from the deadly disk. William primed the engine; the odor of gasoline seeped from the exhaust.

'Hot!' shouted William.

Clark gave Burrows a nervous smile, gritted his teeth, and pulled on the prop. The engine burst to life, and the propeller spun up like a buzz saw. Startled by the little motor's fury, Clark fell back against the tail-plane and momentarily tipped the machine to one side. William glanced over his shoulder and shook his head with a grin while Clark carefully disentangled himself.

After letting the motor warm for a moment, William nodded, and Clark and Burrows each tugged on a chock. The Porter lurched forward, and they sprinted to keep up, holding the wingtips in order to help William steer as he built up speed. After a few short paces they were forced to let go, panting, and the biplane jumped up into the air like a huge and angry wasp. The machine fled, climbing, to the further end of the pasture, then made a steep turn to the right and headed back toward its starting point; it began to descend, its motor whining as it built up speed; the machine whizzed past the lieutenants, only ten feet above their heads. Both men were spellbound as the machine approached; at the last minute they were forced to dive to the ground when it flew by too close for comfort.

William tested the machine's handling with a string of

maneuvers, each escalating in boldness; he began with several steep turns and ended with a loop. As he climbed for more altitude from this last maneuver, the lieutenants were distracted by the hoots of the children gathered at the fence; the group had somehow, unnoticed, grown to seven. They were running around each other in circles, bumping into each other with outstretched arms, and growling at the top of their voices through wide-open mouths. 'Look, I'm a flyin' machine! I'm a flyin' machine!' Suddenly, they stopped their antics, simultaneously, distracted by something up in the sky. Then they began pointing, up and to the west. 'Look! Look!' they cried. There, in the distance, just barely visible against the side of a cloud and appearing little larger than the head of a pin, hung a Prussian dirigible sailing toward them on one of its regular patrols. 'Here they come! Here they come!' chanted the children. 'They're gonna gong us! They're gonna wong us! The Westerns are gonna bomb us!'

William, unaware of this, made another low pass and began a gentle turn near the far end of the field as if intending to land; both officers dashed out into the pasture and gestured madly with their arms, pointing up toward the airship. William aborted his landing, rocked his wings, and buzzed out over the fields to the north. By now the children had swarmed over the fence and stood in a loose pack around the lieutenants—all stared up at the sky, openmouthed. 'He's gonna fight 'em! Lookee there, he's gonna fight 'em!'

The Porter climbed at such a steep angle that its forward progress slowed to a standstill; all the while the unsuspecting airship sailed closer and closer. It took several long minutes for the two machines to close on each other, and the urchins began scrapping with each other in their impatience. The Porter's form shrank to little more than a tiny cross. Eventually, the faint sound of gunfire came down to them. It continued in short bursts until the Porter passed directly beneath the larger ship. William's gunfire seemed to have had little effect so far.

The Porter made two more passes, both uneventful, both disappointing to the crowd below. Suddenly, one of the boys shouted, 'Look!' and all observed a second cross-like form drop from the belly of the airship. It fell straight down for several hundred feet, before it began to fly. Now there were three machines, two of them swirling around the larger. The guns on the two aeroplanes crackled, each with its own distinctive rhythm: the Prussian aeroplane with sharp cracks, the Porter with the slow, heavy thud of its Hugo.

The twisting melee had progressed without any conclusive event when suddenly the Porter broke away and fell toward the earth in a steep spiral that eventually slackened to a lazy circle before it straightened out and turned toward the pasture. The enemy aeroplane circled its airship like a bee about its nest; both turned west and disappeared from view.

At first the spectators had hung their heads in disappointment at the attack's failure, but by the time the Porter touched down and as it bounced across the pasture, all cheered and jumped in triumphant joy, man and child alike. The lieutenants did their best to shepherd the children back behind the fence, unsuccessfully, before racing toward the approaching aircraft, eventually grabbing each wingtip, and steering it to the point at which they had first let it go. William cut the noisy motor with the flick of a switch, and the machine became silent, but everyone's ears were left ringing.

Black stripes streaked across William's face, soot blown back from the machine gun's firing chamber; it made the children giggle. 'It's Laughing Raven, the great Indian chief!' William's stern visage relaxed and then spread into a big smile as the children danced around the craft; they yelled war whoops. Clark and Burrows hauled him from the cockpit.

'I didn't get close enough,' gasped William as he climbed down. 'The shells faded almost immediately. I didn't get good hits until the third pass. Then I ran out of ammunition. I didn't have extra canisters.'

'What was it like?' asked one of the children. 'The other plane . . . was it just like this one?'

William gave an irritated glance at him before noticing that the very same question had almost popped out of Clark's mouth. 'Well, it's bigger, it's faster, and it can climb better! See, look at this!' William walked around the Porter and pointed out no less than ten round, dollar-sized perforations in the starboard wing tip. Then, more to himself than the others, he said, 'And it was yellow, not red.'

'So what are you gonna do?' whined one of the children. 'Are you just gonna let him get away? Are ya yellow?' William booted the child in the seat of his pants, which sent the whole pack scurrying over the fence.

'We'll wait until this evening and try again,' said William.

This most unusual of duels had proved a novel sight for more eyes than those looking up from farmer Druther's pasture—it had been observed by the entire city of Natchez. No sooner had William extricated himself from his flying suit, while the lieutenants chocked and refueled the Porter, than a caravan of horses, carts, and motorcars clambered up the dirt road that followed the railway bed. It took the efforts of all three soldiers to hold the curious civilians at bay, and at times they were forced to threaten the most rowdy to keep them from damaging the strange looking flying machine. In the end, the soldiers were forced to cordon off the area with several stakes and some baling wire, and Lieutenant Burrows kept his carbine on display for all to see. 'You boys ain't gonna keep us waitin' here all night are ya? We came out for a show! You wouldn't send us back home empty handed, would ya?'

The onlookers resigned themselves to observing at a distance and seated themselves on the fenders of their motorcars, or in the beds of their wagons, or perched themselves on Druther's fence and let their horses chew on the grass. They were unwilling to depart as long as there seemed the slightest chance that the aeroplane might fly again. William had tried to dissuade them and shouted out that the flying was finished for the day, but they were unconvinced and remained just the same.

The soldiers erected two tents, built a campfire, and prepared a simple dinner; they hoped this might encourage the onlookers to go home. In the end the men gave up and enjoyed their meal with their backs turned to the crowd.

Finally, shortly after nightfall, most of the crowd dispersed, and later, close to midnight, Clark's snores convinced the few remaining diehards. The men slept until the early morning hours. At three o'clock they rose and distributed dozens of empty tin cans that had been filled with kerosene and stuffed with rags; they placed them at twenty-yard intervals in two long parallel lines. They hauled the Porter to the end of the pasture, sat themselves down on a tarp, wrapped themselves in their jackets, and waited—groggy, but not quite ready to fall back asleep.

'I bet right about now you're asking yourself how in the world you got here,' said Burroughs.

William laughed and nodded, 'Yes, something like that.'

'Well, *I'm* glad you're here, Lieutenant. Those dirigibles give me the chills. And I don't like it that the Westerners are having it all their own way. The newspaper's been saying all kind of mean things about the troops here in Natchez. Sayin' we was caught off guard, and poor old Captain Porter getting the blame and all. I figure we owe those Westerners a thing or two.'

'I can't say I blame you for feeling that way. I've been wanting to settle a score of my own these past few weeks.' William said these words with vehemence, but the truth of the matter was his passion for revenge seemed to have cooled somewhat. Or at least it seemed to have become more focused on the Prussians in general, rather than on Heinrich specifically. His thoughts returned to his experiences with Heinrich and the crew of Dora Nine; he found himself wondering where the Prussian might be, and what he was up to. The past weeks in this unfamiliar land surrounded by its unfamiliar people had left him feeling rather lonely. And though, if asked, he would certainly have denied it, he found himself missing Heinrich—just a bit. 'So what are those West Carolinians so unhappy about anyway?' he asked. 'You must have done something awful to get them all worked up like this.'

'Oh, that story would take hours,' said Burroughs. 'First of all, they've got kind of uppity because of all that oil money they've been makin'. They feel that since they got all the money, the folks in Charleston got no right to tell 'em what to do. And, of course, the president there in Charleston thinks he's got every right to tell 'em what to do—since he's president and all—so he put some new taxes in place just to show 'em. And the Westerners say they won't pay those taxes; that they don't get much in return for their tax money anyway. In fact, they say the money's bein' used for secret stuff, that people been linin' their pockets with it. It's all a confusin' mess. Are you sure you Brits really want to get involved in all this?'

'I have no doubt there are many in government quite happy to get involved,' said William. 'America is a nice, fat goose pie, and they want their slice of it. Besides, trouble in America keeps everyone from talking about troubles at home. And remember, a fair chunk of that oil you're talking about goes to keeping the British navy going. You don't think they're just going to ignore that, do you? They'd have to dust off all their old sailing ships.'

'I suppose that makes sense. Boy, that old governor sure stirred things up alright. But he might get more than he bargained for in the end.'

'I keep hearing about this governor of yours. What's his name—Collier? What's the story with him?'

'He's a strange old bird. I saw him once at an inauguration in Charleston. There's all kinds of funny stories about him. People say he's real smart, that he could have been the next president. Some people think he's just plumb crazy. There's all kind of rumors that he was brought up Tabeth when he was real young.'

'What does that mean . . . Tabeth?'

'Oh, they're just a crazy religious group holed up in the mountains out West. They been there a long time; I'm surprised you never heard of 'em. I don't know how they got their start, but it seems that every poor Tom, Dick, and Harry who gets beat down finds a welcome home out there. A lot of the old Indian tribes made their way there, and most of the slaves went that way too—though that was a long time ago. I don't quite know how their system works, but it works pretty well for 'em. The Carolinians, the Virginians, and the Pennsylvanians all got stopped cold when they tried to get through those mountains. It seems that the Indians and the slaves, after gettin' a taste of how white folks treat 'em, decided they'd rather die fightin' than get the short end of the stick again. They fight real mean.'

'So what does this have to do with Collier?'

'Oh yeah, that's what we was talking about. Anyway, some people say the Preacher—that's what we call the governor around here—was brought up in Tabeth, but he left 'em when he was a young man. See, Tabeth folk stick to themselves and never come down from those mountains; that's why it's so strange if what they say about the Preacher is true. I ain't never met a Tabeth. Anyway, the story goes that he went to a seminary college in Charleston, then worked as a traveling preacher in the East before he ran for mayor in Augusta. From there he worked his way up into the government and eventually got appointed governor of West Carolina; that was several years ago now. But whatever it was he did to get that appointment, he stopped doin' it when he moved out to Buffalo. He's been acting like his own king ever since he got there. A royal pain in the ass if you ask me.'

Clark let out a laugh and said, 'Now that the Preacher's out of the way, it'll be clear for old Isaac Pinchon to run for president.' Burroughs laughed at this as well. But Clark stopped suddenly, looked over at William and said, 'Sorry, I didn't mean any disrespect.'

'Not to worry,' said William. 'I've met Sir Isaac.' Both lieutenants looked at him in surprise. 'I can't say I'd want him telling me what to do either. Personally, I get the impression that we Brits might be overstaying our welcome here.'

The two Americans sat silent for a moment, both seemingly uncertain about how much to say. 'It's kind of complicated,' said Clark. 'Although nobody would admit it, I think we're all just a little embarrassed that we had to ask for help in the last war. To be honest, not all of your friends are quite as polite as you. They act like we can't be left to stand on our own two feet. It gets everyone riled up.'

William chuckled. 'I've never been accused of being polite before.' The three sat quietly for a moment. 'So tell me more about these Indians. I saw pictures of them when I was in school.'

Burroughs let out a long whistle to emphasize the seriousness of the subject. 'Well, the head of the Tabeth Church—his name's Elijah—he tried to help them back when there were all these wars with 'em. Everyone kept pushin' the Indians further and further west. We'd go and promise them things; the Virginians would promise them things; the Pennsylvanians would promise them things; then we'd all turn around and change our minds. They'd get mad and kill some of our people; we'd get mad and kill some of theirs, and so on. This kind of thing kept up till the frontier reached the mountains. Of course the Indians couldn't win, everyone knew it . . . I suppose they did too. But just when things were getting real ugly, when there was going to be a big fight, probably the last one, this Elijah stepped in. He organized a big meeting called the Great Indian Conference—most people just call it the Big Pow-wow—and invited all the politicians from Charleston and Richmond and Philadelphia to meet with the chiefs of the Indian tribes at a big church over in St. Louis. They negotiated a peace treaty there, but I don't guess any of them thought it would last very long. Anyway, this is where Elijah was real clever. That treaty bought him enough time to get the Indians organized. You see, part of the reason the Indians kept gettin' whooped was they were always fightin' with each other and never got together about anything. Well, Elijah—don't ask me how—got them to agree to work together; they call him the Proud White Voice because of it.

'So when the Virginians changed their minds about the treaty and headed back out West to get more land, they found all the Indian tribes acting just like one big tribe. They had occupied all the land north to south, just east of the mountains, and joined forces with those crazy Tabeth people. Well, they whooped the Virginians, and good. But it was real ugly—they didn't take any prisoners, just killed everyone they captured. And that's where things still stand today, even though that happened a long time ago. Everyone's tried to tackle them—even we tried, but everybody just gets their noses bloodied. They're crazy. Fanatical. Anyway, these days, we just let them alone.

'But you got your own crazy folk over on your side of the ocean too. Take those crazy Prussians for example. I don't rightly know where Prussia is, to be honest. I guess they're wantin' their fair share of our oil too. England and Prussia will be goin' at it hammer and tongs pretty soon, wouldn't you say?'

'I suppose so,' said William. 'It won't be long before the rest of Europe jumps in. The Prussians can't really get at England unless they cut through France and Belgium, and I don't suppose the French will stand by and simply let them stroll through. It seems like the whole world's about to blow up.'

'Well, I don't plan to slog it out on the ground—that's for sure,' said Burrows. 'Lieutenant Hastings, you seem to have pretty good connections. I don't suppose you could get me and Clark, here, transferred to a flying regiment?'

'I don't know that my connections are all that good, and I don't actually know of any flying regiments. But if you want to fight in the air, I guess it shouldn't be too difficult to make that happen. All we need is another one of those gasbags to come drifting by tonight.'

The conversation carried on for a bit longer, passing from the situation in Europe to events in the other sovereign states. Eventually each man dozed off and was soon breathing deeply of the cool night air; they dreamt of home and war, and none woke when the throbbing whirr first filled the air as the airship returned. The dirigible had reached a location only five miles north of Natchez when William finally stirred. He shook his head; it took him a moment to become coherent and to harden his will in the disorienting predawn darkness. He shot an elbow into the side of each of his companions. Both jumped up out of their cold sleep; they instantly recognized the sound from above and trotted down the rows of tin cans with a box of matches in hand. The makeshift lanterns flared up easily in the calm morning air.

By the time they completed their task, William had buckled himself into the Porter and strapped on his flying cap. The lieutenants agreed that it would be safer, considering the darkness, for Clark to start the motor again, he being slightly more experienced at the harrowing task than Burrows. The well-tuned motor started easily, and the Porter was soon whizzing down the faintly illuminated grass strip. It began to climb into the night sky where it would have disappeared from view but for the flickering spurts of fire shooting from the motor's exhaust tubes. So long as the aeroplane was pointed away from them, Clark and Burrows could track its progress by these small jets of flame.

The two spectators returned to their dying campfire, each selecting a big warm stone to sit on. The buzzing of the Porter surged and faded at intervals as William made changes in his course, hunting for his quarry.

'How in the world can he fly that thing at night? He'll never been able to find it. I don't imagine he can hear it like we can.'

The gap between the noises of the two machines did indeed widen—the buzz of the Porter and the throb of the airship diverging, as William hunted in the wrong part of the sky.

'Look, Clark, out east, the sun's coming.' There was only a hint of blue in the sky in that direction.

The noise from the Porter's engine changed tone again. It began gradually heading back toward the airship which was now directly over the city. Whether simple luck, or because the airship was silhouetted against the glow of the city lights, the Porter now made a direct line toward its opponent, the buzzing noise of one and the throb of the other merging together into a single continuous hum. The thud of the Porter's gun floated down to them, and the lieutenants could just make out the tiny darts of the incendiary bullets, much like the shooting stars that they had observed earlier in the evening, only a bit more golden in color.

With the help of these darting lights, the men were finally able to locate the dirigible in the darkness above and were eventually able to discern its long form in the deep purple sky. As the Porter circled the ship, its gun chattering the entire time, the airship dropped a bit lower, and now as it sailed closer to the pink light of the city, it took on the same pinkish tinge. The echoing bang of the Hugo hammered away above them. Then, to the lieutenants' surprise, the airship started to glow—not with the reflected light that surrounded it, but with some pulsing internal energy. Its internals throbbed as if it were a mystical beast enraged by the irritating stings of an insect flitting about it. A small, slow-moving tongue of lambent flame emerged from the top of the dirigible, only for a second, before it evaporated. Then just as the lieutenants began to think they had only imagined this brief spout of flame, the nose of the craft plunged suddenly downward. The machine fell slowly at first and then more quickly. The Porter's gun went silent. A soft, ethereal crackling, like a tree creaking in a distant wood, reached their ears. The ship continued its tumult toward earth;

soon it was pointing straight down. Long ribbons of brilliant orange flame trailed behind it; Clark thought to himself, 'This must be what Lucifer looked like as he was booted from heaven.'

'Oh my goodness, it looks like a Chinese lantern,' whispered Burrows.

Clark gawked in amazement and horror.

The hellish vision lasted another long minute before the ship crashed down on the town of Natchez. The morning sky flickered with the explosion, and loud thuds rolled over the countryside. Both men let out a long exhale; each had been holding his breath for the duration of the doomed ship's fall to earth.

*

William, Burrows, and Clark left their motorcar idling as they stepped out into the street. Debris was scattered everywhere; pieces of airship and fragments of homes were horribly intermingled. They walked toward the crumbled girders that jutted up in places. All three were silent. William felt sick; the nausea had followed him down from the sky and stayed with him.

At first, when the doomed ship had started to glow, he had screamed with joy and triumph, but then, when it had started to pulse and when the flames had shot out of it like golden fountains, he had panicked. He had thought of Heinrich; the Prussian's face had appeared in his head; he could see the Prussian flier's pistol pointed at him, shaking. But it had been too late—he couldn't take it back. It had been awful.

The three men marched past the guards surrounding the wreck; the guards were there to prevent the irate mob from pilfering souvenirs or causing injury to themselves. The smell was overwhelming; wood still smoldered and oil still burned and there was another odor in the air.

Burrows and Clark looked at no one thing in particular; they just gazed at the sight in its entirety, but William's eyes hunted through the wreckage. He walked on, following the perimeter of the scorched ground; he hopped over the tumbled walls of the houses that had been flattened; he searched through the tangled remains. Eventually he found what he was looking for—the scorched and twisted frame of an aeroplane. There were a few patches of its yellow fabric still visible.

Chapter 25

CLUSTERED SWORDS

Mrs. Clarice Withers darted about Hilltop like a woman possessed. She shot incomprehensible and often conflicting instructions to her bewildered servants; she straightened the curtains; she repositioned the furniture; she reworked the recently delivered flower arrangements. Mrs. Withers offered helpful but unwanted advice on how best to polish the crystal chandelier, on how best to polish the silver, on how best to polish the surfaces of her mahogany tables, and on how best to clean the windows. She wreaked havoc wherever she went, and her loss of composure frightened her servants; the women in the kitchen prayed she would stay out of their way until the various dishes were prepared, or at least until the pans could be gotten into the ovens.

The reasons for Mrs. Withers' hysteria were many: first there were her ongoing nightmares; they had plagued her ever since the devastating attack on Fort Natchez, and the associated loss of sleep had only increased since that recent and horrible crash of a dirigible onto the very roofs of the city—not so awfully far from Hilltop. And there was the growing realization that Natchez was perfectly placed, geographically, to ensure more violence would follow. The first signs of mass panic already had erupted; many families had begun relocating to the homes of relatives living further east, and this resulted in a continuous drain of the town's population—particularly of the female population, including some of Mrs. Withers' closest friends.

Amidst all this dreadful confusion, Mrs. Withers had been approached by the mayor of Natchez to host a reception for several government dignitaries—'personalities' he called them—who were to descend upon the bruised city that very day. The guest list was heavily weighted with men from the Carolinian and British military, newly arrived at the fortress which was rapidly being put back into fighting condition. The only names on the list that Mrs. Withers recognized were those of Lieutenants Burrows and Clark, and they were bringing with them that reckless English flier who had destroyed the Prussian airship—clearly a man with little regard for Carolinian life and property.

The most significant cause of her discomfort—right at the very top of the guest list—were the names of General Wiley Preston, who was in the process of relocating his headquarters to Natchez, and Secretary of War Charles Tillock, the right-hand man of the president of the Sovereign State of Carolina. The mayor informed Mrs. Withers that the secretary intended to tour some of the battle-damaged regions and then join in the development of the army's war plans for the Mississippi region. While there had been dignitaries to Hilltop many times before, Mrs. Withers had never had such a lofty type as these; it threw her off her game, quite.

A jingling, like the warbling of a small bird, caught her attention and sent her scurrying out of the kitchen, to the relief of the two frantic cooks. In the sitting room she picked up the receiver of her telephone; she had been waiting all morning for the call, and after several loud clicks and hisses, she heard a faint voice break through from distant Charleston.

'Charlotte, dear, is that you?' asked Mrs. Withers. 'I can barely hear you! I'm doing fine, thank you, Charlotte. Now let's not waste time. I had hoped you would have called before now. Yes, I know the lines are busy, dear. What? Only ten minutes?' Mrs. Withers' face filled with panic. 'Tell me right away then. Start with this Mr. Tillock. Tell me everything and don't stop until you're finished.' This request was willingly fulfilled, and Mrs. Withers limited her comments to a string of 'Astonishing's, 'Lord's, and 'Oh my's. When all but two of the allotted minutes were consumed, she interrupted Charlotte and nudged the discussion over to General Preston. Three more minutes passed. Then, once Mrs. Withers realized the operator was not keeping accurate time, she returned the discussion to Mr. Tillock and received an extra three minutes of insight that neither she nor dear Charlotte had bargained on. By the time the operator finally cut them off, without warning and without explanation, it had been a very productive telephone conversation. She would need little more than pretty women and alcoholic libations to ensure the evening was a diplomatic success. Mrs. Withers relaxed. She wandered back through the house, her composure restored and apparent to all.

*

As the sun set, Hilltop was descended upon—not by dirigibles, not by an enemy army, but by the aforementioned dignitaries as well as eighty-three other guests that included as many unattached ladies as Mrs. Withers could muster—seventeen total, from a city becoming sparse in the commodity with each passing day; several noteworthy belles attended: Miss Cora Taylor escorted by her brother, Miss Maria Tavistock escorted by her brother, Miss Edna Williams escorted by her father, Miss Theresa Condit escorted by Major Andrew Ward, Miss Henrietta Grudel escorted by her grandfather, and Miss Stacey Wallace escorted by her sister, Miss Eliza Wallace.

Hilltop was absolutely stuffed with army cotton, political wool, and rustling taffeta. The fireplaces were going strong; the candlesticks were all alight; the ovens were still cooking; the place quickly grew warm. The Champagne and the punch and the liquor were going down easily—a result of the natural predilections of the military men, the heat, and the compressed emotions that had been building in the community ever since the onset of war. All was in nervous splendor.

Mrs. Withers relinquished any hope that the evening's discussion could be channeled in a direction other than the war, and she waded in as deeply as any veteran marine. 'That was quite an accomplishment, Lieutenant,' she congratulated William. He stood between Lieutenants Burrows and Clark in a new ill-fitting uniform that made him look skinnier than he already was. 'I'm so sorry I was asleep at the time. I understand from my neighbors it was quite a sight. It must have been thrilling for you.'

'Ma'am, honestly, it was the most hair-raising experience of my life,' said William without the hint of a smile. Then, feeling he perhaps ought to keep things light, he added with a grin, 'I can't sleep at night for fear of being ordered to go up and do it again.' Everyone laughed.

'Well, Lieutenant, next time you must endeavor to kill the beasts over the river, if ever you can! Another encounter like the last will surely obliterate little old Natchez and everyone in it. And you, Lieutenant Burrows? Are you intent on flying up there with the birds as well?'

'I am indeed, ma'am,' responded Burrows. 'I've only been up once, compliments of the lieutenant here, and I found it the most excitin' experience of my life. You wouldn't believe the view—Natchez, the river, the fortress—it all looks wonderful from one thousand feet up. I actually flew over Hilltop, Miss Clarice. I have my heart set on bein' a flier.'

'Really? The last time you were here I had the distinct impression that dancing with Miss Condit was the most exciting experience of your life. Well, you have more courage than I. My heart could never stand such a thing.'

'Oh come now, Miss Clarice! We'll make a pact. Once I learn to fly, you must join me up in the clouds, just once.'

'Oh Lord, I don't know how I would find the nerve.'

'Pardon me,' interrupted Mr. Andrew Wright, the editor of the *Natchez Spectacle*; he had just joined them. 'Might I ask whether this is our famous flier, or rather our infamous flier?'

'Mr. Wright, I'm so glad you joined us,' said Mrs. Withers. 'I'm desperate for familiar faces. Yes, indeed, this is Lieutenant Hastings, and these are Lieutenants Burrows and Clark—perhaps you remember them from our last reception. All three were involved in the event this week, but it was Lieutenant Hastings who was actually flying the aeroplane. Lieutenant Burrows has just been promising me a ride once he learns how to fly.'

'It is a pleasure to make your acquaintance, Lieutenant Hastings,' said Wright. 'My boys have told me a lot about you, and I'm sorry we haven't met before now. I would love to write an article on the downing for the *Spectacle*. And I'm sure our readers would love to hear about your adventure crossing the Atlantic. There's been more excitement this past month than there's been in the past hundred years.'

'I would be willing, for my part,' said William, 'but I've been instructed not to say much on either account—you'd likely be snapping photographs of me in the brig.' Everyone laughed.

'Then for now, I'll just have to be satisfied with tonight's story,' said the editor in mock disappointment.

'And what story might that be?' asked William.

'Oh my,' said Mr. Wright as he glanced over to Lieutenant Burrows, 'I seem to have put my foot in it.' William turned to Lieutenant Burrows, who shrugged his shoulder and grinned sheepishly before darting from the group in search of another glass of punch.

'Lieutenant Hastings, there you are,' said a new voice. William turned to find Mr. Smith standing behind him. The editor, Clark, and Mrs. Withers slipped away, following in the path of Lieutenant Burrows.

'Hello, Mr. Smith,' said William. 'I wondered when you might turn up again. Are you happy with the results?'

'Very happy. Although I would have been happier still if you had not destroyed quite so many city blocks. I'm very satisfied though; you've demonstrated to everyone that these machines are not invulnerable, and you've made it much easier for me to secure funds for further aeronautical ventures. I would say we are ready to move on to the next part of our bargain.' Mr.

Smith paused for a moment, gathering his thoughts. 'There exists a small and rather ragtag company of fliers stationed up near the border with Virginia, along the Tennessee River. I would like you to go up there and teach them the trade. They have their own machines, and I'll provide the weapons.'

'Alright,' responded William. 'I believe I've met these fliers. They dropped by the Porters' farm while I was there. When must I leave?'

'Tonight!' said Smith. 'You don't have much time. There's something brewing down South, and we need you in New Orleans right away. We need the skies cleared there within seven days!'

William's eyes went wide. 'Seven days? That's ridiculous! You can't be serious. It's too soon. These fliers seem like decent chaps, but I haven't worked with them. I haven't inspected their aircraft, and I have no idea as to their flying skills. Seven days is ridiculous. You'll get them all killed!'

'I'm sorry, Lieutenant, there really is no choice. The operation I spoke of will go forward whether you're ready or not. And whether you like it or not, you now have many lives in your hands . . . American lives . . . and *British* lives!'

William suddenly felt sick. This was too much responsibility being shoved down his throat. He felt like pushing Mr. Smith away, but somehow he managed to hold his temper. He wanted to leave the reception; any momentary joy he had been feeling had certainly evaporated now. If he was going to be saddled with such an impossible mission, he wanted to get it over with as quickly as possible.

'Is there any word regarding my sister?' he blurted out.

'Nothing new,' responded Smith. William frowned; he was disappointed. His first thought upon recognizing the intelligence agent was that there might be news from home. 'But as we agreed previously,' continued Smith, 'once our bargain is concluded, you shall return home. And once your personal affairs are sorted out, hopefully for the better, you may return to Carolina and continue assisting us in our aeronautical efforts if you like. What do you say to that? We will certainly be in need of experienced fliers to deal with the Prussians, and we'll need assistance starting up our aeronautical industry. Both represent rare opportunities for someone with your experience.'

'You know I can't make that commitment right now, not knowing how things will turn out at home. Besides, I'll likely be killed anyway.' Then, calming himself, exerting control over his thoughts, thinking carefully about what next came out of his mouth, he said, 'I'll consider it.'

'Very well, Lieutenant. Now, there is another person who wishes to speak to you.' Mr. Smith led William through the crowd; it wasn't until Smith had conveyed him to the center of the main room, near the brilliance of the chandelier, that William discovered the diminutive form of the secretary of war.

'Mr. Secretary,' said Smith, 'I hope you remember Hastings, our young British flier.' Tillock turned and gazed sternly up at William.

'There you are, Hastings. You've done a good thing. I'm proud of you, boy! Let me shake your hand.' The secretary then gave William a good pumping. 'You keep doing it just like that. Shoot'm all down if you can. I'll pay for as many bullets as you need. Hell, I'll even buy you a new aeroplane.'

'Thank you, sir,' said William, trying not to laugh at the little man's bravado.

The secretary was about to continue when Smith interrupted him. 'Mr. Secretary, it's time.'

'Time? What do you mean, *time*?' Mr. Smith reached over and patted the secretary's jacket pocket in a knowing manner.

'Oh yes, of course! I've had too many of these mint juleps.' The secretary then looked about himself as if he had lost something. He gazed up and frowned at the tall forms surrounding him and then pushed his way between two women and clambered up onto the sofa, spilling much of his drink in the process. 'May I have everyone's attention!' he shouted, but his voice failed to carry, and the throng continued to roar. The secretary puffed himself up to try again when another man's bark stopped every voice in an instant.

'*Attention!*' shouted General Preston; the ladies conversing near him reached up and covered their ears.

'Thank you, General,' said Tillock, equally startled by the man's vocal strength. All eyes turned toward the secretary, awkwardly balanced on the sofa; the chandelier hung above his head like a giant crown. 'We are privileged to have with us tonight a most distinguished guest. This is Lieutenant William Hastings, lately of Her Majesty's Army Expeditionary Force of North Africa, and now the sole representative of Her Majesty's aeronautical forces in America—an unlooked-for, but very welcome, guest of the Sovereign State of Carolina. You will know him best for his recent exploits against the Prussian menace, the downing of the first Prussian airship, and we have invited him here tonight to celebrate his dramatic success.' Cheers went up around the room, for the most part, and William stood there in stunned silence. 'Come here, Lieutenant! Stand right here in front of me!' William joined Tillock at the sofa. 'I am proud to present . . . ' here the secretary halted for a moment, recognized that he had gotten ahead of himself, and fumbled around inside his right-hand jacket pocket. He became flustered trying to extract whatever was contained within and handed his glass to William. 'Hold this, boy.' Eventually he produced a red velvet case. 'As I was saying, I am proud to present Lieutenant William Hastings with the highest acknowledgement the Army of Carolina can bestow. No foreigner has ever before received it.' The secretary then pulled from the case a long gray ribbon on which dangled a glistening silver medal: four small swords crossed together at their hilts, wrapped together with a band of small gems. Placing the ribbon over William's head, Tillock said, 'Lieutenant Hastings, I present you the *Clustered Swords of Carolina*, and I thank you on behalf of the nation of Carolina for your daring and successful attack on an enemy flying machine. Well done, boy! Well done!' Applause filled the room.

William smiled. He was astonished by the applause; he turned red and nodded bashfully, thanking the secretary and exchanging the empty drink glass in his hand for a full one from the nearest waiter. It was a dizzy feeling to be standing before so many strangers, so far from home, so far from anything familiar, and then to be applauded for an accomplishment that had been the direct result of blackmail. Nevertheless, he found this brief taste of glory oddly enticing. It was indeed a strange world. When he downed his drink in a single gulp, the applause transformed into warm laughter and cheers; hands patted him on the shoulder and slapped him on the back. Mr. Wright's camera, which had been standing unobserved on a tripod in one corner of the room, burst with a flash and stung everyone's eyes.

'Now, son, that's enough fame for any one lieutenant,' said the secretary. 'Me and Smith want to talk with you. Follow me.' The secretary was about to step down from his plump dais when Mr. Smith held up his hands and stopped him before he could dismount; Smith silently communicated something to the secretary by tapping his own shoulder in a deliberate manner. 'Oh yes,' said the secretary, 'I almost forgot about that.' He shouted out, 'One more thing, ladies and gentlemen!' pausing until he had regained their attention. 'I have been deputized by Sir Isaac Pinchon and by Her Majesty's government in London to perform this final task. I am happy to announce the promotion of Lieutenant Hastings to the rank of *Captain*—in what I suppose is termed the Royal Air Service. In addition—and I do not need to be deputized for this—he is being given the honorary rank of captain in the Army of Carolina. Please wish him success in this new and highly responsible capacity. Now, Hastings, let's go!'

The secretary hopped down and led William through the applauding crowd and onto a porch to one side of the library; there he lit a cigarette and waited for Mr. Smith to catch up.

'Now tell me, Hastings,' said the secretary, 'do you think you could teach that trick to some other fellas?'

'Yes, of course, provided they have adequate machines.'

'Well then, that's what we want you to do.' Mr. Smith then explained to the secretary that they had already discussed this next step. 'But there is one other thing,' continued the secretary. 'For reasons that I'm certain you can understand, and despite your new honorary rank in the Carolinian army, we feel there might be difficulties if we were to assign you direct command authority over these particular fliers. So we are going to assign two Carolinian officers to work with you and to take on formal responsibility for the men. Can you live with that arrangement?'

'Yes,' said William hesitantly, 'who?'

'Why, Lieutenants Burrows and Clark, of course. Your friend Captain Porter speaks very highly of them. And you three have clearly demonstrated that you can work together.'

William nodded. He turned and searched through the crowd until he discovered Burrows deep in conversation with another Carolinian officer, a captain. Clark was nowhere to be seen. 'Do they already know?' asked William.

'They are being told as we speak,' said Smith; he nodded his head toward the man speaking with Burrows. 'That is Lieutenant Burrows' commanding officer.' William glanced back a second time to find Burrows' face flush with emotion. He looked up and glanced at William with such a tremendous grin on his face that William could not help but smile as well.

It was at this particular moment that a strange experience befell William. His eyes happened to stray to a group of women conversing just behind Lieutenant Burrows. William didn't have a perfectly clear view—only part of her face was clearly visible—but one of the women seemed shockingly familiar to him. His heart skipped a beat and he could feel the blood drain from his face. He abandoned Mr. Smith in mid-sentence and plunged through the party toward the woman, unable to get a good look at her until he broke in upon the small group in which she was conversing. There he received a second shock—a disappointment. He had been mistaken; it wasn't his sister after all; it was young Cora Taylor. On close inspection there was perhaps some slight resemblance to Emily, but nothing more. He wondered if the Champagne had gone to his head. William had startled the poor girl by his sudden approach, but she recovered quickly and, gazing up at him with a concerned expression, asked, 'Are you alright, Captain Hastings? You look unwell!'

'What's the matter with him?' the secretary asked Smith after William bolted. 'He looks like he's seen a ghost.'

'I don't know. He's a strange soul . . . perhaps the limelight . . . perhaps the wine. He'll be alright when the time comes.'

'I suppose so. He is an odd one. So you didn't tell him about his sister?'

'No,' said Smith. 'It would serve no purpose at this point. His task would remain the same regardless. And if I tell him now, it will only unbalance him. That could easily get him killed.'

'He's going to want someone to blame when he does find out. It'll probably be you.'

'Perhaps. If he lives.'

Chapter 26

A GUN TO KILL WITH

Heinrich knew that his hands were shaking. He needed room to breathe; his throat was tight, and his stomach churned. He slipped unnoticed out of the airmen's barracks; the other crewmen, some from his own ship, many from Dora Four and Dora Seven, were sleeping like lambs; their heavy breathing, their shallow wheezing, and their unctuous snoring infuriated him. He pulled the barracks door shut with a bang.

Once outside he felt no better. In fact, the pitch-black night and the chilly breeze made him shiver in his boots. He had never felt this lonely in his life, never so sure he was in the wrong place. He didn't want to return to the slumbering barracks, and he felt uncomfortable in the murky darkness, so he wandered over to the dirigible pit that housed Dora Nine.

The airship pit was an amazing engineering contrivance—an entirely novel approach to housing an airship. The governor's staff had chosen this particular design to avoid detection. Tall storage sheds of a design like those back in Prussia would have been visible for miles and would have alerted the local populace, and eventually the government, well before any dirigibles had actually arrived from Prussia. So instead, the governor's instructions had been to dig down into the earth, to excavate great pits that would have the appearance of quarries, or mines. In fact, they looked a bit like giant graves, long and slender and deathlike.

An arriving dirigible would sail into the prevailing wind and approach a mobile mooring derrick that had been erected on the back of a railroad engine; the railroad engine rested on a narrow-gauge track that encircled the pit. Once the airship was secured at the bow, a second mast on a second railroad engine would motor around to the opposite side, and a cable would be attached to the dirigible's tail from behind. Then, with the engines working in concert, the dirigible would be rotated so that it's length hung directly over the pit where it could be pulled down inside by a variety of winches and cables, all hidden from view by a telescoping set of large, canvas-covered shutters. The railroad engines, and the men who drove them, were called *gravediggers*.

Heinrich followed the gravel path that led him across the railway track encircling Dora Nine's pit and eventually down a wide cement access-ramp that descended into the earth at one end of the pit. He proceeded slowly; the surface of the ramp was smooth and damp. At the bottom he entered the pit itself through a door embedded within a still larger door, much like the wooden gates of the old castles Heinrich had visited back home as a child.

Inside, despite the cavernous space before him, he felt more at ease. The place had a protected feel to it, and it was silent; he was able to think in peace and pace about while doing so. Dora Nine hovered just a few feet off the ground; her bulk consumed much of the cavernous void before him. Golden floodlights, which were suspended far up on the walls, illuminated her. The repairs to Dora Nine were complete, and she seemed to rest contentedly. She had been damaged while being lowered into the pit when returning from her last patrol over the gulf, but this had been easily repaired.

Heinrich's footsteps echoed off the sloping sides of the pit. In some places the walls of the pit were constructed of poured concrete, and faint horizontal lines of the plywood forms were visible; in other places cold hard stone served, and the rough surfaces were stained with the brown residue of the explosive charges that had been used during excavation. The angle of these cavernous walls was forty degrees from the horizontal, and while some of the more dexterous and energetic mechanics could sometimes mount them, most workers traveled between the surface and the pit floor via narrow wooden staircases that had been built at regular intervals along the walls. It was almost like an amphitheater that might have been used by the ancient Romans for their gladiators.

The echo of his steps followed as he wandered about the pit. Heinrich ducked under metal cables that were stretched tightly against the buoyant pull of Dora Nine. He stepped over all sorts of supplies: coiled ropes, pieces of lumber, wooden chests filled with bronze spark-proof tools, boxes of parts and provisions, rolls of fabric, drums of varnish, spools of wire. Rubber gas hoses snaked along the floor and seemed intent on tripping him. Usually, this place was teeming with men focused on every imaginable task required to keep the airship operational; the mechanics fought day and night against the wear and tear of a grueling flight schedule. Now, though, the place was silent as a tomb. The men had been given a single night off to rest and prepare for whatever was to come in the next few days. Heinrich could feel the tension building.

His adventure across the Atlantic and his first few days in the new world had been bewildering. But the recent news about the loss of Dora Two over Natchez had transformed bewilderment into trepidation. While none expected their operation would come without cost, most, including their leaders, had not expected the loss so quickly. Two dirigibles had now been destroyed—one by accident at Chickasaw Bluffs, and one by action. The gas plant had proven to be undependable and was operating only intermittently, and while Dora Nine had long ago had her hydrogen exchanged for helium, this had not been the case for Dora Two and Dora Five. General Stanton had all but disappeared from their midst; he was consumed with preparations for the imminent land battle and communicated his orders to the admiral by telegraph. Despite the fact that Stanton's driving nature bordered on military mania, he conveyed such competence, such utter confidence, that every man—Heinrich included—felt the West Carolinians' audacious scheme for secession might just be within their power to complete. The Prussian admiral inspired no such confidence.

Suddenly, Heinrich's musings were harshly interrupted; a glinting object fell from somewhere high above and struck the floor with great force; a bronze wrench bounced with a reverberating ring and came to rest at his feet; the clatter echoed throughout the pit. He looked up to find a scruffy face peering down at him from a hatch in an engine gondola. 'Sorry, pardner,' shouted the man, a mechanic. 'I don't suppose you could hand that back to me?'

Before Heinrich could reply, the face disappeared; a few thumps came from inside the gondola; the man returned and sent a small cloth sack down, suspended on a thin piece of wire. Heinrich placed the errant wrench in the bag and watched as it disappeared back up into the gondola. 'Thanks, pardner. Just making a few last minute adjustments. Didn't mean to scare you. You jis go on about your business and don't let me bother ya.' The man disappeared.

Heinrich continued staring at Dora Nine; his eyes followed along her belly and stopped momentarily at the hatchway that gave him access to his aeroplane when the airship was in flight. His little red machine rested on the concrete floor a few feet away; it seemed to be waiting patiently to be hoisted up onto its trapeze. Heinrich continued his inspection of the airship; the burned and blackened skin, the mangled keel, the ruptured gas bags, and all the damage inflicted by the lucky mortar shot over Fort Natchez had been long ago repaired. There were, however, still signs left from the wounds—slight wrinkles in the ship's canvas covering.

The wrinkles, those insignificant little wrinkles, bothered Heinrich. It was a telltale scar; it signified that all was not quite right. Although the repairs had been made by skilled mechanics under the direction of the ship's new engineer, the frame—the underlying structure of the craft—must still be ever so slightly out of alignment. She would probably never be the same. He was *sure* that he would never be the same.

Heinrich wandered over to his aeroplane. He had

meticulously inspected the craft over the past couple days, every bolt, every weld, every cable splice, every wire. He had badgered the mechanics to brush on a new coat of dope resin and to paint those surfaces that had worn thin during their journey from Europe, the only difficulty being the shade of red they used; it was different from the original paint and left the machine with a patchwork appearance. He had personally polished the entire machine, and for this he had received a phenomenal amount of ribbing from the hundreds of men climbing about the pit during the airship's repair; every last one of them had seemed to make the assumption that his efforts were from some misguided vainglory. The truth was that he simply could not sit still.

His attacks of nervousness had become much more frequent now, always just below the surface, ready to emerge at the slightest provocation. The attacks had become so crippling that he was certain it would be visible to anyone who conversed with him. By zealously polishing his aeroplane, he prevented anyone from noticing how much his hands shook. Intent on this task, he didn't have to speak to anyone, and they wouldn't notice the high pitch of his voice, or the fact that it quivered at every word. Heinrich knew that Peter Dürr was aware of his strained condition, but there was little his friend could do; they were in the Prussian navy, and the Prussian navy was at war. As best Heinrich could tell, Dürr had said nothing about it to the admiral and seemed to be intentionally keeping Heinrich out of any awkward situations with other officers.

The red aeroplane glinted and sparkled before him despite the dim artificial light. He desperately wanted to take it out for a flight; he knew the rush of the air, the growl of the engine, the distance from the ground would make him feel better. But there was no way to get it out of the pit; it was trapped beneath the airship. Besides, it was night outside. His last flight, earlier that week, had been a disaster; he had made the mistake of testing the machine gun. He had done this out of misplaced hope—hope that his fear of being shot might be unwarranted. Perhaps it had only been an aberration on that very first occasion when he had been wounded; perhaps the engineers had been right all along. So he had ducked his head, pulled the trigger, and hoped for the best. But no, it had been a fool's hope. Within a couple of seconds of pulling the trigger a deflected bullet had clipped off the tunic button on his left shoulder, and then before he had time to release the trigger, another one had nicked his collar. The bullets had not drawn blood this time, thankfully, but that was little consolation. This brief experiment had only validated his fears and left him in worse shape than when he started.

Once or twice he had probed the other fliers about their experiences with the forward-mounted machine gun; he asked them how they felt, blasting away at their armored propeller as if it were a roulette wheel, every black number sending a hunk of hot lead screaming back at one's brain. But each had recoiled violently from such inquiries: the first had gotten angry and had blurted out, 'This is war! What do you expect!' and turned away with a scowl; another had just laughed—an insane, high-pitched, hyena laugh; still another acted as if he didn't understand the question, at first—then he went on to state that his gun had operated perfectly, marvelously, beautifully. Each faced this trial of annihilation in any way other than talking about it.

After circling the craft and finding no new items in need of attention, Heinrich climbed into the cockpit and sat there mired in his thoughts. A request for transfer back to Europe was all but impossible. The real demands on his skills had barely begun. Besides, now that Britain had declared war on Prussia, it was very likely that Europe would be plunged into violence well before he could get back.

As he thought on this, he began to notice a faint rattling noise. Perplexed as to its source, he looked up, and then to each side; he wondered if another mechanic were lurking about the place. But eventually he discovered, to his dismay, that *he* was the source of the noise—he had been gripping the control stick with his trembling hands, and the vibration had been transmitted along the control lines, through the pulleys, and out to the hinges of the ailerons. Heinrich released his grip in horror, and the rattling ceased. He climbed out of his machine; he was disgusted with himself. He began to sweat again, despite the coolness of the air.

Heinrich hesitated. He didn't want to return to the barracks, so he retraced his steps toward the airship's bow. Then without clearly understanding why, he climbed the rope ladder leading to the control cabin. The interior of the cabin was dim and silent; he had never seen it so still and empty. Heinrich moved on, deeper into the officers' deck; the dim light faded as he groped his way along the narrow corridor. All power to Dora Nine had been switched off, but by counting doorways he managed to find his own cabin. He entered it and lay down on his cot. It felt safe and quiet there; he was alone; soft dim light fell on him through the small porthole in the wall of his cabin. He thought he might spend the night here instead of in the barracks with the others.

Heinrich reached under the mattress of his cot and pulled out a Carolinian newspaper—it was three days old. He had looked at it so often that it was now wrinkled and torn. There, on the front page, was a photograph of the Englishman; Heinrich had all the words down from memory; the article related the details of the attack on Dora Two over Natchez. His eyes moved to a specific paragraph, one that he had read over and over; that single paragraph had been consuming him. In it, William Hastings had been quoted, 'We're coming! We're coming to get those Prussian ships! We're going to down every last one of them.'

Heinrich crumbled the paper in a fit of rage; he smashed it into a tight ball and threw it on the floor. He buried his face in his hands and wept. His sobs shook his whole frame, shook the cot, and seemed to shake the entire cabin. His mind had become as fragile as the dirigible that enclosed him; the framework was bending; the girders were buckling. He felt like he was imploding, that he was about to disintegrate. Strangely, part of him desperately wanted to disappear, to vanish. He didn't want to be killed; he wished that he had never existed.

The image of his father flashed through his mind, silent, unyielding, unsympathetic, filled with contempt. His father's face transformed into that of his grandfather; the old man scowled at him, laughed at him, pointed his gnarled finger at him and shook it. The laughter grew and grew; it was joined by the laughter of others, by the laughter of barons and baronesses he had met throughout his life, by the laughter of their daughters, by the laughter of the admiral, by the laughter of the kapitanleutnant, by the laughter of the entire crew of Dora Nine—all of them were laughing. The governor was grinning at him. Stanton was smiling at him.

All of these faces faded as another face overshadowed them—an angry face, a vengeful face. The Englishman, William Hastings, now filled his mind, not speaking, not laughing, not scowling, only staring, unflinching, unblinking. The Englishman continued to glare at him. Then suddenly, the Englishman pulled out a pistol, Heinrich's pistol, and pointed it at Heinrich's face just as he himself had done to the Englishman so long ago in the desert. A grin spread across the Englishman's face as he pulled the trigger. *Bang!* A bright flash went off within Heinrich's skull. He cried out in panic. His eyes shot open and he searched about him, frantic. The crack of the pistol had seemed real to him, as he lay curled up on his cot.

But something brought Heinrich back to reality; he felt a presence. Heinrich looked up and about the cabin and through the door into the hallway. He felt someone there; a shadowy form filled the doorway. Heinrich was unsure whether the figure was real, or just a product of his tortured imagination. The longer he stared, the more certain he became. Eventually he recognized the twisted shape; it was Lothar. Of course—Lothar never left the ship.

One dark form stared at the other, silent, still. Then Lothar took a hesitant step into the cabin and tugged at Heinrich's pants leg; he wanted Heinrich to follow him. Lothar then disappeared down the corridor. Heinrich sat up, dried his eyes, ran his fingers through his hair, and took a moment to regain his composure. Eventually he stood and followed.

He found Lothar standing on a stepladder perched over the engine of his aeroplane. Lothar pointed with a wrench at a second stepladder positioned on the other side of the engine; Heinrich climbed up as directed. Lothar then pointed at the back of the engine block where the crankshaft stuck out from the rear bearing. Heinrich noticed that something had been changed; a new mechanism had been installed, one that hadn't been there the day before. A coupling was attached to the end of the crankshaft and it had two small nipple-like protrusions welded onto it, 180 degrees apart. As well, onto the rear side of the engine block was welded a small, spring-loaded sleeve that enclosed a vertical shaft; it extended upward and pressed against a spring-loaded rocker arm mounted on the upper edge of the block; the end of the rocker arm penetrated into the firing mechanism of the machine gun.

Heinrich examined the new installation closely; he was uncertain as to its purpose. He lifted his eyes and gave Lothar a questioning look—no reaction; Lothar jabbed again at the mechanism with his wrench as if he thought Heinrich ought to be able to figure it out on his own. Heinrich ran his fingers up the shaft and across the rocker arm; he felt around the firing chamber and the gun's hammer. Then, suddenly, he got an inkling of what Lothar had done. He reached over and pulled on the propeller, and a miracle unfolded before his eyes. It was ingenious. Just before each blade rotated in front of the machine gun's muzzle, the protrusion on the coupling came in contact with the spring-loaded shaft, which pushed up on

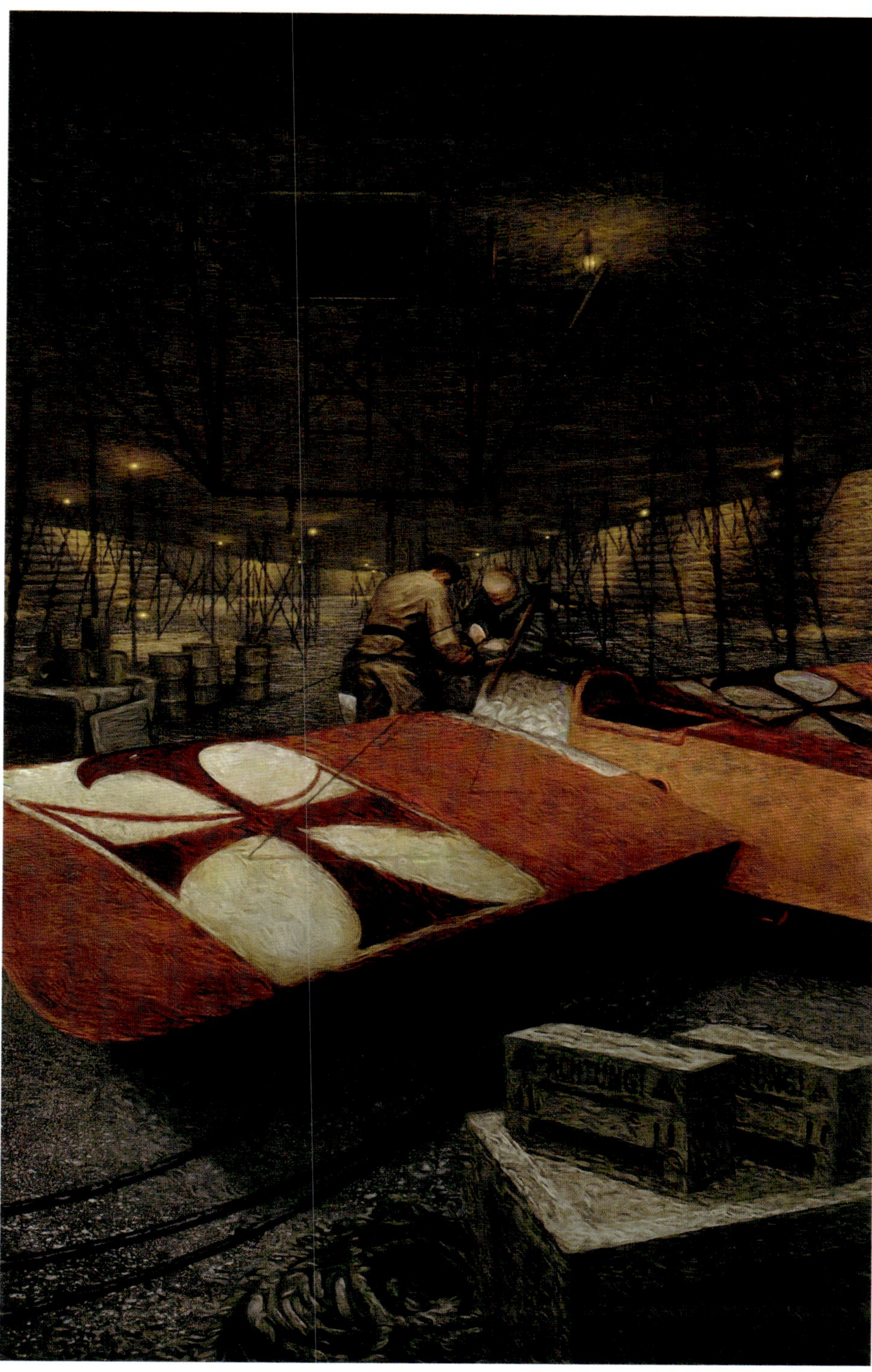

the rocker arm; the opposite end of the rocker arm slid into a small slot next to the gun's hammer. The gun's firing would be interrupted every time a propeller blade passed in front of the muzzle.

'Thank God!' gasped Heinrich. His whole world transformed in an instant. His reaction was physical; it was visceral; he could hardly breathe. He was like a prisoner before the firing squad, saved at the last moment by an official pardon. He had a way out. He need not be killed, automatically. He now had a fighting chance. His machine was no longer that two-edged sword, just as likely to kill its pilot as the enemy. A manic joy filled his soul. Never had he felt such a surge of majestic relief. He looked up at Lothar and grinned—a grin so broad it fell just short of being painful. There was no answering grin on Lothar's face, but the man did give a curt nod to acknowledge the significance of the moment. He then stepped down, strode off toward Dora Nine, and disappeared up the ship's ladder, as if he had done nothing more than remedy an insignificant oil leak.

Although the fear, the anxiety, the terror of his situation had not actually disappeared, the feelings had lessened so much that absence seemed but the nearest thing. In their place was an intense, new-felt confidence; he was now master of his fate. If he were killed it would not be the result of an unlucky spin at the roulette wheel; instead, it would be a result of his direct actions, a result of his skill as a flier; he knew he could live with those odds. He was saved!

He let out a deep laugh that echoed off the cold, hard walls of the pit; only a short while ago this place had been his own personal Hades. He laughed at the figures from his vision, just as they had laughed at him. And he laughed at the Englishman. If William Hastings chose to try his luck against Heinrich and his new gun, so be it. Heinrich had shot him down once; he could certainly do it again. William Hastings had better look out for himself! Heinrich laughed again; he gently stroked the ugly gun that rested beneath his hand.

Chapter 27

THE FIRST SQUADRON

Over the years, colorful names had been ascribed to various geographical regions that composed the long, winding, and bloody border between Carolina and Virginia. The salient formed by the Mississippi and the Tennessee Rivers, just north of Chickasaw Bluffs, had earned the title of *The Crucible*—so many vicious battles having been fought in that narrow, confined space. This narrow slip of land represented Virginia's only access to her lands west of the Mississippi; it had always been her jugular, so to speak. The *Drowning Stretch* referred to the southernmost portion of the Tennessee River near Big Spring, soldiers of both nations having drowned by the thousands over the past fifty years whenever one side or the other attempted to cross the river. The *Palisade*, a narrow ribbon of countryside ten miles wide, butted up against the southern bank of the Holston River between Whitfort and Salt Lick and was another exposed border region that had historically been exploited by both sides. It was a geological and, therefore, military crossroads and an irresistible temptation for any force intent on invasion via the Shenandoah Valley or the Cumberland Gap.

The Treaty of 1873 designated the Palisade—a ten-mile-wide, nonmilitary region, south of the Holston—as part of the negotiated withdrawal of Virginian forces from Carolina; Virginia wanted a buffer to forestall any thoughts of revenge. The Short War of 1872 had been a misguided and abortive attempt by Virginia to conquer Carolina. The Virginian advance had been halted and beaten back, but only with the assistance of British divisions obligingly provided by the King of England—once the Government of Carolina had formally agreed to give up the slaves. Carolina had been forced to choose: relinquish slavery or lose its independence. It had been a difficult choice, but necessarily a quick one.

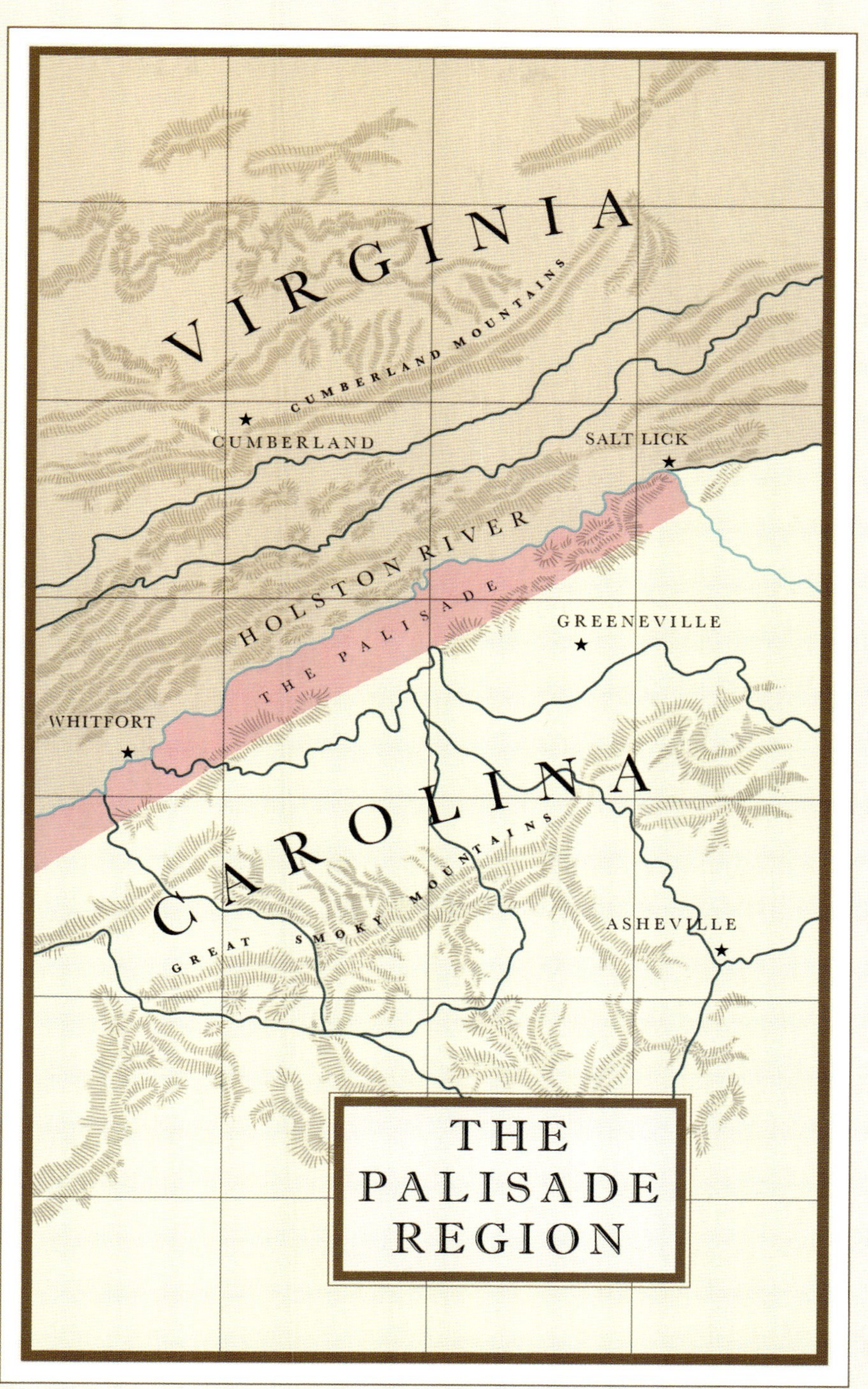
VIRGINIA
CUMBERLAND MOUNTAINS
CUMBERLAND
SALT LICK
HOLSTON RIVER
THE PALISADE
GREENEVILLE
WHITFORT
CAROLINA
GREAT SMOKY MOUNTAINS
ASHEVILLE
THE PALISADE REGION

What had once been a bucolic paradise, the Palisade was now little more than a no-man's-land between two massive, armed camps spread out over a hundred miles of tense borderland. Two standing armies lay on each side of the Palisade; they had been held apart for over thirty years now; the suspicion and distrust between the two countries had abated little through those years. The northern bank of the Holston was littered with Virginian fortresses, artillery emplacements, and army camps like so much flotsam washed up by the river. Carolina's side of the Palisade was set back ten miles from the river and was guarded by an equal number of soldiers, swords, and cannons. It was a strange site—this lush vacant countryside brooded over by high mounds riddled with tunnels and bristling with guns; war leaned over the edge of the ten-mile limit like a frozen tidal wave that wanted only the heat of some political fracas to turn it's latency into smothering destruction. The gunboats of both countries chugged up and down the narrow river, and the sailors eyed each other with malevolence through the narrow slits of their armored hulls; they challenged each other with collision in a never-ending game of riverine brinksmanship.

At the moment, Carolina's forces in the Tennessee Valley were commanded by General Samuel Armstrong—a tough, abrupt, country boy who had learned his trade during the Short War. His forces were an essential discouragement to further attempts at conquest by Virginia. It was an odd defense by its very nature; the ten-mile space between the opposing troops left them feeling somewhat theatrical as no soldier ever caught sight of his potential enemy except during those periods of leave when the Carolinian soldiers might visit Whitfort or Salt Lick or Chattanooga. There, enjoying the hectic riverfront nightlife, they could not help but observe the Virginian batteries, firmly encased in tons and tons of steel-reinforced concrete; the guns rested silently and patiently with their barrels pointed always in a southerly direction.

Although the political relationship of recent years had been relatively stable, and although there was open and mutually beneficial commerce between the two countries, debate continued across Carolina about the risk implicit in the Palisade. Many considered the Palisade an irresistible temptation to the Virginians; it provided them the opportunity to cross the river with little or no opposition and renew their assault on Carolina whenever they might choose. Most thought such an event unlikely and that a breach in the treaty on Carolina's part would tarnish an already questionable reputation within international diplomatic circles. General Armstrong did his best to deflate the country's fears and remained adamant that he could move his men up in a hurry at the first sign of the *Ginnies* coming across.

Despite the general's assurances, there were some who remained deeply suspicious of the Virginians and lobbied for advancing troops right up to the river—treaty be damned! However, these men had so far failed to consolidate themselves into an effective political force, and as a result their efforts were limited and piecemeal. What these men lacked in political influence however, they made up for in boldness. One ingenious move was the expenditure of significant sums of money on experiments with flying machines in the hope that such devices could help keep the Ginnies in their place. Half a dozen volunteers were transferred from across various units in the Tennessee Valley and attached to the Twenty-Eighth Artillery Regiment; the volunteers were placed under the command of Captain Joshua Prentice. Instruction was provided to these volunteers by such aeronautical tinkerers as Mr. Perry Porter of Greeneville, and they were, as well, given a few aircraft to play with. Whenever the weather wasn't too unpleasant, and whenever their machines happened to be in airworthy condition, these volunteer fliers would take off from a field near Craig's Station and gaze down at their 'enemy' along the Holston; they looked for—nay, almost hoped for—signs of impending hostility.

After the attack on Fort Natchez, and as the gears of the Carolina military machine turned faster and faster, Captain Prentice began to feel that this ridiculous experimental posting represented a risk to his career, that it might be akin to him paddling along a shallow, dead-end creek. So when probed by his superior about a posting with the forces on the gulf coast, he jumped at the opportunity. This lovely autumn morning found Captain Prentice sitting alone in his tent, anxious for his replacement to arrive. He sat in the dim light with his legs stretched out on his tightly packed footlocker, and he listened to the conversation of his men as they sat down to breakfast at the table outside his tent. They recently had dragged the table out of the nearby mess tent to enjoy what remained of the fine weather.

'You boys ain't gonna believe this,' cried Johnny as he joined the other fliers at the table. Private Johnny Stewart was a tall, dark haired, good-looking boy from Augusta. 'They already blowed one up!' He threw down a week-old copy of the *Asheville Banner*; on the front page was a large photograph of Captain William Hastings standing amid the wreckage of Dora Two with folded arms and a grim face.

'Who?' cried the others, ' Where? When? How?'

'It was that Jack we met at Porter's farm!' growled Johnny. 'I knew as soon as I seen him something like this was brewing. I got a beef to pick with old Prentice. How'd he let this Jack get ahead of us in line? This ain't England!'

'There ain't going to be any left for us,' whined Private Rice, a short, scrawny boy from out West. 'I heard they only got a handful of 'em. By the time anyone makes a decision 'bout us, the whole thing's gonna be over. Maybe we oughta head down there on a little expedition of our own. We could be gone and back before the captain even noticed it.'

Private Caldwell laughed out loud. 'I'm not sure the local ladies would permit that. The thought of doing without Private Cletus for more than twenty-four hours is likely to start them howling. The captain would find out for sure. Miss Shepherd would surely betray us.' Good-natured laughter erupted around the table.

'I'm serious! I'm willin' to go,' said Rice. 'I got all my stuff ready. Instead of us experimentin' on old barns, we could practice on the real thing. As soon as we knock one down for ourselves, we'll be heroes, just like this fella. They'll give us whatever we want. Bigger engines, bigger aeroplanes. Just think of the women, Cletus, once you get your picture in the papers like this English fella.'

'I hope we ain't gonna hear any more about this exploding yo-yo of yours,' laughed Johnny. 'You'll blow a hole in yourself one of these days. Or more likely, blow a hole in one of us. I saw what happened last time.'

'It'll work!' cried Rice. 'And it's not a yo-yo. It blew a hole as big as a man in the roof of farmer Brewster's old barn. You gotta have a little more confidence. You sound like my grandpa. He was always sayin' flying was for the birds. I tell you—if that Jack can do it, we can do it better.' By this time the other men were grinning at Rice, and his face turned red with irritation.

'Like when you dropped that steel dart through Mason's wing the other day?' interjected Caldwell. 'What we really need are bombs. Do you think the captain would let us get a few made up at the garage in town? I heard they've been dropping them on people and churches and everything over in Europe. I bet we could even take an artillery shell and weld some fins on it, make it fall as straight as an arrow.'

'I tried that, too!' growled Rice. 'Not with a live round—I took a can of lard and screwed some wood feathers on it. It worked just fine! I dropped it right through the hole in Brewster's barn from two hundred feet.' The others continued to trade sidelong glances with each other, clearly wanting to egg Rice on but not wanting to cross the line that would send him into one of his conniptions. 'Maybe we could get one of those European parachutes I heard about,' he continued. 'You know, kind of point the Porter right at it and jump out at the last minute.' Again, no one took this idea seriously. 'I guess Perry wouldn't like that. He might stop making aeroplanes for us.'

'All we need is a good gun,' said Cletus, entering the fray as he dug into his eggs. 'Punch enough holes in one of those gasbags and it'll come down. That's how this here paper said it was done. There ain't no need to go reinventin' the wheel.'

'Well that's it then,' said Rice. 'We just fly down to Perry's place and get him to fix us up. We tell him he's got to treat us fair. Anything he done for that Englishman, he's gotta do for us. Besides, ole' Cletus here wouldn't mind another crack at Miss Esther, now would you?' Cletus produced an irritated glare of his own, his last 'attempt' at Miss Esther having been somewhat discouraging. 'C'mon, Cletus, I'm only teasin' about Miss Esther. Let's go and get one of those airships before it's too late. Everyone else will go along if you say so. You can talk the captain into it. I know you can. You can talk anybody into anything.'

'I know what we can do,' snickered Caldwell. 'We can drop Captain Prentice on one of those airships. He's got so much enthusiasm for flyin' that when he grabs onto it, it'll surely sink to the ground, quicker than an anvil.' Everyone burst out in laughter, spraying chunks of breakfast all over their table.

Captain Prentice stepped out of his tent. The men did not realize the officer had been sitting inside, and they immediately straightened up and piped down. But it quickly became apparent that their commander had no interest in them or their conversation. He stared over their heads with his eyes glued to an army truck puttering up the road toward their camp. 'You men hurry up. We got visitors!'

Cletus leaned back on one leg of his stool and peered over his shoulder. 'Hey! It's that Jack! And those other fellas look like the ones who work for Perry's cousin. You know . . . they came and visited the farm a few months ago.'

'Huh?' questioned Rice.

'Burrows and Clark, I think. You remember them, don't you?'

'Oh, yeah,' said Rice. 'By the way, I heard Captain Porter got in trouble for lettin' Natchez get blowed up. Suppose these fellows did too? Got themselves transferred to the flying regiment as punishment.' Everyone broke into laughter.

'Guess they ain't in too much trouble,' said Cletus, getting up with a piece of sausage in his mouth and a biscuit in one hand. 'You better not mention it though. They might be sensitive. 'Hey there, Lieutenant Burrows,' said Cletus, approaching the officer as he climbed out of the truck; Cletus added a sloppy salute with the biscuit still gripped in his hand. Burrows' eyes followed the biscuit's path; he smiled.

'Howdy, Cletus,' said Burrows. He then acknowledged each of the other fliers with a nod, but their eyes had already moved on to William. Clark stood at William's side and smiled. 'Men, I'd like to introduce you to Captain William Hastings, of Her Majesty's Army Flying Corp. He's an honorary captain in *our* army too, so be polite.'

'Yeah, we already met,' said Cletus.

'You the fella that shot down that airship?' asked Rice.

William smiled and said, 'Yep.'

'How'd ya do it?'

Before William could open his mouth, Burrows explained, 'He took Perry's aeroplane and mounted a French automatic gun on it. Flew up and shot it down on his second try.'

The Carolinian airmen let out whistles of appreciation. 'Wish I'd been there to see it,' said Cletus. 'Don't suppose you got any more of those French machine guns?'

'No, not with me. Sorry, it wasn't my gun. An official chap in Charleston let me borrow it. *He* might have some more.' William glanced over at Burrows as he said this, barely disguising a grin.

'Hey, Burrows,' said Rice, 'you and Clark in trouble?'

Lieutenant Burrows hesitated for a second. 'Well, we were in a bit of a pickle, that's for sure, but I wouldn't really call it trouble until now.'

'Why's that?' asked Rice.

'They relieved me and Clark over in Natchez.' Expressions of concern spread across the fliers' faces. 'Then they said we got to come over here and tell you fellas what to do.' This was followed by a few seconds of stunned silence until in unison they burst out in shouts of jubilation, slapping Burrows and Clark on the back and jumping on each other in a very unruly and unmilitary fashion. A broad smile spread across Burrows' face. Cletus reached out and shook his hand, then reached over and shook Clark's as well. 'Captain Hastings is going to be runnin' the whole shootin' match . . . if you fellas don't mind too much.'

'Lovely to have you with us, old chap,' said Rice as he saluted William with a big grin. 'Just wait 'till Mason and Donnegal hear about this.'

*

On the last day of October, Halloween Day, the six flying privates, their two new lieutenants, and William erected four large tents that were to serve as hangars while they modified their aeroplanes. William's own Porter, still on loan from Perry, was towed by motorcar down the dusty roads from the Asheville railway station. By the end of the day, it sat snuggly under cover with the other six aeroplanes.

It required the fliers' combined efforts over the course of a week to make the structural changes indicated on several large drawings prepared by Perry, whose bold black lines were softened by his sister's neat and graceful lettering. The drawings documented the many small changes to be made in the airframe, rigging, and controls in order to compensate for the shift in the center of gravity that would accompany the mounting of a Hugo automatic gun.

Perry was familiar enough with each flier's individual

aeroplane to include specific notes intended to anticipate particular problems. Each craft was of a slightly different construction, a result of the rapid and constantly changing ideas that percolated in Perry's brain. No sooner had one craft been completed at Kemper's factory in Charleston, than Perry was ready with an updated design.

Unbeknownst to Perry, his sister had included little warning notes of her own, directed at the idiosyncrasies in each man's individual flying characteristics, such as: *Remember, Billy Caldwell, don't cross your controls*, or *Remember, Joey Rice, don't make such steep approaches*. Esther had gathered these insights surreptitiously; she had overheard her brother's critiques of their flying skills during their frequent visits to the farm. Cletus refused to share with the others the note that Esther had directed to him.

The modifications to the aeroplanes were complete by the morning of the seventh, and the fliers sat around waiting for the delivery of the Hugos. They debated their next course of action. Most agreed it was high time to get back in the air, even if it required placing a sack of dirt in the nose of each aeroplane to compensate for the weight of the as yet undelivered guns. Lieutenant Burrows had disappeared a couple of hours earlier; none could say where he had gone.

William sat amongst the rambunctious Americans, trying to learn their individual natures. He refused to acknowledge the social barriers that came with the difference in their rank. In fact, he was intent on leading these men in a manner very different from what he had experienced in Sir Maxim's regiment. He was going to stay close with these men. William had never known a time when he was at peace with the people around him, whether it was his family, his school mates, or more recently, with his fellow fliers in Sir Maxim's regiment. He was now astonished to find that these men, only a couple of years younger than himself, were hanging on his every word. William found it ridiculous, but they actually seemed to admire him; this was an altogether new experience for William. He found that he liked them in return, that he enjoyed being with them. These men were rough, fierce, and straightforward; they said what they meant.

While they waited, they pressed William for the details of his adventures. The story of his arrival in Carolina by airship left them amazed. William then obliged them with as much detail as he could remember about the dirigible's construction and flying characteristics. They also forced him to recount his duel with the airship over Natchez and used this as a basis for proposing new tactics that would allow them to approach an airship during daylight hours, when they would be forced to deal with the more advanced Prussian aircraft and, perhaps, a more experienced Prussian pilot. He also shared with them the sobering experience of being shot down.

'So how do you suppose we ought to go about all this?' asked Curtiss Donnegal, a thin, serious boy from Mobile. He had recently grown a beard and mustache in an attempt to hide the deep scar that cut across his mouth from his upper lip to the lower one; he had been injured in a crash while learning to fly.

'Well,' said William, 'the very first thing we must do is distract the Prussian flier when he drops free. That shouldn't be too difficult with several aeroplanes. If we approach from several different directions, we'll overwhelm him.'

'No, wait,' said Johnny Stewart, 'what we need is some bait. And I got the perfect feller for you. I hear Prussians just love small fry.' Stewart slapped Rice on the back; Rice punched him in the shoulder, hard.

'Actually, that's not a bad idea,' said William. 'We could take a couple of planes and drag the Prussian down to a lower altitude and leave the rest of the group free to bang away at the airship without having to constantly look over their shoulders. What do you think?' The other fliers just stared at each other and grinned; they were unsure as to whether William was serious.

'I suppose it all depends on who the bait is,' said Johnny.

'Well, I volunteer,' said William. 'I've a score to settle with one of those Prussian fliers. Anybody want to give me a hand?'

The others hesitated. Eventually, Cletus spoke up, 'I'll fly with you, Captain. What the hell, my ma and pa would be real proud to see my picture in the paper—as long as I ain't layin' in a coffin.'

'You know, I was thinking,' said Tommy Mason, a dandy from Chickasaw Bluffs. He wore patent leather riding boots and a brilliant blue flying coat that the others suspected was a dinner jacket belonging to his father; they also suspected that the coat had been tailored to fit by his mother. 'We should try to shoot it down on our side of the river, just like Captain Hastings did in Natchez. Can you imagine the fuss the newspapers will make? We might even get a decoration, just like the captain.' The others liked the idea as well, and it was agreed that if at all practical, the attack should be made over East Carolinian soil. The fliers bubbled over with excitement at the prospects of an aerial fight. They quickly agreed on each man's role; William and Cletus were to distract the Prussian flier and the others were to go after the airship one at a time until they had expended their ammunition. If the dirigible tried to escape by climbing higher, everyone was to jump in immediately.

'One word of caution,' added William. 'Please take care not to shoot each other.' Everyone glanced over at Rice.

Before Rice could object, Lieutenant Burrows returned in the squadron's motor-truck, which was so weighed down that its rear tires scraped the inside of the fenders; wisps of white smoke and the smell of burning rubber trailed behind the vehicle as it chugged into camp. The fliers raced around the vehicle before it came to a halt, expecting to find the much-anticipated weapons piled up in the truck's bed. Instead, they found boxes filled with cans of motorcar paint, manufactured by the Grissom Paint Company of Augusta. Most of the boxes were labeled Turkey Down Gray, but several were labeled Emergency Red. The men were a little disappointed at first, but after receiving the lieutenant's instructions, their spirits quickly revived.

The guns finally did arrive packed in plywood crates and stacked in a horse-drawn wagon. But the fliers had become so thoroughly engaged in redressing their scraped and scuffed aeroplanes that at first they failed to notice. Up to this point, each machine had acquired its own unique and somewhat eccentric paint scheme, which varied depending on the flier's mood at the time of its construction, and on whatever colors Mr. Kemper had available in his factory. The craft had been like so many brightly colored horses on a carnival merry-go-round. Rice had suffered many insults because of the pale yellow coating applied to his craft; the other men had nicknamed it the canary.

By day's end the aeroplanes had all been dressed in a homogenous coat of Turkey Down Gray. The tail surface, the top surface of each upper wing, and the bottom surface of each lower wing had been decorated with an elongated red X—a stylized version of the Carolina flag, as well as an identifying numeral—one through seven—each man having pulled a numbered slip of paper from Johnny Stewart's flying cap.

William didn't want to ignore his own martial heritage, so he painted a British lion on the nose of his Porter; he did his best to remember how the emblem had been drawn on the tail of his aeroplane back in the desert. The others were quite happy for him to do this; they were proud of their flying Englishman. But they did not want to be outdone; the American fliers debated what sort of mascot they should themselves adopt; they eventually decided on a turkey, and used the illustration they found on the empty cans of Turkey Down Gray paint as their model.

The men worked through the night under the flickering glow of lanterns to complete their war chariots. By morning many fingers had been smashed, many foreheads had been bruised, and many angry words had been spoken, but each craft sprouted a Hugo air-cooled, canister-fed machine gun. So it was at first light that Lieutenants Burrows and Clark stood before their men, with William standing off to one side; they were surrounded by the contemptuous grins of a few curious onlookers from the Twenty-Eighth Artillery. The fliers lined up, shoulder to shoulder, in their best uniforms. Burrows stood at attention, ramrod straight, with a glistening green bottle dangling from his right hand. A reporter from the *Craig's Station Banner* stood near with his camera perched on a tripod.

'Men, I now christen this squadron, both man and machine, the First Aerial Assault Squadron of the Sovereign State of Carolina.' He then strode over to aircraft No. 1, William's aircraft, and swung the glistening bottle of Champagne. It burst against the dew covered gun barrel and sent a shower of fizzing spray down the nose of the craft and down the front of the lieutenant's uniform. More than one flier silently wished the bottle had been spared for their breakfast, rather than sacrificed to martial pomp.

Chapter 28

INVASION

Captain Porter stood on the bridge of the *Partridge* as it wallowed at anchor in Pensacola Bay. He watched the sun set as he had done hundreds of times from his lofty perch atop Fort Natchez. The view was not so grand, but the colors were the same—distant green fields sandwiched between a pink sky and pink water. He had to admit his circumstances had changed dramatically and his unspoken desires had been granted; for better or worse, he no longer whittled away his time beside that lazy country river.

The *Partridge* was surrounded. Nearby, the *Fox*, the *Weasel*, and the *Penguin* lay at anchor, the last with the captain's artillery company crammed into its tight spaces. And around the four transports floated the entire British navy—at least it seemed like the entire British navy to Captain Porter, though it was only Her Majesty's Caribbean squadron.

The water was calm and the evening air was still, but the sky was becoming polluted. As the black smoke hung in the air, the soft pink light transmuted into an angry red. Jets of black smoke poured from the funnels of the warships. The deep, pervasive grumble of the ships' engines had long ago frightened the birds away. Small cutters swerved around and between the great vessels, transporting officers and mechanics between the various ships that were building up steam.

The sluggish and unkempt oilers had all but finished their task of topping up the tanks of the hungrier ships. The last oiler was at that very moment disengaging itself from the mightiest of them, the *Gorgon*. Black fluid dripped from the long steel spout as it was hoisted back aboard the oiler, and a black mess fell into the water below.

A string of colorful pennants unfurled and whipped up the mast of the *Gorgon*, signaling to the others that the time had come. Immediately the air began to vibrate. The water began to vibrate. Thousands and thousands of hearts began to vibrate. Bottle-green water bulged up behind each ship, and the surface began to churn; white eddies burst up and sent spray flying about. Shallow waves ran from each of these cataracts, only to be overwhelmed by the rush of waves from all the other ships. At first, this disturbance seemed to have failed of its purpose, but then slowly, only by contrasting the ships with the stationary foliage on shore, Captain Porter perceived the ships' movement. Anchors came clattering up, more cataracts of water, then streams of mud and silt dripped down the pristine bows of the warships.

The *Gorgon* began to build momentum, as did the other battleships and cruisers: *Ajax*, *Swiftsure*, *Resolute*, *Indomitable*, *Ulysses*. Finally, the small escort vessels moved on: the destroyers, the oilers, and the coal tenders. It took over an hour for the ships to clear the bay. It wasn't until the sun had disappeared and the last light was beginning to fade that the *Partridge* and her companions found themselves alone, left to breathe the smoggy air while the surface of the bay again calmed itself.

'Lord Almighty!' cried General Caruthers as he came up from below. 'They're gone!'

'Yes,' said Porter. 'It was quite a sight. It makes one fear for the fate of the world.'

'Indeed,' said Caruthers as he sniffed the air. 'I'm sorry I missed it. But I've agreed with the ship's engineers exactly where to cut the hull for our landing. We've marked everything out in chalk so there will be no confusion later. I regret you'll not be with me during the *Partridge*'s beaching. I'm sure it will be a curious sight.' Porter gazed over at the general, uncertain whether he was trying to be humorous. The two men had been together day and night for the past few days; they had worked out the details of Porter's artillery support and then discussed one alternative after another in anticipation of the things that could go wrong. Porter was reassured by Caruthers' thoroughness, and he gained a deep respect for the man's intelligence and his drive; the other British officers seemed equally competent, if not entirely enthused.

Porter and Caruthers had discussed things at such length that each could be fairly certain about how the other would react in any given situation. They would have to depend on one another, and they would be separated early in the fray as soon as the *Partridge* and the *Weasel* moved in for a landing. It was during this period that the landing would be most vulnerable, when half the force would be disembarking and the other half would be waiting in Galvezton Bay. Once the landing had succeeded, the cavalry and artillery would be brought in next.

It hadn't taken Porter long to realize that their operation was a long shot. He completely understood the need to strike quickly, before Galvezton Bay had become impregnable, but Caruthers' force was too small. Captain Porter shared General Caruthers' belief that, while the British battle fleet was quite imposing, it was not likely to reduce the shore defenses by the degree necessary for such a small landing force to succeed. But Porter did not spend much time musing on this. He was a soldier.

*

Lothar sat on a small stool in the aft starboard-side motor gondola, leaning his head out the open hatchway. The slipstream buffeted his head roughly, but he enjoyed the way it felt. At first his eyes had filled with tears from the rushing air, causing the view to go blurry, but he had scrounged around the gondola and found a pair of flier's goggles; now all was fine. The sun was setting, and the surface of the earth had become a smooth, dark plate; the fading light that reflected off the venous streams and stagnant swamps only served to make the areas of dry land that much more black and impenetrable.

A golden flash suddenly lit up the ground below, but before

Lothar's brain could decipher what he had seen, it disappeared; he was blinded for a moment or two. There, again, another flash came, and another. He realized they must be crossing over New Orleans again, heading west. Yes, he made some quick mental calculations—not the mathematical, trigonometric kind of calculations that a navigator might produce, but rather something more visual, like an intricate architectural drawing; the solution presented itself as a whole at a single moment to his mind's eye; it was the same combination of reason and emotion that had resulted in the creation of the interrupter-mechanism he had installed on Heinrich's aeroplane. Yes, that would be just about right; it must be New Orleans down below. Now he understood the flashes of light. The artillery battle raged on and on. The forces below grappled with each other at a distance, separated by the river. Lothar watched intently; he leaned out further to get a better view.

A flurry of flashes came, one overlapping the other, faster and faster, almost a continuous stream of light now that enabled him to observe the landscape in detail. He could identify the curving loop of the river, the city center, even individual buildings, warehouses, and homes; much of the town was burned out and devastated. The lightshow was stupendous—more brilliant than the biggest of the fireworks displays he had observed as a child from the balcony of his orphanage back in Berlin. Lothar could feel his heart beat quicker and quicker with each subsequent burst of fierce, orange light. He could imagine the rending vibrations accompanying each shell burst; he almost wished he were down there, with his feet firmly planted on the ground where he could feel the thumping and quivering of the earth.

If someone had been standing on the narrow gangway that connected the main body of Dora Nine with the engine gondola, they would have noticed an uncharacteristic display of emotion sweeping over Lothar's pale and twisted visage. With each bright and searing illumination his expectant eyes widened in the oval metal frames of his protective goggles; a smile of sublime and utter happiness rested on his lips. He seemed at risk of toppling off his perch as he reached out a hand; he filled with a desire to touch the harsh glow of the battle.

Lothar knew at this moment that he had found his home. He had been homeless in every sense of the word as far back as he could remember. With the exception of the recently departed Otto Rass, the crew of Dora Nine had become the closest thing to a loving family he had ever experienced—a family that followed rules, a family that insisted on order, a family that didn't strike without a reason—there had still been something missing, until this very moment. He realized now that he and the crew and the ship had only been biding time. Dora Nine was much more than a traveling domicile, a place in the clouds to work and eat and sleep; it had a purpose unto itself. It was a magical machine. Its very reason for existence was to convey him and the others to this new and fantastic world. Below him was a world that coursed with powerful forces—the kind of forces that made the weak strong, that made the crippled strong, that made the orphaned strong. It was a world biblical in its drama, and a world in which injustice could be righted with a Jehovian vengeance.

*

The Crescent Express came to a halt within sight of the rail station at Baton Rouge. It was dark now, and the train was six hours late. This was not the typical Express; it trailed ten extra passenger cars and several flatbed freight cars. Soldiers and civilians shared the space aboard, and they all crowded against the windows to one side. Silent flashes pulsed across the firmament, like distant lightning with no visible storm to produce it. As dusk had turned to night, the brilliance of the distant conflict had increased, and soon there seemed to be more flash than night. The last ten miles had required an hour to traverse; roaming packs of West Carolinian rangers had again crossed the river and damaged several stretches of track between Baton Rouge and the beleaguered city of New Orleans. The rail yard was in confusion, and the civilian passengers were forced to disembark onto the rail bed well short of the platform; from this point they picked a path through the scrub and the railway ballast for the last hundred yards.

Once the civilians had disembarked, General Preston ordered the train back out of town, to a location five miles north of Baton Rouge where he had observed a relatively flat and open field. Here the train halted again and dozens of soldiers assisted in unloading the seven Porters. They hauled them across the field by rope, along with barrels of fuel, crates of incendiary ammunition, cans of oil, dope and varnish, cartons of signal flares, spark plugs, magnetos, spare propellers, tents, cooking gear, piles of spruce, and bundles of cotton fabric. Once Lieutenant Clark had the unit's material completely off-loaded, General Preston's soldiers returned to the train. The Crescent Express left the fliers standing in the lonely night and chugged its way around Baton Rouge; it circumvented the confusion in the yard, and then disappeared into the ravaged land to the south.

The members of Aerial Assault Squadron One, their numbers increased by five enlisted men who had been transferred from the ranks of Fort Natchez, spent the night erecting tents—sleeping quarters for themselves and maintenance tents for the machines. The early morning hours were spent organizing their various stores and laying out the wings, struts, and bracing wires of their disassembled aircraft, in preparation for a speedy reassembly during daylight hours.

A little before dawn, all fourteen men turned in, hoping for at least four hours of sleep; however, this was not to be. Two hours later, they were awakened by the sound of chaos: motorcars, nervous horses, and the murmur of hundreds of voices. As he crawled from his tent, William expected to find an audience similar to the one that had appeared in Natchez before his duel with Dora Two; word of their arrival had traveled quickly during the night.

William couldn't have been more wrong. There was indeed a crowd, but it was not for him. A dirt road lay on the far side of the rail bed, and on it, for as far as the eye could see, north toward Natchez or south toward Baton Rouge, were clusters of dust-covered refugees, lumbering under the weight of their possessions; most walked; some led animals and wagons stacked high with furniture; a few were in motorcars piled high with tins of gasoline. The motorcars seemed to offer little advantage to their owners as they were forced to drive at the same slow pace of the pedestrians clogging the road; many of the motorcars already were trailing steam as they began to overheat in the cool morning air.

The wanderers talked in hushed tones. They were choking on clouds of dust. One woman dropped to her knees and then wore herself out even further with deep shuddering sobs. When she found no relief to her suffering, she picked herself up and continued on her way. Many of these folk stopped their conversation and raised their eyes from the road to gaze over at the fliers in their camp. The Porters poked out of the tents and were quickly recognized as flying machines. One lanky young man who had been dragging his wife behind him, shouted at William, 'You damn well make those cowboys pay for this!' William raised an eyebrow and responded with a sarcastic salute; the young man somehow seemed satisfied with this and returned to dragging his wife roughly down the dusty road. The sight of these despairing folk lowered the spirits of the fliers, and they were grateful for the occasional gaps in the stream of suffering. The fliers worked quickly and silently, assembling their aircraft inside the tents where they could avoid the keen stares from the road.

The assembly of the machines was complete by late afternoon, and the men sat around a small fire; it had been placed so the tents blocked their view of the road. Their afternoon meal was of biscuits, coffee, and cold sausage; a small boy had brought them the meal from a mysterious provider in town. A note accompanied it: *The General says we are to look after you. You are in our prayers. Miss Maude.*

The food, though well prepared, sat like a stone in William's stomach; he tried to ignore it. He was anxious—not about the upcoming fight, not from fear of the personal risks he was about to embark upon, but because of the men. Perhaps for the first time, he had some inkling of why the officers he previously had served under behaved the way they did. It was one thing to sit around a campfire and talk about his exploits in the desert, or his adventure over the Atlantic, or his distress in the wasteland of West Carolina; it was quite another to have these men act as he would have them act. As the tension within the squadron grew, each man's behavior had started to change. As a group they became unruly and unpredictable. Mason and Donnegal seemed to have lost all of their vim and were constantly asking for instructions about what they should do next. Rice and Stewart had become sullen and self-willed; they ignored advice and bristled at orders. William suddenly found himself wishing he were still operating on his own; he had a growing sense that his chances of success against the airships dropped proportionately with the number of other fliers involved.

'Well, Clark,' said Rice, slurping his coffee from an empty can, 'what now?'

'The general's orders were pretty simple. He said *just go at 'em, right away.*'

'And where exactly do we go at 'em then?'

Clark disappeared into his tent for a moment, returning with a colorful map prepared by the army engineers. He spread it out on the grass before the men under the light of a lantern. 'It's pretty simple, fellas. We're here. The river's here. New Orleans is here. Recent reports say the airships typically patrol anywhere along this line, near the coast.' The men squinted down at the chart.

'It's kind of hit or miss at the moment,' added William. 'Flying from Baton Rouge we get less than an hour over the city, even less down by the coast, and there's not enough of us to keep up a constant patrol. I'm hoping we can get word from New Orleans when a ship's passing. Then we would be assured of being there at the right time.'

'It's a good idea,' said Burrows. 'I'll get hold of the general's headquarters and see what I can do. '

'Why did they stick us way up here?' complained Caldwell. 'If we were flying from a field near New Orleans, it would be a heck of a lot easier.' The other fliers murmured in agreement.

'Well, Caldwell,' said Burrows, 'you ask me that after you've taken a look at that part of the country. You fellas get up and test out your machines first thing tomorrow. If everything's alright, then head south and perform a reconnaissance around New Orleans.'

'A reconnaissance?' cried Rice. 'What the hell for? The general said go right at 'em!'

'A step at a time, Rice,' said William, supporting Burrows. 'Lieutenant Burrows is correct. Get the lay of the land first. You know we might not be the only army with aeroplanes. The Westerners might just have some sitting around on their side of the river waiting for us. And we need to find some emergency landing fields.' Rice was clearly not satisfied with the explanation but said nothing more.

'And another thing,' said Burrows, 'our troops probably never heard of us. Watch out, they'll probably shoot at you. So don't fly too low.' That comment seemed to get Rice's attention.

*

Dora Nine sped through the morning air as quickly as she could. Events were unfolding rapidly. She had more than enough fuel to run at full power for the next forty-eight hours. And if she used it all up, Dora Eight would soon be ready and waiting.

The admiral had rejoined the airship, to the discomfort of all. He stood behind the men in the control cabin: Oberleutnant Dürr, the two helmsmen, and the captain. Heinrich leaned against a corner in the back of the cabin and remained silent; the paint had worn off the bulkhead on which he leaned and it could be seen, by anyone who cared to notice, ground into the shoulder of his tunic. At times he would glance at the swarm of ships below, all pointed toward the gulf coast.

There had been a few shots fired at them from the larger ships below, but the captain had ordered frequent changes in altitude to avoid presenting an easy target, and the shells had burst well below or occasionally above the dirigible. Observing the ineffectiveness of their gunfire, the British squadron resigned itself to the irritating observation from above and decided to conserve its ammunition.

'We are now only one hundred miles from the line, Admiral,' said the captain. 'What do you wish to transmit to the submarine boats?'

'I see only warships in the fleet below, no troop transports; the warships are not our target. Have your navigator estimate the time at which this fleet will pass our submarine boats, assuming current course and speed.' Ober Dürr disappeared from the control cabin and returned several minutes later.

'The navigator estimates that they will cross the line at approximately zero six hundred hours, sir.'

'Instruct the boats to remain submerged from zero four hundred until zero eight hundred, after that they are to return to their original schedule of surfacing at the top of each hour for ten minutes. They must remain hidden while this battle fleet passes.'

'*Jawohl*, Herr Admiral!' said Ober Dürr, and he retreated to the wireless cabin.

The admiral's eyes followed Dürr as he departed the cabin, and after Dürr was gone the officer glanced over at Heinrich. Heinrich met his gaze evenly and without emotion. A questioning look flashed across the admiral's face. Heinrich continued to stare back, unflinching; he remained silent. The admiral withdrew his eyes and peered down through the cabin windows to continue his observation of the ships below.

'What now, Admiral?' asked the captain.

'We will track this squadron until we are certain of its destination, or until we receive word that the troop ships have sailed.'

Dürr returned to the control cabin. 'The message has been sent and received by the boats.' The admiral nodded. 'And the wireless operator has just received a weather report from Natchitoches. There's a storm coming.'

*

A red pennant shot up the mast of the *Partridge*; the troop transports weighed anchor and steamed out of Pensacola Bay, out into the gulf in search of their escort ships. They made fifteen knots and were expected to arrive on the gulf coast at dawn on the day after next; by then Sir Henschell's squadron should have pulverized the Galvezton shore. As the transports left the protection of the bay, they began to roll in the heavy swell. Captain Porter left the bridge of the *Penguin* and made his way down through the ship's lower decks. The men were in high spirits. They seemed ready for a fight. They were unaware of the odds.

'Hey, Captain,' shouted a private, 'you're just about to get your chance. Give 'em a dose a what they gave you!' Porter grinned and squeezed the man's shoulder. Those within earshot cheered and grinned. There were hundreds of noisy soldiers packed into the open deck; they milled about with cigarettes between their fingers; they sprawled on bunks with books; they sat on the floor playing at cards and huddled in corners shooting dice.

'Put a little extra powder in every shot for me,' said another.

Porter made his way down the stairwell, down into the ship's hold. The floor of the hold was so jammed with cannons and caissons that there was now no room left to walk. Dim light reflected off the polished barrels. With each roll of the ship, the cannons shifted position ever so slightly, not enough for the guns to roll about, but enough to cause the spoked wheels to rotate a degree or two. The cannons seemed like some strange breed of steer, nervous, packed too tightly in their pens—pens that led to the slaughterhouse. Assured that his weapons were secure, Porter returned to the upper deck and climbed back out onto the bridge. He scanned the sea; the wind was kicking up and the crests of the swells were frosted with a hint of white foam; the bows of the other transports plunged roughly into the rolls of the mounting sea. General Caruthers was standing on the bridge of the *Partridge*, braced against the guardrail. Porter sucked in his breath as a thought suddenly came to mind; he reached into the pocket of his coat and pulled out a thick envelope addressed to Perry and Esther Porter, Greeneville, Carolina; he had forgotten to mail it. 'I'll just have to mail it from Buffalo,' said Porter to himself; a grim smile spread across his face.

*

'Kapitan!' cried the wireless officer as he burst into the control cabin, knocking the navigator to one side. 'We have received the signal! The enemy transports have departed Pensacola.'

'Excellent!' said the admiral. 'Navigator, what is our current position?'

'One hundred miles due east of Galvezton, Admiral.'

'According to its current course, what is your best estimate as to the British battle squadron's destination?'

'Galvezton, sir!'

'Inform Natchitoches immediately, and give them our current position.'

'*Jawohl!*' responded the wireless officer as he disappeared.

'Kapitan, turn the ship around and head directly for Pensacola.'

'Admiral, a direct line from our current position will take us over New Orleans. Perhaps we should deviate to the south.'

'It doesn't matter. It will be difficult to find the transports if they travel far into the gulf. We must make for Pensacola immediately, at top speed!' Then, as if the elements, on some sudden whim, had decided to countermand the admiral's orders, a hard turbulent chop struck the airship and knocked the officers against the port side of the cabin. They regained their balance quickly, but from that moment on they would be required to spare a hand for the nearest bulkhead as the rough air built in force and regularity.

'Navigator, when will we intercept the transports?' asked the captain.

Karl glanced up at the airship's airspeed indicator and scribbled some calculations on his notepad. 'If the wind remains this strong, in about two and a half hours, sir.' The admiral seemed dissatisfied, but remained silent.

Karl glanced over at Heinrich and rolled his eyes. 'Here we go!'

Heinrich shrugged and remained silent.

Chapter 29

A BATTLE IN THE SKY

The day opened under a gray sky. A stiff breeze swept the airfield. Gusts combed the grass in long, arch-shaped waves. It promised to be a difficult day for the aviators. The canvas hangars swayed with the impact of the wind; the lanterns swung back and forth. The aeroplanes, however, tucked inside, rested still and secure for the moment. The roadway was empty and silent; there were no onlookers and the breeze was sufficient to kick up the dust without the assistance of the refugees from the day before.

The men rose early and hauled the flying machines of Aerial Assault Squadron One into the open air; the Porters were positioned in the southeast corner of the field, noses pointed into the breeze. The fliers then stood around the remains of their campfire, its embers coming back to life, pulsing with a deep orange glow, nourished by the steady flow of morning air. The aviators sipped coffee and nibbled on biscuits left over from their dinner the evening before.

Lieutenant Clark had motored into town during the night to telephone General Armstrong's headquarters; he had waited for hours in the lobby of the Baton Rouge police station until a connection could be made. It had been worth the wait. He learned that one of the dirigibles had been crossing back and forth over New Orleans with increasing regularity, and though it seemed to be patrolling under no specific timetable, the squadron stood a decent chance of an encounter if they arrived over the city as the sun rose. So the fliers stood around and waited for Lieutenant Clark's pocket watch to strike six o'clock, the hour William had set for their departure.

At the appointed time, the fliers, tense and silent, climbed into their aeroplanes. The machines twitched in the unsettled air—wings rocked ever so slightly; ailerons, elevators, and rudders jerked back and forth with the gusts, and occasionally banged against the stops. Once buckled in, each man donned his flying cap and primed his aircraft's engine. The scent of gasoline spread quickly through the damp air.

Private Jubil Cates, hands trembling, lips tight and bloodless, eyes locked with a steely will onto the hub of the propeller, succeeded in swinging William's aircraft to life; he then did the same for Cletus Martin, Johnny Stewart, and Joe Rice. Cates was out of breath by the time he finished, but he had tamed his fear of the whirling props and the harsh whining motors.

Private Carter Vance went through the same perilous motions for Billy Caldwell, Henry Mason, and Curtiss Donnegal; he seemed to experience much the same feelings as his new friend Cates. Both privates gazed on and, for the first time in their lives, watched as seven flying machines bounced across the pasture before miraculously popping into the air. They watched as the turbulent air batted the machines about; Martin and Stewart slid so close together that a collision seemed imminent; Caldwell dropped down so close to the ground that Cates thought the flier might be forced to repeat his takeoff altogether. Rice's craft, however, received a powerful lifting hand and shot up a hundred feet above the others. Eventually, the fliers managed to wrangle their machines into a loose formation as the squadron circled the field.

William maintained the lead and continued to glance back at the others; he climbed as he circled. He had just completed the first revolution around their new aerodrome when he noticed that Stewart was lagging behind in both distance and altitude. Within a few seconds, Stewart broke off and was soon gliding back toward the grass with a dense trail of blue smoke pouring from his motor. Once certain that Stewart had made a safe landing and that those left on the ground were rushing out to help him, William banked his Porter sharply to the right and led the remainder of the squadron southward.

None were prepared for what they saw on the ground below

as they approached the city of New Orleans. There had been no difficulty finding the city; it hadn't even been necessary to follow the river, for columns of smoke rising in the distance provided all the assistance they needed in their navigation. Puffs of white smoke from long rows of artillery emplacements, bursts of brown smoke from shells exploding on their targets, eddies of black smoke from the city as it burned were smeared together into a homogeneous haze of somber color. When this haze combined with the heavy overcast, it created a dreary pall that spread as far as the eye could see. The gloom of war seemed to be spreading over the entire world.

The squadron approached the city at two thousand feet, trying its best to weave between the oily black clouds. One or another of the aeroplanes would suddenly disappear into the edges of these dark fogs only to reappear a moment later either further away or frighteningly nearby. William kept an eye on the fliers behind him; he had not thought to have the men practice formation flying, and he was now concerned that they might run into one another. At one point Caldwell indeed flew too close to William's tail; William momentarily released the stick and raised his arms above his head and then slowly extended his arms out to each side. Caldwell, after several long seconds, deciphered the signal and increased his distance.

Almost upon the city now, William decided to descend to a thousand feet; it was difficult to get a clear view through the swirling cauldron of smoke. The haze was more impenetrable at higher altitude; it had been more thoroughly mixed by the wind. By flying closer to the ground, where the puffy columns had not yet had time to disperse, the fliers were able to pick a path that permitted them to remain in sight of one another. There were large swaths of scorched and blackened earth below; whole city blocks had been razed on both sides of the river. As William tried to estimate how much of the town remained intact, there came a noiseless burst of smoke near the riverbank. It sprouted up like a powdery gray mushroom. Then there were more, forming a close cluster that continued to spread like a growing fungus. Soon, dark bursts began sprouting up on the other side of the river as well—bursts of a slightly darker shade; apparently the East and West Carolinians each used a slightly different cocktail of high explosive.

William caught the attention of the fliers behind him by rocking his wings—left, right, left and back to level. He led them in a wide, meandering circle around the city. All eyes searched across the terrain below. It had indeed been a good idea to search for emergency landing fields. Everywhere, heavy forest struggled with water and marshland to overcome the dry earth. There were a few open level places in the area immediately surrounding New Orleans, and there would be little chance of a safe landing in the city itself, even on some of the wider streets. And to the south, the terrain worsened dramatically. If they were forced to fight near the coast, there would be few if any places to land should something go wrong. Downstream of the city there were only a few thin strips of farmland, bordering the river here and there as it extended to the gulf.

Orbiting the devastated city eventually grew dull; William turned away and led the squadron south over the edges of the swampland that spread toward the coast; he pointed out to the others with exaggerated arm movements the rare patches of ground that could be utilized in an emergency. Glints of quiescent, black water sparkled amidst the foliage and forest of ancient trees below.

When the squadron emerged from the region of densest smoke, well south of the city, William was surprised to discover that the atmosphere high above them had darkened significantly, without the assistance of any man-made conflagrations, without the alchemy of war. Strange twisting wisps of mist slipped down from the dark layer above like the tangled gray tresses of an old witch peeking from the hood of her cloak. The thick, sluggish cloud layer was moving slowly, ponderously, but in such a heavy, drunken manner that it defied any worldly force to resist it. As they flew along beneath the cloud layer, the color of the sky began to change, reflecting the light in some strange new way. William thought his eyes were playing tricks on him, that perhaps engine oil had started to coat the lenses of his goggles, for the sky was turning a faint green color—like the old vinegar bottles on the shelves of his mother's kitchen back home. He had never before seen a sky like this; it unnerved him in a way that the dangerous clouds of war had not. It appeared as if the sky was becoming ill.

The air had grown shockingly rough as well. His aeroplane bucked from sharp punches of turbulence; the jolts flung him with bruising force against the restraint of his harness. William grew concerned that their machines might not be up to such punishment; it was certainly becoming difficult to keep his own machine on a level, steady path. He looked about him; his squadron was scattered all over the sky; the loose formation they had been struggling to maintain had now entirely disintegrated. He realized they would have to return to their airfield and wait for calmer weather.

No sooner had William decided on this, and just as he glanced over his shoulder to signal his intentions to the others, he was startled to discover Rice peeling off to the west; the bright red cross on the underside of Rice's Porter was plainly visible—it conveyed a strange sense of warning to William. Confused by this errant turn, William followed Rice; Caldwell followed William; the others followed Caldwell. Then, just as William's ire began to rise, first at Rice's disobedience, and then in frustration at his inability to communicate with the man, William suddenly understood. Ahead of them, and slightly above, sailing right between two twisted stalactites of white vapor was a dirigible pursuing a course that would take it directly across the path of AAS-1.

William signaled with exaggerated arm motions that the squadron should proceed directly toward the dirigible just as they had planned back at camp. Rice allowed the others to catch up to him by making tight turns, back and forth, right and left; he eventually slid into his proper place in formation and relinquished the lead to William.

William pulled back on the stick of his Porter. His aeroplane and the others of AAS-1 began to climb.

*

Heinrich had wedged himself into a corner of the control cabin and gazed down at the inhospitable swampland below. The helmsmen were being knocked roughly about, and though they steadied themselves by reaching a hand to the bulkhead above their stations, they still inadvertently jerked their control wheels, which amplified the impact of the turbulence and wrenched the entire ship about. Vomit spread across the floor of the cabin from between the feet of the rudder-man.

'Bayous they were called,' thought Heinrich, as he concentrated on the scenery below to distract himself from his growing nausea. 'What a strange name.' Down there everything seemed calm and still, stagnant even. The land was choked with forest that was nourished by thick arteries, winding veins, and delicate capillaries of gloomy water. His gaze had become trance-like. That watery jungle must be absolutely teaming with life—a dangerous sort of life: snakes, insects, and disease. There would be nothing but death for a man down there. Heinrich's trance was broken by another hard knock; his head bounced off the window with a loud clunk. This turbulence was of a new and tricky sort; it seemed perfectly suited for disturbing the men's balance. Dora Nine groaned with displeasure; Heinrich could feel the ship bend and twist as it sped through the disturbed atmosphere.

The control cabin was crowded. Behind the helmsmen stood Ober Dürr, the captain, the admiral, the navigator, and the wireless operator, all peering with strained eyes through the cabin's mullioned panes. Dora Nine was quickly passing New

Orleans; the city now sat off on her port side. Soon Dora Nine would be shooting back over the gulf water where the officers expected to catch sight of the recently departed troop ships. Heinrich alternated between staring at the backs of the men before him and glancing out the window to his side.

Every pair of eyes aboard Dora Nine searched the surface of the gulf water off the starboard bow; the airmen hunted for their target. Everyone aboard had been assigned duty as a lookout, placed at strategic points about the ship to give a comprehensive view toward every point of the compass. And they spared some of their attention for the surrounding skies as well; the loss of Dora Two over Natchez—shot down by an enemy aeroplane—had proven the need for such caution. Two men were posted on the mooring platform in the nose of the ship, their arms weary from supporting heavy naval binoculars as they peered through the arched glass panels. Two men were stationed, unhappily, on the upper surface of the ship where they were harnessed to the exposed sighting platform and brutalized by the eighty-mile-an-hour slipstream; they both knew it was only a matter of time before the wicked clouds above them let loose a torrent of rain that would flay every square inch of their exposed skin. Even the doctor had been handed a pair of binoculars and told where to look. He now stood peering out the window of his infirmary. But the doctor was lax in his duty—the others surely were more qualified than he for such things; besides, his stomach was upset. He experimented with his binoculars and tried to get a better look at the unfamiliar ground below; all the while he cast worried glances at the dark clouds percolating around them.

Every once in a while Ober Dürr would turn around and look back at Heinrich; Heinrich met his stare calmly and coldly. A concerned expression passed over Dürr's face, but Heinrich ignored the question implicit in the expression. Dürr frowned, shrugged his shoulders, and turned back to his duty.

'Sir!' shouted Airman Thomas Schilling as he burst into the

control cabin. His nose bled from a fall he had taken in his dash from the mooring platform. Everyone turned toward him, instantly. 'There are aeroplanes coming! There are aeroplanes coming! Down there!' He pointed toward a spot to the north, just below the horizon. The officers jumped to the port side windows. All eyes hunted. They searched—nothing. They kept at it—the longer it took to spot the aeroplanes, the more frantic their eye movements became. Eventually each man locked his attention onto distant specks, pale and insignificant against the dark terrain. The admiral turned toward the rear of the cabin and shouted, 'Oberleutnant von Gotha!'

But Heinrich had already gone.

Heinrich strode down the keel. He didn't run. He didn't rush. He walked, occasionally reaching up to steady himself against the turbulence. He ignored the other men as he passed; whenever Heinrich approached one of them, the menace in his eyes caused them to step out of his way. Heinrich slipped down the ladder and opened the hatch that gave him access to his aeroplane; he scanned its surfaces; all was in order.

Heinrich pulled on his flying cap, slipped his goggles down, and dropped into the aeroplane's cockpit. The wind tugged at his uniform, but he was oblivious to it. He buckled himself in and unlatched the mechanism that held the aeroplane's propeller in a stationary position. The slipstream pressed against the blades of the propeller and caused it to begin wind-milling, slowly at first, and then faster. Heinrich tested his controls, opened the fuel cock, and closed the ignition switch. After a few more revolutions the engine sputtered to life. As the motor sped up, the aeroplane throbbed and wrestled against the steel trapeze from which it hung. A thrust of rough air pushed up from below and gave the machine a good shake.

Heinrich glanced up to find Ober Dürr kneeling on the platform above him with a hand on the release lever. The noise was too great for Dürr's voice to carry, but the words 'Good luck! Be careful!' were easily read from his lips. Heinrich nodded and made a pulling motion with his fist.

Dürr released the lever and Heinrich fell.

Heinrich flew up from his seat, weightless, only his harness keeping him from flying out of the cockpit as the aeroplane plummeted; the aeroplane's nose immediately dropped toward the earth. He held the joystick loosely in his right hand as he watched the needle of the airspeed indicator; it wobbled for a moment, then began moving across the face of the dial. Another bump in the air caused the plane to spin around to the right, but Heinrich counteracted the motion by firmly pushing the rudder pedal in the opposite direction. When the needle reached the number eighty, he pulled back on the stick, and the machine began to fly. He banked to the left to get out from beneath the airship and then began to climb.

*

The distance between the Carolinian aircraft and Dora Nine diminished rapidly. William signaled to the others. As planned, he and Cletus Martin broke away. Caldwell, Mason, Rice, and Donnegal continued their climb. William and Cletus leveled off and pointed their machines directly at the airship. They were less than a mile distant when William saw the bright red aeroplane drop from beneath it; he immediately recognized Count Heinrich's monoplane. A lump formed in William's throat. He felt strangely anxious; he wasn't certain of its exact cause; perhaps it was from the responsibility he felt for the men behind him; perhaps it was regret at having to kill, or be killed, by someone who was not a stranger; most likely it came from the realization that his men, even more than he, did not possess the skill of the Prussian flier, and that some of them were going to die in the next few minutes.

The three aeroplanes approached one another—William's marked with its proud British lion, Cletus's with its pugnacious American turkey, Heinrich's with its black Prussian eagle.

William gave a quick glance over to Cletus, who was now positioned directly on his left-hand side and bobbed up and down in the invisible currents. William saw wisps of white smoke come from Cletus's gun; Cletus was firing his Hugo in a long continuous stream in a frantic effort to wound the red machine on the first pass. William grimaced. Over anxious, Cletus was using up all of his ammunition before the fight had even started; once his ammunition was exhausted, there would be no time to change the canister on his gun. William withheld his fire; he realized that very shortly he would be the only one in a position to keep Count Heinrich occupied.

The opposing machines shot past each other. Cletus slid beneath Heinrich's craft. William passed alongside. Goggled eyes blinked at goggled eyes, and then Heinrich was gone.

The red aeroplane pulled up into a steep climb and banked sharply to the right. It twisted around and dropped behind Cletus's aeroplane just as the Carolinian craft began a slow turn to the left. William banked his machine onto its side and pulled on the stick to force the craft into a tight turn; the motor lost fuel momentarily, sputtered, and then came back to life. William lost altitude during the maneuver, and when the other machines came back into view, he could only watch as Cletus flipped his aircraft onto its back in a frantic attempt at getting away from Heinrich. Short, sharp bursts of smoke came from the Prussian's gun. It took only three bursts before Cletus's Porter was spinning downward, out of control.

William split his attention between Cletus's spinning aeroplane and Heinrich. William filled with hot rage; he was back over the desert again. He was ready to kill Heinrich now. Distracted by Cletus's fall, William lost the opportunity to slide in behind Heinrich. The two fliers ended up glaring across at each other from opposite sides of a wide, circular course. They circled and circled, buffeted by the rough air. It was as if they were being sucked into a great whirlpool; each tried to gain on the other while both dropped toward the earth and away from the other fliers. But the red machine was faster, and it began to gain on the gray machine. William began to lose sight of Heinrich as the red aeroplane edged in behind him. Every time William diverted his attention away from the task of flying his own aeroplane, it would wobble slightly, and thus cause him to lose more ground and more altitude. They had fallen a long way by now. But William remained calm.

William knew he couldn't stay out from under Heinrich's gun for long, and he contemplated some new maneuver. He considered diving steeply toward the ground to entice Heinrich to follow him further away from the airship; something like that had worked back in the desert. But Heinrich broke off his attack. He turned his machine away from William and began to climb steeply, up toward the airship and toward the other aeroplanes that were now far above them.

William turned and followed, climbing after the red machine as best he could; he now had a moment to track down his fellow fliers. They were stretched out in a long line as if playing follow-the-leader; each in turn swooped down and along the airship. William was too far away to see smoke from the muzzles of their guns, but he had little doubt they were using their Hugos to good effect. The airship had reacted by pointing its nose up sharply and was beginning a steep climb.

Heinrich climbed. William climbed. The distance between them continued growing. The Porter's motor wasn't powerful enough for William to keep up, and in that instant, he resolved to find a bigger motor for his machine; it was the only way he would ever be able to fight on even terms with the Prussian machines.

The harsh currents of air knocked William from side to side; his harness bit painfully into his waist with each jolt. The steep angle of his machine meant the entire scene before him was filled with the bile-green storm clouds above; they were turning darker and darker. The gloomy thought that none of them might make it back grew in his mind.

Heinrich closed on the airship and the other Carolinian aeroplanes. To William's dismay, he recognized that the others were unaware of Heinrich's approach. The fools, oblivious, were making lazy turns and followed one another as they casually prepared for another pass at Dora Nine. Heinrich burst into the Carolinian formation from below. Again, William was unable to see the ammunition flying about, but it took no more than ten seconds for one of the Porters to explode into a fireball. The explosion dispersed quickly and left behind twisted and fragmented wreckage that began tumbling down toward the earth; pieces of wood and metal scattered as the wreckage fell; portions of the wings were caught in a momentary updraft and seemed to levitate for a few seconds before following the rest down to earth.

'No! No! No!' screamed William as he watched a body separate from the wreckage. Anger coursed through him, along with another feeling—a strangely familiar feeling. It was as if he had just done something wrong, like when he had interfered with Emily's wedding. A strong sense of guilt surged through him. Two men had been killed thus far, and it was his fault.

The red aeroplane immediately turned onto another of the Carolinians, almost running him down; the gray plane twisted and turned as if it were one of God's archangels wrestling with Satan. None of the Porters could manage the red plane, and none were able to avoid the tracks of its bullets; they simply could not remain on its tail long enough to do it any damage. William began to feel their only hope was for Heinrich to run out of ammunition.

William's Porter continued to plow upward. At one moment, the turbulent air would shove him back, maddeningly; the next moment it would fling him upward as if from a slingshot. He no longer thought about the risk to his machine; he prayed for more of the violent thrusts that might get him back into the battle raging above. He had to get back in the fray before it was all over. William noticed the airship's attempt to climb seemed to be faltering; he could only assume that his men had punched enough holes in it to make higher altitude unattainable. Unfortunately, the ship seemed in good enough condition to avoid any unwanted descent.

It was at this moment that William observed something very odd. Again his first conclusion was that his eyes were playing tricks on him, and that the excitement of battle had warped his senses. Up high, above the tangle of aeroplanes and the beleaguered dirigible, up in the churning bottle-green storm clouds he saw something that appeared almost to be the finger of God; a long, thick tendril of vapor reached down and felt around beneath the clouds, as if it wanted to pluck the dirigible up to heaven. Then, as suddenly as it had appeared, it withdrew back into the clouds and was gone. William shook his head in disbelief and returned his attention to the task at hand. He was almost there.

Suddenly, one of the gray aeroplanes flipped on its back of its own accord and started to cartwheel; it was Caldwell's machine he thought; it came hurtling down, whipped passed William, and fell to pieces as it went by. William couldn't fathom the cause; Heinrich was far away now, busy with another Porter. It took another bone-jarring shock for William to understand that Caldwell's Porter had simply fallen to pieces; it had been torn apart by the thrashing currents of air; the delicate machine had not required enemy bullets to drive it past its breaking point. And now another flier was tumbling down to his death. William gritted his teeth; his jaws ached. His mind reeled from his helplessness.

The red aeroplane and the two remaining gray aeroplanes were whirling around each other, and around Dora Nine. William was now close enough to read the numerals on the tails of the Porters; number three belonged to Donnegal, and number five belonged to Rice. These two men were all that remained of his squadron. It was Rice's aeroplane that Heinrich seemed to have in his sights at the moment; he was close up on Rice's tail and ready to fire. Then William gasped as Rice turned directly toward the tail of Dora Nine. William could only imagine that the man was hoping to use the spritely nature of the lightweight Porter to swerve out of the way at the very last minute; this maneuver would force Heinrich to choose between breaking off his attack, or risk smashing into the very airship he was trying to protect.

But Rice misjudged the distance. He waited too long to make his turn. He seemed to recognize this, and as William watched in horror, Rice's aeroplane pitched up sharply—too sharply. The Porter shuddered and wobbled as if it were balanced on the point of a pin. After a couple of heart-stopping seconds during which Rice's machine seemed almost to levitate, the craft suddenly dropped a wing, corkscrewed, and bored straight into the side of the dirigible. Rice and his Porter disappeared from view and left only a gaping black hole edged with torn fabric and twisted aluminum. A few seconds later the dirigible seemed to sag slightly at its mid-point; the fin and elevator on the starboard side flopped down and dangled limply below the ship's hull.

William flew along the side of Dora Nine. Hoping for some sign that Rice had survived, he tried to peer into the gash; but the gaping hole was little more than a blur as William shot past and flew out into the open air behind the airship. Just as he was about to pull his Porter around to fly up the other side of Dora Nine, he saw the strangest and most frightening sight of his life. There before him for the second time in the past few minutes, and not much more than a mile away, hung that vengeful finger of God. A twisting, rotating cloud, tapered like a giant whirlpool, had descended from tormented skies above; even now its pointed bottom was descending down, down, toward the earth; the whirlwind was coming directly toward him. This funnel was much bigger than the last one, and it would not go away un-sated.

William yanked his Porter around in a desperate attempt to

reverse course and get away from the hellish sight. He wanted to interpose the stricken dirigible between him and the demonic storm in the irrational hope that this would keep him safe. The violent, churning air sucked at him. For a moment he seemed to be standing still, and then suddenly he was flung forward at an unbelievable speed.

Apparently the other fliers had become aware of the funnel cloud as well. Heinrich and Donnegal flew away from each other at a diverging angle; the fight was clearly a secondary thought as they all struggled to escape the monstrous cataract. Dora Nine continued to fly along as if unaware of the menace approaching her from behind. Her aft end, with all of its elegantly constructed control surfaces, disappeared into the churning gray spiral. The funnel tore at her. The shearing wind stripped off her outside covering from the aft end forward as if she were being skinned alive; her delicate and neatly organized skeleton was exposed now for all the world to see. She flipped upward into a perfectly vertical attitude and was sucked into the maelstrom; she was devoured entirely—the only thing wanting was a scream of agony to make the slaughter complete. The cyclone ripped Dora Nine in half and flung the pieces out the back. The two halves, each still with significant buoyancy from the remaining undamaged gasbags inside, began to sink slowly toward the earth and were completely at the mercy of the confused winds. The whirlwind seemed to have expended its fury with the destruction of such a majestic creature and suddenly changed course, away from the circling aeroplanes.

William's attention was diverted from the mesmerizing sight of Dora Nine's destruction by the familiar experience of his aircraft losing some of its important pieces around him. A bullet ricocheted off the barrel of his gun and left it vibrating on its mount. The controls began to grow sluggish in his hands. He pulled back on the stick in an attempt to execute a half loop—a maneuver he had just seen Heinrich perform in order to avoid colliding with Dora Nine while chasing Rice. William's aeroplane rebelled at the rough handling; the engine groaned under the stress; the Porter stalled at the crest of the loop and dropped into a spin. The plinks from the deadly bullets stopped and allowed William to concentrate on controlling the machine. The panic he had experienced in his first fight with Heinrich was entirely absent now, and he worked swiftly and fiercely; he applied every combination of stick and rudder to bring the machine out of its deadly spiral. Eventually one of the combinations worked. The rotation slowed. William pushed the stick forward, and the machine began to respond. Soon he was flying again. The controls were sloppy but workable; the engine clanked and thumped, but it still pushed him forward.

William looked around him, beneath him, then back over his shoulders. Heinrich shot past in a dive that brought the red aeroplane so close to William that exhaust swooshed into William's face. Heinrich pulled up and exchanged the momentum of his dive for altitude; soon he was in a tight turn that brought him onto a course directly back toward William. They were now flying toward each other head on.

The muzzle of Heinrich's gun flickered with a bright hot light, but only for a second; then it went dark. William pulled the trigger on his Hugo and let loose his bullets in four long bursts. Many of them seemed to hit the red aeroplane. Suddenly, the pounding of his gun ceased. He couldn't tell whether he was out of ammunition, or if the gun had jammed, and there was no time to look.

William's weakened aircraft now began to disintegrate around him, but he held his course as the distance separating the two aeroplanes evaporated. Heinrich began to pull up to avoid a collision. William was frustrated by the failure of his gun and believed this might be his last opportunity to inflict lethal damage to the red aeroplane. So, he yanked back on his own stick and sent the top wing of his Porter crashing into the bottom of Heinrich's aeroplane. Splinters of wood burst from both machines.

After they separated, William observed that Heinrich's machine was still flyable, albeit with no wheels; William discovered that his own machine was not. Looking over his shoulder to inspect the upper wing, William found two big gashes in its leading edge, gashes that were lengthening. Soon the entire wing would come off. He somehow managed to maintain a level attitude as the craft began a steady, rapid descent.

He cut the switch to his engine and held the stick rigidly in one position in an effort to prevent a dive. He tried not to exert any new forces on the fragile and deteriorating structure. As the needle on the altimeter swung through 800 . . . 700 . . . 600 feet, the image of Perry Porter telling him 'This machine is solid, it'll keep you alive' floated through his mind. Then as the aeroplane sank through 400 . . . 300 . . . 200 feet, the image of his sister Emily appeared before him, expressionless, neither frowning nor smiling. He shook his head to banish her from his thoughts as he frantically searched for a hole in the jungle rushing up at him. Lastly, the image of Esther Porter, her warm green eyes and her long black hair, emerged before him. She smiled at him.

D9
4

Chapter 30

CAUGHT IN A SWAMP

Rain poured down. Lightning flashed across the sky. The wind whistled through the trees. By the time General Preston wound his way through the debris-strewn streets, around the shell craters and the dead bodies, and had galloped the last two miles to where the two halves of the stricken airship had slammed into the earth, a frenzied mob from the outskirts of the city was swarming around the wreckage. He whipped his horse as it plowed a path through the mob, while most of his staff frantically tried to catch up with him. He arrived just in time to find three gray-uniformed Prussians kicking spasmodically in the rain, each at the end of a long rope that had been hastily thrown over the thick branch of a moss-bearded oak. He fired his pistol into the air; he emptied it, all seven shots necessary to divert the mob's attention from the gruesome task at hand.

'You will cease immediately!' he screamed at the top of his voice. 'Immediately!' The general grabbed a second pistol from his aid's holster and pointed it at a large man at the center of the violence. The man held a fresh, unused rope in his hands and had been trying to put it over the head of bloody and angry Private Rice; the private's frantic explanations as to why he had been found amidst the airship's wreckage had been ignored.

While some of the mob—curious, angry, destructive—swarmed over the smoldering wreckage or closed in on those crewmen who had managed to crawl out, the group around the lynching tree seemed to vacillate, uncertain whether to reach for another victim or to run. In the time it took them to decide, the remainder of the general's staff rode up, and the increased numbers decided the issue. Soon, soldiers on galloping horses were chasing the civilians away. The expression of fear on the faces of the dazed Prussians remained for they seemed to think that their fate had not changed.

The officers dismounted their horses, skittish from the noisy storm, and rounded up those crewmen still ambling about through the mud in confusion; the officers guided them toward the small cluster of men who lay on the ground groaning from their wounds; Captain Timmer, Peter Dürr, and Emil Dreckmesser were among the dead. Airman Thomas Schilling seemed to be the only man without so much as a scratch, the rain having washed away any remnants of the bloody nose he had received just prior to the battle up in the sky.

While the cavalry officers were occupied, an odd-looking crewman—hunched, battered, and bleeding—slipped out from the far side of the wreckage. Limping awkwardly, dragging an injured leg behind him, he made his way unseen into the tangled overgrowth of vines and stunted trees that surrounded a nearby swamp. There he disappeared from view.

The general climbed down from his mount and briefly examined the twisted mass that had once been Dora Nine; he wrinkled his nose from the stench of burning oil and gasoline. He glanced at each of the soiled faces before him and inspected the uniforms that had been reduced to a homogeneous mass of ripped and bespattered gray fabric. Eventually his eyes alighted on Admiral von Ramstein and halted.

'Speak any English?'

'*Ja*, a little.'

'You in command?'

The admiral let out a snort and nodded dejectedly.

Suddenly, just as General Preston was about to ask another question, he noticed, out of the corner of his eye, a streak of light shoot across the open ground a few yards away. A young man, dirty, scrawny, and bearded, whisked by with a flaming torch that he had made from a piece of lumber and some oil-soaked rags. The man rushed up to what remained of the airship's bow, a still inflated gasbag protruding like a blister out of the confining tangle of aluminum girders. He screamed as he thrust his torch into it like St. George piercing his dragon. Two soldiers pointed their rifles into the air and fired shots to discourage him, but they were too late. Every cavalry soldier nearby took off in a furious dash or dropped to his knees and covered his head.

General Preston flinched but held his ground. As his gaze traveled across the faces of the exposed Prussian crew, he quickly noticed that not a single crewman flinched at the flaming assault. In fact, they gazed on complacently and seemed amused by the young man as if he were a common variety lunatic. The general turned back to the admiral.

'Why didn't it burn?'

The admiral looked up at the general and shrugged his shoulders.

*

Captain Jefferson Porter stood at the bow of the *Penguin*. The excitement and fear that had begun to rise the moment the transport hit the first gulf swell was still there. It was not long after their departure that he had begun to feel that his position on the bridge beside the vessel's skipper was not a sufficiently forward one; so he had descended to the *Penguin*'s main deck and from there had made his way forward to the bow.

Porter stood between the ship's anchors and leaned forward against the rail. It hadn't taken long for his uniform to become damp from the invisible spray, but he did not mind. His thoughts were on the landing ahead. Turning to glance at the *Partridge* off the *Penguin*'s port beam, Captain Porter recognized the upright stance of General Caruthers. The general seemed to be suffering from the same sense of anticipation and had made his way to the bow of his own ship. The two soldiers faced each other across two hundred yards of heaving gulf water and grinned

The four transports and their escort of destroyers approached

Point Eads, rounded it, and turned due west. They passed over the line of submarine boats, right over the trap set for them, without ever learning of its existence. The noise from the transports' churning propellers echoed clearly through the hulls of the two nearest submarine boats hidden in the mud below, and the submerged sailors looked upward in confusion as the sound grew to its gurgling crescendo and then faded away. Three hours later the submarine boats would surface, according to their prescribed schedule, and then finding no transports within sight and receiving no signal from above, they would sink back into their slimy burrows, their skippers slightly confused by the sudden peacefulness that seemed to surround them.

As dusk fell, echoes of thunder continued to roll across the tempestuous water. Captain Porter felt a certain dread at the thought that the already difficult landing would be made more so by the rough and stormy seas. The boom and crash of the sky seemed only to increase the further they sailed along, but then Captain Porter understood; his throat tightened with the realization that he was now hearing the guns of the British naval squadron going about its task of reducing the coastal defenses. The rumble of each salvo merged into the next; Captain Porter tightened his grip on the railing. He stared at the horizon, hunting for signs of land, but found only the faint flashes of the great cannons. He gazed out at what lay before him with a grim face and a hardened will. His moment had arrived.

*

The sun faded and the noise from the insects began to grind and throb as they vied with one another in communicating whatever things insects communicate. The gnats and mosquitoes assaulted William as he sat on his small waterlogged island of stinking mud, while he debated his course of action. Heinrich's low pass over him as he had climbed out of the wrecked Porter, now half submerged in the murky swamp water a few hundred feet away, seemed like a distant memory.

The twisted, vine-tangled trees hung over him like tortured gargoyles. They had begun to block the light late in the afternoon, and the shadows had lengthened and crept across the turbid water. It had become more and more difficult to keep track of the reptile, giant and grotesque, that popped up at times in different locations about the island, never further than a hundred feet, and never closer than fifty. William shivered in his wet clothes. His last attempt at standing had made it painfully clear that his ankle was again injured. It was going to be difficult to crawl or swim out of his jungle prison.

In which direction should he turn? Which way should he begin swimming, or crawling? This region west of the river was nothing but expansive swampland. He could head south hoping to find the coast or east hoping to find the river or north where there would be dry land that was likely to be crawling with West Carolinians; or he could head west in a hope that he could exhaust the swamp and end up in a safe but unpopulated area. All choices could prove impossible, but the wrong one would *certainly* kill him.

He reached up and pulled another hunk of rotten wood from the trunk of the uprooted tree he leaned against; he flung the missile out at the protrusion in the otherwise still water twenty feet away. There was a monstrous swoosh of the creature's tail as it bolted away and left William spattered with a new coat of ooze. He let his mind roam where it would, and the image of his sister that he had banished just before his crash appeared again; it formed out of the thin strands of mist that curled around his small island. He did not try to dispel the ghost this time; he let her rise up out of the swamp and walk over to him. She gazed down at him, patiently, as if waiting for something.

'I'm sorry,' William said, bowing his head as a tear slid down his cheek, momentarily washing a thin line of mud from his face. 'I should have come home.' When he lifted his head again, she was still there, shimmering against the mist. 'Can you forgive me?' he asked.

At first there was no reaction, just the same somber stare, but as his shoulders began to slouch in defeat, his sister suddenly turned her head, gazing upward as if she had been disturbed by something. She returned her gaze to William and considered him for a moment. She smiled at him, blew him a kiss, and then evaporated into the dusk. William shook his head and as his focus returned to the waking world, he found the blinking eyes of the swamp creature and its long rows of dirty teeth visible in the shallow water only ten feet away. Then, before William had time to reach for another projectile, the creature bolted away as if frightened by an unexpected presence.

Suddenly, the dripping, empty marsh was blasted by the roar of an aeroplane tearing through the dusky air just above the treetops. It had been visible for only a second through the small gap in the foliage above. Although William had lost sight of it as quickly as it had appeared, he could hear the intonation of the motor change as the machine turned and eventually began circling the area, hunting for something, seeming to hunt for William. After a short pause, the craft again ripped across the small patch of fading sky directly above him. William jumped to his feet and cried with pain as he hopped on his one good leg.

The aeroplane's engine seemed to go quiet for a moment. Then, again the craft whipped overhead, but this time a small object, about the size of a human head, came tumbling down, bounced off a branch, and landed with a splash in the exact spot that had just been abandoned by the creature.

It took a moment for William to identify the object as most of its bulk rested well below the water's surface. However, the color of the object seemed vaguely familiar; it was a large metal can, labeled with green and yellow stripes. As it gently bobbed in the rippling water, it rotated slowly. The front label, which had faced downward up to this point, rolled into view, and William's stomach grumbled in response. The word

APFELMUS appeared for a moment and then again disappeared from view as the can continued its roll.

William looked up into the sky above him, fiercely angry. He could hear Heinrich's new aeroplane circling around for another pass, probably the last as it was becoming too dark to navigate. Whoosh! Another pass, and another similarly shaped projectile came down; this one missed the interfering tree branch and landed with a plop in the muddy pool five feet in front of William.

William waded out into the gripping mass and scooped up the can just as the first can disappeared in a gushing torrent of water and teeth; the creature's tail slapped the water and doused William again. After quickly retreating to his island, William discovered that this new and unlabeled can contained something other than applesauce; one end of the can was covered by a thin skin of rubbery material that was held in place by several windings of string. William fumbled with the knot for several minutes until his cold fingers found enough slack to break the twine.

The all too familiar smell of apples escaped as he removed its cover. Inside, William found four objects. The first and heaviest was a pistol of Prussian make, Heinrich's pistol, very likely the one the Prussian had aimed at his face so long ago. William immediately pointed it at the returning monster and fired two rounds into its long forehead. The alligator thrashed and bolted away, back into the swamp with an angry roar, never to be seen again. The second object was an apple from which William took a large bite before thrusting the remainder into his jacket pocket. While he chewed, he identified the third object, a box of matches; he successfully ignited one after a couple of tries. Lastly, there was a thin rectangle of parchment. William released the empty can and let it fall back into the mud. He carefully unfolded the document.

Crouching down in the mud, William spread the paper across his knees and exposed its surface to the golden illumination of the flame. In the soft radiant circle he found a detailed map of the region around New Orleans. In the center of the map he noticed a hand-drawn arrow pointing to a swampy area named Bayou Tremont; the point of the arrow rested on the very eastern edge of the swamp. At the other end of the boldly arching arrow were written three words:

YOU ARE HERE!

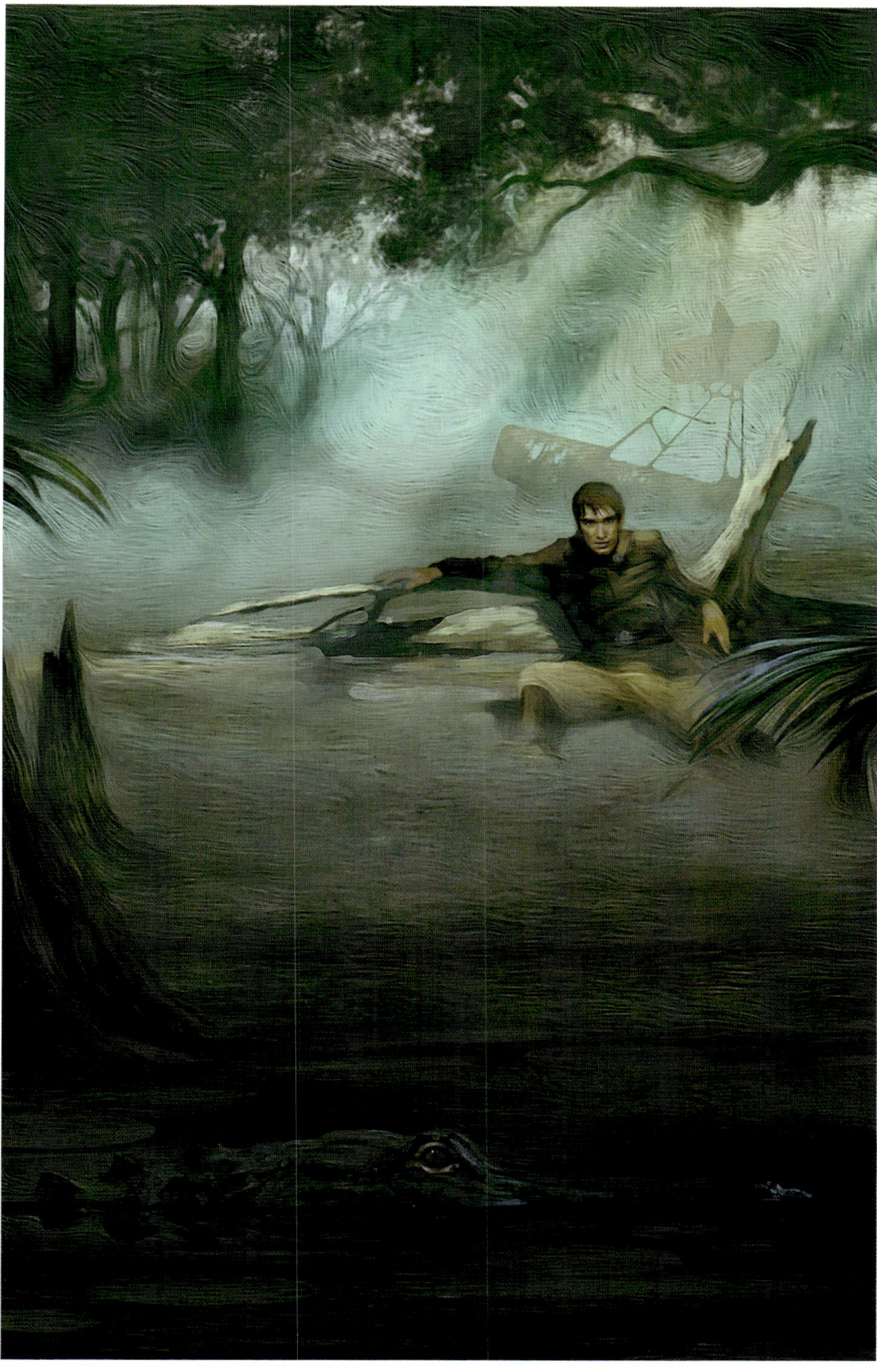